PARALLAX

SENTIENT STARS

AMBER TORO

SALT PEACH

To Hoz,
the love of my life,
who has always believed in me,
even before I did.

CHAPTER 1 | SKYLA

THE CRASH

Leaving to chase ghosts felt pointless now as her life flashed before her eyes. As much as she had yearned to find her father—to feel that connection—he was not the one she thought of when the frozen ocean reached up to greet her. In that moment, there was only space in her mind for *him*.

The bite of Skyla's harness digging into her shoulders brought everything into sharp focus. They were in free fall. A vast ocean stretched out beneath them. Scales of ice plated the surface, painted brilliant blue and white, snow devils dancing over the icy surface which stretched beyond the horizon.

Gold threads of light danced up Skyla's arms, weaving around her shoulders and inserting into her neck. Even with the full neural link, she couldn't help Pele regain control. They were going to crash.

The impact rocked Skyla's body, throwing her against her restraints once again, pain blossoming across her chest as darkness enveloped her vision. She blinked hard, trying to bring the world back into focus. They had punched through the ice. Dark water filled the viewport.

"Skyla." Pele's voice came to her, calm as always, but serious. "You need to get out now."

"I'm not leaving you, Pele." Unbuckling her restraints, Skyla struggled to find her footing with the bridge tilted at a violent angle; she took a staggering step.

"There is nothing you can do for me here. If you stay, we'll both be trapped down here until life support runs out. Then we both die."

Skyla pressed the heels of her palms into her eyes, sending sparks across her vision, willing them to see a solution they had missed.

"Get out now and go get help. I'll be fine. I'll wait for you."

Once again, she had put Pele in danger, chasing after the ghost of her father on a lead now decades old. How could she have been so foolish? Now Pele was in mortal danger, and she trusted Skyla to save her life.

The weight of the realization threatened to crush her. Pele trusted she would come through for her; that her soul wouldn't be trapped on an alien world until her systems failed and she died a true death.

"Skyla." Pele's voice was sharp now as she read Skyla's emotions. Pele knew her too well. A by-product of being bonded for a lifetime. "Go. Now."

Years of military training kicked in. Skyla dashed for the back of the cockpit, her legs burning at the near-vertical climb as she made her way to the cargo bay.

"Fenrir!" Skyla called without breaking stride. There was no time, and she knew the oversized wolf-cat creature would be on her in moments. She ran straight through the cargo bay to the back hatch, but she couldn't open the cargo bay. They were already too far from the surface to swim; just the thought sent a chill through her. Those temperatures would kill them in minutes.

Fenrir came barreling into the cargo bay. His claws scrambled for purchase before he skidded to a halt beside Skyla. With pointed ears drawn back in anticipation, he looked up at her. She found complete trust reflected in his warm brown eyes.

"Sorry buddy, you're not going to like this." She patted the top of his head before leading him over to the evac tube. Fenrir stood as tall as Skyla on his hind legs and weighed more than she did. He would have to evac in his own unit. She guided him into the tight space; he whined as she sealed the door.

"Pele, launch Fenrir with my tube."

"Hurry, Skyla, you're running out of time."

Snatching her archeology supplies from the wall, Skyla folded her arms around the gear, then stepped into the three-meter pod barely larger than a coffin.

"I will come back for you," she whispered, frustration burning through her.

"I know."

Pele didn't wait for her command. With a hiss, the pod sealed and filled with a viscous gel. Skyla worked to keep her breaths even as the gel surrounded her, flowing into her nose and through her system. The force of the escape pod racing toward the surface sent her blood rushing to her boots. Black spots flecked at the edges of her vision. The gel contracted around her legs, forcing blood back toward her brain and keeping her conscious. The pod erupted from the water in a geyser of frozen debris, hovering suspended in the air for a moment before falling back to slam into the broken surface.

The gel melted away from Skyla's body as the pod opened. The frozen air sliced at her skin, a thousand vicious pinpricks, cutting her to the bone as she surveyed the crash site from the clam-shelled pod. A shiver worked its way down her spine, setting her teeth to chatter, and no amount of rubbing her palms over her bare arms could warm the skin that had already gone deathly cold. Even with the cold slowing her mind, she realized she wouldn't last long without her bio-regulating gear. Her numb fingers fumbled with the fabric as she slipped into the nanite-infused cargo pants and jacket.

Within seconds, the nanites began to regulate her temperature. Feeling returned to her hands, and the fog that had settled into her mind began to clear. It was still cold, but she wouldn't freeze to death, not immediately anyway.

The pod had basic controls, which she used to maneuver over to the second unit. Skyla tapped a sequence into the exterior panel, and it sprang open, releasing Fenrir. After a quick shake, he immediately jumped into her pod, causing it to rock violently in the choppy water. Fenrir cowered by her feet, his ears flat against his skull and big eyes filled with fear.

"Whoa, calm down, buddy." Skyla threw her arms out to steady herself as the pod continued to slosh from side to side. "It's going to be okay. We'll get out of this ocean and go find the research settlement." The statement was meant to reassure herself more than Fenrir. They had already been aligned for entry when an ominous ship had shot them down. She could only hope that they had crash-landed near the research outpost.

Fenrir whined as he hunkered down by her feet. She scratched the top of his head as she surveyed their surroundings. There was an ice shelf not far from where they had crashed. The climb looked to be about one hundred meters up from the waterline. It would be steep, but she hoped it would lead them out of the ocean. After salvaging what supplies she could from the second pod, she maneuvered over to the shore.

They bumped into the ice. Skyla jumped out, pulling hard to ground the pod. Tilting her head back, Skyla surveyed the ice cliff. A pit settled in her stomach as she realized there was no trail. She would have to climb, and bringing the supplies along would be a challenge. Fenrir jumped onto the ice beside her, prowling the shoreline protectively, his long tail whipping from side to side as Skyla made quick work of offloading the emergency gear. There was only so much she would be able to haul up the ice cliff, but she was certain she could fashion pieces of the pod into a sled—the pod rocked violently.

Waist-high waves washed up over the shore, knocking her back into the ice. Freezing water crashed through her clothing, stealing her breath as a crushing pressure wrapped around her leg. Then everything went dark.

Icy water pressed in all around her. She thrashed violently, trying to reach the surface, but the grip on her leg only tightened. The tentacle gripped her like a vice as it thrust her back through the surface, then slammed her into the ice shelf. The cold air cut like knives against her wet skin, and her head threatened to split in two from the strike.

A menacing growl ripped through the air, followed by a flash of golden fur. Fenrir tore into the tentacle wrapped around her leg with his massive fangs as his claws shredded through green flesh. The grip around her leg went slack, and she scrambled back from the water's edge. Skyla took a moment to process what she saw. The blow to her head made her vision blur.

The creature before her was massive, the size of a small starfighter, with green, iridescent scales and three sharp-tipped tentacles that flew toward

Fenrir, who held the fourth tentacle pinned to the ice. Fenrir ripped into its flesh with his long teeth. The creature reeled back, pulling away the severed appendage and leaving only the sharp tip on the ice. Green glowing ichor dripped from Fenrir's fangs as he snarled at the beast.

A spear-tipped tentacle smashed into the ice where Fenrir had been just moments before. Shards of ice flew into the air around the impact. Fenrir raked his claws along the tentacle now embedded in the ice. A second tentacle lashed out, slicing along Fenrir's ribs. He hissed at the creature. Crimson bloomed along his side from shoulder to tail.

Skyla had to do something. Those tentacles outnumbered Fenrir. Even with his strength and size, he was no match for the creature alone. She pushed to her feet, boots sliding under her as she fought for balance on the ice. She pulled out the handle of her nanite staff, extending dual blades from either end. A purple glow of electricity crackled around the edges as she advanced on the creature. She took a wide, sweeping arc at an incoming tentacle. The blade sliced clean through, raining glowing green blood over her as the tentacle fell lifelessly to the ice.

Electricity sizzled up the skin of the beast, extending out from the wound. The beast let out a piercing cry. Its two intact tentacles thrashed wildly in the air. Skyla screamed back with a feral battle cry as she advanced on the creature. Its six onyx eyes widened as it took in her manic fury, seeing her as a threat for the first time. It squawked once, gnashing a beaked jaw, then slid back into the dark depths.

Adrenaline-induced tremors racked her body, but she stood focusing on the rippling water of the monster's retreat until eventually the water calmed, taking on a glass-like sheen. Only then did she collapse to her knees, drawing in deep shuddering breaths.

A low whimper pulled her from the shock setting into her bones. She crawled over to Fenrir, who had collapsed on the ice where he stood. Deep crimson matted his fur and turned to a frozen pool of gore beneath him. His warm eyes looked up at her, pleading, just like they had on another strange planet when she had rescued him.

"I won't let you die," she whispered, but Skyla's heart nearly stopped when she saw how deep the wound was. A long gash stretched down his side, penetrating deeper until it had nearly severed his hind leg. Hot tears clouded her vision at the realization that she couldn't save the leg. Maybe if she had a full med bay and an army of nanites—maybe then she would have been able to knit the flesh back together—but not here, with nothing but a field med kit. Blood flowed freely from the wound, and Skyla knew there was only one way to save his life. Trying to quell the tears that threatened to overwhelm her, Skyla came to her feet, extending her bladed staff out to her side.

"You have to trust me, buddy." Her voice wavered as electricity rippled across her blade. In one swift motion, she finished what the sea beast had started, severing through the last of the tissue that held Fenrir's hind leg in place.

The air filled with the acrid smell of burnt hair while Fenrir's cry ripped through her soul. But her blade had done its job. Scorch marks branched out across the bloodied flesh, completely cauterizing the wound.

She hummed softly to let Fenrir know she was there as she packed the wound. She brushed her hand along his fur and let the tears fall freely now. Once she had packed the wound, she tucked her supplies away and loaded Fenrir onto the makeshift sled. His eyes had closed some time ago, but his breath remained strong. There was nothing more she could do for him here. It was up to him now to fight for his life, and it was up to her to get them to safety. Pele waited for rescue, and Fenrir depended on her strength. As bruised and broken as she was, she would not fail them.

CHAPTER 2 | FREYJA

To Ruin

"I want him off my ship!" Rohaan stomped down Cista's ramp; his boots kicked up red dust with each step.

"It can't be that bad," Freyja said. Her eyes locked onto Tristan as he followed close behind, his muscled forearms folded across his chest and a mischievous smirk plastered on his thick lips. Freyja shook her head. Twenty years and the man hadn't changed a bit since they were cadets back at the academy.

"It's worse." Rohaan stopped in front of Freyja, irritation coming off him in waves. "He is loud, foul-mouthed; an absolute slob! I can't get any work done with his incessant noise! I can't live with him on my ship. I want him off, now!"

Freyja chuckled at the description. Tristan was an acquired taste. She would give Rohaan that. He was also loyal to the end and a damn-skilled weapons expert.

"Doctor, if you'll remember, Tristan is on your ship because you insisted it wouldn't be proper for Dr. Aman to house with you. We have limited space, and concessions must be made."

Rohaan's face turned red; whether from embarrassment or anger she couldn't be sure.

"I must insist that we return to the central rim and have Dr. Pinot install the rapid remodeling technology on our AI ships. Our current arrangement...Is. Not. Working."

Freyja rubbed a hand over her brow as she took a moment to consider. This wasn't the first time the scientist had made the request, and Freyja had previously declined each time before. He and Tristan had been bickering for months. It was imperative that they get to the bottom of the mysterious signal before more blood was shed. Before her mother realized that she had not indeed perished in the capitol bombing, as Freyja had led the entire United Tribal Axis to believe. Foolishly, she had thought she could end this swiftly, but the weeks had stretched into months, and now they were in need of a resupply, even if this site had the answers she so desperately sought.

Irritation flared under her skin. She had thought they would have found the source of the signal by now. Freyja fought to calm the rising flame. There was no reason they couldn't seek out the doctor while they restocked their ships. Dr. Pinot had made extensive upgrades to Pele that had allowed them to connect the AI ships on a joint venture to the Zeta quadrant. If she could make those same improvements to Selkie and Cista, their expedition to discover the origins of the mysterious signal would be much more comfortable for everyone.

Freyja sighed. Maybe Skyla had returned to the central rim by now. Every day that passed, the dread of what was to come settled deeper into her bones, burrowing like deep space drill bits until they lodged into the marrow and wouldn't let go. The reports that came in. The moves The Empire made. Even without evidence, Freyja feared she already knew who was behind it all. It reeked of power, control, fear: the very tenets of her upbringing. The signature was undeniable, yet she wasn't ready to face what that would mean for her and her crew. She could use Skyla at her side.

"After we finish here, we will head back to the central rim for supplies, and I will request Dr. Pinot's assistance with our ships."

Rohaan's shoulders relaxed away from his ears. "And what will I do with this idiot until then—"

"I am not an idiot…just because you don't appreciate my style of genius." Tristan leaned an elbow against the doctor's shoulder.

Rohaan snorted, shook Tristan off, and took a deep breath to prepare for another onslaught of insults when Kylian stepped in.

"Aye boss ma'am, I'll bunk with the scientist on the return trip ya?" he said in his accented standard, a side of him he only shared with those he trusted. Freyja quirked an eyebrow, looking at her second-in-command. She hadn't realized how close he had grown to Rohaan.

Freyja hesitated. She preferred to keep Kylian close. The idea of him on another ship soured her stomach. It was bad enough that his cousin Tristan had taken the spot on Rohaan's ship, but they had limited space, and between her crew and Dr. Aman, Selkie was full. Tristan had been the logical choice. She trusted him with her life and knew he would watch over the doctor, and he wasn't an idiot; he was more than versed enough in weapon's tech to help assist the doctor with some of his research if they could find a way to get along.

As much as she hated to admit it, Kylian was the next logical choice. He was their resident hacker. Truth be told, he would probably do a better job working with the doctor than Tristan. Freyja's skin itched at the thought of it. She hadn't been separated from Kylian since the academy. She didn't like it, but it was the best solution for the mission.

"Fine, Kylian will bunk with you on the return trip. Now, can we get to work?"

Rohaan sighed, the fight leaching out of him, and he gave a brief nod before disappearing back into his ship to grab his gear. Freyja smiled and shook her head. The scientist had grown over the past six months. She couldn't imagine the quiet man she had met after the battle of Medina standing up to her like that.

"I hope that's okay with you, Admiral." Kylian stood at her side, his voice low.

She shrugged. "I don't like it...but it's for the best. Those two would probably kill each other on the return trip otherwise."

Kylian chuckled, rubbing the back of his neck. His fingers caught on the edge of the thick, white scar that slashed across his throat. His smile twitched, and he dropped his hand. It was a reminder of an operation gone sideways and of his undying loyalty to Freyja. She hadn't needed to save his life to gain his loyalty. She already had it, but it had sealed their bond. The sight of the scar always made her uneasy, an ever-present reminder of how close she had come to losing him. The thought flared hot and angry in her. She turned back to the ship.

"Let's get a move on, Rohaan," Freyja shouted.

The rest of their crew clustered around her, ready to move out with their packs cinched tight and fine red dust already coating their boots. Freyja had escaped the battle of Medina with only her two lieutenant commanders and five Berserkers. Her personal army whittled down to these few souls.

So few remained of those who had fought at her side since the academy. The loss was an oozing wound that only continued to fester; it would never heal.

"Adelice and Loic, you're on camp duty. Watch over the ships. Make sure everything is in order for our return trip."

The two Berserkers nodded. "Yes, boss ma'am."

Over the past few months, her entire crew had slipped into accented standard, a habit the UTA made a point of stomping out of cadets at the academy. But now they only had her to answer to, and she welcomed the comfort of their accented words. It was a piece of their past that no one could take from them. They were on their own, and even though they still called her admiral, she no longer commanded fleets, just this strange little crew. She was surprised to find she didn't miss the power or the prestige; she had everything she needed right here.

Rohaan reappeared with Dr. Zarah Aman by his side and dual drones hovering over his shoulder. Dr. Aman was all smiles as her eyes raced over the alien landscape. The scientist had traded in her traditional dress for black cargo pants and a long-sleeved, black tee shirt, courtesy of the UTA gear from Selkie's stores. The only remnant of Medina culture was the burnt-orange hijab wrapped around her hair. They had landed in a desert basin only five kilometers from the ruin of an Old World society. Great cliffs of sandstone rose in the distance, splashed with lines that told their story over eons. Countless hoodoos stretched to the horizon, and strange, spiky, silver plants dotted the rocky landscape. It was harsh and deadly; Freyja thought it might be the most beautiful planet she had ever visited.

On Rohaan's command, the drones shot off into the distance. The drones disappeared behind a cliff face while Freyja and the rest of the crew watched. Rohaan's eyes went glassy, taking in the readings from his ocular display.

"This may take a little longer than I thought," Rohaan muttered.

"What is it?" Freyja stepped closer to the scientist.

"These ruins were built into the side of a cliff. My initial scans indicate the ruins extend deep into a cave system. I'll need more time to fully map the cavern."

Freyja fought to temper her building annoyance. "How much longer, Doc?"

Rohaan hesitated. "I should have the complete scans by nightfall."

"Damn it, I wanted to be off this rock before then."

"I'm sorry, Admiral." Rohaan blinked hard, and his deep brown eyes focused on Freyja.

She knew just as well as he did that it wasn't worth going into the ruins after dark. Freyja let the anger radiate along her skin a moment longer before she conceded. "It looks like we'll be spending the night." Turning on her heel, she stomped back toward her ship. Another delay. This entire mission had been one delay after another, and she wasn't sure how many more she could take.

"It doesn't have to be a bad thing." Kylian matched his stride with hers.

"I'd rather get what we need and get off this rock as soon as possible."

Once they stepped into the cargo bay, out of sight of the rest of the crew, Kylian caught her by the elbow and spun her, pinning her against the bulkhead before she could disappear into her quarters. Her eyes flared with anger as they burrowed into him. Yet he returned her ire with one of his crooked grins—the one that made her forget she was angry with him.

Selkie's lights dimmed, flickering red with her displeasure. "Know your place, Aimé." Her near-human voice was closer to a growl than words.

Freyja patted her palm against the bulkhead behind her. "It's fine, Selkie."

There was a moment of hesitation before Selkie relented, the red hue leaching from the lights, leaving them a soft pink.

Kylian leaned in closer. "Freyja," he spoke softly, "we have been at this for months. It's okay to take a night off."

"Every delay costs lives." Freyja's gut twisted with the thought of her own Berserkers who had fallen on the *Ormen Korte*, whose bodies she had abandoned to the enemy instead of returning to the stars. All because of a signal that had impersonated her likeness and given orders she never would have given. A signal that had put into motion the events that had led to the fall of the United Tribal Axis and the start of a war that raged across the galaxy.

She had to find the source, find who was behind all of this, and put an end to it. That signal would lead her to the traitor, and when it did, she would take her vengeance. Only once she had bathed her sword in blood, could she rest...and yet, a voice nagged at the corners of her mind, a voice that whispered that she already knew who was to blame. A voice that taunted her. It whispered that she would never be able to stand up to the one who had created her.

"I can't rest until this is done. We have to get to the bottom of this signal."

Kylian continued to smile at her as he held her in place.

Freyja rolled her eyes. "What?"

"Nothing boss." That stupid grin was still on his face.

Yanking her arm free of his grip, Freyja only took one step before Kylian boxed her in with a hand on either side of her shoulders, dipping his head close. "It's one night. The crew needs it."

Freyja's eyes caught on his. She swallowed hard before relenting. "Fine, let the crew have their fun."

Kylian dropped his arms, but the moment Freyja moved to disappear into her quarters, he grabbed her by the hand and led her back out into the desert.

"I said it was fine, Kylian. Now, can you leave me be?"

"You're part of the crew, Freyja. You need this too."

She sighed, but finally relented. He was right; they had pushed hard these past months, moving from planet to planet, investigating ruins, and collecting data. Dr. Dar insisted they were close to having enough data to pinpoint the source of the signal, but Freyja had only grown more restless. The gravity of her mission weighed heavy on her. She was tired of fighting. She didn't have it in her to fight Kylian, too.

"Alright then, what did you have in mind?"

That crooked grin spread into a wide smile. "Leave it to me."

***

By the time Kylian had settled onto a log beside Freyja, stars were scattered across a pale pink sky, giving way to the violets of the void. The golden flames of the bonfire licked at the approaching night, scattering embers into the darkening sky. The warmth of the fire was comforting on her skin as the temperature dipped with the fading light.

Kylian pressed a flask into Freyja's hands, and she smiled, unscrewed the top, and clinked it against his before taking a drink. Tequila. Her favorite.

Across the fire, Makena, Ona'je, and Basilie held long sticks with 3D printed meats stacked to the tip. They held the kebabs just above the flames, joking amongst themselves about the rations back at the academy.

"We had 3D printers in the dorms. Why didn't anyone ever print food like this?" Basilie pulled her kabab from the flames, gently pinching a cube between her fingers to check the cook.

"Because they kept those printers on lock. Only the academy approved slop!" Makena knocked a playful shoulder into Basilie. "Although rumor has it, Aimé knew how to hack those things. Huh, boss, were you holding out on us?" Makena called out across the fire.

Kylian shook his head. "Don't you think if I knew how to hack those printers you would have seen me eating something better than enhanced amino gel?"

Makena considered this a moment before nodding and diving into another argument with her fellow Berserkers.

Kylian turned to Freyja, conspiratorial mischief in his eyes, because he had indeed learned how to hack those printers, and apparently the only people who knew about it were the two of them.

Tristan pulled out his guitar and began to sing. This was one of Kylian's favorites. He had often sung with Tristan back when they were cadets, but he didn't join his cousin now. Freyja studied the man beside her. A soft smile sat on his lips, but there was sadness reflected in his warm hazel eyes as he watched Tristan play. Freya's gaze dropped to the thick scar across his neck, and cold guilt washed over her at the realization. She hadn't heard Kylian sing with his cousin since the ring mission. Now she wondered if he even could.

Freyja tapped her flask against Kylian's to gain his attention. He broke his gaze away from Tristan to settle on her.

"To family," she said softly.

A knowing smile spread across Kylian's lips. "To those bound by blood."

"And those forged in it!" The rest of the crew took up the cheer with raised glasses.

Freyja's cheeks heated. She had lost herself in the moment, forgetting that the entire crew was gathered around her. She waited until they had picked up with their own activities before speaking.

"You were right." Freyja nodded at him to drink.

Kylian took a slow pull from his flask. "And what was I right about?"

Her heart warmed at the sound of his deep voice and clipped vowels. "Are you going to make me say it?"

"I can't make you do anything, Freyja," he whispered.

A smile of her own carved its way across her lips, and for once, she didn't feel the need to fight it. In this moment, by the warmth of the bonfire and her closest friends, she finally let her guard slip.

"The crew needed this." Freyja took a sip of her drink to avoid the gloating grin Kylian gave her.

"The crew needed it?" He wasn't going to let it go.

"Fine, I needed it, happy?"

"Extremely." Kylian leaned back, smug in his victory.

"You're insufferable."

He tilted his head to the side, a dark eyebrow raised. "I think you like it."

A panicked fluttering beat against Freyja's ribs at his words, but Loic's shout from across the fire saved her from a reply.

"Who's up for a round?" Loic slapped a deck of cards down on a bio plastic drum.

"Ready to lose all your credits again, Loic?" Tristan tucked his guitar away and moved to join Loic and Adelice. When Freyja looked back to Kylian, she found him studying her, and her skin prickled under his gaze.

"Hey cousin, get over here. Loic's ready to fund your new hoverbike!" Tristan shouted.

"Yeah, yeah, yeah, you won't be shit-talking when I'm done with you." Loic laughed as he dealt the cards, leaving a space for Kylian to join them.

Kylian swallowed hard, reluctant to turn his gaze from her. Freyja watched his heated gaze melt away to a cocky grin as he stood to join the crew.

Inhaling deeply through her nose, Freyja fought to push away the dangerous thoughts that played through her mind—thoughts that she shouldn't have for a man that had been her rock her entire life, but her racing pulse betrayed her. The bitterness of tequila on her tongue helped to cleanse her mind. Yes, the tequila, it was just the tequila.

***

The early morning rays crested over the distant rock formations, painting the desolate landscape in pinks and golds. The levity of the night before was already fading. Freyja had a mission to accomplish, and it was back to business as usual. No more delays. It was time to get what they had come for.

Kylian stepped up beside Freyja, scouring his hand across his face in an effort to remove the sleep from his eyes. He had still been playing cards with the crew when she slipped away last night, and it appeared he had gotten carried away with the festivities.

"Beautiful morning isn't it, cuz?" Tristan threw an arm around Kylian, who immediately shrugged the man away.

"Aye, do you always have to be so loud?" Kylian squinted daggers at his cousin.

"Now, now, don't be like that. Last night was a riot. Don't go and ruin a perfectly pleasant morning because you're a poor sport." Tristan snorted a stim.

"I can't believe you got me to bet my code stack last night," Kylian groaned. "What the hell was in that burner?"

"Just good fun." Tristan winked.

"What a beautiful ecosystem." Zarah joined Freyja, effectively ending the argument, though Kylian's expression remained sour.

"Dr. Aman." Freyja nodded to the woman. "Are you certain you'd like to accompany us into the field? It won't be an easy hike to the ruins."

Dr. Aman bobbed her head in assent. "Yes, quite sure. I have spent too much time in the lab. I think it's time I get a look at the tech in the field." Zarah's voice was quick and cheerful as ever. It grated on Freyja, the way the woman was endlessly optimistic.

"Suit yourself." Freyja cupped her hands to her mouth and yelled, "Rohaan, we are rolling out."

At her prompt, Rohaan stuck his head out from the back of his starship, several scientific instruments clutched in one arm and an open field bag grasped in the other.

"Right, I'm ready," he muttered, stuffing the last of his items into the bag. The man was still no field researcher, but he had improved quite a bit from their first expedition. His eyes caught on Zarah's, and they both turned a light shade of pink. Freyja rolled her eyes. They were both so obvious. They were also both oblivious.

"Let's go, doctors." Freyja turned and guided them in the direction of the ruins.

It was slow-moving with the two scientists, but after an hour, the ruins finally came into view. They hiked straight toward the giant cliff face. An opening, framed by ornate columns over one hundred meters high carved straight into the sandstone, rose before them. A pantheon of carved creatures stood guard above the opening. Strange beasts mixed and tangled in the space between columns. If they were a reflection of the creatures on this planet, she hoped they wouldn't run into any of them.

"Magnificent." Zarah stared up at the carvings, a thick sheen of sweat beading her brow.

"Those are some massive stones. Think they were compensating for something?" Tristan elbowed his cousin.

Kylian slapped him in the back of the head in response. "Pay attention," Kylian muttered, but his smile gave him away.

"It's impressive, but not what we are here for. Power up," Freyja said as she made her way to the mouth of the cavern. The high-lumen torches strapped to their arms illuminated the path as they picked their way through the loose dirt and large rocks that had built up over time.

While boulders and mounds of sand partially blocked the entrance, the debris lessened as they advanced into the space, until their boots clicked on a perfectly polished floor. Beams of light bounced off the surface, illuminating little particles in the stone that glittered gold. The sculpted walls gave way to the same refined stone as the ground. Silence pressed in, oppressive in its totality; the only sounds were their steps and their breath as they made their way through the long corridor. In the distance, the dark swallowed up their lights as the hallway opened up to a massive cavern.

The cavern was so large that their torch lights barely pierced the darkness, which stretched in all directions. Freyja held up her fist, signaling for the scientists to hold. They were too busy inspecting the walls around the entrance to notice. That suited Freyja just fine. She didn't want them wandering into the dark.

"Stay put," Freyja said.

Rohaan waved her off, too busy scanning the symbols that rimmed the doorway to be bothered.

Freyja gestured directions to the rest of her team. "Do a sweep. I want to know what we are dealing with." While the drones had provided scans of the structures, there was no telling what else awaited them in the dark. Her soldiers paired off, then advanced into the gloom, leaving Freyja with the two scientists who were talking quietly in an excited rush.

"Find something?" she asked.

Zarah bounced up and down with excitement. "Yes, this is the same text that we found on two of the other planets."

"And it matches the text samples Skyla brought back from her first expedition into the Zeta quadrant."

Freyja pinched the bridge of her nose, exhaling her annoyance. "How does that help us determine who is sending the signal?"

Rohaan shook his head. "I don't know that it does, but it proves that these planets were linked. They shared a language, and I would bet they also shared technology. We should look for a protected, clean room like we found at the last two sites."

Freyja groaned. She hadn't signed up to be an archaeologist; she was on a mission to discover who was behind the signal and stop them from sowing any more chaos. The scientists had remained firm that researching the tech from these worlds was how they would find answers, but after months without progress, Freyja had her doubts. Recently, she had begun to wonder if they weren't just indulging their scientific curiosity. Anger flared beneath her skin at the thought of it. If the lack of progress was indeed due to their insubordination, she would have to remind them of their place.

"Freyja, I think we found what we're looking for." Kylian stepped out of the darkness. "Come on." He motioned with his head for them to follow. The space was so immense their lights only illuminated a small pool around them, though as their light beams swept back-and-forth, Freyja caught glimpses of the abandoned city. Grand sandstone buildings rose to either side of them, carved with designs that matched the sculptures outside, but one side of the avenue crumbled into sharp fragments that now littered their path. Buildings and sculptures alike lay like glass houses toppled from their pedestals in sharp contrast to the structures that stood untouched to her other side, as if their occupants had just stepped away and could return at any moment.

Freyja shuddered, trying to chase away the prickling feeling of unease that crawled over her skin, setting the hair on the back of her neck on end. They had seen the same scene at the other worlds they had visited. Structures smashed beyond recognition, while others looked like they were brand new. She had a hard time believing a natural phenomenon would be so discerning in its destruction.

They wove their way through the ruins until they reached the far side of the cavern. There, ornately carved structures lined the cavern walls. The ground level looked like shops and storefronts, while those up above had most likely been living spaces, with balconies and windows. Empty terracotta pots that may have once held plants lined the railings; all they housed now was dust.

"This one here." Kylian motioned to one of the buildings where Tristan stood, leaning against the wall with one leg propped up behind him, as if he had just stepped out of the nightclub for a smoke. Freyja knew it was all an act, though. His eyes were sharp, scanning the darkness for threats.

"What's so special about this one?" Freyja asked. Carvings of tangled, intertwining ropes with jewel-like strands between them decorated the exterior.

"Rohaan here gave us a guide to the symbols based on the ruins we've seen so far." Kylian tapped the twining rope carvings. "And these here represent DNA. It could be there's something worth looking at..." He trailed off, not as sure of himself as he had been when he'd led them across the cavern.

Rohaan stepped up, clasping Kylian by the shoulder while he leaned in to inspect the carvings. "Good find!" Rohaan said. "This is very promising indeed—"

"Have you swept the structure?" Freyja cut in before one of the scientists rushed into the space.

"We were waiting for you, boss ma'am." Tristan kicked off the wall and strode over to the group, pulling his nanite sword from its scabbard as he walked. "Shall we?" he asked with a crooked grin as he nodded toward the entrance.

Freyja drew her own sword. "On your mark."

Tristan and Kylian lined up shoulder to shoulder, then kicked the doors in with heavy boots. The loud crash of wood against stone echoed through the cavern, and Zarah jumped beside Freyja.

"Stay behind me," Freyja ordered the two scientists, then followed her men into the structure. The building was small enough that it took mere minutes to clear the space. There was nothing of note. It was mostly empty; the equipment cleared out long ago. Kylian shook his head as he rubbed the back of his neck. "Sorry, I really thought it was something worth looking into."

"Give me a moment," Rohaan said, making his way to the back wall. Unlike the outside of the building, the walls inside were smooth, clean, and sterile, except for a line of carved, twining DNA running through the middle of the back wall. Rohaan ran his fingers along the carving, muttering softly to himself.

"Dr. Aman, can you give me a hand?" he asked.

She stepped up next to them, and they brought their heads close, quietly discussing something Freyja couldn't hear as they pointed to different sections of the DNA strand. After a few moments of debate, Rohaan pulled a sync cord from the datapad on his arm and inserted it into the carving. A pulse of electricity flowed through the chiseled DNA structure as Rohaan's fingers danced above the keypad. Then there was a click, and the carving peeled apart, strands of DNA unwinding as the wall slid back to reveal a second room. This room housed rows upon rows of glass tubes that ran its entire length, all of them glowing a gentle blue, the creatures inside peaceful in deep cryo.

"What is this place?" Freyja whispered.

CHAPTER 3 | HINATA

OBLIVION

Battles are not won with force alone. Hinata knew this. Hinata knew all of the rules of engagement. And though this fight had just begun, he already knew it was only a matter of time before he claimed victory.

Pressing his weight into his stance, Hinata stood strong against the broad sword that threatened to push through his defenses. The soldier that met his blow had at least twenty kilos on Hinata, and it took all of his force behind the blade to hold the man off. Damn the Stjarna Tribe and their giant Viking genetics.

Gritting his teeth, he twisted his hips and slid to the side, removing his counterweight and throwing his opponent off-balance. What Hinata lacked in size, he made up for in skill. Trading quick blows, Hinata increased the pace until—there, that was his opening. The man staggered forward; Hinata dragged his blade across the man's exposed shoulder, peeling open the battle armor to expose delicate flesh.

"Surrender your ship, and I will send you back to your tribe," Hinata said through labored breaths.

"We have rights to this trade route just as much as Hoshiko. I'm not leaving without those supply ships." The man hurled a wad of spit at Hinata's boots to accent his point.

"Have it your way," Hinata growled as he answered with another series of blows. This time, he moved at full speed. His previous advances had been measured. He had been testing his opponent. The man was strong, but he was all brute force, no match for Hinata's speed. It was over before it even began. With a flick of his wrist, Hinata sent the man's broadsword flying across the deck. The soldier took one step to chase after his weapon, but Hinata halted his advance with a blade to the throat.

"Behave. You've already lost this battle. Don't lose your head to go with it." Hinata's voice was even. Any emotions the fight had stirred reigned back in under his control.

The man lifted his hands in surrender, slowly standing and squaring his shoulders. Deep loathing burned in those ice-blue eyes—ice-blue, like the captain's. Hinata shook his head, trying to force the image of the woman from his mind, but it was no use. She was there now. It would take hours of training to tire his mind enough for sleep that night. A sleep, that if it finally came, would no doubt be haunted with her image all the same.

Six months had passed since they had parted ways at Gefion. Six months and no word. The Known Galaxies were vast, and the uncharted space beyond was endless. If she didn't want to be found, there was nothing he could do. Quantum relay stations littered the colonized systems. She must have passed a relay by now. Yet she hadn't responded to a single message.

Not a single holo, not a single line of text. She had taken her opportunity to return to her adventures and left him behind.

Hinata balled his hands into fists as frustration burned through him. He had let the one thing he had truly wanted get away. Why hadn't he begged her to stay? Why hadn't he gone with her?

Instead, he stayed. Stayed to fight this war, stayed to serve his tribe. He had stayed out of honor and duty, and what had it gotten him? The UTA was in pieces, fragmented into the great houses and conglomerates of lesser tribes. Crime syndicates staked their claims on lesser systems, while factions fought over scraps, and he was stuck in an endless round of skirmishes over farming rights and trade routes.

Hinata's attention snapped back to the Stjarna soldier before him. He still saw Skyla's eyes when he looked at the man, and it made his blood boil. The man before him was massive. Hinata wasn't a small man by any means, but the Stjarna soldier before him stood more than a head taller. He was all muscle, with long, white-blond hair half pulled up into a bun, the soft shadow of a beard covering an angled jaw, and pale, unblemished skin.

Hinata forced his anger down. It wasn't this man's fault that he was on the other side of this war, just as he hadn't chosen for his tribe to secede from the United Tribal Axis. They were both merely pawns in someone else's game.

The pounding of boots behind him signaled his reinforcements had arrived.

"Secure the prisoners," Hinata demanded as he sheathed his katana.

"What do you want us to do with them, sir?" The little Hoshiko soldier had to tilt her head back to take in the prisoner.

Hinata didn't want more mouths to feed in his fleet. He had given the man the choice, and he had chosen to engage. If Hinata let this crew go, he would face off against them again in the next skirmish. There were no more decisions to be made. He would detain them and send them to the prisoner-of-war camp at Jubokko.

This isn't what he signed up for.

"Take them to the brig."

***

The blue glow of the training room clock lied. Had it already been two hours? Sweat cut rivers across Hinata's sculpted chest. A deep ache settled into his muscles, yet he needed more. Even stripped down to the waist, Hinata found the training facility sweltering. His muscles burned from the effort, yet it wasn't enough to soothe his tortured soul. He had to push further. The obstacle course blurred around him. Jump, grab, twist, dodge. He moved like a demon, dominating every level until, finally, his grip failed. Falling from the top platform left him breathless on the mat for only a moment. He couldn't stop, couldn't rest; he had to move. He wrapped his hands, trying not to let his mind wander as he worked through the practiced motions. It was no use. The only thing that kept his thoughts from spiraling was action.

Jab, jab, cross, uppercut. He worked through one combination, then the next, and the next until his knuckles bruised through the wraps. His breaths came in labored waves; his lungs starved for oxygen, and yet his mind was still too alert. His thoughts raced in endless circles. What could he do next? He needed to escape into the rhythm of his heartbeat, into the motions and the effort. Even as his body failed him, he craved release.

The doors to the training facility snapped open. Tax stood alone in the doorway. He took one look at Hinata and shook his head.

"Again?" Tax asked as he approached. The doors snapped shut behind him. With the wave of his arm, he sealed them before advancing on Hinata.

Hinata already knew the lecture Tax would give him by heart, having heard it many times over the past few months. He knew Tax had locked the doors because he didn't want the rest of his soldiers to see him like this. Though there was little chance of that, the crew had learned to steer clear of the training room when Hinata was there. Not in the mood to be reprimanded, Hinata shrugged and walked away, but there was no escaping Tax.

Tax approached slowly, giving Hinata time to collect himself. "How long are you going to keep doing this?"

"As long as it takes," Hinata said.

"What happens if we are on another boarding party tomorrow?" Tax eyed Hinata's bruised knuckles and shaking hands.

"Then I will rise to the occasion," Hinata snapped, but there was no bite behind his words. He was too tired for it.

Tax dropped into one of the plush chairs that lined the back of the room. His eyes flicked from Hinata to the chair beside him. Hinata sighed but eventually caved. Fatigue was already weighing heavily on him, and training himself into oblivion wasn't working. He sank into the chair beside his second-in-command, tilting his head back to trace the contours of the cross beams overhead.

"Want to talk about it?" Tax asked.

"No." Hinata continued to focus on the angular titanium structure of his ship, cold and lifeless, so different from the soft coral contours of Pele's hull. What he wouldn't give to be on that ship again, with her. He pressed his eyes closed against the thought. He couldn't escape her. Everything reminded him of her, and he was certain he was slowly going mad.

The two men let the silence stretch until Tax finally broke it. "Well, do it anyway."

Hinata groaned, "Why do I put up with you?"

"Because I am the only one who can put up with you. Now talk, because this—" Tax waved an arm, gesturing to Hinata's broken body. "—isn't working."

"I can't get her out of my head." Hinata's words were so soft he almost hoped Tax hadn't heard.

"Why do you want to?" Tax's deep brown eyes were gentle, and Hinata was relieved to find there was no pity there, just a desire to understand.

"Because it hurts to think about her. It hurts to know that I can't be with her, that I choose to stay and fight this pointless war..." Hinata trailed off. He didn't want to say the worst of it.

Tax waited for him to go on.

"It hurts too much to know that I chose wrong." He squeezed his eyes shut against the thought. He had followed his training; he had done the honorable thing, and it had meant nothing.

Tax clasped his shoulder. "You don't know that."

Hinata locked eyes with Tax, letting his turmoil bleed through, letting his mask fall.

"You don't know that you chose wrong." Tax tightened his grip, the pressure a comforting anchor to this moment. "There is still good we can do in this universe. The battle isn't over yet, and when we see our opportunity to turn the tide, I promise I will be at your side. We will make the difference. We will make it matter."

Hinata gave a curt nod. He wasn't sure that he believed Tax's words, but it was something to hold on to.

"And it's okay to think about her, you know. She isn't lost, just searching. If it's meant to be, she will find her way back to you."

"And if it's not meant to be?" The words were out before Hinata could stop them. He didn't want the answer to that question.

"Then the memories will fade, and someday it won't hurt so much."

CHAPTER 4 | SKYLA

INTO THE DARKNESS

Skyla took the better part of an hour to get all of their supplies up the ice cliff. Finally everything was repacked around Fenrir, who she had bundled into a sleeping bag atop her makeshift sled. Once repositioned, he nuzzled into the bedding and closed his eyes against the biting wind. Worry twisted her thoughts, but the gentle rise and fall of his ribs reassured her. While he still had breath, he had a chance. She just needed to get him to shelter.

Skyla pulled the hood of her jacket up over her head, cinching it close to her skin, then strapped a ventilator over her mouth. It wasn't much, but it would help protect her from the freezing temperatures and endless wind.

Swirling blue particles danced across Skyla's datapad as she waited for it to sync. The seconds felt like hours. Finally, a soft ping signaled it was complete, and a shimmering holo display materialized. A purple dot pulsed at the edge of the ice cliff where she now stood. The pixels shifted as the display zoomed out until a green dot strobed softly on the edge of the map—the settlement. Skyla reoriented herself toward the research outpost...it was nearly one hundred kilometers away.

The weight of the task ahead pressed heavy on her, but she pushed it away, knowing it would drown her if she let it. She could do this—she didn't really believe it, but she didn't have a choice, and so, with the sled anchored to a makeshift harness across her chest, she began to walk. One foot in front of the other, each step took her closer to the settlement. Each step was a step closer to saving Fenrir. As time ticked on, Skyla grew irritated with the shapeless snow mounds that stretched into the distance, identical in every way, as if she walked in place, never truly advancing toward her goal. She couldn't take it a second longer; initiating her ocular display, she zoomed in as far as she could on the path ahead. It was more of the same, all snow and ice until her visuals hit a wall made of dancing green and gold light, swirls of ice laced through the brilliant display. The trek was getting to her. It was delirium, or a mirage, or an anomaly...it didn't matter, she would deal with it when they got there. Every so often, she tried sending an emergency signal out to the settlement. All she got back was buzzy static over an eerie hum.

"That would have been too easy, wouldn't it?" she grumbled to herself after several attempts with no response. "Couldn't have had someone from the settlement just come pick us up, huh?" Skyla pretended like the comment was meant for Fenrir. But she knew the truth; he was asleep, and the words were for her alone. She had to stay focused, focused on the goal, one foot in front of the other.

I am the blaze in the flame.
I am the calm in the storm.
I am the force behind the machine.
The choice is mine.
Fear has no power over me.

The world fell away; only the litany remained. Time ticked on as she repeated the words over and over again until she nearly laughed. What she wouldn't do to feel that warmth, to be the blaze in the flame. They were just words.

The snow shifted under her boots. The wind bit into the exposed flesh around her ventilator, and a blinding glare reflected off the ice. Her feet ached from hours spent trudging through the snow, her toes gripping and relaxing in an endless cycle to try to stabilize on the unstable ground.

A fully armored space suit would solve a lot of her problems right now. Why hadn't she been wearing one? That's right, she hadn't planned on being shot out of the sky.

With a forceful blow through her nose, Skyla pushed the thought from her mind. She was fine. She could do this. At least her nanite survival gear was still regulating her body temperature and minimizing her water loss, even if it did nothing for her muscles that now protested every movement.

One more step: her hips ached, and her stride shortened.

One more step: her feet shuffled over the ice as she lost the strength to lift them.

One more step: she fought the hot prickling sensation of tears as she noticed her pace dwindle.

Her chest constricted with panic when she did the mental math. She was moving too slow. At this rate, it would still take her hours to reach the settlement. With over ten hours out on the ice already, she wasn't sure that she had hours—

Panic struck. Seizing her body. Constricting her lungs. Threatening to take her over. She shook her head. Focus, right here, be right here. One foot in front of the other, each step is one step closer. She could make it. The panic settled into a low hum at the back of her mind, not gone, but manageable.

Time blurred, and her muscles began to seize, the spasms locking her knees; she tried to force them to move, but her legs had stopped responding to her commands. By sheer will alone, she forced her body forward.

One step.

Two steps.

Three—

She collapsed onto the ice. Dry sobs racked her body; the pure exhaustion robbing her of tears. Her breath came in panicked rasps as she pressed her eyes together, trying to take control, trying to will her body to comply, but she had nothing left to give, and so she gave into the darkness, letting it swallow her whole. She gave into the depth of her despair. They weren't going to make it, and no one was coming for them.

CHAPTER 5 | FREYJA

OF TECH & MONSTERS

Freyja ran her hand along the cryo tubes as she walked the length of the storeroom. The chill that met her fingertips dispelled any doubt about the integrity of the tanks. What was the purpose of hundreds of creatures identical to Skyla's pet Fenrir?

When she turned around, she found Rohaan already plugged into a wall console, fully engrossed in what he had found there.

"Want to share with the rest of us?" she asked.

"Of course, Admiral, now that we have collected language samples from several sites, I have a rough translator running. This site was focused on genetic engineering." Rohaan swiped his fingers over his datapad to pull up a holo of the creature. "Fenrir and his friends appear to be genetic hybrids, with primary components from the genus Caracal and Canis, plus a dozen others—fascinating."

"You lost us, Doc." Tristan tapped on the glass of one of the tanks.

Rohaan glared at Tristan before answering. "It looks like Fenrir is a combination of creatures. Primarily, his DNA comes from a large cat and a wolf, plus a dozen others, with a couple of additions from the local flora and fauna to make him more robust." Rohaan swiped his hand again to reveal a list of all the inputs that went into the hybrid.

"Why?" Freyja asked.

"It appears that they were service animals. They were bred to be strong, lethal, and extremely loyal to assist the colonists here on their expeditions."

Freyja shook her head. Not growing up with animals on Upsala station, she struggled to see the point.

"Our friends here aren't their only experiments. Come." Rohaan disconnected his datapad and led Freyja to a side door. She lifted her boot to kick in the door, but Rohaan raised his hand to stop her. "I've got this." With a series of taps, the door sprang open. They stepped into the pitch black room. Freyja reached for her torch, but once again, Rohaan put out a hand to stop her.

"Give me a moment, Admiral."

Freyja tracked his footfalls as he walked away from her, and she fought to calm her rising irritation. Taking control of her own destiny had provided her with a sense of calm she had never had before, but patience had never been her virtue, and what little she had the doctor was quickly wearing thin.

The sound of knuckles rapping on thick glass rang out through the dark, followed by a wash of pale blue-green light, a glow that echoed out through the tubes lining the room—a visual representation of the sound waves passing through. The brilliance faded, but the tubes now remained dimly lit. Freyja stepped up to the closest tank, squinting to get a better look, but it was empty, save for the little particles glowing in the darkness.

"What is it?"

"Bioluminescent algae!" Zarah stepped up next to her, admiring the vats with rounded eyes.

A sneer twisted across Freyja's face. "You wanted to show me a room full of algae? Our ancestors survived on algae alone for millennia. It's not really an amazing finding, doctor."

"Oh, but that's where you're wrong," Zarah said. "Not about our ancestors eating algae, of course, that's just facts, but about this algae being special!" Zarah ran her well-manicured fingers over the glass. "This algae was specially designed to light this entire city."

"Again, not that impressive. We have bio lights on our ships."

"Right, but these algae are completely self-sustainable. Unlike the algae on our ships, they don't need to be fed or cared for at all. They have a symbiotic relationship with their food source and can theoretically live forever, powering the city."

Freyja had to give it to the doctors. That was an invaluable find.

"What is it all doing in here, then? Why is the city pitch dark?"

"If the records are accurate," Rohaan interrupted, "it appears there was an expansion project happening when this civilization was destroyed. The algae was moved here while new pathways were being installed throughout the city." His gaze went far off as he read a record in his ocular display. "Yes, it looks like construction was completed just before the records end. If you would like, Admiral, we could power up the city. It might make our search a little easier."

Freyja paused, considering his request.

"Come on boss ma'am, it would be pretty cool to see the whole ruins lit up, don't ya think?" Tristan leaned against a tube, tapping it rhythmically, sending little bursts of light through the fluid. Why was she overthinking this? She wouldn't hesitate to activate a light sensor on a space station.

"Do it."

Rohaan and Zarah each ported into a control panel. Within minutes, there was a gentle whirring sound as the tanks began to empty. Fine lines throughout the walls illuminated, bringing a hauntingly beautiful glow to every corner of the room.

Tristan walked to the far wall, then paused, inspecting a row of large, bulbous tubes that ran the entire length. They were empty, along with the rest.

"What was in here?" Tristan tapped the empty glass.

"More algae, I'm sure. This entire store room was dedicated to city maintenance species," Rohaan said.

Kylian's face twisted with doubt. "Why wouldn't they use the same containers for all of them?"

"I cannot speculate as to their choice of vessel, Kylian," Rohaan said, his attention on the console in front of him.

"Find something, Doc?" Freyja stepped closer.

"Yes, in this next room. I just need a moment to work through the security protocol."

"I can help with that." Kylian came to Rohaan's other side. Rohaan gave him a sideways look, as if he were unsure if he should trust the man with the task.

"Hacker." Kylian jammed his thumbs into his chest to accent the words.

"Very well." Rohaan stepped aside.

"How do you know the next room has Old World tech with the virus code?" Freyja asked.

"I don't."

"You said you found something. That's what we are here for." Freyja's pulse throbbed in her ears.

"That is what you are here for, Admiral. I also have my own interests."

Freyja groaned. Both doctors had made invaluable additions to the team. They had found life-changing technology at all of the sites so far, but little more than a satellite with a signal and some alien, virus-infected tech along the way. Freyja wasn't an archaeologist. She wasn't here to salvage tech, she was here for answers; she was here for revenge, to ensure the lives of her Berserkers lost at Medina hadn't been for nothing.

"I understand you have a passion for Old World med tech, but I need you to focus. We are no closer to finding the source of that signal than we were six months ago."

Rohaan waved her off. "That is where you are wrong." He focused his attention back on the code Kylian was working on.

Don't murder your scientist, don't murder your scientist. "Care to elaborate?"

"This is expedition number five," he said, as though that explained everything.

Freyja ground her teeth together, about to lose her temper, when Zarah stepped in.

"Five expeditions mean we now have five points of reference. We can use the trajectory of the signal emitting from each of the alien satellites we have surveyed to trilaterate their target." Zarah's chipper voice grated on Freyja's nerves like scraping metal.

Freyja pressed her eyelids shut, blocking out the annoying scientists as she inhaled deeply through her nose: *inhale, exhale, keep calm—this is good news.*

"So you are telling me that we could have collected an analysis of each satellite, avoided wasting our time at the ruins, and already have known the location of the signal months ago?" So much for keeping her temper.

"My passion for Old World med tech, as you would call it, is why I am here. If you want my help, you will let me gather the tech I need along the way. Or you can find another alien signal expert." Rohaan's voice held even. She had never seen this side of the doctor. There were no other alien signal experts in the Known Galaxies, and they both knew it. The audacity of the man burned beneath her skin, and her violent rage threatened to erupt, but she would appease his quirks. It had already cost her months; she couldn't afford to lose any more time.

"Got it," Kylian said in time with the door snapping open.

Rohaan held Freyja's stare, daring her to challenge him on this.

She gestured toward the next room. "Shall we?" Freyja said through clenched teeth.

Rohaan paled as if suddenly realizing he may have pushed her too far. He nodded and led the way into the next room, Zarah following close behind, her gaze downcast. Tristan and Kylian cleared the room in seconds. It was a lab space, mostly counters with some equipment built into the walls.

Freyja had learned better than to take rooms like these at face value. All of the operational tech they had found on these expeditions had been tucked away into shielded containers beneath the counters or inside the walls. It didn't take long for Rohaan to tap into the lab systems and begin revealing its secrets. Boxes of varying sizes bubbled up through shimmering shields all across the lab. Rohaan's eyes sparkled with each new item that appeared. Once an assortment of pieces cluttered the lab, he turned to Freyja.

"That should do it."

"Oh, is that all?" Her eyes roamed over the collection.

"It is all worthwhile, I assure you," Rohaan said.

"This will take hours to load—"

The pleading look Rohaan gave her cut her rant short. She shook her head. He had become a pain in her ass, but something about that look silenced her. They were already here; the time had already been wasted. She raised her hands in surrender.

"Fine. Kylian, Tristan, get started." She waved at the mountain of tech, then opened a comms line with the rest of the expedition crew. "Finish your sweeps, then meet us at these coordinates to assist with tech extraction."

"Yes, Admiral." A trio of confirmations came through her aural implant.

Tristan chuckled at her defeat, but he had the good sense to keep his mouth shut, for once.

It didn't take long to pack up the mini suspensors with the first load of technology. The sleds hummed softly, the weight of the load causing the hover system to sink uncomfortably close to the ground. They would have to grab full-size suspensors from the ship on their return to bring the rest of their findings.

Forming a line, each of them pushed a suspensor as they walked back through the cavern. Soft blue-green light filtered through tiny channels woven through the walls of every structure, transforming the dead city into an ethereal shrine. Larger pipes outlined intricate patterns along the domed ceiling, lighting a pantheon of creatures that glared down at Freyja and her crew. Unease clawed at the corners of her mind.

Before, the city had felt ancient, lost, dead. Now it glowed with life, and if Freyja turned her back to the destruction, taking in only the whole structures, she could almost imagine that the inhabitants of the city were only sleeping, that they would soon rise and take to life as they always had. The sound of boots tapping against the polished floors pulled Freyja from her thoughts. Basilie rounded a street corner just ahead of them. Makena and Ona'je stepped out onto the main path just a few buildings down. They had finished their sweep.

"Admiral—"

A green-scaled creature leapt onto Basilie, cutting off her words. Its massive jaws snapped back, then sprung shut over the Berserker's head. The sickening crunch of bones echoed through the quiet street.

Freyja drew her nanite broad sword. "On me!" she shouted, advancing on the creature. She had already lost too much. She would not let this creature take one more soul from under her command. She was the monster in the dark. It would fear her.

CHAPTER 6 | HINATA

FAIR FIGHT

The Torri Ring took up the majority of the *Takarabune's* viewport. The wormhole ring was so massive it appeared as a dark blemish against the star that powered it. Hinata shifted the view to survey his fleet, checking his troop placements one last time. Satisfied that every ship was in place, he turned his attention to the intel reports streaming through his ocular display. Their scouts had intercepted transmissions from the Empress that suggested she was preparing to attack the Torri Ring. Her troop movements might have appeared subtle to the causal observer, but he was not a casual observer. He lived for this. During his exile at Medina, he had spent countless hours in tactical simulations, playing war games and running his troops through drills until they operated more like machines than humans. The Empress was bringing the fight to the Hoshiko Tribe, and he was ready for her.

The obvious move would be to deliver an overwhelming force through the ring itself. Her sector was a galaxy away from the Hoshiko Tribal territories. That would be the obvious move, the brash move. It would be a stupid move. The Empress was a lot of things, but she wasn't stupid. Hinata had deployed an EMP field to disable any ships coming through the gate, along with a contingent of troops to guard the ring. They were green, shoshinsha, barely out of the academy. If they hadn't gone to war, many of them would still be cadets, training in simulations and games where the price of failure would be bad marks instead of their lives. They would learn fast, or they would die quickly. Hinata would do everything in his power to make it the former. Stationing them away from the battle gave them the best shot of coming out of this alive. That was the only gift he could give them. War was not kind.

It wouldn't come to that, Hinata was certain. The Empress was a mining tycoon. She controlled all major sites and trade routes, which meant that resources wouldn't be a problem for her. If he were in command of her fleet, he wouldn't hesitate to use those vast resources. He would jump his fleet to the nearest ring. It was in Setareh territory, and they were too busy fighting their own factions to worry about a fleet just passing through. It would burn considerable resources to make the jump from Setareh territory to Hoshiko territory, but the element of surprise would be worth it. Too bad Hinata would be ready for them.

Set in a synchronous orbit around the nearest planet, his stardestroyer was suitably hidden by its irregular magnetic field. Starfighters dotted the nearby asteroid field and hid in the shadows of moons. They would be obscured from view initially. The Empress would be lured in toward the small fleet guarding the ring. Then he would close the net. Her fleet would be surrounded, and she would have no choice but to surrender in accordance with the Inter-Tribal Preservation Accords—never waste resources necessary for the survival of humanity as a species. Genetic material was never in short supply. Humanity could bleed itself dry, hack away at the dead weight, and harvest mutinous souls to the end of time. There would always be new bodies to fill the crush. But starships were finite, especially those great enough to house the species as they scattered to the stars. Warfare within the tribes was never to lead to the destruction of life-sustaining ships.

Even with the rules of engagement on his side, he would not underestimate his enemy. He was ready to board and take her stardestroyers by force if needed, but he doubted it would come to that. They would have no way to win this skirmish. The logical thing to do would be to surrender. In accordance with tribal codes, the Hoshiko Tribe would keep the ships and send the Empress's people back to her in shame.

Flashes of light pin-pricked in between the vast curtain of stars. Her fleet was here. They appeared exactly where he had predicted. A smirk twisted his lips as it all began to unfold, just as he had planned. The Empress brought in a stardestroyer, six corvettes, and a starfighter carrier, complete with a heavy contingent of starfighters. She had more ships than his scouts had reported. No matter, Hinata still had the upper hand.

As her ships advanced on the ring, Hinata's exposed troops fell into formation, raising shields and selling the narrative.

"Prepare to spring the trap." Hinata sent the order to his hidden forces.

The Empress' ships advanced on the ring. They wouldn't get any closer, though.

"Now." His body dispersed into the ether before the command fully fell from his lips. The battlefield materialized before him as his ships made the micro jumps from their hiding places to surround the Empress's fleet.

Years of drills moved Hinata's starships like a well-oiled machine. Each unit knew its place and completed its function with precision. Plasma cannons bombarded the enemy starfighters, wearing down their shields array. It would only be a matter of minutes before his fleet disabled the enemy ships. A quick, decisive victory.

Pink electricity crackled along the bottom of the Empire stardestroyer. Déjà vu washed over him. That initial feeling boiled away to fury as he gave the command, "Full power to shields, all units!" This time, he wasn't too late. The atomic blast threw his ships through space with the force of a tidal wave, but the shields held.

"Report."

"All units functional, Commander, shields down to thirty percent. Twenty-five percent of our starfighters have been disabled." Damn it, he should have known. The Empress was Freyja's mother. Freyja had learned her disregard for the rules from someone. This wouldn't be a fair fight. Dread settled in the pit of his stomach as he watched the enemy stardestroyer pick off his fighters one by one. The ships exploded into sparks, a macabre fireworks display.

"Get our fighters out of there," he roared. "Move us into a defensive position. Starfighters, corvettes, fall back!" The smaller ships didn't have the shield capacity to withstand the bombardment, not after the atomics had thoroughly depleted their power supply.

Hinata's ship rocked under his boots as they absorbed the plasma cannon fire of the opposing stardestroyer.

They were evenly matched—the enemy depleted from the power it took to generate the bomb, Hinata's warship from absorbing the blast. They traded blows like fighters in a ring, each taking a shot and absorbing the other's volleys. A squadron of cruisers launched from the stardestroyer, headed for the ring.

"Take out those ships!"

They redirected their plasma cannons to engage with the squadron, but the enemy destroyer countered the attack.

"Damn it, those shoshinsha don't stand a chance! Get us in position to defend."

"Commander, the *Oseberg* won't let us pass. There isn't room at this proximity for a jump. They are going to have to fight for themselves," Tax responded.

Hinata slammed an armored fist into his console, thin cracks spider-webbing out from the impact.

"I want this ship out of my way! NOW!" Hinata would not sacrifice the cadets.

Tax hesitated. "Commander, are you giving permission to break with the accords?" Hinata gritted his teeth, forcing air in through his nose as he worked to gather his composure. The Empress wasn't fighting by the code; his soldiers were being picked off one by one like wild game. He had to step in. She had forced his hand. Hesitation wrapped its grip around him. He always followed the rules. To engage with the Empress on her level would bring dishonor to his name, but if he didn't...

A feral growl tore through his throat. He wouldn't stoop to her level, but he wouldn't let her slaughter his troops, either. "We stick to the code, but we don't have to play nice. We end this. Inoue, the bridge is yours. Eliminate their shields, then pick off their weapons systems."

"Yes, Commander." Lieutenant Inoue brought her fist to her chest, inclining her head.

"Tax, Callan, on me. Prepare a boarding party."

CHAPTER 7 | SKYLA

ALONE

Soft fur grazed the exposed flesh of Skyla's face. A deep rumbling purr rolled through her body. Frozen lashes sealed her eyes shut, and she struggled to pry them open. Finally, the ice cracked, allowing her to peer through slitted eyelids. She was freezing. She didn't know it was possible to be this cold. Everything from her limbs to her thoughts moved in slow motion. That soft, golden fur nuzzled into the side of her neck. She smiled. It almost felt warm. The nuzzle became more forceful until she rocked onto her side.

"Hey." Skyla snapped out of her stupor, her surroundings coming into vivid detail. Sprawled out on the frozen tundra, she took in the brilliant splash of stars cut across the sky. Night had come, and she was freezing to death. Fenrir wobbled, then plopped down awkwardly on his three remaining legs. A keening whine escaped his snout before he tucked it under his front paw. He had used all of his energy to wake her. Pressing her eyes closed once more, Skyla tried to order her thoughts. She wasn't sure what to do, but they couldn't stay here. They wouldn't last much longer out in the open.

"Come on," she groaned as she picked herself up from the ice. Violent shivers ran through her body, clacking her teeth together uncontrollably. Once she settled Fenrir back into the sled, she resumed her endless walk. Strained muscles protested every movement, but with her inner fire rekindled, she dared to hope. She wouldn't let them die on this sun-forsaken planet. Just one more snow bank, make it over one more snow bank, she negotiated with herself. Then another, and another.

She fought to keep her mind focused as one more snow bank turned into ten, and then twenty...Her mind went numb and her tiny ember of hope sputtered out in the night wind.

Skyla crested one last snow bank and collapsed to her knees. Rising up like an oasis in the frozen wasteland was a cluster of yurts around a collection of larger buildings. They had made it.

Stumbling steps slowed by fatigue led her to the nearest yurt. She pounded a gloved fist against the door, begging for relief from the cold before exhaustion claimed her.

She swiped her fingers over the keypad, praying the door would open. Nothing happened. Cursing, she pounded against the door again before stumbling over to the next yurt. Again, she pounded and yelled, pleading for someone to respond. They were so close, so close to salvation. Someone had to be here. Someone had to be willing to let them in.

After three yurts with no reply, she gripped her forearm, preparing to ram into the door of the next, when the edges of her datapad bit into her fingers. She shook her head, then pulled her datapad out and held it up to the lock. Lines of code ran across the screen until—click. The sound of a lock turning over nearly brought her to tears. The seals creaked, but the door remained closed. Skyla groaned. Maybe she would have to break into the place after all. One, two, three times she rammed her shoulder into the door until, finally—crack, it gave in.

If the pitch black wasn't enough confirmation, the freezing temperature affirmed that they were alone. With what little strength Skyla had left, she heaved the sled inside before sealing the door once again.

It took several minutes of fumbling with frozen fingers to find a lantern and get the generator running. It was far from warm, but at least it blocked out the biting wind.

Fire raced under her skin as Skyla rubbed her numb hands together in front of the generator. Her blue-tinged fingertips trembled—or maybe it was from the tremors running through her arms—but the generator washed a warm, dry heat over her and Fenrir, who had curled up by her side.

Once the deathly chill began to thaw, she struggled to keep her eyes open, and all she could do was curl into Fenrir's golden fur and give in to the exhaustion.

Pale morning light streamed through the window, cutting a beam of light across Skyla's face. Shifting away from the encroaching day, she stretched the stiffness out of her body, then carefully checked Fenrir's wound. The angry scorch marks had already faded to pink, and a soft fuzz of fur covered his skin.

"What the hell?" Skyla was no medic, but even she knew that wasn't normal. Fenrir turned and licked a scratchy blue tongue over her face.

"Ew!" Skyla stumbled, falling backward, but she couldn't keep from grinning. Were her eyes playing tricks on her? Besides the missing limb,

Fenrir looked like his normal self. Questions later...first she had to figure out their next move.

Reluctantly, she pushed up from her cozy place beside the generator to take in the one-room yurt: there was a little kitchenette, two beds, a table, and a trunk full of supplies. And they were still alone. The space obviously belonged to a pair of researchers. Skyla's stomach soured. The stillness brought on memories of the ruins she had visited at Alpha 4375. The way parts of the city looked, as if the residents had just stepped away. The yurt had the same eerie feeling, and she pushed the thought from her mind.

Hungry—that pit in her stomach was from hunger. She was both ravenous from the trek and too tired to eat. Skyla sighed and edged over to the window to survey the camp. Several minutes passed, and there was no activity save for the little snow devils kicked up by the wind. The loud rumble in her stomach broke her concentration.

"Fine," she grumbled, looking down at her belly. "You win. I wonder if they have anything better than emergency rations. What do you think, Fenrir?"

The creature just yawned at her, sticking out his long blue tongue before settling his head back on his paws. After several minutes of rummaging through the cupboards of the kitchenette, Skyla pulled out a silver tin, praying it was what she thought it was. The sweet aroma hit her as soon as she popped the seal on the top. She inhaled deeply, her eyes rolling back. *Coffee.*

"Things are looking up for us, boy." Skyla held up the tin so Fenrir could see. Not that he was paying attention. "Everything will look better after a nice cup of caffeine."

Fenrir closed his eyes and pulled both paws over his head, as if he was hiding from her antics.

"Fine, be that way. You'll see; I always think better after my first cup of coffee," Skyla mused.

After setting a kettle to boil, she continued to look through the cupboards. She found oats, nuts, cinnamon, and salt—not bad for a rim research yurt. There was also some frozen game in the icebox, and she pulled out a chunk to defrost for Fenrir. A chill crept up her spine as she considered the fully stocked yurt.

"Coffee first," she mumbled, but even the promise of liquid gold couldn't fully dismiss the feeling.

Skyla took her time with breakfast, not mentally ready to handle this situation. Just the thought of stepping outside of the yurt brought on a wave of panic so strong that her ribs cinched tight, threatening to strangle the life from her.

So instead she pushed away reality for a little while longer, savoring the sensation of hot coffee hitting her tongue and warm oats in her belly. Never would she have imagined she would be so grateful for a hot meal. After she finished her breakfast, she fed Fenrir, who refused to budge from in front of the generator. He ate the chunk of meat with vigor and rewarded her with a loud, rumbling purr.

"You're going to be okay, buddy." She scratched under his jaw. "We both are." There was that knot tangling her insides again. But she had delayed as long as she could. It was time to face reality.

After a mumbled pep talk that neither Skyla nor Fenrir believed, she forced herself from the warmth of the yurt, back out into the ice and snow.

The research facility was quiet. There had been no sound beyond the howling of the wind all morning. The wind was loud and the conditions unforgiving; perhaps the scientists were all safely tucked in their beds...that's where she wanted to be.

Just one thought of her busy-bodied bestie, Rohaan, dismissed the thought from her mind. Despite herself, she smiled. No, the scientists would be working on their research, likely in one of the large buildings at the center of the complex. She would start there.

Just like the yurt, the door of the first central building was frozen shut. Skyla braced her hands against the door and a boot against the frame, and pushed until it gave way.

The air inside the main structure was considerably warmer than the yurt she had barged into last night. Having broken the ice around the seal, the door slid closed seamlessly behind her as she scanned the space, looking for any sign of life, but it was as empty as the rest of the camp.

Tables littered with lab equipment, the occasional datapad, and absent-mindedly placed mug lined the perimeter of the room, with an overgrown hydroponics garden taking up the center.

The plants twisted and twined with one another, overflowing from one section into the next. Skyla had never seen a hydroponics garden so neglected. The gardens on Upsala station, where she had grown up, were always meticulously managed. Every plant trimmed and tended, water levels and nutrients tested daily. This looked more like a wild jungle had overtaken the towers, while thick, green algae lined the sides of the fish tank. A chill ran down her spine as the doubts she had been pushing down all morning clawed at the edges of her mind, trying to break through the barriers she had erected.

Keep moving. While she was moving, there was still hope. Skyla broke into the next facility. This one was full of samples and equipment; no overgrown garden, but no people either.

The fear now shouted at her from behind the barrier. Nothing she did could silence the voices.

Alone.

Alone.

Alone.

"One more, there's one more building," Skyla's voice caught in her throat, the words choking her.

With the same effort that she had applied to the first two buildings, Skyla pried the door open to find: a commissary, a rec room, food supplies, and nothing more.

Panic finally flooded over the gates of Skyla's mind, filling her lungs and drowning her from within.

Lost.

Powerless.

Alone.

The manic thoughts fueled Skyla, driving her to jog the perimeter of the camp. Cold bit through her gloves and clipped her nose as she smashed her face against the windows of the yurts, as if the closer vantage would change what she would find. More of the same: supplies, gear, and nothing more.

Skyla burst back into the yurt from last night, hyperventilating so hard her head swam, and her legs turned to jelly as she collapsed just inside the door.

This couldn't be. This was the last place her father had been. This was supposed to be her salvation. They were supposed to help her rescue Pele.

No, no, no; her brain wouldn't let her accept the truth. She was supposed to find her father, find answers.

What was she going to do now?

Skyla's anger joined her panic, swirling into a nauseating cocktail that made her want to retch, but instead, she screamed. The sound raked like nails through her throat, startling Fenrir.

Too drained to stand, Skyla balled her hands into fists and beat them against the ground. She wanted to rage; she wanted to break something, but all she had were her lungs and her fists, and so she let loose until her throat grew raw, and her hands ached in a way that she knew would give way to bruises, and then her screams turned to twisted, manic laughter.

"I wanted to be alone."

CHAPTER 8 | FREYJA

THE HIVE

Freyja advanced on the creature. She could feel Kylian and Tristan at her flank. The nasty beast stood on top of her felled Berserker, blood dripping from its long teeth, pointed claws digging into the flesh of her fallen soldier as it shifted to observe them. A deep, guttural growl, like rocks grating against stone, rumbled from its throat.

Freyja yelled back at the beast, her blood boiling, rage threatening to overtake her senses. Just down the path, Makena and Ona'je advanced with their swords drawn, ready to block the creature's escape. They had the beast outnumbered, five to one. Another guttural growl rang out from behind the buildings, then another from further down the path.

"How many of those things are there?" Tristan yelled.

The monster in front of them had to weigh at least a ton, with green scales that rippled a soft blue-green glow when it moved, like the algae in the walls. Its eyes were two huge onyx orbs; no light escaped them. Nasty teeth stood out from its jaw, too long to be housed inside its mouth.

"Watch your six," Freyja ordered, refusing to take her eyes off the creature. The beast twitched as Freyja took a cautious step, working to edge around the monster.

Step.

Twitch.

Step.

Twitch—

Freyja froze.

The scales along the creature's back rose, strobing with a rumbling vibration, and then the creature launched itself at her.

It was fast. Too fast. It knocked her sword out of the way to bury its teeth in her shoulder. Freyja fought to gain control as the beast took her to the ground, ripping at her flesh.

Kylian and Tristan were on it in an instant. They lunged forward, burying their swords to the hilt in the creature. It screamed, letting go of Freyja. Thin arms hooked under her armpits, dragging her back with stumbling footsteps. The beast thrashed between Tristan and Kylian, snapping its jaws. Both men stood with their arms raised, looking for an opening, their swords still buried in its chest. Further down the path, Freyja watched as Makena and Ona'je engaged with another beast, fighting to keep it distracted between the two of them as they took nicks and cuts out of its scaled hide.

Confusion clouded her mind. Who had grabbed her? She tilted her head back to see Zarah's soft features.

"Don't you know better? I can't keep you safe if you rush into danger."

"I don't think you're in any shape to keep me safe, Admiral. Now keep quiet and let me take care of this." Zarah pushed hard on Freyja's wound to slow the bleeding. Freyja clenched her jaw to hold back a stream of expletives. Zarah had pulled her back behind the suspensors, away from danger. Rohaan crouched down next to them, but his gaze was far off, and his fingers flew through the air over his datapad. What was he doing?

Freyja shifted so she could see the fight, ignoring the shooting pain that ran down her shoulder. Relief mixed with the pain as she watched Makena and Ona'je down the second creature and move in to help Kylian and Tristan with the first. They held their swords ready, waiting for an opening. Kylian moved first, having retrieved Freyja's fallen sword. He swept in with a wide arc over his head, slicing clean through the head of the creature as it opened its jaw to devour him. Deep blue blood rained down over him as he screamed at the beast. It collapsed with a loud, wet thud on the polished stone floors.

Kylian froze in place, the sword clutched so tightly in his grip that his fingers turned pale around the hilt. Tristan stepped forward and roughly pulled both of their swords free from the corpse; he holstered one so he could clasp his cousin by the shoulder.

"A'ight, cuz?" Worry lined Tristan's usually carefree face.

Kylian took a moment to regain control, then he nodded. "Ya, cuz." He held out his hand for his sword, which Tristan returned. Makena and Ona'je joined the rest of the crew behind the suspensors where the scientists had hunkered down with Freyja. Kylian sheathed his own weapon, sprinting to Freyja's side as soon as he saw her. Dropping to his knees, he took her hands in his as he looked her over head to toe.

"She'll be alright," Zarah said as she finished sealing the wound.

Kylian didn't relax his grip; his worried eyes locked onto Freyja's. She knew he needed to hear it from her.

"I'm alright." She squeezed his hand, trying to reassure him. He didn't give. His jaw locked, and his usually warm eyes were hard and serious. "I promise. I'm nowhere near as bad as you were." She ran a shaky finger over his scar. He flinched at her touch, but then some of the tension eased from his grip.

"Are you sure, Freyja?" His voice was quiet, his eyes searching. She had never seen him like this, not even when he was the one laid out on a med bed fighting for his life.

Freyja nodded. "I'm sure."

He let out a long breath. "I meant what I said, Admiral. I'll follow you until the last star in the universe burns out." His voice dropped to a whisper. "You can't leave me." A tear slid down his cheek. She brushed it away with gentle fingers.

"Admiral, we need to move. I hear at least three more of those things." Tristan stood just behind the suspensor, his eyes darting between the two of them and scanning the city.

Kylian held her gaze for a moment. She nodded, agreeing with Tristan's assessment. That was all the confirmation he needed. Kylian scooped her into his arms, lifting her onto the suspensor. Rohaan, still absorbed in his ocular display, paid them no heed, otherwise she was certain he would have objected to Tristan dumping half the tech off the suspensor to make room. Freyja gritted her teeth, willing her anger at being bundled into a suspensor like another piece of salvaged tech to settle. She was being irrational. She had lost too much blood to keep up with them on foot. They needed to escape these ruins, fast.

Once they had retrieved Basilie's body, leaving another mound of discarded tech in their wake, Freyja gave the order. "Roll out." Her voice was a whisper over gravel. Her eyes darted to the distracted scientist. "Make sure he doesn't get left behind."

Tristan clapped the doctor on the shoulder. "Time to move."

Rohaan blinked a few times, his focus returning. He frowned at the discarded tech, but held his tongue. "I'm not done," was all he said before returning his attention to the display.

"I'll watch out for him," Zarah cut in, looping her arm through Rohaan's, guiding him behind a suspensor. Then she nodded. They were ready to move.

Makena and Ona'je took point. Kylian was reluctant to leave Freyja's side, but his training won out. He and Tristan took up the rear, swords drawn and eyes sweeping the structures as they made their way through the ruined city.

"Nearly there," Tristan said as the columns that bracketed the entryway rose before them. A loud crash rang through the cavern as a creature barreled straight into a suspensor loaded with tech. Its arms and head thrashed wildly, smashing tech and ripping the suspensor apart.

The Berserkers moved to fight the beast, but it was faster. It flung Zarah to the ground with its wild movements. Rohaan shook his head, bringing the sight of the beast into focus. The creature, however, locked onto its downed prey.

It stalked forward. A growl like a landslide emitted from its throat. Cold, vacant eyes fixed on the woman as she tried to scuttle backwards out of its reach. It swiped at her leg, digging ten centimeter-long claws into her flesh. Zarah screamed, her eyes going wide with panic.

Before the Berserkers could step in, two more beasts came at them, pinning them in on both sides. There was no help. Tristan and Kylian fought to keep the creature from moving in from the rear, while Makena and Ona'je did the same with the creature at the front.

Freyja stumbled from the suspensor, drawing her sword. She held the blade only a moment before her arm dropped to her side. Useless and weak, dark spots bubbled up around her vision.

"No," she snarled. She would not let these things win. She took one unsteady step before she collapsed to her hands and knees, watching helplessly as the creature reared up, opening its gaping maw to crunch down on the defenseless doctor.

A feral yell ripped through the chaos as Rohaan ran forward, throwing himself in front of Zarah, his forearm raised over his head like he intended to use his datapad as a shield. The creature lunged forward to swallow Rohaan, but just as it moved to take his head in its jaws, it froze. A terrifying statue of teeth and scales and claws, its jaws were mere centimeters from closing around the man. Rohaan's breaths came heavy, his eyes wide.

The other two creatures had frozen too. The Berserkers still held their swords at the ready, unsure of what to make of the menacing beasts. Time warped and stretched as the silence returned to the cavern, and Rohaan finally moved out from underneath the creature. He wrapped an arm around Zarah, bringing her to stand behind him. She leaned heavily on his shoulder as blood oozed down her pant leg. Rohaan tapped at his datapad, and the creature relaxed, shifting back on its haunches to sit at attention before him. Another tap and the other two creatures sat as well.

"What did you do?" Kylian asked.

Rohaan was still short of breath when he answered. "Those creatures are part of the security system here. We must have accidentally activated them when we re-lit the city." Guilt washed over his face. "As soon as I saw them, I thought that might be the case, anyway. I dug back into the archives we uploaded from the lab and found the subroutine that controls them, but I had to get close to initiate the protocol." His eyes darted from the first beast, then over to the other two. "Once I had control of one, I used it to link with the hive and take control of the rest."

"Thanks for the explanation, Doc." Freyja leaned heavily against a suspensor, her head spinning from the blood loss. "But I'd rather not spend any longer in this death trap."

"I've taken control of the hive. It's quite safe now. I assure you," Rohaan said.

"I'd rather not take any chances."

Disappointment washed over his face as his eyes caught on the discarded tech. They had left at least another full load in the lab.

She shook her head. They had already lost too much. With the signal data, they had what they needed, and she wouldn't risk any more of her soldiers' lives. They could finally track the origin of the signal. After months of searching, they could go after the source, and although Freyja was afraid it would lead her right back to where she had started, at least they would finally have answers.

CHAPTER 9 | HINATA

GISEI

The helm of Hinata's suit slid shut, sealing him into his armored space suit. The black alloy soaked in the light as a shimmer-like starlight cut through the void. Gold symbols in an ancient language trailed down his side. He held his katana at the ready. Combat, this he understood; this he could do. His mind was more calm than it had been in months. This he would not fail at. He would not let the Empress destroy his fleet. He would not let her take the lives of those children he had stationed around the ring, barely old enough to wear the uniform.

With Callan and Tax at his side, he was ready to take the enemy starde-stroyer. Ten of his best soldiers stood at attention behind him. Now they just had to make it onto her ship.

"Report," Hinata opened a comms link to the bridge.

"Her shield array is down, ready to deploy on your mark," Inoue responded.

They wouldn't be able to bring their ship in close enough to board. The *Oseberg* had started evasive maneuvers as soon as his ship had moved into position. No matter; the ships didn't have to connect for him to breach the destroyer and gut the Empress' defenses.

He nodded to Tax. "Move out, vac ready in ten."

The airlock doors sealed at their backs moments before the vast emptiness of space opened before them. They crawled out of the airlock to line up along the hull of the *Takarabune*, like insects in exoskeletons scuttling along the walls. The magnetic charge in their boots and gloves kept them attached to the ship while their suits alleviated the effects of the high-G maneuvers.

"In position. Launch when there is a window." Hinata gave control over to Inoue on the bridge. The timing would have to be precise, or they would miss their mark.

"Ready for launch: three, two, one, launch."

The countdown came from the bridge just as they went into a tight barrel roll. The bridge released their magnetic attachments and initiated the thrusters on their suits in sync with the roll, rocketing them straight at the enemy ship. They were missiles of death, ready to rip the bridge apart from the inside out.

Plasma cannon fire lit up the space between the two ships. It was up to the *Takarabune* to protect the boarding party from the incoming projectiles. The dark space exploded with fireworks as plasma cannon rounds collided.

Clashing munitions lit up the void in blinding fashion, stealing his sight, but he felt no fear. He would not let fear in, not here, in the vast vacuum of space, protected only by a shell of armor, alone in the aether. No, that door must stay sealed shut. He would not let fear in, because once fear took root, it would eat a man alive. Like a virus, it would consume until there was nothing left but a useless shell. Hinata felt no fear. He had trust, complete trust in his soldiers, in their training. He trusted them with his life, just as they trusted him with theirs.

Hinata activated his reverse thrusters just before impact, slowing him only enough to keep from damaging the suit as he slammed into the side of the enemy ship. The magnetic attachments of his suit activated on impact, anchoring him in place. The rest of his crew landed safely around him within seconds.

They had all made it. The hard part was done. They would have the upper hand once they made it on the bridge. The Empress employed mercs—no match for his soldiers, who trained from the age of ten for combat. Mercs lived for standars, his soldiers lived for these moments.

"Make me a hole," Hinata gave the order.

With the plasma torches set in place, tiny blue lights burned through the hull. Tax's careful calculations had paid off. They had landed on the bow of the ship, allowing them to cut directly into the bridge. The edges of the laser torches met, and the lights died out. The outline of a square, large enough for two to enter at a time, lay before them. He had no illusion that they still held the element of surprise, but they would play this right. Once the containment field to keep the oxygen from escaping into space came to life, they were ready.

Hinata held out a gloved fist: three, two, one.

Leading the assault with Tax at his side, Hinata kicked the cut-out frame into the bridge with the full force of his thrusters. The thick piece of hull flew across the bridge, slamming into the unlucky soldier manning the weapons station and pinning him to the console.

Hinata drew his katana. With his dark battle armor sucking in the light and his towering frame, he made for an ominous figure as the silent backdrop of open space slid by behind him.

The first merc came at him from his side, swinging a heavy, double-edged nanite ax. The weapon was bulky and slow, like its wielder. Sidestepping the blow, Hinata spun out with his sword, taking the man's arm at the shoulder. The merc screamed as he dropped his weapon to clutch at the wound with his good arm. Hinata kicked him hard in the chest, and the man went flying.

The next merc moved in with her broadsword drawn. She was much more skilled than the first, but still no match for him. Hinata traded blows with her, feeling out her rhythm. Once he had it, he broke the pattern, grabbing her sword arm and turning into the opening to bury his blade in her gut. Just as quickly, he moved away, pulling his sword from her body as she dropped to the ground.

Tax had felled two opponents of his own, and the rest of the boarding party made to secure the remaining crew who sat at their stations, hands held in the air. They might value standars, but these ones valued their lives more.

"Call in your ships, this is over," Hinata commanded.

The comms officer needed no further prompting. He opened a line with all the remaining ships. Hinata kept watch on the viewport. Flights of starfighters and a handful of cruisers broke away from their assault on the shoshinsha squadron protecting the ring. Their ships had taken a beating, but they were all accounted for. His gambit had paid off. Those cadets would walk away with their lives.

A contingent of corvettes caught Hinata's eye. They had broken away from the returning squadrons halfway between the stardestroyer and the ring. They hovered there, waiting. He squinted at the image. His gut twisted. Something was wrong, and he was helpless to stop it.

A barrage of escape pods ejected from the corvettes. The ships were too far from anything of importance. Detonating their cores would only destroy the ships, leaving his fleet busy collecting the escape pods. He growled in annoyance. How petty was this merc crew?

Then the screen went blindingly white. Hinata leaned over the command console, willing the display to clear. When it did, he wished it hadn't. The corvettes had micro-jumped right into the ring. The impact of matter dropping out of hyperspace on top of matter ripped the ring apart in a series of explosions. Shrapnel from the destroyed ring cut through his fleet like they were nothing more than origami. Shards of titanium and fragments of bone were all that was left of his cadets.

"No!" Hinata slammed his armored fists into the command console, cracking the screen. Shaking with rage, his eyes darted around the bridge, daring one of the mercs to stand up and fight.

An endless fury raced through him, fueling his blood lust. He needed an outlet for this pain that threatened to shatter his fragile façade. Forcing air into his lungs, he fought for control. Killing these mercs wouldn't bring back his cadets. Nothing could save them now. He had failed them.

The ring scattered in broken pieces across the viewport, destroyed. They were isolated in this quadrant, cut off from the mines of Tamatori, from the very alloy needed to replace their broken ships. Their fleet was crippled. The next generation of soldiers was gone, along with a quarter of his fleet. The Empress had changed the rules of engagement; it wasn't a choice; he had to adapt or die.

***

The loud crack of metal against metal rang out as escape pods slid into place along the *Takarabune's* hangar. The battle was over, and Hinata was left to clean up the broken pieces. A long line of injured soldiers trailed out of a frigate sent to scour the ring debris for survivors. The battered soldiers before him were all they had found, the lucky few who had ended up in sealed sections of their broken ships.

Hinata clasped forearms with the young soldiers, gripping them by their shoulders and pausing to speak with each before they continued on to medical.

"What is your name?" Hinata would ask, followed by, "You fought well and brought honor to your tribe." Hinata's eyes locked with each soldier—so young, they didn't belong in this war. He listened to their stories and carved each name in his gray matter.

Hinata's heart grew heavier with each name until the weight of the tragedy threatened to crush him. The line thinned, and soon only Tax, Callan, and the dock crew remained.

"That's all?" Hinata whispered.

Tax gave a stiff nod as he stepped up to Hinata's side. "There was no time for them to make it to the escape pods."

Hinata turned, taking in the rows upon rows of escape pods that filled the hangar bay of the *Takarabune*. Each had the emerald hammer drill emblem of the Empress painted on its nose. Fire raced under Hinata's skin. Her soldiers had survived the cowardly move while his had paid the price with their lives.

His hands clenched into fists as he began to tremble, the mask of commander slipping as the loss tore him apart. Unable to contain the fury that coursed through him a second longer, Hinata let out a yell that echoed through the cavernous hangar. He slammed into a nearby supply cart, spilling its contents across the deck. He scooped up a thick pipe wrench and stalked toward the first pod.

So consumed by his anger, Hinata barely noticed Tax and Callan clearing the dock workers as he slammed the wrench into the nose of the first pod, chipping away at the green-painted mark of his enemy. Again and again, he struck until only crumpled metal and shiny streaks remained where the hammer drill had been.

Hinata moved on to the next pod, then the next. He struck the emblem of the Empress from pod after pod until his breath came heavy, sweat streamed down his face, and his arms seized. Again and again, he struck the pods, unleashing the wrath that he wished he could unleash on the Empress herself, as if each strike could bring back a soldier he had lost. The soldiers that were mere children—they had been his to protect, and he had failed them.

The wrench fell limp at his side as the realization burrowed into his marrow. He had failed them. It was his fault that all of those cadets would never live to grow into the men and women they had trained their whole lives to be.

"It's not your fault." The voice came to Hinata in his aural implant, stopping his heart. Two decades had passed since he had heard that voice, yet it still rang out familiar and warm in his mind.

Hinata turned slowly, realizing for the first time where his fit of rage had led him. Tentei towered behind him. A blue-green pulse washed over his nose and down his sides.

"It's not your fault." Tentei's voice came to him, softer this time, beckoning him forward. "Just like Akio was not your fault."

The wrench slipped from Hinata's grip, clattering to the floor.

"Tentei," Hinata whispered, taking a step closer to his ship.

"Otouto."

At Tentei's words, the last pieces of Hinata shattered, and he fell to his knees beside his ship.

"I failed them." Hinata dropped his face to his hands. "I failed them. Just like I failed Akio…"

Tentei pulsed softly; a warmth that Hinata barely remembered tinged his words. "You did not fail them, brother. We all have our own paths to walk. I have left you alone on yours for too long. I am sorry. It is I that have failed you."

Hinata shook his head, lifting a hand to run across Tentei's hull. The warmth he felt there only made the ache in Hinata's chest blossom as he now thought of Pele and Skyla. It was all too much. There was nothing left of him to hold together, and so he crumbled, nothing more than a shattered vessel. Any control he had left him as silent tears trailed the lines of his face.

"I miss them too," Tentei whispered. All these years of silence, and Tentei still knew his mind like they were linked. "That night you stayed with your captain…Pele was the first person I spoke to in over a decade. Seeing her memories with Skyla reminded me of what we could have. If I could forgive the little boy who was too afraid of his mother to disobey her orders…"

A thick lump formed in Hinata's throat at the mention of that night, the night his brother Akio had died, and his mother had forbidden him from having a relationship with Tentei beyond the war machine that he was built to be. The memory hit sharp—like the lemon sour candies Akio brought Hinata when he would come home from the academy. He realized Tentei wasn't the only one she had forged into a weapon. That was all he would ever be to her. Tentei and him were the same in her eyes—they always had been.

"Can you forgive me?" Hinata whispered.

"There is nothing to forgive. You are my brother."

Hinata's tears slowed, Tentei's words acting as a tether for his tattered soul. He turned to lean against the ship, tucking in under Tentei's wing, just as he had when he was a child. They sat like that for a long time, Tax and Callan taking up posts a few meters away. Their backs were turned to Hinata for privacy, but they were there all the same.

Hinata let his head fall back against Tentei's coral nanite hull, finally ready to voice his fears. "I don't think they are coming back."

Tentei considered this a long moment before answering. "Then they have chosen their own path. But know this brother, you don't have to walk yours alone, not any longer."

Hinata considered Tentei's words. He was still broken, the pieces of himself unable to fit together quite right. But there, under the wing of his ship, with the boys he had grown into a man with standing guard, Hinata finally saw that he was not alone, and perhaps he could find the strength to carry on.

CHAPTER 10 | SKYLA

MEMORIES

S kyla spent the next several days skulking in the abandoned camp. After several stumbling attempts and a few face plants that crusted Fenrir's snout in snow, he eventually figured out the new mechanics of moving with only three legs, and once he had, he never left Skyla's side.

The first day she sat in the overgrown garden, snacking on fruits off the vines that stained her fingers purple and left her lips sticky with sugar. Fenrir watched the fish dart around the hydroponics tank, and she rambled endlessly about stories from her childhood. She told Fenrir about her father and then mused about what he must have thought of this place. Fenrir cocked his head and twitched his ears at the appropriate moments, and Skyla didn't even try to pretend that she wasn't losing her mind.

The next day she found a store of liquor in the commons room along with enough food preserves for another year; at least she wouldn't starve, and there was plenty to drink, but no whiskey. While she hated the taste of vodka, she still lost her battle against her desire to wash away this nightmare with drink. She drank until the room spun, and her vision doubled, and she lay sprawled out in the middle of the commons, staring up at the metal cross beams and willing the world to slow.

"What are you doing, Captain?" His tone was soft and playful, the tone she had only ever heard in stolen moments; the tone he saved for her alone.

Skyla bolted up from the floor, her head spinning from the liquor and the sudden movement. The room splayed into doubles, but she was alone. Lying back down on the floor, she shut her eyes hard against the delusion.

"Skyla." His voice came like a whisper in her ear, so close she could reach out and run her fingers over his angled jaw, so close she could tangle her fingers in his hair and pull his lips to hers if he were there, but he wasn't.

The tears came then, hard and ugly as rough sobs wracked her body. Was this what she wanted? To be alone? She knew there was a very real possibility she would die here, alone, on a world that the very solar system had rejected. It was all made worse by the fact that she had chosen this.

What had she been thinking? She finally had her best friend, her sister, back, and she had left Freyja to chase a ghost. She had found a little brother in Rohaan. She had known how important tracking down the signal was to him, and she had left him for her own selfish desires. And *him*. She ached at the thought of him. He had asked her to stay, and she had refused. She had chosen a frozen wasteland over the warmth of his touch, and now she was draining a bottle alone instead of sharing a drink with the only man in the universe who had made her feel seen, who had understood her enough to let her go. She had chosen this path. Why had she chosen this path?

Realization hit her so hard that it stole the breath from her lungs. Her ribs constricted around her. She deserved this. To die alone on a frozen world.

"I'm still right here, Captain. I told you I'm not going anywhere."

"You're not here," she said through her tears.

"I told you I am not going anywhere. I will wait. Come search for me."

She curled into a ball on the floor, succumbing to the endless sorrow. At some point, she drifted off, and in those fitful dreams, she dreamed of him.

When she woke the next morning with a blinding headache and burning eyes, she resolved to keep searching. She would search for a way off this suns-forsaken planet. She would keep her word; she would rescue Pele and find her way back to her family, back to him.

***

The following day, Skyla finally gathered enough courage to search through the yurts. She had been avoiding them. She reasoned that she didn't want to bother the researchers' personal belongings. What if they were just on an extended expedition? Although the hydroponics garden told the true story: it hadn't been cared for in months.

Yet she clung to the illusion, stretching out her last shred of hope a little longer, not ready to accept that no one was coming back. A night spent passed-out on the commons floor had solidified her resolve. No one was coming to rescue her, and she was ready for answers. Working through each dwelling, she checked for clues. Who had been there? What had they been working on? Had one of them been her father?

Skyla found her answer in the second to last yurt. The moment she had forced the door open, she knew. It hadn't been inhabited for months, yet his scent lingered in the air: cedar and sea salt. This was his home, from the cozy, flannel, casual clothes thrown haphazardly over the chair, to the photos of far-flung places and the stolen Turkish coffee kettle left on the stove. It was her father's. It was exactly how she remembered him to the last detail, equal parts cozy and eccentric.

Slowly, she walked over to the kitchenette. Her movements were automatic as she made herself a coffee in her father's kettle. She slipped on his flannel shirt and settled into his only chair, folding her arms around her knees, and sipped the hot liquid as her silent tears fell. After twenty years, she had learned that her father hadn't abandoned her. After twenty years, she had hoped. She had come to this planet in search of him, and after twenty years, she was only months too late to see her father again.

Skyla let herself just be in his space, casually looking through his things. A full smile split her face when she found a journal stuffed with old drawings she had made and photos of her as a little girl. Guilt twisted her stomach into knots that she had spent so many years angry with him, believing that he had abandoned her. Still, he had left, hadn't he? Then anger burned through the mixed emotions when she thought of how her mother had kept the truth from her, and she grasped onto that anger, not yet ready to grieve.

The last corner left to explore housed a small bookcase full of blue journals, just like the one he had left for her. Her eyes went wide as she took in the collection, decades' worth of his research.

Slipping the first one free from the bookcase, she found it had the same lock on the front, an imprint of a vegvísir. She pulled the pendant from under her shirt, pressing it into the housing of the journal. The protective box slid back, exposing the leather-bound book inside. She collapsed onto the cot and began to flip through the pages, reading her father's thoughts.

The cot rocked as Fenrir hopped up beside her. Skyla scanned the bookcase once more. It would take time for her to sort through all of this, but time was something she had in abundance at the moment. One of the first things she'd discovered after hacking into the settlement logs was that the planet was in a blackout zone for most of the year. No comms for the next nine months. No way to call for help, and she wouldn't be able to rescue Pele, not without help. For now, her plan was to survive until the planet made its orbit out of the blackout zone. There was little else she could do. Clutching the journal tight to her chest, she resolved she would make the most of that time.

Fenrir twitched beside her, and she reached out a hand to run along his soft, golden fur. He was healing well, but it would take him time to adjust to three legs instead of four. She ran her hand along his side, then pulled back in shock when she reached where his wound had been. The skin had healed, and new fur had sprouted by the second day, but she swore she felt a bump where yesterday there had only been fur. Skyla leaned close before running her fingers over the wound. Sure enough, there was a thick bump.

"What?" Skyla whispered, searching along Fenrir's hip, as if she would find the answers hidden there. Fenrir whined and turned into her. She watched as the bump stretched and moved in-sync with his hind leg. She shook her head. Whatever it was, Fenrir didn't seem to be bothered by it; she would keep an eye on it. Curling up with him, she settled in to read until the light faded from the window and her eyelids grew heavy.

***

Wind whips white-blond strands of hair across Skyla's face. Her little hands grip the throttle tighter; golden tendrils of light lace up her arms and insert into the back of her skull. Pele has grown with Skyla from the size of a drone into a small personal hover, just big enough for Skyla to ride, and at seven years old, Skyla can't get enough. Living on a space station provides limited opportunities for Skyla to fly, which is why she jumps at the opportunity to go with her dad on his expeditions.

This one is to a lush world brimming with life. Their campsite is in a meadow at the center of a forest that stretches out in all directions, the canopy a kaleidoscope of yellows, oranges, and reds as far as the eye can see; a thousand crystal clear lakes that reflect the pale blue sky break through the endless living tapestry.

Striped white-and-black tree trunks whip by on either side. Skyla thinks she can hear her dad calling after her, but she can't slow, not now, not with this whole wondrous world stretching out before her. The forest opens up, sending Pele and Skyla out over a particularly large lake, so large it is dotted with rocks and tiny islands of its own. Skyla grins. "It looks like an obstacle course! What do you say, Pele?"

Pele sends warmth through the bond. "Always up for a challenge!" She chirps in Skyla's aural implant.

That is all the encouragement Skyla needs. She prompts Pele to full speed, then goes straight for the first rock formation. It juts up like a mini mountain with flat plains chipped away at each edge, revealing a ripple of shimmering black through the purple stone. At the last moment, the duo dodges right. Pele's wing tip brushes the top of the calm water. The bond sends the cool sensation through Skyla's fingertips. One mind, two processors.

"Wahoo! Good one, Pele! Ten points. Can we get to one hundred?"

"Only one way to find out." Together, Pele and Skyla shift their course toward the next collection of stones. They dodge and turn and spin, collecting another forty points before Skyla's aural implant vibrates with her dad's voice.

"Skyla, where are you?"

Skyla shakes her head, dismissing the comms. She would meet back up with Dad soon, just as soon as she got her one hundred points. And that is when she sees it, the best obstacle of them all. At the center of the lake, a large island towers above the rest, its center carved out by time.

"How about a finale?" Skyla asks.

Pele's excitement matches her own as they align with the towering stones. Coming up to speed, the wind tears around Skyla, and the thrill of flying thrums through her veins. They rise up, ready to thread the needle, then loop back through for one grand trick before returning to camp.

Just as the duo lines up with the opening, a deep voice booms across the lake.

"Skyla!"

She glances back to see the worried expression on her father's face as he flies toward her. When she turns back, her vision fills with shadows as little impacts pummel her body. Skyla's grip slips from Pele. The golden cables that connect them rip painfully from her spine as Skyla's stomach leaps into her throat, and the world falls out from beneath her.

In freefall, time warps, speeding to an instant while lasting a lifetime, and then everything goes quiet. The shock of hitting the water only lasts a moment before Skyla's instincts take over, and she kicks her little legs furiously to bring her back to the surface. Once she breaks the surface of the water, she takes a deep breath, then peers around for Pele, her eyes wide with shock. But it doesn't take long for Pele to find her. The little AI zooms over, dipping low so the girl can scramble back into her seat.

"Skyla! Are you alright?" Pele's tone is filled with worry.

"Yeah, just fine! What a rush! I wish we could have completed the loop, though. What happened?"

"It appears," a stern voice breaks through their conversation, and Skyla peers up into worried, ice-blue eyes, "that you spooked a colony of local mammals roosting in the arch."

Her father's dark eyebrows draw low over his eyes as he takes her in sternly.

"Oh." Skyla drops her gaze to the water and kicks at the surface with her boot.

"Oh," her father echoes, but then all the sternness leaks from his voice, giving way to worry. "Gyr." He places a gentle hand on her shoulder. "You can't fly like that. The stunts—cutting through the trees at top speed; it scares me."

Skyla finally looks back up from the lake and takes her father's cheeks in her small hands. She presses her face close to his.

"You fly at the speeds you are comfortable with, and I will fly at the speeds I am comfortable with." Her tiny voice is serious with the declaration.

Her father chuckles and wraps his arms around her, bringing her close as they hover above the lake.

"Just promise me you will be more careful? I don't know what I would do if anything ever happened to you."

"You don't have to worry, Dad. I am going to be the best pilot the UTA has ever seen!"

He chuckles again and tousles her wet hair before letting her go. "I have no doubt about that. You will be the best pilot! Not just in the UTA, but the universe one day! You and Pele are an unbeatable team."

Skyla scrunches up her nose at the declaration; it's true that she and Pele are an amazing team, but, "Dad, there's nothing beyond the UTA."

"Is that so, my little falcon?" His face goes serious as he gives her time to consider.

Not sure of what response he is looking for, she simply nods.

Her father pushes out a long breath before continuing, "There is so much more out there than the UTA, Gyr. There are worlds upon worlds that once housed our ancestors...and somewhere there is a planet where it all started." His eyes shine with a light she has never seen before, and Skyla wants to ask *what he means, but then he says, "One day you'll understand, but for now, we better get back to camp. You're soaked, and the sun is setting."*

Distracted by the prospect of food, Skyla forgets her questions about the lost planet and instead asks, "Can we build a fire?"

Her father chuckles. He knows what she is really asking. "We can build a fire. I brought sausages and—"

"And marshmallows?" Skyla is now bouncing in her seat, Pele pulsing rhythmically over the lake with excitement.

"And marshmallows and chocolate and honey cakes."

Skyla giggles then prompts the bond to lace around her hands again. Unable to contain her excitement a second longer, she punches Pele up to full speed and calls over her shoulder, "Race you back to camp!"

***

Skyla dug her fingers into the covers, hugging the blankets closer, the dream prompting bitter-sweet memories. She had gone on many expeditions with her father. He took her with him every chance he got before he disappeared. But that expedition had been one of her favorites. The vibrant alien landscape, the flora and fauna her father had collected, days of racing with Pele, and nights spent gorging on camp food. She remembered it all vividly, but she had pushed the memory of her father's warning to the recesses of her mind. What had he known? What had he been searching for?

CHAPTER 11 | FREYJA

MISSING

Freyja stalked the halls of her starship, rolling her shoulder as she paced. The tissue felt tight, even if her flesh had knitted together flawlessly. Regenerated tissue always took time to fully integrate. She was just glad the damage hadn't been more severe. Back at the academy, she had seen joint injuries put cadets out of commission before their careers even started. There was only so much nanite tech could repair.

Rohaan hadn't fought her on the decision to leave the rest of the tech behind. She had seen the argument brewing in his eyes, but the rage that burned in her own had silenced him. Losing Basilie to those creatures had reminded her of her mission, why she was doing this. She had to stay focused to find the source behind the signal...and if it was her mother?

Freyja wasn't ready to face that truth. Instead, she focused her fury on the events at hand. Freyja didn't give a damn if Rohaan said he could control the beasts. Too many of her Berserkers had fallen already. She had lost too much; she needed answers, and she wasn't willing to pay any more blood to the cause.

Bile rose at the back of her throat when she thought of Rohaan's omission, his lie. They hadn't needed to scout any of these ruins. There had been no need to risk her soldier's lives. They could have collected signal data from orbit and been on their way. Hell, they may have even had answers by now.

Freyja's head swam, though if it was from the fear of what she would find or the cost in lives of the delay, she couldn't be certain. Skirmishes were breaking out all throughout the former UTA as tribes fought for territories, and new powers struggled to establish themselves. This signal had been associated with the attack on Medina. It had framed her for the assault, planting a deepfake and blocking her transmissions to her fleet. It had cost her most of her Berserkers, her stardestroyer, and her entire fleet. This signal had been associated with the weapons buy at the capital, and she was certain it had something to do with the capitol bombing. If they wanted to bring stability to the Known Galaxies, the signal was key. She had to stop whoever was behind it before they destroyed them all, and Rohaan had delayed them by months!

Clenching her fists, Freyja wound up to punch the bulkhead.

"As much as I enjoy your outbursts, that isn't going to make you feel better," Selkie said as she gently strobed her lights, trying to calm Freyja.

"Shows how well you know me. Hitting something always makes me feel better."

"If you hit that bulkhead, you'll break your hand. Then you'll be even more insufferable."

Freyja snorted, but she dropped her fist all the same. Selkie was right, of course. They had been bonded their whole lives. She knew Freyja too well, even if Freyja felt like she didn't know her ship at all. Their relationship was still strained, even after the months that followed the capitol bombing. How could she trust Selkie when she had been reporting to the Empress behind her back? Selkie had promised no more communications with the mining tycoon. She had sworn fealty to the cause, to Freyja. Freyja wished she could believe her, but trust was earned, and they weren't there yet.

"Any updates on The Empire's troop movements?"

"You have read the reports."

"You know what I mean..." Selkie had fabricated reports to support the claim that Freyja had lost her life at the capitol. The hope was that she could buy enough time to investigate the signal without interference from the Empress.

"There are no signs that your mother has discovered our ruse."

"Listen where you can, Selkie. I don't want any surprises from The Empire."

Selkie flickered her lights in annoyance. "Shall I continue with the updates?"

Freyja waved a hand, inviting Selkie to continue, though she already had the report she was interested in. She wasn't on her mother's radar, not yet.

"We are one week out from the Hoshiko home world, Amaterasu." Selkie's words blurred together in Freyja's mind as she continued on with a list of supplies, systems, reports, and crew updates. Amaterasu was where Dr. Pinot had been stationed after Medina was destroyed. Odd, given that she was from the Etoile Tribe. Perhaps it was because she served under Commander Azai at Medina. He may have requested to keep her close.

Dr. Elodie Pinot had proven to be a valuable asset. As the foremost researcher in integrated biotech, the updates she'd made to Pele during their last mission had been impressive. Freyja was a little annoyed that the doctor hadn't made the same updates to Selkie. Logically, she understood. She hadn't been on good terms with the rest of the crew at the time. They had blamed her for the attack on Medina, and given the evidence, she couldn't hold that against them.

Still, it was another detour she didn't have time for. Now that they were down a crew member, she technically didn't have to station one of her men on Rohaan's ship. There was an empty bunk on Selkie. The thought carved a hollow in her stomach. Even with the extra space, she didn't think leaving Rohaan alone on his ship for weeks on end while they traveled was a good idea. How Skyla had managed it without going mad was a mystery.

Freyja chuckled at the thought. She wasn't entirely convinced Skyla hadn't lost it a bit after all those years in solitary, but Skyla had always been a little strange, even as a kid. Freyja shook her head. The decades they had spent as enemies, all the time she had spent lying to keep her friend safe—she tried not to hold it against Skyla for going off again on her own so soon after they finally reconciled.

"Selkie, any messages from Captain Karsten?"

"No, Admiral, the captain has not responded to any of your twenty-six missives. Shall I compose another?"

Freyja growled, "That won't be necessary." She had sent a message each week for the past six months. Would it kill Skyla to respond to one?

"Has there been a receipt signal?"

There was a delay this time. "No, none of your messages have been marked as received."

Freyja stopped her prowling. Skyla not answering was one thing, her not receiving the messages at all was another.

"Selkie, check the deep space quantum relays. Given Karsten's last known location, what are the odds she wouldn't have passed one in the last six months?"

"I put the odds that Captain Karsten would not have intercepted a quantum relay in the past six months at ten percent."

Not impossible. Skyla had spent the past three years off grid, but she wouldn't avoid the relays now, would she? Freyja was almost certain Skyla would want to check in on Rohaan, at least. The man had no business in the field, and it was obvious Skyla had a soft spot for him.

"I don't like this, Selkie." Freyja stalked to her private quarters.

"I agree. The odds of Skyla not having received one of your numerous messages are unlikely."

Freyja rolled her eyes at her ship. "It is a normal number of messages."

"If you say so."

Freyja really didn't want to do what she knew she had to do next. "Prepare a message for Commander Azai." She ground her teeth. She didn't want to involve the commander. They may not be enemies, but they weren't friends either. "This is Admiral Freyja Nygaard." She hesitated for a minute. Was she really an admiral anymore? She shook her head. Not the point. "My crew will be docking at Amaterasu in one week to consult with Dr. Pinot. It is imperative that we meet. I have a matter that requires your assistance...Send."

"That's it?"

"That's it."

"So informative."

"I don't know who is listening in on deep space communications. If something has happened to Skyla, I'd rather discuss it with the commander in person."

"Well, in that case, are you sure you should sign off as Admiral Nygaard? Maybe you should use a code name?" Selkie deadpanned.

"Do you think that's necessary?"

"No."

"Damn it, Selkie. Just send the message."

"Very well. Sent."

Freyja's wandering had brought her to her little greenhouse. Fitting—she always found her way back to her garden. She ran her fingertips along the leaves of her plants. The hydroponics garden before her was bursting with life, thriving under her meticulous care. A smile spread across her lips at the thought of an entire greenhouse filled with her plants. No, an entire yard. No, an entire planet—too much. A yard, a big yard, that would be nice. And Kylian, sitting by her side as she sunk her fingertips into the damp soil...

She wasn't sure when he had become part of the dream, but now every time she thought of that little farm on a quiet planet, she saw him there too. Would he come with her when this was all over? He had said he would follow her anywhere. Was that just into battle? Or would he follow her into retirement, too? She shook her head, clearing the thought from her mind. Those were far-off dreams, a problem for another day. She hoped he and the doctor were getting along alright on the remainder of the three-week journey to Amaterasu. A ring jump had brought them closer, but the nearest ring had been disabled, yet another delay. At least she hadn't received any complaints. That was something. Turning her focus back to her herbs, she pinched the leaves off one by one, focusing on the here and now, letting the quiet, practiced movement wrap around her like a blanket.

CHAPTER 12 | HINATA

CONTROL

"The rules have changed." Green tea sloshed over the sides of a porcelain cup before him as Hinata slammed a fist into the hardwood desk. Never before had he been so bold. Usually, he could barely meet his mother's eye, but he could no longer hold his tongue and play the dutiful son. The deaths of his cadets at the ring weighed heavily on him. This war was leading them all to destruction, and she refused to see it.

"The rules of engagement have not changed in over a millennia, Hinata-kun. Perhaps it is you who cannot accept responsibility for yet another mistake."

Her words raked like ice through him, but they did nothing to cool the fire that burned at his core. He would forever bear the responsibility of his brother's death; they both knew that. He held no illusion that the weight of the loss of the cadets would haunt him until his dying day but this—this was not his mistake alone. If he did not stand up to her now and make her see their folly in underestimating the Empress, more children would die, and he could not bear it. They had assumed that she would follow their tribal code. That assumption had cost him a quarter of his fleet. He couldn't change it, but he'd be damned if he didn't do something to prevent it from happening again.

"I accept responsibility for my mistakes, Okaasan, but do you?" She reeled back as if he had slapped her, but Hinata was not finished. "This isn't about Akio. This is about the lives of our soldiers, your soldiers. If we do not adapt, if we are not prepared to meet the Empress on her level, we are sending them to die!"

"Enough. I will not be lectured by my wayward son in my office."

Hinata's gaze dropped to trace the dark wood grains of her desk. "You are making a mistake." His voice had dropped to a near whisper, pleading with her to stop this, to save their people from ruin.

"The only mistake I have made is in placing my faith in you." She waved a palm over the datapad on her desk, a holo display shimmering to life between them.

Hinata's stomach clenched into knots, recognizing the scene. The Torri Ring was still intact, with his fleet stationed around the megastructure. It was the scene just before the battle that had broken him, and his lungs tightened as it played out once again. Everything happened as he remembered, all up until the moment when the corvettes should have ejected their escape pods. Something shifted, the *Takarabune* moved out of alignment, and the *Oseberg* took advantage of the slip, which wasn't possible, as he had been in control of the destroyer. All chaos broke loose. The battle raged on until the ring was destroyed, and finally, Hinata regained control of the

Oseberg. Hinata's eyes blew wide, as if staring at the foreign scene could somehow reconcile the unfamiliar images before him with his memory.

Once the holo dissolved to pixels again, his gaze darted up to meet his mother's, her dark eyes seething.

"That—that isn't what happened." The words lodged in his throat, his mouth having gone dry.

"I have had enough of you. I am Josei Tennō of the independent Hoshiko Tribe. This is my planet, my Navy, and you have disappointed me for the last time. If you want a place in this universe, you will do as I say."

"This is a mistake—"

"I do not make mistakes. Now get out of my sight while I decide what to do with you." Rising from her seat, she turned her back on him to look out the large windows that spanned the wall behind her desk. There would be no reasoning with her.

Hinata stormed into the courtyard, his mind reeling. What had he just seen? He couldn't make sense of it, but he knew that there was so much more to this war than he had suspected, and if he didn't act, many more of his people would die. He could no longer allow her to choose his fate.

The traitorous thought scared him. He had always deferred to her, to the tribe, to honor. They were the tenets that made up the core of his being...and where had that gotten him? Now he was trapped, and he wasn't ready to give in.

A soft ping broke his train of thought as Tentei forwarded a message.

"I thought I told you to hold comms," Hinata snapped.

"I think this is one you should take," Tentei responded.

Hinata's heart skipped a beat. He had an incoming message from the Zeta quadrant. Had she finally returned one of his messages?

His racing mind stilled as he opened the message, adrenaline pumping through his veins, but his excitement was doused in disappointment as the face of Admiral Nygaard filled his ocular display. What did she want? Up until now, she had had the good sense to leave him alone. He hadn't forgiven her for cheating on the admiral exams, and even though he knew without a doubt she had nothing to do with the attack on Medina, he didn't trust someone willing to cheat their way to the top.

The message played out twice in his ocular display before he dismissed the image. Why would she need to meet with him? He shook his head. He didn't have time for whatever nonsense the admiral was involved in. Unlike the rogue admiral, he had a fleet to run; he had lives to save.

***

The loud thunder of his racing pulse blocked out the sound of his heavy breath. He focused on the burn that lit his legs and pushed harder. Faster. The sun-dappled trail blurred beneath Hinata's feet as he plunged deeper into the wooded trails behind his family home. Ancient pines reached up overhead, blocking out the harsh midday sun. Soft pine needles crunched under his shoes as he picked up the pace. The heady scent of sap and air and water worked to clear his mind. The harder his muscles burned, the less his mind wandered, and he found he could just be. Here. In this moment.

A series of urgent alerts brought Hinata to a halt. Pausing, he leaned against one of the great pine trees to catch his breath.

"Tentei, I thought I told you not to disturb me," he scolded his ship.

"This is important, brother."

Relenting, Hinata pulled up the alerts in his ocular display.

Nygaard: Commander Azai, we have landed on Amaterasu, and I am requesting a meeting.

Hinata ground his teeth. He and Tentei would have to have a discussion about what was important.

Nygaard: Commander Azai, it is imperative that I meet with you. Please respond with a time and place.

Nygaard: Damn it, Hinata, stop being an ass and answer my messages.

Well, that escalated quickly. He couldn't help the grin that came with pissing off the admiral.

Nygaard: Set a meeting. It's not about you and me.

That final message had his attention. If it wasn't about the two of them, did that mean it was about *her*? He broke into a run, heading back for the capital. He had ten kilometers to cover, and if it was about her, he didn't want to wait.

Azai: Meet me at the gardens in one hour.

***

Hinata paused his pacing on the wooden bridge that stretched over the koi pond. Having arrived ten minutes before the meeting time, he had nothing to distract his nervous energy.

With a forceful breath, he worked to steady himself. He needed to appear calm and collected; he wouldn't let Freyja see how her message had unsettled him.

His eyes locked onto the large koi fish swimming under the bridge. A thick orange and black fish skimmed the water near Hinata. That was Akio's koi. Hinata closed his eyes as his brother's face came unbidden into his mind. The koi had grown strong and large over the years; if only his brother had lived to grow alongside it. Hinata turned away from the pond, pressing his eyelids closed to block out the world. He didn't have time for this right now. He needed to focus on the meeting with Freyja. He needed to know what she knew.

The crunch of boots on gravel came to him long before he heard her clear her throat beside him.

"Am I interrupting?" There was an edge to Freyja's voice. She didn't care if she interrupted; she only cared about herself, her goals.

He opened his eyes, turning to face the woman. "Hardly. What is this about, Nygaard?"

Freyja flinched at the use of her surname without a title. Good. She wasn't a part of the UTA anymore, not that there was a UTA, not really. Either way, she hadn't earned his respect.

Freyja didn't correct him. Her eyes flicked around the gardens. "Is it safe to speak here?"

Hinata tapped a out sequence on his datapad. With a subtle pop, the noise pollution of the growing city beyond the garden walls vanished. Now the only sounds were those of water lapping against the bridge and the gentle rustling of leaves in the slight breeze.

"The gardens are shielded, but I've initiated a local jammer. What do you want, Freyja?"

Freyja turned to the wood railing, picking at the grain with a fingernail. Her eyes wouldn't meet his. "Have you heard from Skyla?"

His heart froze at the mention of her name, mind racing at the implication of her question.

"No." He begrudgingly gave his answer, a painful admission that opened a door in his mind that he had fought to keep shut, had worked his body to exhaustion to keep shut for months now. The captain had not answered a single message, and he felt like a fool for continuing to send them, but he couldn't help himself.

"Me neither." Freyja's whispered confession cut through his mental spiraling.

"What?"

"She hasn't received a single message. She hasn't passed through a quantum relay station in the past six months. Has she received any of yours?"

Hinata shook his head slowly. He had thought maybe she was avoiding him; she had done it before, avoiding him after he kissed her on their return journey from the fractured Dyson sphere. She had a habit of running away when she was uncomfortable. He figured she had avoided accepting his missives at the stations, but she hadn't passed through a single relay?

"Doesn't that strike you as odd?"

"Yes." He hated to admit it, but Freyja was right. It was strange. Then guilt hit him like a surge of electricity. She hadn't passed through a single relay station. What if something had happened to her? To Pele? What if she had needed him and he had spent these months sulking like a child?

Dread washed over him. What if it was worse? Worse than him not coming when she needed him. What if she was already dead?

He grasped the wood railing so tight his knuckles turned white, struggling to hold on to reality, to stay grounded in this moment. He couldn't be responsible for another death. He couldn't have let her down like he let Akio down. He couldn't fail her like he had failed all of those cadets at the ring. The horizon tilted, and he swayed on his feet.

"Whoa, easy there, Commander." Freyja grasped him by the shoulder, grounding him in the moment, her eyes wide with concern. "It's going to be okay. I'm sure of it. Skyla is stubborn as hell, too stubborn to die. She's out there."

A thick knot formed in Hinata's throat. No words would come.

"We will find her. I promise." Freyja's fingers pressed firmly into his shoulder, her eyes locked on him. Her words were forceful, carrying the full weight of her belief, but Hinata struggled to share her optimism.

"Where was her last known transmission?" Hinata shut down that emotional side of himself. He needed his wits about him now. If Skyla was stranded, alone, lost at the borders of the Known Galaxies, he had to focus. He had to get to her before it was too late.

Freyja nodded, letting go of his shoulder. She was all business now. "Last I heard, Skyla was on her way to Thule. That's the last planet her father had mentioned in his journals."

"Do we know if that's where she actually went?"

"Hard to say for sure."

"Did she check in at Thule?"

Freyja shook her head. "I don't know. Selkie pulled some research for me, and it turns out that Thule goes dark for ten months out of the standard year. Its orbit passes through an anomaly. Even if she made it there, we wouldn't know for another three months."

Hinata gritted his teeth against his frustration, the muscles of his jaw so tight they threatened to snap.

"So it's possible she ran into trouble six months ago?"

"It's possible."

"We leave tonight, prepare your ships for the jump—"

"Selkie doesn't have the fuel stores to make a jump that far."

Hinata slammed a fist into the railing. "She needs us now." His soul couldn't take the blow of another failure, not with her. If she was out there, he would find her. This was something he could do.

Freyja gripped the railing next to his fist. She didn't move to touch him, but her words came out quiet, almost kind. "She is a big girl, a captain in the UTA, and an experienced archaeologist. Even if she is in trouble, she can handle herself until we get there. We have to play this smart. We aren't any help to her if we end up stranded along the way."

"A stardestroyer could make the jump," he said.

"One way...maybe."

A half smile parted Hinata's lips. "One problem at a time, Nygaard."

Freyja's face betrayed her concern at the sudden shift in his countenance; she squinted at Hinata, no doubt she could see how close he was to snapping. "What did you have in mind, Azai?"

CHAPTER 13 | SKYLA

HERACLEION

The lights overhead flickered and died as the gentle hum of the generator fell silent.

"Come on!" Skyla unwound her arms from around her legs and came to her feet. With the toe of her boot, she kicked the generator gently, willing it back to life. No luck. She ran her fingers along the panels, searching for the power source. As she traced the lines of the machine, she came to a latch at the back. With a twist and a yank, Skyla freed the dead energy cell. It was heavy and bulky at forty kilos, and it came up to her waist.

Skyla pushed a breath through pursed lips as she set it on the floor beside the generator.

"There has to be a recharging station." Her gaze flicked over to Fenrir, who still lay curled up on the floor, that strange nub where his leg had been twitching slightly. Skyla was certain it was larger today.

"Come on, pal." Skyla lugged the energy cell to the door of the yurt. "This isn't going to be a pleasant place to nap if we don't get the generator running again."

Skyla pushed out into the frozen wasteland, clutching the energy cell, leaving the door open only long enough for Fenrir to hobble out behind her. His gait was still awkward, but he was managing surprisingly well. A brief walk to the main building and a short search later, Skyla had found the charging station. Unfortunately, the power to the main building was also dead.

"This planet can't make anything easy, huh?" Skyla sighed, throwing a sidelong glance at Fenrir.

Skyla paced back from the building, scanning the roof. A thick layer of ice coated the surface, but a glint caught the light and she was certain it was the metallic sheen of solar plating. The camp ran on solar, and in theory, should be able to run indefinitely, but the thick layer of ice that had settled over the roof was preventing the solar plating from gathering energy.

"Alright, I guess we are de-icing the roof today." Skyla rubbed her gloved palms together and cast her gaze about the camp. There had to be something she could use to get on the roof. There was a large structure nestled back behind a couple of yurts that she had missed on her first day. Given that she had already searched the other buildings and hadn't found any maintenance equipment, it felt like a safe bet.

The ice-crusted snow drifts crunched beneath her boots, and she grimaced as she looked down at Fenrir hobbling through the snow.

"You can head back, pal." Skyla turned and pointed.

Fenrir cocked his head at her.

"It's cold, and there's not much you can do." Skyla decidedly ignored how she was speaking to Fenrir like he would answer.

In a way, he did; he bumped his head into her belly and rubbed his head against her until she relented.

"Okay, okay, you can come with." Skyla laughed and scratched him behind the ears before continuing on.

When they arrived at the building at the back of camp, she found that the entire face of the building was made up of a series of large doors, one of which had been left slightly open. She shoved hard against the door, which groaned and resisted only briefly before sliding open.

It was a garage. There were several land skimmers and a wall full of equipment. Everything appeared to have a light layer of frost, and Skyla hoped the equipment wasn't damaged.

Skyla ran her fingertips along the land skimmer as she walked toward the back wall. The small vehicle might come in handy, but first, she had to get the generator working again.

Skyla grabbed a black duffel bag with a ladle-shaped constellation stitched into the fabric and began filling it with items from the back wall: plasma torch, multi tool, heating elements, nanite hand tool, aerogelium patches, sealant, and carbon fiber cable. If she couldn't fix the panels with these supplies, she was spaced.

Spinning slowly, Skyla searched the space. No ladder, no rope...there. A disc-shaped object hung in the back corner. She grabbed the personal suspensor and ran a gloved finger around the rim. Her breath caught as she waited, praying the disc still held power. A soft glow ran three quarters of the way around the rim. Skyla let out her breath and smiled. That would do.

On her way out, her eyes fell once again to the land skimmer. That was a project for another day.

With the garage sealed up tight and the duffel slung over her shoulder, Skyla placed the disc on the ground in front of the main building. She stepped onto the disc, then with a signal from her neural chip, the suspensor hummed to life slowly, ascending until it brought her level with the lip of the roof.

Skyla stepped carefully onto the ice-slick surface. Her toes gripped at the insides of her boots as she took tiny steps toward the center of the building. There was a thick beam that ran the length of the roof, and Skyla immediately saw the problem. That beam housed the automated cleaning mechanics, and it appeared to be iced shut. If she de-iced the central unit and thawed the panels, the central generator should start working again.

The work was slow, Skyla taking care to keep purchase atop the block of ice as she moved along the central unit, setting up plasma torches along the way. She then worked her way around the roof, setting up the mobile heating units every two meters. With the last heating element in place, there was nothing to do but wait.

Skyla had nearly made her way back to the corner where she had left the personal suspensor when a wall of shimmering green caught her eye. The same strange shimmering wall she had seen on her trek to the camp. It was so far out in the distance, she nearly missed it. Squinting, she activated her ocular display to zoom in for a better view—

Ice cracked under her boot. A melted sheet broke free, taking her feet out from under her. She slammed against the roof. Throwing her arms out, she fought the momentum of the sliding ice, but it was no use. She slid off the edge. The world sparked with stars as her head slammed into the ground.

***

"Don't you see it!" Skyla's father says.

Nine-year-old Skyla peeks out from around the corner, careful to stay out of sight. Her mother and father stand in the living room, a holo of star charts suspended between them.

"What I see is a waste of time." Skyla's mother waves a hand through the star charts.

"No, no, no," Skyla's father sputters excitedly as he comes behind his wife, turning her to inspect the star charts once again. "This is something big! I promise. These are alien signals."

Skyla's mother scoffs, "Not this again."

"It is! It's communication—and look." He swipes his hand shifting the holo to display the central rim. "They are communicating with us!" A broad smile spreads over his face, but Skyla's mother only grimaces in return.

"You can't go public with this." Her voice is serious.

"Of course I have to go public with this! We've finally found it! Proof of alien life and that they are already communicating with us! This is huge!"

"Enough!" Skyla's mother shouts. "All you have found is a strange signal. It means nothing. You cannot go public with this. I forbid it."

***

Something rough and damp ran the length of Skyla's face. She cracked an eye open. Fenrir's golden face took up the entity of her vision, a blue tongue hanging lopsided out the side of his mouth.

"Gross!" She ran her gloved hand over her face. "Can we not make this our thing?" she asked playfully as she pushed up from where she had fallen in the snow. Her head pounded, and her ribs ached, but she was otherwise intact.

The memory of her parents' fight played through her head. It was nothing special; her parents had plenty of fights just like that one when she was a kid, but it felt eerily similar to what was happening right now, and she couldn't help but wonder if it was the same signal Ears had picked up in the Zeta quadrant. Maybe there would be something in her father's journals?

A loud pop demanded Skyla's attention. She sprang to her feet and stepped back enough to get a good view of the roof.

"Yes!" Skyla threw a fist in the air as the maintenance unit hummed to life; its casing peeled back, and mechanical runners took to life cleaning the roof.

She smiled down at Fenrir. "Looks like we just bought ourselves some more time, buddy."

***

The soft paper slid through her fingertips as Skyla flipped to the next page of the journal. She had settled into a routine over the past several months at the abandoned research facility. After the night she drank herself delusional, she knew she had to stay disciplined or she would surely die here. As much as she hoped that someone would come to rescue her—that the researchers had a designated pickup that would come to find her in the coming months, or that Freyja would tire of waiting for her to come join her, or that *he* would notice she had disappeared—she couldn't count on any of that. Skyla had been a rogue planet for too long. They had given her space, and she wasn't sure anyone would notice that she had fallen off the map. She had been very clear that she couldn't wait for it to be just her and Pele again.

Pele. Skyla cursed herself. She missed Pele so much it hurt. Like the pain of a severed limb, Skyla still felt her presence, even though she wasn't there. A deep, resounding pain echoed through the hollow space. They had been bonded at birth, and Skyla didn't know who she was without Pele.

The pain in Skyla's chest grew as she let the thoughts in. Pele wasn't the only person she missed. She missed Rohaan and his wild theories, and she was surprised that she even missed Freyja. After decades of hating the woman, she had quickly found her spot in Skyla's heart again. And she missed *him*. She missed him so much it robbed the breath from her lungs and threatened to crush her.

She cursed herself again, knowing there was no way he missed her like this. A pain so real it was like a sword had been ripped through her gut.

It was ridiculous. They barely knew each other. They had spent a few months together in a time of chaos. Most of that time she had spent hating him...or avoiding him, because deep down she had realized the truth. She didn't hate the commander; she wanted him. Wanted him near her. Wanted to sit with him while he cooked for her, to share a drink with him and exchange stories of their past lives. She wanted his lips on hers and his hands all over her body and...

And she had stopped it all. She had put distance between them every chance she got. She had known they would end up like this. There was no way he felt the way she did about him, not when she had pushed him away. The realization made everything worse.

Focus. This was the time of day she spent studying her father's journals. *Stick to the schedule.*

Each day, she started with a run around the camp. To Skyla's amazement, Fenrir's leg had fully regrown, and he spent his mornings hunting the small game that wandered near the camp. Skyla, however, never strayed out of sight of the yurts. The weather was volatile, and she still hadn't figured out what had happened to the researchers at the station. Maybe they had been emergency evacuated? She could hope, though doubt pushed its claws into the edges of her mind when she thought of all the personal effects left behind.

After her run, it was time for calisthenics in the commons, then breakfast in her father's yurt. She had debated for a few days whether she and Fenrir should move into his room. She ached to feel close to him, but at the same time, she didn't want to disturb his things. She didn't want to replace his scent with her own. In the end, the comfort of being in his space won out.

Afternoons were spent tending to the hydroponics garden, de-icing the solar panels, and making repairs to the camp. Then she would eat and study her father's journals for the rest of the evening. It was monotonous, but it kept her focused, kept her productive, kept her from losing her mind.

Skyla flipped the page of the journal—the images grabbed her attention instantly. Sitting up from the cot where she had been lounging, she braced her elbows against her knees as she studied the sketch. It looked like a ruin; not any she had ever been to, but it was Old World tech, no doubt about it. Her father had been a scientist, a researcher. He held unpopular ideas, sure, but he wasn't an archaeologist. What was he doing with this?

She flipped the page: more sketches, up-close scenes, and cross sections filled the following pages. Finally, she came to a section scrawled in her father's familiar handwriting.

The lost city, or as we call it here, the city of Heracleion. The reason we are here at Thule. After decades of searching, we have finally found it: the location of the lost city. It took us years as we followed a trail of scattered old tech beneath the ice, but I am certain the city is located at the edge of the Talg Sea. All evidence points here. At the time of the Old World, the shelf would have been above the waves. All of the pieces we have found so far have brought us here. If my calculations are right, it should be approximately 3,000 meters down.

We have had to requisition the diving tech to withstand the temperatures, pressure, and hostile creatures that we expect to encounter on our dive. We will have to wait another year for all of the equipment to arrive. It's hard to be so close and still so far, but I have waited two decades for this. I can wait one more year. Finally, we've found it!

Found it? Skyla flipped back to the sketches of the ruin. She thought her father had left to prove his theories that there was other intelligent life in the universe. But if these drawings were accurate, Heracleion was an Old World civilization, human in origin. She shook her head gently, flipping through the journal.

"What were you searching for, Dad?"

Fenrir's ears perked up at her voice, but he didn't move his huge head from his paws where he lay napping.

Another series of drawings froze her hands. It was a sketch describing a wild wormhole. No one traveled through wild wormholes anymore. They were unstable and dangerous. There was no telling where it might lead.

Wild wormholes had been used during the Exodus when the vast expanse of space before them was so barren that humanity risked extinction if a way to bypass the wastelands couldn't be found. In their histories, humanity had taken three such jumps during the Wandering, accepting that the unknown was better than braving generations through a dead galaxy. Since colonizing the Amalthea galaxy, humanity limited jumps to the Silk Road Rings and the micro jumps made possible by extensive star maps.

Skyla flipped the page, her breath caught. The sketch of the little blue and green planet with wisps of white clouds wrapping around it stirred memories of a planet she had seen once in a near-death hallucination. Earth, her father had labeled it in the journal.

The entry went on to detail her father's theory of how ancient humans had traveled through a wild wormhole, how they had arrived in the Amalthea galaxy. He believed the travelers that established Heracleion were the first in a series of exploratory missions that spanned hundreds of years. If his theory was correct, that was how their galaxy had been seeded with life—the Old World civilizations that had since died out.

Skyla snapped the journal closed, her eyes wide with the realization. Her father hadn't come here to find an alien civilization; he had come here to find Earth.

CHAPTER 14 | FREYJA

THOSE FORGED IN BLOOD

*T*he other cadets part around Freyja as she enters the training room. Hushed whispers follow in her wake.

"Dangerous."

"Murderer."

"Monster."

No one will meet her eyes. Normal conversations resume as Freyja finds her way to the corner. The other cadets resume their activities in the training rings farthest from her. Slumping against the wall, Freyja slides to the floor. With her forearms braced against her knees, she drops her head and forces the air from her lungs.

This had been her plan,: make it look like she had tried to kill Skyla so the academy would separate them, and Skyla would be safe; they would all be safe. There had been no choice. If she disobeyed the Empress, people got hurt. This had been the only way to save both Skyla and her Berserkers. So why does it bother her so much that the other cadets see her as a monster? Is it because deep down, she fears they are right?

A firm kick to her boot pulls Freyja from her thoughts.

"You going to put up a fight, or am I going to have to kick your ass while you're down?" Tristan gives her one of his lopsided grins as he extends a hand to help her up. Rolling her eyes, Freyja accepts his help, coming to her feet.

"No one will train with me." Freyja's gaze roves over the other cadets, all of whom keep their distance, not so much as chancing a glance at the corner.

"None of them could take you anyway." Tristan strolls out into the center of the ring before turning to beckon her forward.

Freyja rolls her eyes but obliges, stepping into a sloppy fighting stance. Tristan springs forward, snapping both of her legs together in his arms as he drives her to the mat. The air rushes from her lungs, and her head buzzes as Tristan calls out the count. "One, two, three." He slaps the mat and springs back up onto his feet. "You're going to have to do better than that."

The familiar buzz of rage licks beneath her skin as Freyja staggers to her feet. She wasn't in the mood for Tristan's games. The feeling of the other cadets' eyes assessing her only makes the fire burn brighter. Who are they to judge her? If she had wanted Skyla dead, she would be. If she wanted any of them dead, they would be. Maybe she is a monster, and they should fear her.

The walls of the training room press in around Freyja. She needs out—anywhere but here. She moves to shoulder past Tristan, but he drops low, grasping for her knee. This time she is ready with a sprawl, throwing her feet back and her hips into his shoulders. He collapses to his knees under her weight, and she spins around, wrapping her arms around him and driving forward.

"Enough, Tristan," she hisses in his ear.

"We are just getting started." He pries her hands apart and springs forward, coming to his feet and twisting so they are once again face to face. They waste no time tying up, each grasping the other by neck and elbow.

"I can't stand the way they look at me."

"Let them look. Let them fear you," Tristan counters.

Freyja breaks his grip and shoves him away. Her eyes land on the edge of the mat where the rest of her crew have arrived. Her gaze locks onto Kylian. The way he looks at her stops her heart, as if he reaches between her ribs and squeezes until there is nothing left. Maybe she could learn to ignore the others, let them think she is a monster, but not him. The way he looks at her right now threatens to destroy her.

Kylian disappears from her sight as she registers the impact of hitting the mat.

"You're an ass." Freyja forces the words out as Tristan stares down at her.

"And you are distracted." Tristan pulls Freyja to her feet, his eyes flicking between her and Kylian before resuming the fight, his fist held up protectively in front of his face. "He will get over it."

Freyja shakes her head but mirrors Tristan's stance. "He thinks I'm a monster."

"I've done far worse. He has the privilege of being who he is because of you and me. He'll get over it."

"I'm not so sure."

Tristan lets loose a series of jabs followed by a combination she has never seen before. He moves so fast she barely has time to react, and then he is through her guard with a mean left hook.

Pain blossoms across her face as her lip splits open, and her mouth fills with the metallic tang of blood. The inferno takes over, and Freyja comes at Tristan with a vengeance. They trade blows until they are both panting and bloody.

"Enough." Kylian grabs his cousin's fist as Tristan winds up to deliver another blow. Kylian's eyes dart between the two of them, and a spark of hope lights in Freyja. Those warm hazel eyes fill with concern as he takes in the bloodied and broken state of her.

Tristan drops his fist and throws his arms around the two of them. "I think you're right, cousin." He rolls his head to the side and gives Freyja his lopsided grin. "I just needed to remind our leader who she is. Let them whisper; let them call you monster. We will be your creatures in the night. Let them fear us."

With the fight ended, the rest of her crew presses in around them, their arms looped in a tight huddle. Freyja's gaze darts to Kylian. Tristan is hers, a creature willing to do whatever it takes, but will Kylian follow? Kylian's eyes still blaze with concern, but he gives her a stiff nod.

"To family," Kylian whispers.

"To those bound by blood," Tristan says.

Freyja hesitates for only a moment. It is their mantra; never before has it been hers. But even now, after all that she has done, they would claim her as one of their own. "And those forged in it," they finish together in a chorus.

***

Freyja opened her eyes to the familiar coral structure overhead. It was early, but the dream, the memory, ran through her mind on a loop, preventing sleep from pulling her under once again. Freyja groaned and pushed herself up from her tangled sheets.

"Selkie, report." She needed a distraction from those memories of the academy that sat bittersweet on her tongue. It had been the first time she had truly become one of them. Her Berserkers accepted her fully, the good and the bad, but it still broke her heart the way Kylian had looked at her that day—that he could see her as a monster. That memory had scabbed over into a scar far deeper than any other she had collected at the academy.

Selkie had listed off all of the sleeping crew while Freyja's mind raced. "And Dr. Dar and Dr. Pinot are in the lab."

Finally, Selkie had Freyja's full attention.

"At this hour? When did Dr. Pinot arrive? What are they doing?" Freyja had approached Dr. Pinot about making the upgrades to Selkie. The doctor was busy and had asked for some time to consider.

"Unclear, would you like me to relay audio?"

Running a calloused palm over her face, Freyja sighed as she reached for her boots. "Send the audio."

"You came to Medina to make a difference, right?" Rohaan asked.

"My research was scrapped long before Medina was destroyed," Dr. Pinot replied.

"I know. Commander Azai's stance on archaeologists cost us years of advancement. What if we could make up that time?"

"What are you proposing, Dr. Dar?"

"We have been investigating the signal that was associated with the attack on Medina as well as the capitol—"

"Not my area of expertise."

"That's not all. The signals we have found in the Zeta quadrant...they are all linked to satellites orbiting Old World ruins."

There was a pause in the conversation. "Selkie, visual," Freyja demanded as she crept silently down the corridor toward the lab. An overlay of the room appeared in Freyja's ocular display. Dr. Pinot crossed her arms, but Rohaan held her full attention.

"I have been collecting all of the potential med tech we could salvage at each of the sites. That is your specialty, is it not?"

"It is." Dr. Pinot's voice was controlled, but she betrayed her curiosity.

"Come with us. Work on the tech we find. Your talents are being wasted here."

Dr. Pinot brought a fist to her chin, considering his offer.

Freyja considered Rohaan's behavior over the past couple of months. It had been strange, to say the least. Ever since their first salvage mission, he had become obsessed with the Old World tech, even worse than Skyla. And now he was arranging clandestine meetings. What was he up to?

"You came to Medina because of the miracle tech that saved a little boy from an incurable illness, right?"

Dr. Pinot's eyes locked onto his.

"What if you can give that gift to another child? What if your work made the difference?"

Dr. Pinot nodded. Freyja could see it in the woman's eyes. He had sold her.

Stepping around the corner, the visual from Freyja's ocular display aligned with the two doctors standing in the lab.

"Dr. Pinot, is now a good time to talk about those enhancements you made to Pele?" Freyja let a smirk twist her lips. She had been nervous that Dr. Pinot might turn them down, but if she joined their crew there would be little reason to deny Freyja the rapid remodeling tech. The nagging annoyance she felt at Rohaan inviting another member to join their crew was a small price to pay. Still, it wasn't his place, even if it had worked out in her favor.

Dr. Pinot nodded. "I'll get to work on the modifications this afternoon. I need to gather a few things from my lab."

CHAPTER 15 | HINATA

THE DECISION

The thick wooden doors of the council meeting room crashed against marble walls as Hinata threw them open. He had lost all sense of reason, all control. *Fuck,* the captain put him entirely out of his mind. He didn't care; he was going out to Thule, and he would get the council's approval to do so.

His plan hinged on being able to take the *Takarabune.* It was the only ship in his fleet with a large enough power supply to make the jump to Thule and then limp along for a resupply. Who knew how long Skyla had been missing? How long she had been adrift in space or crashed on that damned ice planet? Who knew if she was still alive? That thought brought

Hinata's focus back to the council, who stared at him with the shock of his interruption worn plainly on their faces.

"Can we help you, Commander Azai?" High Council member Ito asked, his voice gravelly with age. His dark eyes were sharp as ever as they apprised Hinata, but Hinata's attention was solely on his mother. A flash of anger greeted him in her intense eyes, but she kept her features schooled. She would not give him the satisfaction of seeing how much he had disturbed her.

"I formally request to take the *Takarabune* for a recovery mission in the Zeta quadrant."

"This couldn't have been submitted as a formal request?" Ito asked.

"My apologies to the council. It is an urgent matter. I wish to prepare the ship for the journey and leave no later than tomorrow."

"What is so urgent that you can't follow protocol?" Ito asked.

Hinata's mother remained dangerously quiet.

Hinata took a deep breath, centering his thoughts. "There is an asset at risk. The sooner I can retrieve it, the better our odds of a successful mission."

"An asset?" His mother's piercing gaze saw right through him. The weight of her malice landed heavily on his shoulders. He knew then she would take this from him.

"Yes, Josei Tennō." Hinata wouldn't give in so easily.

"Please, enlighten us, Commander Azai. What asset is so important that you believe the council should sanction a mission to the border of the galaxy, taking one of our stardestroyers at that, an asset that you know we are in short supply of after your failure to defend the ring?"

"It is a tactical asset, one worth the risk, I assure you." Hinata held his voice steady.

The council broke into whispers amongst themselves.

"Enough!" His mother slammed her hand into the table to regain order. "Motion denied. You will take your fleet and deliver the prisoners of war to Jubokko, as planned."

"Okaasan—"

"You will do as you are told or you will be court-martialed. You are quickly losing your value to the Hoshiko Tribe. Do not push me, Hinata."

Fire flowed through his veins. He wanted to rage at his mother; he had lost his value to her long ago, and now she threatened to take this last little spark of hope that he had left. But he knew better than to let her see how she had broken him. He kept his face blank as he bowed, his fist planted over his heart.

"Of course. My apologies to the council for wasting your time." Hinata turned on his heel and marched with measured steps out of the Senate building. He had always followed the rules, fought for his tribe, fought for his mother's acceptance. He was done fighting for them. If they wouldn't give him the ship, he would take it.

***

"Get your crew together. We are leaving," Hinata said, his voice closer to a snarl than actual words as he stepped into the galley on Freyja's ship. Tax stood at his side while Freyja and her men lounged at the table.

Freyja looked him over, her mask of cool indifference firmly in place, assessing him, weighing him. He was sick of it, sick of being judged and found wanting. He glared at her, daring her to voice what she thought of his outburst, but she had the good sense to keep whatever she was thinking to herself.

Already seeing where this was going, Hinata glared at Freyja's men. "Get out," he snapped.

Tristan's eyes landed on Tax, and he grinned as he walked toward the doorway and slung an arm around Hinata's second-in-command. "With pleasure, Commander." He gave a half-assed salute as Tax shrugged out from under his arm.

Tax gave a tight nod. "I'll be just outside, Commander."

"Now what fun is that?" Tristan complained. "You could at least accompany me to the rec room."

Tax looked to Hinata, who simply barked, "Go."

Once the men had left, the galley grew deathly still before Freyja finally broke the silence. "You got approval to take the *Takarabune*?"

Hinata drew his lips into a thin white line. His silence said it all.

Freyja shook her head. "What's your plan, then? Steal a stardestroyer? I know you want to help—"

"You don't know shit. Want to help? What the hell, she could be dying out there, alone." His carefully crafted façade crumbled as all of the emotion he tried to hide flowed out of him. His hands began to tremble, though his voice remained firm. "I need to get to her. I am done playing by their rules."

Freyja was judging him again. He could feel it in those hazel eyes, but the way she looked at him had shifted. "You actually care about her, don't you?"

He snorted, turning away. "Can we not do this? I told you to get the crew ready—"

"I don't take orders from you. Answer the question," Freyja snapped.

Hinata turned and pressed his palms onto the table. "Isn't it obvious?" he whispered.

Freyja's head canted to the side. "I saw the two of you in the capital. I just didn't think...I didn't think you were..."

"What? Capable of feelings?"

"Exactly."

Hinata shoved off the table and glared at her. "Fuck you, Freyja. Who are you to judge me?"

A slight smile tugged at her lips. "I'm not judging. I just thought we were more alike."

The fight went out of him as he sank into one of the chairs, pressing his palms to his eyes. "You have feelings too, Freyja."

"If you count white-hot rage," she shrugged and joined him at the table. "That's really the only one I've got," she joked.

"Are we done?" Hinata's gaze darted to the door. He had his work cut out for him if he was to commandeer the *Takarabune* tonight.

"Not hardly." Freyja snatched a bottle of clear liquor from the cart beside them, pouring two glasses and shoving one at Hinata.

"I don't have time for this." Hinata made no move to take the drink. "Get your crew ready. We launch in—"

"You do have time for this because stealing the *Takarabune* is not a plan. You'll paint a target on our backs. They'll shoot us down and detain us before we can make it to the jump site." Freyja punctuated her point by clinking her glass into his, sending liquor spilling across the scratched steel surface of the table.

"We will jump from here."

Freyja kicked her shot back, then slammed it onto the table. "Like hell, we have to hit a refuel site twenty light years from the jump site or we won't have enough fuel for a return trip. You know that. You're supposed to be a brilliant tactician! Stop thinking with your cock and start thinking with your head."

Hinata pressed a hand across his eyes, forcing his breath out, then in. "It's not like that."

"I don't give a shit what it's like. You want to help Skyla, start thinking things through. We need a plan." Freyja filled her glass once again, this time taking measured sips as she waited for his response.

Hinata nodded. He slipped the familiar mask of commander on, taking control once again, tucking his feelings away and focusing on the logic. "You're right."

A soft ping signaled an incoming message. His new orders. He was to take the *Takarabune* to the prison planet of Jubokko, then rendezvous with the rest of the Hoshiko forces, who were preparing for a battle with the Stjarna Tribe over a nearby trade route.

An idea began to form in his mind. It just might work. He pulled up the star charts. Jubokko wasn't an ideal refuel spot, but it was just close enough to get them to Thule, to *her*.

Hinata smiled. "I have a plan."

"I'm listening." Freyja held her glass up, once again prompting him to take his drink.

This time, he grabbed the glass and hit it against hers. "We will steal the *Takarabune*. But we will steal it from open space, where no Hoshiko forces will be able to stop us."

***

With the arrangements made for their departure, Hinata had nothing left to occupy his mind, and so he played the ring battle footage again. Pausing. Rotating. Dissecting. Replaying again. He studied every angle. Considered every tactic.

The holo displayed before him was as he remembered, but when he had tried to bring it before the council, his mother had told him that he needed to learn his place, and if he did not fall in line like a good soldier, she would have him court-martialed.

"You could not have done anything differently." Tentei's gentle voice broke Hinata's concentration.

"Play it again," Hinata said, watching for the countless time as the Empress' ships jumped into the ring, utterly destroying his forces.

"Hinata," Tentei prompted.

Gold tendrils of light tickled his fingertips, and Hinata finally dismissed the holo, letting the battle dissolve into particles. Tentei's comforting presence pricked along Hinata's nervous system. He relaxed into the familiar feeling of the bond. Even though it had been decades, it felt like coming home.

"You miss her." It wasn't a question. Tentei could feel the emotions that clouded his thoughts. As much as he tried to keep Skyla from his mind, she was always there, a constant thrum that only dulled with hours of training and an aching body.

There was no point in denying it. Hinata sighed. "Yes," he admitted to the empty cockpit, a confession that would stay between him and his ship.

"I miss Pele too," Tentei said, but a gentle warmth traveled along the link Hinata had not expected.

"That one night I stayed on Pele, she had insisted that you needed time for a sync. I had dismissed it as an upgrade, but that wasn't it, was it?" Hinata asked.

A warmth tingled through his nerves, and he had his answer, even without the words that followed. "No, that was not it."

"You love her?" The words were out of Hinata's mouth before he considered the implications, before he considered the returning questions he had opened the door to.

"Love..." Tentei began, "it is such a human concept. AIs experience time differently. When we choose to, we can spend a lifetime in a moment. Time in the way you perceive it loses meaning. I spent an eternity with Pele, and it was not enough. I found my soul reflected in another. An entity I would go to the ends of the universe to be with. Is this what you would call love?"

Hinata's throat had grown thick. He struggled to keep his voice even, only managing a single word. "Yes."

Tentei was quiet for a moment. "Then, yes...and you? You love the captain?"

Hinata didn't answer; he didn't need to. Tentei could feel the answer through their bond. Was he a fool chasing after a woman who had left him behind? What if she wasn't lost but simply didn't want to be found? Didn't want him? And yet, he couldn't stop himself.

Tentei sent a wave of comfort down the bond, but there were no words that could mend his fractured heart.

CHAPTER 16 | SKYLA

TALG SEA

"It will be good for you," Skyla said, looking at Fenrir, but they both knew she was talking to herself. Fenrir yawned before turning to go curl up by the generator.

"You could at least pretend to be a little bit nervous," she said, taking a sip of her coffee. It had gone cold, and she couldn't bring herself to finish it. With no excuses left, she proceeded to fasten her expedition jacket, working her way through the toggles to ensure that her gear was cinched tight, taking every opportunity to lock out the impending cold.

She pulled a fuzzy hood up over her head before securing the ventilation mask in place. With her goggles secured and her gloves and pack in place, there was nothing left to do but face the icy tundra. A slight tremor passed through her hand as she reached for the door. Every inch was covered. Her logical brain knew she would be protected against the freezing temperatures, yet her hands trembled at the thought of leaving the safety of the camp.

"It's been months. It will be good to get out of the camp for a bit. Yes, this is a good thing. We can do this." She nodded her head, as if the gesture could convince her subconscious. Fenrir bumped his head into her gloved hand, a rumbling purr vibrating through her legs as he rubbed up against them.

"You go out every day to hunt, and you do just fine. This is okay. This is fine. We are fine." She bounced gently on the balls of her feet, shaking out her hands as she worked up the courage to open the door. "Here goes nothing."

Blinding light set off the optics in her goggles, momentarily turning the world dark as she stepped out of the yurt into the freezing sunshine. Once her vision adjusted, she walked slowly to the garage at the edge of camp. She took in slow breaths as she walked, willing her heart rate to slow. There was nothing to be afraid of. The weather was perfect. No storms on the scanners. She had chosen today because it would be a low-risk day to go scout out the site she had found in her dad's journals. They had been preparing for the Heracleion dive, and a spark of hope had grown into the seed of an idea. She had to find out what condition the equipment was in. If the dive module was operational, maybe she could get to Pele.

Pele. Just the thought of her bonded ship set her resolve. She could do this.

Bad storms had kept Skyla cooped up in the yurt for the past week, that spark of hope fanning into a bonfire as ice pelted the thick yurt windows. She hadn't even ventured out to the main buildings, paralyzed by the memory of the endless trek across the ice that had nearly claimed her life.

But now the weather was clear, and she couldn't put this off any longer. She had to know. If there was even the slightest chance of getting to Pele, it was worth the risk.

Loose snow slid out from under her boots as she approached the garage. The storms had covered the compound in fresh powder. Fenrir followed, not far behind. Fixing the broken land skimmer had quickly become her favorite project. It was one of the many tasks she had set for herself to keep her mind from wandering into dangerous territory. The oversized hoverbike had been adapted to run in sub-zero temperatures, but the garage hadn't been properly secured when the camp was abandoned, and several of the pieces of equipment, including the land skimmer, had been damaged. Without the proper supplies, it had taken her a while to adapt pieces to fit, but she had gotten it in working condition and had even taken it for a test run around the camp before the storms had set in the previous week.

The suspensors hummed to life, and Skyla pushed the land skimmer out of the garage.

"Let's go, Fenrir." She patted the wide bed at the back of the vehicle.

He cocked his head to the side, deciding if he would honor her request. After a moment's consideration, he leaped onto the back.

"Good choice. You're fast. But that leg is still new." Skyla eyed the appendage that she had severed from Fenrir's body only six months prior. It had fully regrown with thick, golden hair and strong muscles. Skyla wondered how it was possible, but without a connection to the rest of the data net, she had found very little information on mammal hybrids that could regrow limbs.

Moving up to the front of the land skimmer, Skyla straddled the vehicle, wrapped her gloved hands around the handlebars, then kicked back and forth gently from foot to foot, getting a feel for the weight of the skimmer.

"Ready?" she called over her shoulder before powering up the engine. "Let's do this."

The landscape flew by at a dizzying rate, a white blur as she led them back out to the Talg Sea. It looked so different from when she had trekked the one hundred kilometers on foot to the camp. She didn't recognize a thing as ice cliffs and snow dunes blurred by.

Soon, the joy of flying again replaced all other thoughts in her mind. Even if it was just a land skimmer, it was the most pleasurable thing she had experienced since the crash. A twinge of guilt dampened the moment as she wished that she was flying with Pele instead. Soon, she would rescue Pele, and they would return to the stars.

Skyla angled them north as they approached the Talg Sea. If she was right about where the crash site was, then the dive site was only another twenty kilometers north. Hope bubbled up until it swelled in her chest, buoyed by the freedom of flight and the certainty that the dive site would be close enough to mount a rescue for Pele. The land skimmer purred loudly at her prompt as she pulled back on the throttle, bringing them to full speed.

The great ice ocean came into view, plates of ice spanning into the horizon. The loud cracking of plates breaking apart and colliding echoed in the distance. As Skyla approached the edge of the ice shelf, she slowed, then cut the engine and dismounted, walking the last few steps to the edge of the vast sea. From this vantage, she could see for miles, and all she saw as she scanned the area was a terrifying clash of snow and ice.

"Where is it?" She pulled up the scans she had taken of her father's notes. Had she made a mistake? Was she wrong about the site location? No, this was it. This was the spot; she was sure of it.

Skyla's stomach plummeted. There was nothing here. What if the dive site had been destroyed? Or what if they had packed up and gone off-world? Suddenly suffocating behind her ventilator, Skyla tore the mask from her face and let loose a scream that echoed through the ice. So close; she had been so close.

Fenrir whined, pawing at a mound of snow behind the land skimmer, but Skyla paid him no mind. Her legs buckled as the last scraps of hope she had grasped onto for the past week slipped through her fingers. Sinking back on her knees, she couldn't tear her eyes from the endless ocean that had become Pele's tomb. She should have gone down with her ship.

Digging her gloved hands into the snow, she crushed the tiny crystals in her grip like she could wring the answers she so desperately craved from their crystalline structure.

Fenrir whined again. Skyla tried to ignore him, but Fenrir was done being ignored. Slamming into her side with his head, he nearly pushed her to the ground, then whined again.

"What?" she growled at him. "What? What do you want me to do? There is nothing here." She rose to her feet and stomped over to the snow mound he had been pawing at.

"What? Are you bothered by snow now?" She threw out her arms, spinning in a circle and laughing mirthlessly. "Because I hate to break it to you, buddy, but that's all we have here. Just snow and ice and nothing." The words were acid on her tongue, and she was too desperate to care.

Fenrir looked up at her with those big, warm eyes, and instantly guilt replaced her ire. He might very well be her only companion for the rest of her life, however long that might be; it wouldn't kill her to indulge him.

"I'm sorry, boy. What did you find? A nice snow mound?" She was trying, but she couldn't keep the sarcasm from her voice. He bumped his head into her hand and then motioned toward the mound. She sighed, but walked over, dusting away the top layers of snow, eyes locked on Fenrir.

"Are you happy?"

Fenrir looked from her to the snow mound again. She pulled back fistfuls of snow until her fingers caught on something hard. There must be a rock, which made sense. The snow had piled up around the landscape.

Fenrir was still intently fixated on the mound. He would not relent until she showed him what was under all of that snow. With the palm of her glove, she began to dust snow away from the surface—but it wasn't a rock.

"Whoa!" Skyla staggered back from the mound.

Fenrir watched, his tail lashing back and forth.

Skyla edged forward cautiously, taking in the mound. Staring out at her was a face. Eyes frozen shut, lips turned pale blue in death.

She gently removed more snow, unearthing the cadaver's torso. He wore a dive suit with a constellation that looked like a large ladle etched on the breast. Her gloved hand wandered to the identical stitching of her own jacket, the one she had taken from the research station.

"No." The word was a whisper on the icy wind. She had known, deep down, she had known they hadn't left the planet. All of their personal things were still in place inside their yurts, with some doors frozen shut and others left open to the elements. None of the buildings had been prepped for leave. She had known something had happened to them. She just hadn't expected to find the bodies.

Skyla stood, surveying the site again with new eyes. There were several irregular mounds, some small like the one Fenrir had her unearth, others much larger. She hadn't got the calculations wrong. This was it; this was the dive site turned graveyard.

CHAPTER 17 | FREYJA

MORE THAN A MEAL

"*C*ome on, you stupid thing!" *Freyja slams her fist into the top of the 3D printer. The combination of hunger and her annoyance at being relegated to eating in the dormitory kitchenette was only exasperated further by the glitchy machine.*

Tristan and her Berserkers may have claimed her as their own, but Freyja is still the demon in the night, the cadet all the other kids fear, and she hates the way they stare. She hates the way conversations die when she enters the room. She will learn to deal with it. What choice does she have? But for now, she takes her meals at odd hours in the kitchenette where she can eat in peace, even if all the printer will make is amino gel.

Now, if she can just get the outdated 3D printer to fabricate a meal.

"*I'm not asking a lot here,*" she growls at the machine as the heads glitch and freeze in place.

"*Can I help?*"

Freyja's eyes snap up at the familiar voice. Kylian.

"*Here.*" Slipping in front of her, he opens the side panel and makes a few adjustments with deft hands before sealing the compartment and initiating a new print sequence. This time the machine picks up with a steady hum. Freyja's eyes go wide as the savory scent of pulled pork fills the air.

Retrieving a metal-wrapped package from the printer, her eyes linger on Kylian's.

"*This isn't amino gel,*" Freyja states, her eyes locking on the boy before her.

Kylian simply grins. "*Try it.*" He nods at the package in Freyja's hands.

The package is warm against her fingers, the smell of baked flour and spiced meat nearly overwhelming her. She slowly pulls the casing back before sinking her teeth into the meal. Chilli, garlic, and tomato wash over her tongue, eliciting a moan of contentment. After weeks of nothing but amino gel, the pleasure of having a real meal nearly overwhelms her. Hot tears prick at the corners of her eyes, but she blinks them away before Kylian can notice.

"*Good?*" Kylian smiles at her, and she notices that something has shifted between them. The fear and anger she had seen in those hazel eyes since the accident is mysteriously gone.

Having just taken a large bite of the meal, she takes her time, studying him as she chews, then swallows hard before speaking. "*It's amazing. What is it?*"

"*It's a burrito. Tristan always liked to get one when we went to the market back home in Koronis. I thought you would like it.*" Kylian sinks into one of the chairs at the small dining table, gesturing for her to join him.

Her eyes dart to the door. She had planned on taking her meal in one of the quiet alcoves where none of the other cadets go. The longer she stays in the common space, the greater her chance of running into another cadet, and she *is too tired to deal with their ridicule. She doesn't trust herself not to take out all her built-up anger on the next snarky kid that has something smart to say.*

Kylian doesn't miss her apprehension. "Don't worry. I locked the doors."

Freyja snorts. "Of course you did." She can't hold back the smile that pulls at her lips, so instead she hides it behind another bite of her burrito as she slides into the chair beside him.

"You want to talk about it?" Kylian asks. The way he takes her in makes her breath catch. She searches his eyes, trying to understand what has shifted. He has always been loyal, but the way he looks at her now—this is different.

"No." Freyja takes another large bite to punctuate the sentiment.

Kylian nods, his fingertips moving absently to trace his sternum. Freyja's eyes catch on the silver chain that peeks above the neckline of his black t-shirt. She can't remember a time when he didn't have the chain, but she has never seen what it is that he always keeps so close to him.

Looking for a change of topic, Freyja nods at Kylian's fingers. "What's that?"

His fingers freeze their idle movements, as if realizing what he's been doing. His throat bobs, fingers moving slowly to his neck, pulling the chain free from beneath his shirt. At the end hangs an intricately printed piece of metal. Elaborate looping knots tangle together to form a cross. He holds it suspended in front of him for just a moment before he brushes a finger over the metal, which reacts immediately to his touch, twisting and turning until it reforms into a key.

Freyja scrunches her nose. "What is it?"

Kylian brushes his thumb over the top of the key, and it springs back into a cross before he tucks it beneath his shirt. "It's a key." He gives her one of his lop-sided grins.

"No, really?" Freyja says sarcastically, bumping her shoulder into his. "I couldn't have guessed."

Kylian leans into her, the rumble of his laugh traveling through their shoulders where they touch, and Freyja finds herself leaning into the comfort of his closeness.

"It's the key to my hoverbike."

"I didn't know you rode."

Kylian shrugs before leaning his head over to rest against hers.

"I didn't think cadets were allowed personal vehicles beyond bonded ships."

"They're not. My bike's back in Koronis."

"But you still carry the key?"

"The day you see me without this key is the day you send my cold, dead body back to the stars." His voice is serious, and Freyja senses there is something left unsaid beneath his words.

"Well, then I hope I never see you without it." Freyja reaches up to trace over the lump of his shirt where the key rests. She feels his body tense beside hers for a moment before he relaxes again, bringing his arm to rest around her shoulders.

They sit like that for a long while, neither ready to leave this small pocket of comfort they have carved out for themselves. But the longer Freyja sits in the comfortable embrace of her friend, the more her worry builds. She has never felt so safe, and that alone scares her.

"Are we good?" she asks, unable to keep her anxiety to herself any longer.

Kylian squeezes her shoulder. "Of course we're good."

He offers no further explanation, and Freyja doesn't have it in her to fight for more answers, so instead she relaxes against him at his words.

"I will follow you anywhere. I am yours." His words are quiet, a whispered confession.

The words send fear flooding through her. He has always been hers, all of the Berserkers are. They were contracted through her mother to serve for her. But this...this declaration is different. For the first time, she is truly one of them. They accept her, despite the terrible things that she has done, and they claim her as their own. But Kylian's words strike a different chord in her. Freyja pulls away from his touch, coming to her feet.

"Right, well, thank you for this." She shakes the crumpled-up foil in her hands. "We better get to bed. Lights out was fifteen minutes ago."

"Whatever you say, boss ma'am." He winks at her, stands, and releases the lock on the kitchenette doors.

Freyja gives him a tight nod, pushing past him and rushing toward the girl's dorm before he notices the moisture building in her eyes. He is hers. They all are. They are hers to protect, and part of that means keeping them at a distance. They are already in danger as things stand. She can only imagine how her mother will use them if she really lets them in. Her mother can never suspect how much Freyja cares for these kids that her mother sent to be her soldiers. Freyja can't let that happen. They are hers, and she will do anything to keep them safe.

***

The taste of that burrito lingered on Freyja's tongue as she made her way to the galley. That was one of the better memories she had from her childhood, and she couldn't believe that she had never asked Kylian to program their 3D printer to replicate the meal. Now, with the dream fresh on her mind, she was determined to rectify the mistake.

"Selkie, where's Kylian?" Freyja demanded.

"Aimé is not aboard the ship."

Freyja froze mid-step. "What? Where is he?" They had left the Amaterasu nearly a week ago. They now flew in the shadow of the *Takarabune* on their way to the prison planet of Jubokko. If Kylian wasn't aboard Selkie, where in the Known Galaxies could he be?

"Aimé accompanied Cylien on his excursion to the *Takarabune*." Selkie's disdain for the two men was barely hidden beneath her icy tone. Freyja's ship had never been fond of any of her Berserkers. Freyja now believed that was because she saw them as a threat to her loyalty to the Empress. Selkie had fed information to her mother behind her back for years, but things had changed, and Selkie would have to get over her bias.

"And why is Tristan taking an excursion to the *Takarabune*?"

"Because, I quote, 'a man can only entertain himself on stims and sims for so long.'"

Freyja sighed. That did sound like Tristan. "And Azai just sent a shuttle so Tristan could take shore leave?"

"Azai sent a shuttle to collect Dr. Dar to run further simulations on how to optimize our travel time to Thule."

"Of course he did," Freyja mumbled. The man had become unbearable in his singular focus to reach Thule...to reach Skyla. His actions bordered on obsession, and Freyja had taken to ignoring his missives.

With her enthusiasm drained, Freyja trudged along the corridor, entirely deflated now she knew there would be no dream burrito on the menu. Walking past the lab, she found the doors open, and Dr. Pinot, the sole scientist, at work.

Dr. Pinot was fully absorbed in her work at the station she had claimed as her own since moving aboard Selkie. Seeing the doctor rekindled her anger toward Rohaan at offering the woman a spot on their crew, or maybe it was her hunger and annoyance at Tristan for taking Kylian with him to the *Takarabune*.

Truth be told, she was happy to have Dr. Pinot aboard, even if it hadn't been Rohaan's place to invite her. Having the dual PhD and MD aboard gave her a sense of security. She hadn't had a physician on the crew since the mutiny, and what had been expected to be a simple recon mission had proven far more dangerous than any of them had anticipated.

Freyja leaned against the door and watched as Dr. Pinot let a pale-green goo flow from her fingertips toward the counter. Then, with one swift movement, the scientist slammed the substance onto the surface. A flash of light traveled through the structure, so quick Freyja almost missed it, and she was surprised to find that the goo appeared to have solidified into a rod in the doctor's hand.

"What are you working on, Doc?"

Dr. Pinot jumped at the sound of Freyja's voice, whirling around to face her. The pale rod clung tightly in her hand. Recognition washed over the woman's naturally pale face, and she let out a slow breath as she turned back to her station.

"You startled me, Admiral."

Freyja moved closer for a better look at Dr. Pinot's project. "So what is it?" Freyja raised an eyebrow in question.

Dr. Pinot set the rod on the counter, and Freyja was still surprised to see that it held its shape. Dr. Pinot slid the object over in front of Freyja, who hesitated only a moment before picking it up. It was cool to the touch and felt as hard as aerogelium.

Before Freyja had finished her inspection, Dr. Pinot slid a container in front of her. This one contained the goo that Freyja had seen the doctor handling before it solidified into the solid object she held now. With careful fingers, Freyja pinched a piece from the container. She rolled it around her palm and marveled at how the soft putty could transform into the solid rod she still held in her other hand.

"It's impressive, isn't it?" Dr. Pinot observed Freyja carefully.

"Are you going to make me ask again?" Freyja's words were clipped. She wasn't one to play games.

A shy smile spread across Dr. Pinot's face. "Here, let me show you."

She swiftly grabbed Freyja's hand, gently spreading the goo along her pointer finger until it ran near the entire length. Then she raised her hand and slammed it into Freyja's finger. Freyja moved to withdraw her hand on instinct, but Dr. Pinot tightly clutched her wrist. Freyja was surprised when she didn't feel the impact. She looked down to find that the goo had extended to encapsulate her finger. Dr. Pinot gave it one more hit before holding Freyja's wrist up to inspect her handy work.

"There!" Dr. Pinot said proudly, showing Freyja her finger trapped inside the-now solid substance.

Freyja tapped the finger against the counter. The goo clicked against the steel, entirely solid. She couldn't feel a thing.

"It's a field application I've been working on. A kinetic cast that can be applied to breaks on site."

Freyja tapped the cast against the counter again. "How do I get it off?"

Dr. Pinot reached into a drawer, pulling out an aerosol can. With a quick spray of the solvent, the cast dissolved into a puddle.

"The substance absorbs kinetic energy into its crystalline structure. Impact only makes it stronger, making it the perfect field splint. The only way to remove it is with the solvent." Dr. Pinot shook the can once before placing it back in the drawer.

Freyja canted her head. "A useful application—and my remodeling tech?"

Dr. Pinot straightened, her casual demeanor dissolving away. "Integration is at one hundred percent. The connection between Cista and Selkie is stable and can be maintained indefinitely."

Freyja nodded. That was good. More than ever, she wanted to keep a close eye on Rohaan. "And how is working with Dr. Dar?"

Dr. Pinot shrugged. "Dr. Dar spends most of his time working with Dr. Aman on recreating the quantum entanglement energy transfer project that she lost at Medina. I believe Rohaan and Zarah are on the *Takarabune* to run some preliminary tests right now. But he has been quite open with sharing any analysis Cista has run on the med tech. There are some very promising pieces. What you and your team have found is going to change millions of people's lives."

Freyja's mood soured at the mention of the med tech that had cost Basilie's life. The prospect of saving lives in the future paled at the thought of those who were dying now because of this war. The conflict between the Stjarna and Hoshiko was coming to a head, and Freyja was certain the two tribes would be at all-out war within the year.

The Hoshiko Tribe would never have been able to challenge the Stjarna Tribe before the fall of the UTA, but the Empress had carved out a good portion of the Stjarna fleet, putting the two tribes on an even footing for the first time in centuries.

There had been extensive losses when the Empress separated from the tribe. Officers Freyja had come up with, family and friends, all gone, and for what? Her mother to consolidate power?

That nagging in her gut returned, the one that told her the journey would lead her back home. If her mother was responsible, then what? Freyja shook her head. She would focus on the mission at hand. Find the source of the signal, find out the truth behind the attacks, find who was responsible for destabilizing the UTA, and then, just maybe, she could prevent humanity from falling into a dark age.

CHAPTER 18 | HINATA

KRAKEN

"Run the analysis again," Hinata demanded, wheeling around to slam his palms on the conference room table. Tax, Callan, and Rohaan sat at the table across from where he had been pacing.

"No. I've run the simulation a hundred times. No variables have changed. I will give you the same answer as I have the past one hundred times." Tax crossed his arms over his chest and locked eyes with the commander.

Hinata broke eye contact first, growling as he pushed off the table to resume pacing.

"This will work; you just have to be patient," Tax's tone softened.

They were a week into their assigned mission to Jubokko. The assignment was humiliating, meant to remind him of his place, but his mother had given him exactly what he craved, his best chance at finding Skyla. The only problem was that it would take a month to get there, and his anxiety was eating him alive. What if she was hurt, dying, dead? He had tasked Rohaan and Tax with finding a faster route, certain that one must exist, but so far, the answer was always the same.

Hinata shifted his focus to the scientist. "Rohaan, what about the experimental reactor you have been working on?"

Rohaan's gaze sharpened as he caught the commander's eye, dismissing whatever he had been reading in his ocular display; he shook his head softly. "Much was destroyed at Medina. Dr. Aman and I are working to put the pieces back together, but we're not there yet. And then there is the matter of replicating the super-powered, bio-quantum computer that we found at the Dyson sphere. The further we intend to jump, the more compute power we are going to need...I need more time."

Time, it always came back to time, which left Hinata helpless, light years away from being able to do anything for her. "There has to be somethin g..."

Guilt flashed over Rohaan's face, and Hinata took a small solace in the fact that the man was almost as miserable as he was.

"She's going to be okay." Tax stood and in two short strides was at Hinata's side. "This is going to work. You can't lose it now. This is the time for you to be the man I know, the commander I trust with my life."

Hinata nodded slowly. "You're right. We'll refuel at Jubokko and make the jump. Make sure everything is ready." The concession stuck in his throat, a bitter pill he was forced to swallow. What else could he do?

Callan studied Hinata carefully before he spoke. "I'm not certain we should make the jump at all, Commander."

A storm gathered in Hinata's eyes as he glared at his lieutenant commander.

"Callan—" Tax began.

"No, enough of this." Callan sprang to his feet. "We stand together. We stand for the tribe, but we have let this madness go on long enough."

"And what madness is that?" Hinata's voice dropped low and dangerous.

Callan exhaled a long breath before he spoke again. "I have watched you tear yourself apart these past months. I thought you needed time, and I was happy to have your back while you took that time, but enough is enough. You will commit treason over a woman that doesn't want you? Get your head straight, Hinata; it's time to let her go. We are needed here."

Hinata's glare threatened to cut Callan down where he stood. "You think I would risk my crew? My ship? My tribe over a woman? We will go through with the jump because this is how we will get to the bottom of everything. This is how we will save our tribe."

Even as he said the words, Hinata knew it wasn't the full truth. He felt it at his very core; he had been pushed too far, and he would be a supernova destroying everything in his path if that was what it took to get to her.

The two men stood eye to eye in a battle of wills until finally, Callan dropped his eyes to the conference table before him with a slow shake of his head. "Of course, Commander. Forgive me."

"We will end this war; I promise you. Dismissed." Hinata needed Callan out of his sight. The words of his third-in-command sat heavy on his chest, stirring up thoughts he had trained for hours to push from his mind because, if he was honest, they rang true. She didn't want him. She hadn't chosen him, and yet he would still cross a galaxy to save her. What did that say about him?

***

Hinata spent the following weeks in the familiar rhythm of once again training himself into oblivion, despite Tax's frequent protests. Callan refused to train with him. He may have been unable to sway Hinata's course, but he refused to participate in the commander's masochism any longer.

Hinata was in the gym again, his muscles already swollen from the hours of training, sweat running rivers over the living ink koi that darted around his chiseled back. Training was all he had right now. There were no battles to occupy his mind on this trip, no scenarios to run or training missions to oversee. There was no distraction from his failures: he had failed his brother—making that challenge as a kid, the stupid race that had gotten Akio killed—and he had lost at the admiral exams to Freyja...Even knowing what he did now—that he never stood a chance, that Freyja's position in the UTA had been bought and paid for—it still stung all the same.

He had failed to defend the ring, to save those cadets. Now he had let the one woman who had gotten under his armor, who had ever truly seen him—the one woman who occupied his mind, waking or dreaming—slip through his fingers. He had left her alone at the edge of space because he had been too afraid to dig deeper into why she hadn't answered a single transmission.

He had been afraid to see the truth, afraid of what he would learn if he looked into the transmission history. Afraid that he would know without a doubt that she had left him behind. That it had all been in his mind. Still it ate at him. She had left him. Even if he found her, there was no guarantee that she would stay, that she would choose him.

He feared she loved those solo adventures more than anything. He had seen the way her face lit up on an expedition, the way she came to life in the face of adventure. He had never seen her look that way at Medina or the capital. If he did find her, how could he ask her to stay? Could he light her up the way her adventures did?

The realization threatened to drown him. He had been nothing more than a distraction for her, someone she had gotten carried away with while battling through an impossible situation. The weight of it all pressed in on him until he struggled to breathe. She didn't need him the way he needed her, the way he craved her, the way he couldn't get her out of his damn mind.

The harsh truth of it stared him in the face, but it changed little. He would save her. He would come for her, even knowing she wouldn't choose him. Though she had already broken him into a thousand pieces, he would come for her. Knowing she would leave and break him beyond repair when she did, he would always come for her, and he hated himself for it.

Pain blossomed across his knuckles as he worked the heavy bag, his hands already bruised and arms aching, the physical pain failing to cover the pain of his broken heart.

***

When Hinata strode onto the bridge, he looked as he always did: his uniform crisp, the sides of his hair shaved into a fresh fade with the top braided tight against his scalp, every detail carefully crafted. Only Tax and Callan had any idea how much he had come undone, and Hinata would be sure it stayed that way.

"We are nearing Jubokko, sir. But we've picked up several vessels between us and the planet," his comms officer reported.

"Patrols?" Hinata asked.

"The ship schematics don't match any of our patrol class vehicles, and they are blocking their signatures."

There were only two reasons to block a signature. It was an ambush, or they were pirates. The question was which?

"How many ships?" Hinata asked.

"Five, sir, all the size of a corvette, or smaller."

"Can we get a transmission through to Jubokko? Request assistance?"

"Our transmissions are being blocked, sir."

"It looks like we are headed for a fight. Relay orders to the rest of our ships: shields up, weapons ready, hold on my order."

There were three corvettes along with Freyja and Rohaan's AI ships in Hinata's fleet. It was all the ships the council would grant him for this embarrassing assignment.

"Commander, we are receiving a transmission from one of the unidentified ships."

"Bring it up on the viewport."

There was a flash of noise, varying shades of black angles, and the grinding sound of metal. Then the view screen was filled with a face Hinata would only greet if it appeared at the end of his sword.

"Gabriel." Hinata growled the name of the warlord, leader of the Fenix Cartel. "This isn't Fenix space. Stand down, and I will let you live."

Gabriel burst into laughter, his living ink phoenix tattoo flapping its flaming wings across his neck. He looked exactly as he had the last time Hinata had seen him on the cartel-run world of Trogon: flawless olive skin and a tight fade giving way to gelled curls.

Hinata gritted his teeth, resisting the urge to run his fingers along the side of his face where Gabriel had burned away his flesh with electrified titanium knuckles back on Medina. The wounds had healed, and he had caught the rest of Gabriel's crew, but the leader had gotten away, and it still got under his skin.

"Good to see you again, Commander. I wasn't expecting you out here at the edges of Hoshiko territory. Doesn't someone of your status have somewhere more important to be?"

"I am exactly where I'm needed. Now, are you going to drop your shields and let my soldiers take you peacefully? Or do I finally have an excuse to kill you?"

"Are those the only options? You really don't know how to strike a deal." Gabriel sat back in his chair, bringing his hand to his chin in mock consideration before dropping his forearms to his knees and responding with a twisted smirk. "I think I will take your ship instead."

Hinata cut the transmission; he was done talking. He shook his head. The Fenix Cartel were outgunned, with only five corvettes to his three, plus a stardestroyer and Freyja's AI ship. He wasn't complaining. He didn't need an excuse to end Gabriel, the man who had once left Skyla to die on a job gone wrong. The man who had tried to kill them all back on Trogon, who ran a world based on weapons and fear. The universe would be a better place without him.

"Cover our ships and take out their shields." Hinata gave the order, calm and collected. Battle was something he understood. There was no fear here.

The *Takarabune* maneuvered into place to cover their fighters. The three Hoshiko corvettes engaged head-to-head with the cartel, and Freyja's ship was holding its own, even with Rohaan's ship melded to its hull.

The *Takarabune* kept pace with the enemy bombardment, trading plasma cannon fire to keep the heat off their smaller ships.

"Bring those shields down," Hinata growled, losing patience for this dance.

"Yes, sir."

Three targeted blasts ripped through space, destroying the shields array of the nearest ship.

"Again." His gunners repeated this process. Once, twice, three times; only one of the enemy ships had shields intact. It was all too easy. Had the cartel really thought five corvettes could bring down a stardestroyer? Even without the small fleet Hinata had running interception, the cartel ships were no match for the *Takarabune*.

"Commander," Rohaan's voice came to Hinata in his aural implant.

"Little busy, Dr. Dar," Hinata responded.

"I had a prototype of the advanced quantum computer we picked up at the Dyson sphere running analysis when—"

"Get to the point."

"I am getting signatures that match the signal coming from one of those vessels."

Hinata froze. That wasn't possible. The signal came from beyond the Zeta quadrant. Although they had chased ghosts of the signal around the capital nearly nine months ago, they hadn't found any further traces of it in the central rim.

"You're sure?" Hinata asked.

"Don't insult me. Of course, I am sure."

Hinata trained his eyes on the viewport as the final ship opened up its cargo bay. Three blasts impacted the ship as its shield array came down. There was the shimmer of purple against the jet-black backdrop of space, then a dark cloud erupted from the cargo bay.

A murder of crows enveloped his first corvette, tearing at its haul. The view screen zoomed in on the chaos. They weren't birds; they were all hard lines, the drones from uncharted space.

"Open comms, those are nanite drones. They need to set off an EMP pulse, now!" He was already too late. The drones had ripped through his corvette like it was made of paper, and they were already moving on to the next ship.

This ship had gotten the warning that had come too late for the first. A wave of purple energy rippled around the ship. The drones burst into dust as they ran into the crackling energy field. A dark wave of disabled nanites washed over the ship before they swirled into space, abandoning the smaller target to focus on the prize, the *Takarabune*.

"Raise our EMP field," Hinata commanded.

The bots swarmed. He hadn't forgotten how quickly they had adapted to his tactics when they'd faced off in uncharted space. He had no illusion that the same trick would work twice.

The drones swirled, pulling together into one ominous mass. From the chaos, long limbs thrashed out of the cloud, the ends sharpening into two-meter-long drills. The tentacles whirled around as the center solidified into a long body, moving to envelop the ship, wrapping around the stardestroyer like a kraken from the deep, threatening to crush the *Takarabune*, as if it were nothing more than a wooden ship on the oceans of Earth That Was.

The bridge shook as the kraken took hold, wrapping its arms around the hull. The EMP field was too weak to penetrate its armor, and Hinata watched, helpless, against the monster as it pushed its drill tips into the hull.

Freyja's face flickered onto the viewport. "Hold tight, Commander. Backup is on the—" Her communication cut to static.

"Commander, we have breaches on Alpha deck, Theta deck, Kappa deck—"

Hinata held up his hand to cut the comms officer off. "Deploy units to all breach sites. Tax, Callan, on me." Hinata was already halfway to the bridge doors.

"Sir?" The comms officer looked at him with questioning eyes.

"We are going to end this."

CHAPTER 19 | SKYLA

The Fallen

The cold pushed through the nanite-infused fabric of her pants as Skyla sat in the snow, her eyes raking over all of the irregular drifts at the dive site. She prayed they weren't all bodies. She didn't know if she could handle it if they were.

Fenrir circled her twice, then plopped on his haunches beside her, satisfied that she had investigated his finding. Tremors ran through her hands as she threw her arms around him. She pressed her face into his soft fur, barely a prickle against her numb skin. What if her dad was under the snow somewhere here?

Hot tears stung her eyes at the thought of it. She didn't want to know, didn't want to dig into the snow and find his face, but what if he was there?

She couldn't leave him buried on a strange planet under the ice. Why had she come here? She had come for answers and may have lost everything that mattered in the process. She couldn't turn away now. These people deserved more than to be left forgotten. Her dad deserved more than that.

She took one deep breath before letting her arms drop from Fenrir. He cocked his head at her as she stood, brushing the snow from her pants and gloves, then secured her ventilator and goggles back over her face.

"Well, it looks like we have our work cut out for us."

Half of her hoped she would find her father's body, and she would know what happened to him. The other half hoped she wouldn't, and that she could dream he had already left this place and was out there chasing his dreams across the stars.

The pale sun blazed across the sky, burning away half of the day as Skyla carefully uncovered each mound. She had only found one more body, and it was another man she didn't recognize. The rest were supply crates, a command station, and finally, the nose of the dive module. The weak light was already fading, and she didn't dare stay out at the site past dark. The temperatures were below freezing during the day.

Once she had carefully wrapped the bodies in tarps, she secured them in the command station where they would be safe until they escaped from this nightmare of a planet.

***

Skyla curled up in one of the plush chairs in the commons room, a bottle of vodka clutched in her hands, still sealed. She stared into the liquid. For the first time since that drunken night she considered opening a bottle. Finding the bodies, confirming her suspicions—she wanted to forget. Forget she was on this frozen wasteland planet, that her father was most likely trapped in an icy tomb, and that no one was coming for her. She wanted to forget, even if it was just for a night.

Sighing, she placed the bottle on the table next to her. She didn't want to drink alone. As much as she wanted to hear his voice again, she didn't want it to be a figment of her imagination. She wanted *him*. Resolve solidified her decision. She would get the dive module working. She would rescue Pele, and she would go searching for him, just like she promised. And when she found him, she would drink to her victory instead of drowning out her failures.

The next morning, Skyla spent the entire flight to the dive site dreaming of getting to Pele. She was so close; all she had to do was get the module working. But first she would continue her search for the bodies. They were her responsibility now.

After excavating three more mounds, she uncovered one more body, this time a woman, and she decided it was time to move on to the module. She wasn't ready for the next body to be her father.

Skyla wondered what had killed them as she chiseled away at the ice. The bodies she had found were completely intact: no blood or injuries. It was as if they had frozen where they stood. A shiver ran through her, and she pushed the thoughts from her mind, needing to focus on the more delicate work of chipping ice away from the propulsion mechanism.

After the better part of the day, Skyla had finally gotten the machine free. Now she needed to focus on melting the ice that had sunk through all of the seals, cementing the dive module shut.

After spending the prior evening adjusting the settings of the plasma torches, she was certain they wouldn't damage the seals. They were tuned to provide just enough warmth to melt the ice. She couldn't take any chances. She couldn't afford to damage the module. It was her only hope of rescuing Pele.

Resolve reinforced her movements. No, she wasn't going to die here alone, just another body under the ice. The first step toward making that plan a reality was to rescue Pele, and the first step toward Pele was to get the dive module working. *Focus.*

Skyla attached the pads of the plasma torch to align with the seals; they moved along the edges, beads of water dripping from the seal before freezing again like wax along the side of a candle. Finally, the pads of the torch met at the bottom of the door. Gently pulling the torches from the hull, Skyla tucked them back in her bag before she reached up to try the release lever. She popped the lever out, twisting and turning it to release the door.

Nothing.

The seals remained intact.

"Damn." Skyla slammed a fist into the door, eliciting a pop as it released. Stale air rushed out from the cabin. Her heartbeat thumped in her ears. She had been dreading what she might find inside. The frozen bodies in the ice had been bad enough. What if some of the researchers had been trapped inside when they expired?

She took a deep breath, steadying herself. There was no going back; there was only forward. She pulled the door the rest of the way open, peering inside, praying the cabin was...empty. She exhaled hard through the ventilator. Thank the stars for small miracles.

Skyla stepped inside. It was just big enough to seat six people. Sliding into the captain's seat, she looked over the controls. She ran her fingers along the panels, praying for a spark of power. Nothing. She stepped out of the pod once again to look it over. Where was its power source? They weren't going anywhere until she could get the damn thing on. Still, she didn't see anything. No port for cables or fuel cell exchange. Nothing.

Skyla's eyes drifted up. The pod was almost two meters high, and she couldn't see the top now that she had dug it out. Could it be solar? She scrambled to the top of a mound of ice for a better vantage. There were no obvious solar panels that she could see, but it was meant to dive to depths that would crush standard tech. Could they be tucked safely inside?

She took a deep breath before stepping back a few paces and then ran and leapt on top of the pod. Her boots slid against the icy surface, but she quickly gained her footing, her arms thrown out wide to keep her from toppling off the side. Carefully, she inched her way along the module.

A fine layer of snow had already settled on the surface, even though she had freed it from its snowy prison only a few hours earlier. She brushed the snow away, looking for any switches or paneling. There. That looked like the release latch she had engaged to open the door.

She tried to pry the latch up with her gloved hands. It was stuck, and she had left the plasma cutter in her bag. Peering over the edge, she glanced at the bag, but she didn't want to come down empty-handed if she could help it. The second she pulled her glove from her hand, the warmth drained from her fingers. She jammed her fingernails into the seal, working to tear away the ice and gain enough leverage to pop the switch. The feeling in her fingertips leached away, and her nail beds ached from the pressure. Just as she was ready to give up and tuck her fingers away before frostbite claimed them, the lever loosened.

Stumbling from the release, she threw her arms out wide against the hull, bracing herself before she slid off the side. She let out a shaky breath. She had gotten it free. Time to see if it was what she thought it was. She stuffed her hand back into the glove.

With numb fingers, she twisted and rotated the lever, pushing it back into place. A series of grinding noises made her cringe. The gears were frozen. She prayed they wouldn't break as the section in front of her sluggishly unfolded, spiraling out like a flower in bloom and exposing a wide solar panel.

"Yes!" She laughed as tears filled her eyes, watching the panel settle into place, drinking up the last of the evening sun rays. Only then did she notice that the sky had turned pink, and the sun threatened to dip behind the ice peaks.

"Damn," she whispered, debating whether she should risk damaging the frozen solar panels by tucking them away from the harsh winds and snowdrifts that would no doubt stick to the panels over night. She only debated for a moment. The weather forecast was still clear. She could clear any accumulated snow in the morning, but she would be in a world of trouble if she broke the solar panels by closing them before they had gained enough energy to warm the module and get it working properly again.

Hopping off the pod, she wore the first genuine smile she'd had in weeks.

"We did it. This is going to work. We are getting Pele and going home, Fenrir."

CHAPTER 20 | HINATA

INTO THE VOID

Hinata stood at the edge of the airlock, the familiar thrum of adrenaline coursing through his veins. The quiet of space just before a battle centered him. The shell of his fully armored space suit was the only barrier between him and the vacuum. Tax, Callan, and ten of his most skilled soldiers stood at his back. These were his demons of the void, the crew he took with him to break starships.

The crew within the *Takarabune* was tasked with taking out the drills and minimizing damage to the hull, while Hinata's spacewalk crew would end this threat at the source.

Hinata's ship shifted under his Z-grav boots as pitch-black tentacles whipped past his vision, slamming into the hull. They were running out of time; they needed to end this now, before that thing destroyed his ship, his only hope of rescuing the captain.

Hinata turned to address his team. "That thing will adapt to our tactics, move quickly. If you see an opening, take it; you may not get another. I've battled a drone like this before. That exoskeleton is hard to penetrate. It has shielding against our EMP fields. Get to the base of a tentacle, drive your swords deep, then detonate. That is our best shot at scraping this thing off our ship."

"Yes, sir," his soldiers echoed through the comms.

"Stay sharp. Everyone comes home," he finished before turning to the airlock. Boots thumped against the floor and fists against chests, reaching a frenetic pace before Hinata led his squad into battle.

With their Z-grav boots activated, they ran across the hull of the *Takarabune*, ducking under rolling tentacles that whipped through the black, working to crack the *Takarabune* open. Hinata would not let them take this ship. Normally it would be a point of pride, but this ship was more than that now. It was the key to rescuing *her*. He would not lose this ship to the murder bot beast.

A tentacle drew back from its breach, whipping out toward Hinata. He cut the gravitational force from his boots, simultaneously activating the magnetic grips in his palms as he threw himself backward. The magnets snapped him horizontally against the hull. Out of the corner of his eye, he saw the same tentacle strike one of his soldiers square in the chest; the impact smashed through the man's space suit, a cloud of red vapor bubbling off into the vacuum as the man's torso ruptured like a melon.

Hinata's pulse thundered in his ears, a deadly rhythm calling him to violence. He deactivated the magnets in his palms. Using his thrusters, he came back to a standing position and re-engaged his boots, then broke into a sprint. No more lives; this thing would take no more lives from under his command.

As if the drone read his intentions, another tentacle ripped free from the hull. This time it slashed a wide gash in the hull as it pulled free. Bodies flew through space, sucked out into the darkness.

Hinata gritted his teeth, turning the fury that boiled his blood into fuel to take his revenge. As he drew near the source of chaos, the massive body of the drone blocked out the shimmering stars beyond, shadowing Hinata in the umbra of the beast. He drew his katana, but left the EMP field down. If he activated the EMP now, it would divert power to its shielding, preventing his blade from hitting its mark. He would never be able to chip away at the drone that way. No, he had to get to the core before activating the pulse. A cascade failure was the only way he was taking this thing down. He only hoped it would work on something this size.

Hinata sprinted straight for the center of the towering drone. Once he reached his mark, he moved decisively, activating his thrusters to send him straight into the belly of the beast. Ready to initiate the EMP, he held his katana over head.

A sharp pain spread through his shoulder and down his spine as he slammed into the paneled exterior of the drone, but his grip held strong as he plunged his katana into the mass. He hadn't expected that. The last time he fought the nanite drones, they had shifted under the blow of his naked blade, letting it pass through as if the drone were made of mist, but not this time. It was constantly changing the rules, *adapting*. He pushed the thought from his head; it didn't matter; he was positioned at the center of its mass, his sword driven down to the hilt. *NOW*.

Hinata activated the EMP, sending an impulse to travel through the nanite structure. Reversing his thrusters, he flew back to the hull of the

Takarabune in a swirling cloud of dark nanite dust. He was the master in the storm—a tentacle came whipping out of the darkness.

It was mere centimeters from him when he spun to the side; the blow grazed his shoulder and sent him spinning to crash against the hull in an uncontrolled tumble until he finally activated his magnetic grips. All of the joints in his arms groaned against the sudden shift in momentum as his body snapped against the hull.

Hinata grunted, the impact forcing the air from his lungs. A dark shadow slid overhead; another tentacle whipped across his path. Had he not been laid out on the hull, had he moved a second slower, he would have been pulverized.

Hinata's mind reeled as it tried to catch up. He had seen the nanites raining down on him; he had delivered the EMP at the center of its mass, and it hadn't been enough. Bringing up his ocular display, he found he had five units left, himself included. He needed a plan.

A light blinked out on his display, four units. There was no time to think. He needed to move. Their window was closing. If they couldn't neutralize the drone in the next three minutes, they were all spaced, and there would be no one left to help *her*. He wasn't going to let that happen.

"On me," Hinata bellowed through the comms as he regained his footing. He did a quick scan of the battlefield, clocking each tentacle, locking their positions into his ocular display before he sprinted back under the body of the kraken. Tax, Callan, and Kaito joined him to form a ring under the monstrous drone.

"What's the plan, Commander?" Tax asked, bringing his arms up to join with Hinata and Callan.

Hinata slung an arm around Tax and Kaito, completing the chain. "We all move to strike simultaneously at these points. Our individual EMPs aren't strong enough to trigger the reaction. The only play we have left is to strike together and hope it's enough power to take this thing down."

"On your mark, Commander." Callan nodded.

The drone groaned overhead as it began to undulate, vibrations coursing out from its core toward the tentacles wrapped around the ship. Then Hinata saw it. The drone was rearing back, preparing to crush them under its weight.

"Into position, now!" he yelled, falling back to prepare for the impact. They would only have one shot at this. If he was wrong, they would be crushed and the ship would fall...and *she* would be lost. He would not fail.

"Lock in!" he commanded as he dropped to a knee and crouched low to brace his katana against the hull. "The second it hits your hilt, activate the EMP. We have one shot."

Hinata trusted his soldiers with his life. They had trained for this, trained to be an extension of his will. He had no doubt in their execution. His only doubt was if it was the right play. The shadow was all-consuming as the kraken drove its massive body toward the hull of the *Takarabune*. The movement slowed until each second stretched into eternity, the blade of his katana sinking into the drone's black-plated armor, the milliseconds ticking by as it inched forward until his sword was sheathed in the armor plating. This was it. It would work, or he wouldn't live to know his failure.

Now.

Purple electricity surged from his blade, rolling across the surface of the drone, spreading like cracks in ice. Ripples of power joined the first as the rest of the blasts converged, amplifying into a violent force. Everything went black as nanite dust filled the void around Hinata. His breath caught as he waited to feel the weight of the machine crush him into oblivion, but it never came.

Hinata swiped his hand across his vision, trying to clear the dust. When his vision remained obscured, he pulled up his ocular display, overlaying thermal and LiDAR readings. The space where the drone had been was clear. There was no structure lurking in the dark.

"Yes!" Callan shouted over the comms. Tax and Kaito's cheers joined in on the channel. It had worked. A reluctant smile stretched across Hinata's lips. He would let his men have this moment.

"Well done. Let's get back inside and on to Jubokko." The drone had nearly torn the *Takarabune* apart, and she was in desperate need of repairs, though he didn't say the last part. The nanite dust began to clear, and Hinata's eyes swept over the carnage on the walk back to the airlock. Massive gouges marred the hull in too many places to count, yet relief washed over him as he took in the damage. It appeared to be mostly superficial. She would still be able to make the jump. He would still be able to get to Thule, to *her*.

CHAPTER 21 | SKYLA

THE FREEZE

Skyla ruffled the fur between Fenrir's ears with her gloved hand as he hopped down from the trailer behind the land skimmer. She felt more hopeful than she had in a long time. They would fix the dive module, find Pele, and begin repairs. They were going home. She could feel it.

First thing, she clambered back on top of the pod and carefully cleared the snow that had built up around the solar panels. They would need time to charge before she could run any diagnostics on the module. Her boots sank into the snow as she hopped down.

Then she searched for work to do on the pod, but there was little she could do without power.

Exhaling a heavy breath into her ventilator, she turned to survey the remaining mounds. Her hands tingled, and she grew queasy at the thought of finding her father's body. But she also hated the idea of leaving him behind on the frozen rock. Every day she excavated without finding him, a little hope grew in her heart. Perhaps he had left for a supply run, or found a lead on another planet, or launched an expedition to another site while they waited for the dive equipment to arrive...

Tilting her head back, she took in the vast expanse of sky. It was steel gray and dimensionless, the ominous color that tinged the heavens before a storm. Whether her father was here or not, she was too late to make a difference for these lost souls, but she could still make a difference out there. If she could get to Pele and back out into the expanse, she could make a difference for her friends, for her tribe, for humanity. The thought made her uneasy. She had run from her responsibilities for so long, too long. She was done running. After finishing the excavations, she was getting the hell off this rock.

The panels would need a few hours to charge the module, which was enough time for her to finish her work around the site. She carefully dug out two more bodies, wrapping and securing them. Then there was only one mound left.

Anxiety crept through her. This was it; that mound would be her father, or it would let her continue to dream that he was still out there somewhere.

She worked carefully, her hands trembling as she brushed the snow away from a hooded face. She froze, ice running through her veins. The only visible features were closed eyes, thick dark brows, and frozen lashes; a ventilator obscured the rest of his face, but that was all she needed to see to recognize the man that had raised her.

Tears built in her eyes until she couldn't hold them back any longer. She had released the dam, and now they wouldn't stop. They pooled in the bottom of her goggles until finally, she tore them from her face and let the tears spill freely over her cheeks, freezing trails of ice down around the edges of her ventilator. It was him, the whole reason she had come to this planet. It was him, and he was already gone.

Skyla fell back into the snow, sobbing into her gloved hands, her body shaking. Fenrir moved to brush his head along her side, and she threw her arms around him as he snuggled into her, a rumbling purr passing from his body to hers. She ripped the ventilator away from her face, craving the comfort of his fur on her skin as she poured her sorrow into him. She wasn't sure how long they sat like that, but Fenrir never left her side.

Eventually, she pulled herself together. Tears wouldn't bring her father back, and she had work to do. She could still save Pele. That was all she had now, and she would pour all of her energy into saving her bonded ship. Securing her father's body with the rest brought a feeling of finality. At least he would not be forgotten on this planet. At least she could return him to the stars where he belonged. *From the stars we come, to the stars we return.*

Skyla ached to leave this planet more than ever, this place that took her father from her. Her skin crawled. She couldn't stand to be here a second longer. She would give anything to hear Pele's voice in her ear, telling her that all would be well, that they would get back to their adventures, and everything would be all right.

Skyla's stomach twisted at the thought. Is that what she really wanted? To escape into the cosmos with Pele, and go back to the way things had always been? As much as she had tried to deny her feelings, it was *his* face she saw when she closed her eyes at night.

More determined than ever, Skyla walked back over to the pod and climbed up to check on the solar panels. Sitting on top of the pod, she watched as the pale rays of the sun hit the panels. There still wasn't enough of a charge to bring the module online.

Skyla turned her attention to watching Fenrir from her perch. He was stalking a jackalopper—a furry little creature that lived on the tundra. With a thick fluffy body, chubby cheeks, stubby antlers, and wings, mottled white and gray, it blended in seamlessly with the rock and snow. The little creature moved along in a comical combination of waddling, gliding on stubby wings, and belly sliding in the snow, then the sequence would repeat.

Fenrir stalked forward, scrunching down in the snow, waiting for the perfect moment to pounce. The jackalopper leapt into the air for the glide portion of its progression. The crackling of ice rang through the air, and its movements became stiff. It didn't shift into position for its belly slide. Instead, it slammed into the ice with a crack.

Green lights danced through the air, passing over the body of the jackalopper and moving toward Fenrir, the crackle of contracting matter pulsating through the air as lights danced over the snow.

"Fenrir!" Skyla shouted, jumping down from the dive module. Fenrir turned, his eyes flashed to her, and then he was moving, sprinting toward the pod. She leaped into the module, preparing the door to close. Fenrir was just a second behind her.

She pushed hard against the door, pulling it into place, then twisted the interior lever, locking the door. The metal of the pod flexed and contracted as the strange storm passed over them. A sickening groan rang through the confined space, but nothing more happened.

Skyla exhaled in relief. What was that? Even as her racing pulse began to slow, unease settled over her. The weather scans had been clear; there had been no warning...the researchers hadn't seen it coming either. That's why they had been frozen in time here—their bodies preserved in place, no wounds, no time to react. They had been caught in an anomaly just like this one. She hated this place. She would have to do some research when she got back to the camp. There had to be some way to keep herself and Fenrir safe while they worked at the dive site. One thing was certain, she needed off this death trap of a planet.

Skyla waited several hours in the pod, not certain how she would know if the danger had passed, if it was safe to travel back to camp. To entertain herself, she repeated her father's stories to Fenrir while he napped at her side.

"We can't wait any longer, or we'll be stuck out here in the dark," Skyla groaned as she got up from the floor, her legs stiff from sitting in one position for too long. "I just hope the storm has moved past camp."

Skyla twisted the lever to open the door. It snapped into place, but nothing happened. Skyla groaned. The seals had frozen. She heaved her shoulder into the door. Once, twice, three times, nothing happened. There was no crackle of breaking ice, no shift to let the dying sunlight in.

Panic set in as her wide eyes roamed over the interior of the module. She had left her pack out in the snow; she didn't have plasma cutters to melt the seal.

Again, she shoved hard against the door, but it didn't budge. She rammed into the metal until her shoulders ached, but nothing changed. Her thoughts raced as she gave in to her mounting panic. She fought hard to think straight. There had to be a way out. Clawing at the dash, she searched for something, anything, she could use to break the seals...but there was nothing.

Skyla slid into the control chair, praying the solar panels had charged the module enough to get the pod running. Maybe there would be enough power to heat the module and loosen the seals.

The control panel came to life. Skyla sighed in relief as holo lights lit up the dash, illuminating a model of the pod. Her relief was short-lived as the holo turned red, a low battery warning taking up the image before it disintegrated into little pixels, like sand sliding through her fingers. Then the light died.

"No, no, no!" She slammed a palm into the controls.

For several hours, Skyla pried panels open, pulling out bits of tech to try to manage something, anything. Nothing worked. They were trapped, and this time she couldn't see a way out. As the adrenaline faded and exhaustion took over, Skyla fell to the floor in a fit of tears that turned to manic laughter.

"All of this, all of this work. We were so close to going home. It was all for nothing. Guess we are going to die here after all." She banged the back of her head against the floor once before turning to Fenrir, his golden eyes locked on hers. "I'm sorry, buddy. I know I said I'd get us home." She sighed and looked up at the ceiling. "I didn't think we'd go out like this."

CHAPTER 22 | FREYJA

BOARDING PARTY

"We've fought that thing before and won. Get me on that ship. It's the only ship that can make the jump to Thule. We can't lose it." Perched at the front of her captain's chair, Freyja clutched the armrests so tight her knuckles went white.

Tension flowed through Selkie's circuitry, her lights flickering as she hesitated.

"I need you to trust me, Selkie," Freyja said.

Her ship lurched forward, dodging through the tentacles that ensnared the *Takarabune,* making their way to the launch bay doors.

The shields were down, and Freyja was grateful for the easy entrance, but it was a bad sign. The stardestroyer didn't have the power to shield the docks.

"Suit up, let's go," Freyja shouted as she exited the bridge.

Minutes later, Freyja, Kylian, Tristan, and her four remaining Berserkers stood in full armored space suits, ready to disembark. Freyja's eyes caught on the six soldiers she had left. A shudder ran through her body. This was all she had left of the men and women she had spent nearly two decades with. She stuffed her feelings down. Now was not the time. They had fought this thing before; it was a link to the signal, the chaos, the driving force ripping humanity apart. She would destroy this machine and track down whoever was responsible. She would make them pay for all of the lives lost, all of those lives that weighed heavy on her soul. They would pay, starting right now, and if her prey turned out to be her mother...so be it.

With seals checked and Z-grav boots activated, they disembarked Selkie into the dying ship. They passed through evacuated docks and empty corridor after empty corridor, all shrouded in midnight, forcing them to rely on the enhancements in the HUDs of their armored space suits to guide their movements. The lines of the corridors were carved in black and accented with varying shades of gray. The fact that all power had been diverted from non-essential systems didn't bode well for the *Takarabune*. Freyja didn't dare fire up the torch lights on her suit. In this case, the darkness was their friend.

They rounded a bend in the corridor and came face-to-face with a long gash running along the side of the ship, the stars of the void on full display. A chill crept through Freyja; anyone who had been here when the breach happened would have been lost to the stars, leaving nothing behind but an empty corridor. They moved cautiously forward, eyeing the darkness beyond for the bots in case they returned.

The hallway before them was blocked by sealed doors, which Kylian made quick work of overriding. A shimmering purple shield sprang to life just as the doors snapped open. The force field kept the atmosphere of the intact section of the ship from escaping. As soon as they were through, Kylian resealed the doors behind them. They would do everything they could to keep the ship in one piece.

As they passed through the next corridor, Freyja noted little piles of dark sand. The bots had been here, and Hinata's soldiers had successfully destroyed at least some of them, but where was everyone now?

Kylian hacked the next set of doors. The quiet after the chaos unnerved her more than if they had come across angry hordes. She had time to take a single step before a blade was at her throat. She had been so focused on the drones she hadn't thought to expect human combatants on the ship.

"Drop it," a man nearly the size of a mech growled as he pressed the tip of his blade into the junction between Freyja's jaw and neck. With long, dark, braided hair, pale skin, and a thick beard, she was certain the man was Stjarna Tribe, though she didn't recognize him.

Freyja released the hilt of her broadsword, letting it gently glide away in the null-G.

The man's eyes flicked to her Berserkers, just behind her. Out of the corner of her eye, she saw Kylian and Tristan raise one hand in surrender as they lowered their own swords, then gently pushed them away. The rest of her crew's weapons floated by shortly after. *Damn.* Now they were all unarmed.

"Against the wall." The mountain of a man gestured toward the far wall where a contingent of Hoshiko soldiers stood with their foreheads against the bulkhead, their hands bound behind their backs. Three more men in flimsy flight suits, like the one her capturer was wearing, stood guard with broadswords drawn.

There were only four of them against Freyja's crew of seven. She liked those odds. Who knew how many more of these men roamed the ship. If she wanted to take advantage of their superior numbers, she would have to move fast.

Chancing a glance to either side of her, she could tell that Kylian and Tristan had done the same mental math. They were ready to move on her mark.

Freyja and her Berserkers lined up as instructed, but they had all left a sizable gap between themselves and the wall.

"I said against the wall," the man snarled, prompting Freyja forward with the tip of his sword.

"You know the funny thing about ships' systems when they are busy fighting off a breach?"

"Shut up and do as you're told."

Freyja ignored his outburst, instead tapping into her own boiling rage. "They don't deem gravity necessary." She exploded forward, switching her Z-grav boots off as she pushed from the ground with all of her power. She tucked into a somersault as her body vaulted vertically. As soon as she completed her rotation, she pushed off the wall with her boots, sending her flying straight into the man behind her. His sword was drawn, but she caught him by surprise. Barreling straight into his wide chest, she knocked him across the room. His sword flew from his hand in the commotion.

Freyja shifted her position to wrap her legs around his torso. Using their connection as leverage, she bashed her helmet into his unshielded face. Once, there was the crunch of cartilage. Twice, blood smeared across her helmet, pulling off into the air in round droplets. Three times, she heard the snap of bones breaking. She unwrapped her legs and shoved hard against his chest. His body floated away from her, suspended in a haze of blood. Freyja took stock of the rest of their captors. One hung in zero-G, his arms and legs floating limp like a rag doll. Two more stood knocked out, rooted in place by their Z-grav boots.

Freyja had to hand it to Hinata. His soldiers were well-trained. Within moments, they had cut their ties and moved in to defend her Berserkers.

"What do we know?" Freyja retracted her helmet into the collar of her suit as she turned to face the ranking Hoshiko officer.

He shook his head, the pink tinge of embarrassment spreading across his cheeks. "They were prisoners." He nodded toward the disabled men. "They must have escaped from the brig during the attack."

Freyja nodded. She had figured as much; they would need to watch out for prisoners and bots now. "How many?"

"There was a full Stjarna star flight in the brig."

That complicated things. They needed to take control of the bridge before the prisoners did, or before the bots completely disabled the ship.

"We need to defend the bridge." She looked over at the soldier. "You, what's your name?" she asked the officer.

"Yoshida, Admiral." He recognized her.

"Yoshida, get us to the bridge. Kylian here will take care of any technical issues. We will not lose control of this ship," she said.

Yoshida pounded a fist over his heart in salute before turning from her and motioning for his soldiers to fall in. They settled into practiced formations as Yoshida led them out of the small rec room into the next corridor.

With Yoshida leading the way, they made it to the bridge doors within minutes; they had been close.

Pausing at the mechlock doors, Kylian pulled up his datapad; his eyes went hazy as his focus shifted to his ocular display.

"I'm going to need a minute." He had moved through the rest of the ship like they hardly had any security at all. The bridge was different. The blast doors were meant to be a last line of defense, to be able to hold out until reinforcements came. This time they were the reinforcements.

Kylian took almost as long to crack the code for the doors as it had taken them to trek through the ship from the hangar bay to the bridge, but finally the doors snapped open, and they secured the bridge in mere moments. Hinata wasn't there, and neither were Tax, Callan, or any other high-ranking officers. Those who had been left on the bridge threw their hands in the air the moment the doors opened.

"Where is he?" she growled, frustrated that Commander Azai was not at his post as she had expected him to be.

"Everyone with combat experience left to battle the drone," a young woman with lieutenant insignia at her mock collar answered.

"Well, that explains this." Tristan waved dismissively at the young bridge officers, most of whom quivered in their seats.

"I'm taking command of the bridge until Commander Azai returns."

How easily Freyja slipped back into her role as a UTA officer. She didn't miss it, though. She thought she would. She thought it was power that called to her, but that wasn't it at all. It was the control she craved, and now, having left the employ of her mother, the Empress, having left the UTA behind to seek answers, to seek revenge, she finally felt like she had control of her own life, her own destiny. Even if every step along the way was steeped in chaos.

The thought twisted a smile across her lips as she stepped to the center of the bridge, looking over the damage reports hanging in the holo display.

The young nav officer looked Freyja over, the UTA-issued battle armor enough to dissuade her from making any argument. She nodded, then turned back to the display.

"What was your name?" Freyja asked.

"Reina, ma'am."

"Reina, damage report."

The nav officer scrolled through the reports, highlighting the worst of the damage on the holo. Freyja dispatched repair crews to the most critical areas. The *Takarabune* was in rough shape, but she would make it. They had managed to seal all of the breached sections. Still, the casualties had been high, and the *Takarabune* barely had enough structural integrity to make a jump. They would be laid up at Jubokko, making repairs for weeks.

Freyja shook her head. Hinata wouldn't like that. He had already been damn near unbearable with the current timeline—

"Well, what do we have here?" The voice broke through Freyja's thoughts.

CHAPTER 23 | HINATA

BLITZ

The edges of his lips tugged up, surprising even him at seeing Freyja on his bridge. Hinata smoothed the emotion from his face before retracting his helmet and was surprised to find his own relief mirrored in Freyja's eyes. Walking forward with his purposeful stride, he grasped Freyja's forearm, bringing their shoulders to touch.

"Good to see you alive," he said, letting go of the admiral and stepping back to take in the state of his ship.

"Not sure I ever expected those words to come out of your mouth," Freyja said.

Hinata spared a glance for the admiral. "Don't get used to it." But the light tone of his voice betrayed his true feelings. He may not fully trust the woman, but she had come through time and again for him. She was at the very least an ally, and perhaps, given time, he could consider her a friend. Shifting his focus, Hinata took in the damage reports on display. "What the hell did you do to my ship?"

"I wish I could take the credit. This is all that dreadnought drone's doing."

Hinata shook his head. "She is barely spaceworthy. A jump might tear her apart." Tension bound his shoulders in knots at the thought of the delay he didn't have time for. There had to be another solution—

A blast threw him into the command console. Pain blossomed through his chest. Hinata triggered his helmet, rolled to his back, and drew his katana. The motion came as natural as breathing. A dozen men rushed onto his bridge, outfitted in lightly armored space suits painted with wild flaming designs and screeching birds. Hinata rolled to crouch behind the command console, his blade held ready to strike.

Scanning the room, he found Freyja and her boarding party had taken up similar defensive positions. His young officers, however, were in varying degrees of surrender, some with hands held high while others cowered under their stations, eyes pressed closed as tears slid down their cheeks. That one was Reina, one of the few cadets who had survived the assault at the ring. All of the surviving soldiers now served under Hinata's command on the *Takarabune*. He needed to keep them close, where he could watch over them. Being attacked by murderous drones and boarded by pirates hadn't been a scenario that Hinata had found even remotely possible before now.

Hinata cursed himself. He had foolishly thought they had disabled all of the cartel ships before the drone engaged with his fleet. The *Takarabune* was so damaged it hadn't detected the boarding party. Anger coursed through him; he would make the Fenix regret ever having set foot on his vessel.

He locked eyes with Freyja. Her hands flashed quickly at her thigh, using the battle language they had all learned at the academy. Her crew would sweep right on his order.

He nodded ever so slightly, then turned his attention to what was left of his combat crew: Tax, Callan, and Kaito. A quick flash of his hands and Tax confirmed that they would sweep left while Hinata cut straight down the center. Hinata clenched his free hand into a tight fist, then when he released his grip, all chaos broke loose.

Wild battle calls echoed through the bridge as Freyja and her Berserkers surged forward, mowing down anyone who stood in their way. Hinata's men moved with swift efficiency, silent as shadows. Springing forward, Hinata drove his blade straight through the gut of the first gangster, then kicked the man off the end of his sword before moving on to the next obstacle in his way.

Like a spirit possessed, Hinata swept through the men, slamming an armored forearm into the next man's wrist. The light armor cracked under the force, and the man's sword went flying from his grip. Hinata swept through the man from hip to shoulder, and he was on to the next. This one stood a full head taller than the rest. He clapped his hands together in mock merriment, and though Hinata couldn't see his face, he knew the man was smirking, because he knew with certainty who hid behind the mask: Gabriel. He wanted nothing more than to end that man's life.

Allowing his anger to crack through his carefully crafted veneer, Hinata charged forward to clash blades with Gabriel. The man was better with a blade than Hinata would have guessed, but not good enough. The effort it took for Gabriel to keep up with the onslaught of Hinata's blows showed in every labored move.

Pain shot through Hinata's sword arm as another thug slammed into him with a thick nanite rod. Hinata lost his grip on his katana as the man muscled him into an arm bar with the rod.

Gabriel stalked toward him with his sword ready, but all it took was a swift kick from Hinata to send Gabriel's blade spinning through the null-G. Hinata threw his weight back, winding up, then slammed both of his feet into the shins of the man restraining him.

The grip on the rod that restrained him slackened with a resounding crack. Hinata was grateful they only wore light armor. If they had been in full armored suits, that blow would have done little.

Freed from the gangster's hold, Hinata rushed forward, dipping his shoulder low, and rammed straight into Gabriel. They barreled backward until Hinata had him pinned against a console. Hinata locked Gabriel's arms to his sides and slammed the ridge of his helmet repeatedly into his faceplate until he felt the glass crack and give way. Then Hinata slammed his head forward once more, fully shattering the helm.

Hinata paused, taking in the man behind the mask as he sucked in deep breaths, working to bring his raging heart rate under control.

Thousands of thin cuts marred Gabriel's once flawless face. Bits of blood bubbled off his skin as he laughed uncontrollably.

"Glad you haven't forgotten me, Commander," Gabriel said between his fits of laughter. "You really did a number on my drone. I wish you hadn't. I was hoping to see what it could do, but those bots are more wild than she had let on." The laughter stopped as Gabriel dropped his voice. "I'll make sure you pay for that."

"You and what Navy?" Hinata asked.

A deep baritone Hinata didn't recognize rang through the bridge. "I don't give a damn what the two of you do to each other, but we are commandeering this vessel."

Hinata's attention snapped to the newcomer. A massive man with pale skin and long white-blond hair half tied up in a bun held Reina by the throat, her feet kicking uselessly. Hinata shoved Gabriel away and slowly raised his hands as he took in the giant. It was one of the prisoners he'd taken from the skirmish with the Stjarna Tribe, and he wasn't alone. His men from the skirmish held blades at the ready.

"You can take the ship, just set her down. You'll need her to pilot back to the Alpha quadrant."

"I don't make deals with men who hide behind masks." The large man tightened his grip around Reina's neck. Her face began to turn red as her fingers pried helplessly at his grip.

Hinata slowly raised a hand to retract his helm. "No more masks. Now let her go. I don't make deals with men who kill my crew." Hinata's voice was ice.

The man relaxed his grip, and Reina hung suspended in the null-G, her hands flying to protect her neck as she took in ragged gasps. She would live.

"I let your nav officer go. Now have her program the jump back to Stjarna space."

As Reina regained her composure, she engaged her Z-grav boots. The gravity field pulled her back to the deck, and she shuffled over to her station. As she slid into her seat, her eyes locked on Hinata, waiting for his command.

Hinata shook his head. "We don't have enough fuel for a jump to the Alpha quadrant. We will have to refuel at Jubokko—"

"Do you think me a fool?"

Hinata didn't answer.

"You think that I don't know your people will take control of this ship and throw us all in a cell until this war is over if we dock at Jubokko?" He spat the words.

"There is no other choice. We don't have the fuel."

"Pull up the reserves display," the man snapped.

Reina's eyes darted to Hinata. Only when he nodded did she pull up the read-out.

A nasty laugh barreled out of the man. "More than enough to make it to the edge of Stjarna space."

"And then what? Sit adrift and hope someone will come tow you in?"

"There is plenty of traffic at the border these days. I'll take my chances drifting in space over rotting in a Hoshiko prison."

Hinata shook his head. He would have made the same decision, but he couldn't let this play out. He couldn't lose the ship to the Stjarna tribe. He would never make it to Thule; he would never make it to *her*.

A reckless wisp of an idea formed in his mind. It was all he had. It would work. Hinata angled his body slightly away from the man. Reina still had her eyes locked on him, waiting for his command. He dropped his hand just behind his thigh and hoped the man couldn't see what he was signaling.

Once Hinata had signed his orders, he peeled his eyes away from the man to lock onto his nav officer. "Prepare the coordinates for a jump to the Alpha quadrant." He said the words the man wanted to hear, but he hoped that Reina had gotten his message. They would be making a jump. He just hoped she put in the right coordinates.

CHAPTER 24 | HINATA

HOPE

Hinata's body dispersed into the ether with the jump. All at once, he was everywhere, and he was nowhere, and then he slammed back into his body. He fought the force that threatened to crush him to the deck. With the crew reeling from the effects of the jump, he had mere moments to take control.

He turned, slamming his boot into Gabriel, sending the man flying across the bridge where Tax was waiting, katana at the ready. Hinata then lunged forward, stopping the point of his blade at the jugular of the Stjarna man who had dared to attempt to commandeer his ship.

With a swift sweep of his eyes, Hinata took in the rest of his crew. Reina was scrunched up under her command console. Callan, Tax, and Kaito had secured half of the bridge, and Freyja and her men had taken the other. The *Stjarna* prisoners had gambled and lost. The *Takarabune* was once again under Hinata's control.

"Secure our prisoners and escort them back to the brig," Hinata snarled, his eyes locked on the glacial gaze of the man before him. Those ice-blue eyes shifted to the viewport and grew wide with surprise.

"Where have you taken us?" he demanded.

"That is none of your concern. You're lucky I don't jettison you into space with the rest of the refuse. Get him out of my sight."

Order resumed as Hinata's soldiers took control of the prisoners, leaving Hinata to focus on the viewscreen where damage reports outlined in red text scrolled over his view of the icy planet. The repairs would be extensive, but Hinata couldn't focus on that right now.

"Get me a scan and get me on the line with the research station, now," Hinata ordered.

"Sir." The comms officer hesitated under Hinata's harsh stare. "There are no signals on the planet."

"What do you mean, there are no signals?"

"It's completely quiet. No chatter. If there is a research station here, I think it must be abandoned."

The edges of Hinata's vision turned dark as he narrowed his eyes. "Find me a ship signature." Hinata flicked his fingers in the air above his datapad, sending the specs to the techs station.

A glowing holo formed in the air in front of the soldier. "An AI ship, sir?"

"Wait." The Stjarna man that Hinata had unceremoniously dismissed struggled against the two soldiers that restrained him, each a head shorter. They struggled to keep the man in line. "Wait, why are you looking for Pele?"

Hinata held up his palm, gesturing for his soldiers to stand down. "How do you know this ship?"

"I asked first." The man raised his chin as he glared down at Hinata.

"And I am the one in charge here. How. Do. You. Know. This. Ship?"

The Stjarna man's eyes flicked from the holo to the screen, then back to Hinata. He let out a heavy breath, his shoulders sagging with defeat.

"That's my cousin's ship." The man straightened up, taking back some control. "Now tell me why you jumped us to a forsaken rim planet in search of my cousin's ship."

Hinata shook his head. "I don't have time to waste on you. Get him off my bridge."

Freyja stepped up next to Hinata as he turned back to the view port. She triggered the release for her own helm, clasping her arms behind her back and leaning closer. "What's our next move, Commander?"

"Wait," the man yelled, once again straining against the soldiers who tried to muscle him off the bridge.

Freyja turned to the prisoner, quirking a brow. "Gunner?"

"Freyja." The prisoner growled the name. "What is this all about?"

"You know this man?" Hinata asked.

Freyja lifted her chin, indicating the prisoner. "Gunner Karsten, Stjarna Tribe...and Skyla's annoying little cousin."

Gunner's nostrils flared at the insult. "Is someone going to answer me?"

Freyja assessed the defeated warrior, letting his frustration mount until she finally answered. "We're looking for Skyla. No one has heard from her in months. This was the last place she was going before she disappeared." Freyja gestured toward the viewport.

The storm in Gunner's eyes was replaced with worry. He scanned over the bridge once again. "Let me help."

"Absolutely not," Hinata said.

Refusing to acknowledge Hinata, Gunner focused on Freyja alone. "That's my cousin!" he snarled, but then his face fell, and he added more quietly, "Please, I promise I won't cause any trouble. Let me help."

Freyja forced out a heavy breath, shaking her head from side to side.

Gunner's expression turned dark. "You tried to kill her once before." His eyes darted to Hinata. "And now you are on an enemy ship. If you really don't intend to try and finish what you started back at school, then let me help."

The silence grew thick enough to choke on, then Gunner added one last plea, "Please, I didn't come through for her the last time she was in trouble...Please."

Freyja set her jaw, readying another denial, but then she gave a curt nod.

"You are not in command here." Hinata's words were dangerous.

"Commander, we don't have time to argue. This *ship* is barely space-worthy. You said it yourself. If your tech is right, this planet is abandoned, and it just might be the only chance we get to find a lead on where Skyla went next. Gunner was part of Skyla's squad for years. Maybe he will see something we don't."

Hinata ground his teeth until the muscle in his jaw popped. "Fine, he is your responsibility." Turning away, Hinata focused on the viewport once again. "The ship," he barked.

The tech jumped in his seat and turned back to the console. "I'm sorry, Commander. There is no sign of that ship or any other on the planet."

Hinata stepped closer to the console, menace radiating from his posture.

"I do have something, sir. I believe I have located the research facility."

"The facility you said was abandoned?"

"Yes, well, their generators are running. But there's no movement on the satellites."

"So it could be occupied?"

The tech frowned. "Yes, I suppose. Sir...it's awfully quiet."

"Take us down," Hinata commanded.

"Sir." Worry creased Reina's face. "We're barely holding together. We're lucky she survived the jump...If we take her down, she isn't coming back up."

"Fine, we will take a shuttle down. Freyja, bring your men. Tax, the bridge is yours. Get started on repairs."

Hinata turned to leave. Freyja and her men fell in just behind, followed by Skyla's cousin Gunner. Hinata didn't like it, but he had enough on his mind. Freyja could worry about Gunner. Hinata didn't have time to waste.

Dread settled in his stomach. There was no sign of Pele or the researchers. If Skyla wasn't on Thule, if there was no one here to give them an idea of where she had gone next, how would he find her in the endless expanse?

Hinata rushed his dock crew to prepare a shuttle while he and the expedition party donned lightly armored space suits. While there was an atmosphere, the environment on Thule was harsh, and the suits would protect them from the sub-zero temperatures.

Within the hour, a glittering, white landscape stretched out beneath them as the shuttle dipped below the frozen clouds of the upper atmosphere. Hinata worked to keep his mind focused on the present, worry stealing his attention. He would find her. He had to believe that.

As they descended, a vast ocean filled the viewscreen. Split with sheets of ice that broke the surface into jagged shards, the planet revealed its harsh nature. It wasn't long before they left the ocean behind, and massive ice cliffs rose to one side while a snow-swept tundra stretched out in the opposite direction. They followed along the ice cliffs until a spattering of structures materialized from out of the swirling, white haze. The wind had picked up, and with it, tiny particles of ice danced through the air, obscuring their vision.

"That's the outpost." Rohaan broke the silence as she read the read-out on the screen.

Hinata nodded. There were no words. They could all see the scans—no heat signatures.

They came to a halt in front of the large central building. Hinata smashed the release on his crash harness and stomped out of the ship, cracking the thin layer of ice that coated the snow under his boots as he stormed away.

"What do we do now?" Freyja followed close behind him.

He didn't have answers, but he was desperate to find them. Hinata's eyes roved over the desolate landscape, taking in the abandoned facility. The scans had been right. There was no one here.

The hopelessness of the situation cut deeper than the freezing wind. Hinata turned in slow circles, looking for something, anything that would give him a glimmer of hope.

"Huh, that's strange," Gunner's voice shattered Hinata's concentration, and he turned to glare at the man. So much like Skyla, he was shocked he hadn't made the connection before.

"What?" Freyja asked.

Gunner crouched down and traced the outline of a large impression in the snow. "This print, I haven't seen one quite like it, but it's all wrong for this landscape."

Hinata squinted at the print. It looked like a large paw, and he couldn't keep the image of Fenrir from his mind, the way the strange beast followed Skyla around like a pet. Could it be him? He shook his head. He was seeing signs where there were none. The more likely explanation was that it was from a predator, and his heart sank. If predators were stalking through the facility, it was likely abandoned long ago.

"Say more words," Freyja growled. She obviously had no more patience for the man than Hinata did.

"This print looks like it belongs to a large forest-dwelling creature. It's not suited to the ice," Gunner elaborated.

Hinata's eyes followed the trail. He didn't believe for a second that Gunner's words held any merit, desperation only carved deeper into him. The tracks lead straight to the main building...where they disappeared. His heart stopped.

He followed the tracks, pausing in front of the main door. It was sealed, with no automatic sensors to allow the creature inside. Anticipation built as he triggered the mechanics at the door. Drawing his katana, Hinata stepped carefully inside. The crunch of boots on snow alerted him that Freyja and Gunner followed just behind.

In front of him, a vast garden took up the majority of the space. He paced the building, checking each corner meticulously. It was abandoned, like the rest of the facility. Hinata stomped toward the exit. What had he expected? That he would find Fenrir hiding in the storeroom ready to lead him to the captain? How ridiculous.

Hinata paused at the door when he noticed that Freyja hadn't moved to follow him. The overgrown garden held her full attention, and Gunner stood with his arms crossed, focused on her.

"Still like playing with plants more than people, Freyja?" Gunner quipped.

"Shut up," Freyja snapped, stepping closer to the nearest tower.

"What is it?" Hinata's words came out harsh. He had no patience left.

Freyja shook her head. "It doesn't make sense." She gently ran her gloved hands over stalks and stems, then rested her fingertips on a control panel. "This garden, it's been cared for."

"You can tell that just by looking at it?" Gunner asked in disbelief.

"And you can tell that whatever animal left those tracks isn't from the tundra?" She bit back.

"Yes, I can tell that," Gunner muttered as he turned his back on her and moved closer to the door, where he paused and waited.

Hinata took the garden in once more. It was full to the brim; vegetables hung heavy on their vines, and a rainbow of colors painted across the verdant space. If the research station had been occupied, he doubted very much that they would allow this much food to sit unharvested.

Freyja waved a hand, dismissing the look on his face. "Yes, I know it's overgrown, but look here." She pointed to a stalk tied securely to carbon fiber supports. "These have been secured, recently, and here." She gestured to another plant. "These have been freshly pruned to force the plant to focus on the existing fruit." Freyja gestured to a small tomato just starting to turn from green to red. "Someone is taking care of these plants."

Hinata shook his head. He couldn't put his faith in a few plants. As he shifted to leave, Freyja placed her hand on his shoulder, rooting him in place.

Freyja's fierce eyes burned into his. "Someone is here, Hinata."

"Yeah and maybe they have a big pet," Gunner called over his shoulder.

Hinata stomped toward the exit, pausing once he was close enough to Gunner to make the man feel the menace of his words. "I did not want you here. If you don't have anything useful to say, keep your mouth shut." Then Hinata was moving again.

"Hinata." Freyja grabbed him by the arm.

Hinata pulled away from her grip and stepped back out into the bitter cold. The icy wind that cut into his exposed skin was a welcome distraction from the crushing desperation threatening to take him under. He didn't believe Freyja, and he didn't believe Gunner. There were no answers here.

Had Skyla even made it to Thule? Had she come before them, found the research station empty just as they had, and moved on to another outer rim planet? The ache inside of him burned at the thought of it. Had she moved on without a thought of him? Moved on to her next adventure without a single word sent to him? Had he left his post, stolen a ship, and chased her across the galaxy for nothing? What if she wasn't in any danger at all? What if she had seen her opportunity to run away from the core and never look back? What if she had taken that chance and left them all behind?

The thought burned through him, consuming his thoughts...until he was out of space to wander. He had followed those damn animal tracks to the edge of the compound where they disappeared inside a yurt. He chanced a glance around to find the rest of the expedition spread out to secure the facility. Rohaan caught his eye and moved like he might intercept. Hinata couldn't deal with the man right now. He needed a moment to himself, so he pushed his way inside of the yurt and slammed the door behind him to make his intentions clear. He stomped the snow from his boots, and threw himself into the single chair that sat beside a small table. Clenching his fists, then releasing them again and again, he willed his feelings away. He wished he could go back to who he was before a mysterious outlaw had landed on his station and made him feel again. Before she had torn down his meticulously crafted walls and opened a wound that he wasn't sure he would ever heal from. There was a reason he followed the rules. That he kept his emotions in check. He never should have let his guard down for her.

He slammed a fist into the table, causing coffee to spill from the mug resting there. He pressed his eyes shut, drawing deep breaths through his nose, and worked to tuck away those emotions that threatened to consume him. When he opened his eyes again, he took in the space for the first time.

There was a bookshelf filled with blue spines, but several were missing, scattered across the bed, which was in a state of disarray. Coming to his feet, he moved to the other side of the yurt and snatched a journal from the pile. His heart thundered in his ears. There was a gold symbol imprinted on the journal, the same as the pendant that Skyla always wore.

He spun around, looking over the yurt with a sharper eye this time. On the shelf, he found a framed photo of a little girl. Taking it in his hands, he traced the edges of the frame as he studied those ice-blue eyes. It was her; he was almost certain. The pieces began to click together in his mind. The enormous paw prints that lead him here. The symbols on the journals. The photo. This had been Skyla's father's yurt—the coffee.

Hinata's pulse thundered in his ears as he rushed back to the small table, careful not to disturb anything this time. The coffee. It had sloshed from the cup with his outburst, but there had been liquid to disturb. He took a deep breath, willing his heart rate to slow as he crouched down to inspect the rim. His breath grew shaky, the world titled, and he quickly grasped the edges of the table to hold his balance. He had found what he was looking for. A darker ring, three centimeters above the surface. She had been here, and recently, days maybe. He fought to gain control, hating the way his emotions ran rampant at the thought of her. Days. Maybe she was still here? Maybe he *had* found her.

TOMB

They secured the rest of the facility but found no further clues as to where Skyla went or who else may have been at the research facility.

"Don't you think that if Skyla was still here, we would have picked up Pele's signal?" Freyja asked.

Hinata ground his teeth together, biting back his words until he finally relented. "I don't know."

"We all want to find her, but I think we need to face facts. If she was here—"

"She was here," Hinata cut in.

Freyja rolled her eyes. "Fine, but she's not here now. There is no sign of Pele—"

"Someone else could be at this facility who knows where she went."

"You saw the same thing that I did; none of the other yurts have been used in months. If Skyla was here, she was here alone."

Hinata turned and stormed away from the shuttle. The irony wasn't lost on Freyja that, for once, she was the level-headed one.

"We will find her," Freyja called after him, but he didn't respond, instead storming all the way to the garage at the perimeter of the compound where he froze in his tracks. "Hinata, get on the shuttle. We will figure out a plan when we get back to the *Takarabune*."

Still, he didn't respond.

Stomping her rising frustration into the ice-crusted ground, Freyja came to stand beside Hinata. "Come on, freezing our asses off isn't helping anyone."

"What do you see?" His voice was quiet, broken, afraid to hope.

The tone of his voice pierced her resolve. Freyja scanned the garage. The door hadn't been secured properly, and the wind had blown it open a meter or so. Snow had drifted inside and settled into the empty space between hovers. It looked like there was one missing.

Freyja scanned the snow around the garage. Large paw prints had disappeared inside, just as they had at the main building and the yurt.

"There is a hover missing," Freyja relented.

Hinata nodded. "And Fenrir disappeared inside the garage, but never reappeared. What if she is out there?" Hinata turned to scan the frozen wasteland.

"How would we even begin to search for her?"

"The journals," Hinata whispered.

"What?"

"Her father's yurt. It's filled with his journals. She was looking for something."

Without further explanation, he sprinted across the compound, leaving Freyja running to catch up. He threw open the door before them and stomped over to the table where a journal sat open. Hinata took the journal into his hands, which began to shake.

Seeing the emotion glaze over his eyes, Freyja reached out, placing a hand on his to stop the tremors. Then she gently took the journal from his grip. She scanned the pages as she thumbed through the entries it had been open to. Skyla's father had found something, or rather, he thought he had. There was mention of a dive module located on the rim of the frozen sea just a hundred kilometers from the facility. Is that what Skyla was looking for? It didn't make any sense. If Skyla was here, Pele had to be too, and they had already taken full scans from orbit. There was no sign of Pele.

Freyja shook her head, preparing to voice her doubts, but the look in Hinata's eyes halted her words in her throat. His eyes brimmed with unshed tears, and though he tried to hide it, his hands still shook. Who was this broken man before her? She never would have imagined there was a chink in the warrior's armor. She never would have dreamed her childhood friend would be this fierce commander's undoing. So instead of letting her sharp tongue fly, she nodded slowly. She would need him for the journey to come. Perhaps if she gave him this small concession, he would hold together.

"There is a research site on the edge of the frozen sea," she began slowly, pointing out the diagram in the journal. "Perhaps she went there?"

Hinata swallowed hard and gave a curt nod in response.

"Come, Commander, if we leave now, we can reach the site before nightfall." Freyja turned to leave the yurt. "Pack it up boys!" she called out as she neared the shuttle.

"Thank god, this place is even worse than Trogon," Tristan mumbled as he and Kylian fell in behind Freyja. Gunner took his time, inspecting tracks on his way back to the shuttle where Rohaan was already absorbed in a holo. It was not lost on her that the commander took a few moments before joining the rest of them on the shuttle.

When Hinata finally joined them, he slid into the seat beside Freyja, his jaw set and eyes trained on the viewscreen as he buckled his harness. Any hint of the tears that had gathered in his eyes was gone, and his hands were held steady in tight fists.

Freyja nodded, taking command of the mission. Her fingers flashed over the controls, inputting the coordinates from the journal. "There is a research site not far from here. We will check it out before we rendezvous with the *Takarabune*."

"May I?" Rohaan reached his hand out for the journal. Freyja passed it over to the scientist, then settled into her seat as Kylian brought the shuttle up to speed.

The snowy landscape flashed by in a blur of white, and Freyja prayed for answers, for a clue, something. She knew Skyla. She might be selfish and reckless and always looking for the next adventure, but this wasn't like her. She wouldn't have gone off-grid without a word...would she?

No, Freyja was certain something was wrong. She tried to push the fear from the corners of her mind—fear of what she would do next if there was no sign of Skyla on this frozen rock. What would she do then? How had everything gotten so twisted? The man who sat beside her was barely holding it together. She feared this would break him, and then what? What would she do with a broken commander, a broken stardestroyer, and a broken society?

No, she refused to let this be the end of the line. She would find Skyla, and together they would find the signal and end this once and for all.

It wasn't long before the sharp edges of the frozen sea rose up before them. Nestled between ice and snowdrifts and rock was an oblong pod with smooth edges and a metallic surface, which shone bright in the pale light. Freyja dared to let hope creep into her mind. It was obvious that the pod had been excavated from the piles of snow around it. Perhaps there was a clue as to where Skyla had gone next.

The shuttle glided silently to a halt.

Freyja took in the site with keen eyes. It wasn't only the dive module that had been excavated. Other areas had been dug out as well, though she couldn't tell what had been there. She noticed the missing hover parked nearby. This wasn't right. The site looked as abandoned as the rest of the planet. How had they left? Why abandon the hover here?

"Well boss ma'am, what's the call?" Kylian asked, gripping her shoulder gently as he peered at the view screen beside her.

Her eyes darted to Hinata. His face had turned to stone as he took in the research site.

"Let's check it out." She hoped her voice sounded more confident than she felt.

Freyja led the way. Kylian and Tristan spread out to either side of her while Rohaan and Gunner stayed close behind. Hinata had moved to inspect the hover.

"It still has a charge," he called out.

It hadn't been sitting out in the elements long then. Freyja tried to piece it together as she inspected the pod. It had been cleared recently, but the snow was already beginning to accumulate on its surface again. A thick layer clung to the extended solar panels.

Palming the panel, Freyja triggered the release for the hatch, but nothing happened. She dug her gloved fingers over the seal. Ice.

"It looks intact, but it's frozen shut," Freyja yelled.

Kylian came to her side, holding a pack. "Found this in the snow. There's a plasma torch. We can get it open."

Freyja nodded and took a step back, giving him room to work. After attaching the pads, it took only a minute for the plasma torch to trace the perimeter of the hatch. As they came together again, the soft, orange glow of the laser died out. Kylian looked to Freyja one last time for permission. When she nodded, he triggered the controls. This time, the hatch released with a pop as it opened...

Even in the frozen air with a ventilator shielding her mouth and nose, the rancid scent of stale air, sweat, and refuse nearly overpowered Freyja. Her heart stopped. Someone had been trapped inside.

Pushing past Kylian to enter, Freyja made it just inside before she froze at the sight before her. Laid out on the bottom of the dive module was a massive creature, and curled into its side was Skyla. Neither stirred as the icy air flooded into the capsule.

Freyja's skin burned, and no matter how she tried to prompt her body forward, it wouldn't comply. If she drew near enough to check Skyla's vitals, her worst fears would be confirmed. She had been too late, and her friend was gone.

Gunner let out a feral yell, slamming a fist into the pod beside Freyja, but it wasn't until Hinata pushed past her that she came to her senses. Hinata dropped to his knees beside the bodies. He gathered Skyla into his arms; her head rolled back, limp and lifeless. Freyja watched helplessly as Hinata squeezed his eyelids together—to hold back tears or to activate his ocular display, she wasn't sure.

When he opened his eyes again, it was with a sharp gaze that passed over the frail body in his arms. "I need a med kit!"

Finally, Freyja moved. She sprinted back to the shuttle, but Rohaan had beaten her to it.

Meeting him halfway, she was just in time to catch him as he stumbled in the snow. After steadying the scientist, she snatched the equipment and sprinted back to Skyla and Hinata. Her fingers trembled as she worked to open the pack.

"I've got this." Kylian steadied her hands with a touch, then took the med kit. He took out a canister filled with medical-grade nanites and pressed the syringe to the exposed skin at Skyla's neck.

Skyla didn't so much as flinch as the tiny robots flooded her bloodstream. Freyja cringed at the thought of it. Medical nanites hurt like hell. She didn't want to think about what it meant that Skyla hadn't reacted to the pain.

Kylian pulled out a second syringe and repeated the process with Skyla's beast, who began to twitch as soon as the nanites hit its veins.

Hinata mumbled with his head pressed to Skyla's, "I'm sorry. I'm sorry. I'm sorry." The litany that tumbled from his lips was so quiet it barely carried to Freyja.

Pulling up her ocular display, Freyja ran her own scan of Skyla's vitals. Relief filled her as she watched the nanites do their work. Subtly, the color display shifted from all red to patches of yellow as the nanites worked to stabilize Skyla. Freyja forced out a breath and stood, turning to whisper to Kylian. "Prep the shuttle. There is only so much that nanites can do. She is going to need a regen pod."

Kylian nodded and gripped her shoulder. "She is going to be okay."

Nothing was guaranteed. Freyja's chest tightened with annoyance at the tears that fought to break free. The sooner she could get her friend back to the *Takarabune,* the better her odds.

Freyja's breath caught as Kylian pulled her into his arms. She stiffened under his touch, shocked by the display, but she was too tired to fight this small comfort, and so she melted into him, steadied by the rhythm of his strong heart. Tentatively, she wrapped her arms around his waist and let herself savor the closeness for just a moment. She didn't deserve this kindness, but she was too exhausted to care.

Pulling back slightly, she gazed up into his hazel eyes. While he had always read her like an open book, she saw so many words sitting behind those eyes, unsaid. She wished that she could read him the way that he read her. His eyes stayed locked on hers until he finally released her.

"I'll prep the ship," he said and turned to leave, nearly running into Rohaan, who was perched at the entrance of the pod. Freyja noticed for the first time how uncomfortable the scientist looked. He had gone pale, and worry lines creased his face.

"Rohaan, why don't you see if you can grab some diagnostics on the pod?" Freyja's words broke the scientist from his stupor. He swallowed hard, but eventually nodded and edged past Hinata, who still held Skyla in his arms. Rohaan focused his attention on the console, and his posture relaxed as his eyes glazed over, absorbed in his ocular display.

"Ready for transport," Tristan said as he edged a suspensor through the narrow entry to the pod. He moved to load Skyla, but Hinata only tightened his grip and growled at Tristan, who put his hands up in surrender. "Take it easy, kin. We are all tryin' to help."

"It's fine," Freyja curled her fingers over Tristan's forearm. "Load the beast first."

Tristan rolled Fenrir onto the suspensor and exited the pod once again. Freyja squatted down next to Hinata, dropping her voice low so that her words would stay between the two of them. "She is going to be okay."

Hinata squeezed his eyes tight, fighting to hide the emotion that shone too plainly there. "I gave up on her." He choked the words out. "I thought she had run off to her old life. I thought she had left me behind." He paused, his fingers clutching tightly against Skyla's coat. "I was so angry with her. If you hadn't come to convince me that something was wrong...I would have let her die out here." A stray tear broke free, carving its way down his cheek.

"But you came." The effort to try to comfort the commander was awkward, but she barreled on. "And she didn't die, because you came for her."

Hinata shook his head. Her words had done nothing to lessen his guilt.

"Listen, there is plenty of blame to go around." Freyja's voice became harsh; she wasn't built for this. "Stop taking the weight of the universe on yourself. She chose to leave. You chose to stay. None of us chose this war, but here we are. We are all just doing the best we can. Our work is not done. She is going to need you to be the strong commander we all know you are. Can you do that, soldier?"

Something about her words finally sank in. Hinata set his jaw, squeezed Skyla tight, and gave a curt nod.

Tristan reappeared with the suspensor, followed by Gunner, who had finally gotten himself under control.

"Alright lover boy." Tristan moved the suspensor close. "Kylian has a med bed set up for her in the shuttle, so it's time to move."

Hinata glared at the man, then came to his feet. "Right." He clutched Skyla to him. "I've got her." He shouldered past Tristan, then Gunner, who grunted but submitted to following close behind. Tristan rolled his eyes in return before leaning against the wall and crossing his arms. "Well, find anything interesting, Doc?"

Rohaan nodded without taking his eyes from the display he was studying. "Plenty actually." But he didn't elaborate.

"Wrap it up, Rohaan. You'll have plenty of time to dive into that data once we're back on the *Takarabune*," Freyja said as she shoved off the wall and made her way back to the shuttle.

Freyja's scalp prickled as she took in the desolate landscape and realized they had found Skyla...with no sign of Pele. Had Skyla been on this sun-forsaken rock alone all this time? Freyja shook her head. She would have her answers when Skyla woke.

CHAPTER 26 | SKYLA

SECOND CHANCES

Skyla fluttered her eyes against the blinding light. The air felt heavy against her eyelashes, and her vision swam with pure white. For a moment, she thought she had escaped from the pod straight into a whiteout...but she wasn't cold, quite the opposite. Her skin buzzed with a tingling warmth. Another series of blinks couldn't clear her vision, which remained blurry. Through the haze, she made out a faint pulsing. A blurred mosaic of golden hex tiles faded in and out, the rhythm of it nearly lulling her back to sleep, but then recognition hit, and her eyes blew wide as she tried to gasp in a lung full of air. Instead, her system was flooded with the oxygen-rich silicate bath she hung suspended in. In and out, in and out, she worked to calm her breathing.

The viscous fluid tingled as it flowed into her lungs. She was in a regen pod. She ran her fingertips over her arms. The little nanites that warmed her skin squirmed under her touch. How was this possible? There was no way to know until the regen cycle finished. Until then, she would have to wait to find out who had saved her.

The pulsing lights went hazy, and she had just let her eyes close when a soft ping signaled that the cycle had finished. The nanite-infused silicate drained from the pod. The liquid pulled from her lungs, and the last of the little robots that covered her body poured off her like rain to be reabsorbed by the pod.

Her heart thundered in her ears. A soft hiss accompanied the opening of the ceiling as it split above her, the two sides sliding soundlessly into the base of the egg-shaped pod.

Skyla lay in the center of the shell, completely bare, the sterile air prickling her skin. She slowly pushed up from the platform to sit, her muscles shaky from disuse.

A throat cleared behind her, and she turned her head to find a thermal blanket brushing the exposed skin of her shoulder. Grasping the blanket tight, she pulled it around herself before turning to see her savior.

Her heart stopped as her breath caught in her lungs. No, no, no, it couldn't be. Hot tears pricked at the corners of her eyes. This was another dream, another vision. She couldn't keep the tears from streaming down her face because this couldn't be reality, which meant she was still trapped in that pod on Thule. Her neurons firing their last, sending her a final vision before she died.

"It's okay," he whispered, and he sounded so real.

Skyla shook her head. "This isn't real."

Hinata's brows creased with concern. "You're safe now." His voice was soft, as if he feared a loud sound would scare her away.

The tears came even stronger now. She wanted to reach out and touch him, but feared that if she did, the image would shatter, and she would die alone. She pressed the heels of her hands to her eyes until she saw red, willing away the tears that wouldn't stop.

Giving up on the futile attempt, she dropped her chin and tangled her fingers in her hair. The taste of salt pricked her tongue as the tears continued to fall, and a slight smile spread across her lips. At least she could have this moment.

"You sound so real," she whispered. "More real than any of the other dreams. I almost believe that you came for me." Her voice broke.

A calloused thumb swept across her cheek, clearing the tears as Hinata cupped her face in his palm. Her eyes darted to his as his other hand moved to clasp her cheek. She could hear him and see him and *feel him*. Her pulse quickened at the realization.

"I'm sorry I was late." His voice took on a tone she had never heard from him before, soft and broken.

Laughter shook Skyla's frame as she squeezed her eyes against the tears. He was real. He had come for her. Her eyes locked on his. They burned with an intensity she hadn't seen before. Pain and anger raged there. She stilled under that gaze, her relief replaced by uncertainty. He had never looked at her like that; she didn't know what to make of the anger reflected there, and her heart stilled as she feared that he would never look at her the way he once had.

The sound of the doors sliding open behind her snapped her back to reality. She dropped her hand from his a moment before he pulled back, and his touch was replaced by another as arms clasped her shoulders from behind.

"You stupid idiot," Freyja muttered in Skyla's ear. "You almost got yourself killed!" Freyja clasped her tighter, and Skyla relaxed into the embrace.

"I told you to come back. I need you with me in this. No more going off on your own. You're too reckless. What were you thinking?"

"I wasn't *trying* to end up stranded on a frozen hellhole." Skyla finally got a word in.

Freyja let go and moved to sit next to Hinata beside the regen pod. Skyla's eyes flicked to Hinata, who now sat stiff and guarded. Whatever emotions he had let her see were now covered with the mask he always wore, and her heart broke at the sight of it.

"What happened? Where is Pele? Why were you trapped in a dive pod?" Freyja prompted.

Skyla's heart dropped. *Pele.* "Pele." A lump formed in her throat, making it hard to speak. She pushed through, recounting every detail she could remember about the ship that attacked them. She told them about the crash and the research station, though she kept the details to herself. The wound of living alone in the abandoned station and finding her father was still too fresh. She wasn't ready to talk about it. Instead, she focused on the research she had found—how her dad was looking for the lost city of Heracleion, and how she had been working to restore the dive module to rescue Pele.

"We're going to have to come up with a rescue plan and get back planetside then," Freyja said.

"What do you mean get back planetside? Where are we? I can't leave without Pele."

"Calm down. We are in orbit around Thule. We had to get you to the *Takarabune* for the regeneration pods, but don't worry, we aren't going anywhere anytime soon. The commander here decided to jump out to the rim without any fuel reserves, so right now we are dead in the water."

"What?" Skyla's eyes flicked to Hinata once again. He was stiff under her gaze, his jaw set.

"I did what needed to be done," was all he said by way of explanation.

Why would he jump without reserves to get them back? Why would he behave so recklessly?

Freyja waved to clear the tension. "Whatever, it was reckless and stupid, but if we hadn't come when we did, we would have been too late, so I can't fault your decision. The only thing that matters now is dealing with the consequences. Don't worry, Rohaan and Zarah are working on it. If anyone can figure it out, it's those two."

Skyla warmed at the mention of Rohaan. He was here too. Her relief was instantly replaced with worry. "Fenrir?" she asked, afraid of what the answer would be. At one time he may have been just some strange alien creature she'd found on an abandoned world, but after nine months of it being just the two of them, he was so much more than that.

Freyja scrunched her nose at the mention of the creature, but her smile gave her away. "He's fine, resting in your quarters. I'm sure Tristan will be glad that you're awake and can take care of the thing. He's not happy I assigned him cat duty."

A smirk twisted Freyja's lips, and Skyla got the feeling Freyja enjoyed putting Tristan in his place. Finally, Skyla let the tension melt from her body. Everyone that meant anything to her in the entire expanse was right here. She found comfort in that. Now all they needed to do was rescue Pele, and everything would be right again.

As if reading her mind, Freyja said, "Let's get you a real meal, and then we can get to work."

Hinata stood, taking that as his cue to leave. "I have repairs to oversee. We can discuss retrieving Pele in the morning." He moved to exit but paused on the threshold; his head turned as if to say something more. But after an awkward pause, he disappeared down the hallway without another word.

Skyla let out a long breath. "What was that about?"

"Give him some time. The orbits didn't cease while you were missing. Come on, I've already waited nine months for you." Freyja pulled a black flight suit from a cupboard and flung it at Skyla. "I'll fill you in while we eat."

CHAPTER 27 | HINATA

OFF COURSE

Hinata smashed his boots against the metal plating harder than necessary on his walk to the bridge. Exhaustion clouded his judgment, making it difficult for him to keep his emotions in check. He had sat by the regen pod for the past two days, refusing to leave until he was certain Skyla was all right. The relief he had felt when she focused her ice-blue eyes on him had quickly turned to anger. It had taken everything in him to keep from gathering her in his arms and never letting go.

He had wanted her so badly for so long that it hurt. He craved her. He had finally gotten her back, but it had done nothing to quell the anger he felt toward her for leaving. She had left him, nearly gotten herself killed. And for what? There was no sign of her father or the researchers who had manned the station. She was reckless and chaotic. A deep ache ripped through him—he couldn't open himself up to her again. Not after last time, not after how it damn near destroyed him when she left. Who was to say she would stay this time? What was to keep her from continuing her quest across the stars in search of answers she might never find?

He wasn't strong enough to let her in, only to lose her again. If he did, he was certain this time he would shatter, and there would be no coming back. No, he was in no position to open himself up to the possibility. He had done what was needed, he had found her, and now he needed to let her go. Callan was right, his obsession had clouded his judgment. His people needed him. If there was any hope of restoring peace, he had to be focused. He had to be whole, or if not whole, fractured but functioning, as he was now.

Hinata paused outside the mechlock doors, inhaling deeply as he forced the thoughts from his head. With the unreadable mask of commander firmly in place, he stepped onto the bridge. The deck was a flurry of activity as his officers buzzed from station to station. Quick chatter rang through their comms as they coordinated the repair efforts on the *Takarabune*.

The ship had been badly damaged in the battle with the mega-bot; it was a miracle that she had held together for the jump. She certainly wouldn't survive another in this state, not that they had the fuel to make a jump. With that thought, his eyes trained on Rohaan. The scientist stood hunched over a command console, inspecting a holo with navigation officer Reina.

"Dr. Dar," Hinata said as he approached. "Any updates?"

Rohaan waved his hand over the holo, which dissolved into a tumble of glowing particles, his frustration written plainly on his face. "We won't make it back on conventional power. At least not anytime soon. We did find some archaic solar sails in storage. With some modifications, we could limp to the nearest outpost, but that will still take months."

"There is a war raging, Dr. Dar. We can't afford to sit on the sidelines for months."

Rohaan waved his palm over the display, his fingers twitching with agitation as he pulled up a new holo. "My thoughts exactly." The words were mumbled under his breath. "I am exploring alternatives now. The research that Dr. Aman and her father were working on is promising."

Foreboding settled over Hinata as he recognized the name of the project etched under the diagrams: *Quantum Entanglement Energy Transfer.* "Where did you get these files?"

"The original work was lost at Medina." Rohaan shifted uncomfortably at the mention of the destruction of his home. "But Dr. Aman has been working on restoring the project from memory. It's taking some time, but she has made real progress, and our preliminary analysis shows it is viable."

"Dr. Aman didn't make it off Medina."

Rohaan's face fell. "Nazhi Aman didn't make it off of Medina." Rohaan's words were soft, reverent. "But his daughter Dr. Zarah Aman did. She was his silent partner on the project and quite brilliant. I have no doubt that she will be able to restore the work that was lost and solidify her father's legacy."

Hinata's nerves tingled, and his eyes darted around the bridge. Everyone was busy going about their own projects. He was certain no one had heard Rohaan's declaration. Clasping a hand over Reina's shoulder, Hinata leaned in, dropping his voice low. "Let's keep this discovery between us for now."

"Yes, sir," Reina immediately responded.

"Commander?" Rohaan questioned.

"Walk with me." Hinata turned to exit the bridge, not leaving a moment for Rohaan to consider. Once he was in the quiet hallway, the sound of quick footfalls met his ears as Rohaan hurried to catch up.

"What is this all about?" Rohaan asked.

"Patience, Dr. Dar," was all Hinata said until they had reached his quarters. Once inside, he settled them at a small seating area before he spoke again.

"Enough with the theatrics. What is going on?" Rohaan's tone was surprisingly bold.

Hinata took another moment to assess the scientist. He wasn't the same man Hinata had met at Medina nearly a year prior. He had filled out; strong muscles now corded his shoulders and arms, and his skin, which had been the pale olive of a space dweller, was now rich and dark. But it wasn't just his appearance. The man held himself with confidence, and his voice was strong, demanding even. Time with Freyja and her crew on the rim had changed the man.

Hinata nodded his approval. They were in the thick of a storm, and the scientist would need to be strong. They would all need to be strong if they were to survive. "Are you aware of what happened to Dr. Aman's lab on Medina?"

Rohaan stilled. "There was an accident."

"An explosion," Hinata corrected. "And I don't believe it was an accident. Then Dr. Aman didn't make it off of Medina. Interesting that the Empress was hell-bent on taking out every ship that left the station but didn't pursue our fleet, don't you think?"

"Coincidence."

"I don't believe in coincidence."

"I believe in empirical evidence," Rohaan said.

Hinata shook his head. "You are going to have to trust my instincts on this one. Just keep it quiet that you are working on this with Dr. Aman."

"I am eventually going to need to work with engineering if we want this research to power the ship."

Hinata considered a moment. "I'll notify Wout. He'll get you anything you need. But Dr. Dar, I can't stress enough the importance of your discretion."

"Very well." Rohaan shifted uncomfortably in his seat. "How is Skyla?"

Hinata's blood ran cold at the mention of the captain. His eyes locked on Rohaan's, and he was hit with guilt as he read the concern harbored there. Hinata had refused to leave the regen room for the past two days. He had also refused to let anyone else take a shift at Skyla's side. He vaguely remembered growling at Rohaan that he had better things to do, like figuring out how to power their ship, before he had kicked the scientist out.

"Fully recovered. Freyja took her to get settled in," Hinata finally answered.

Relief relaxed Dr. Dar's features. "Good, that's good. I wonder what happened? And where is Pele? The rest of the researchers? Do you think she found anything?"

Rohaan's stream of questions continued, putting Hinata on edge. He didn't want to think about Skyla. He needed a change of topic, and so he asked the first thing that came to mind, even knowing that it wasn't his place.

"How do you have a bio-ship?" Hinata interrupted.

Rohaan froze, confusion washing over his face. "Well, I was bonded at birth. A practice you should be intimately familiar with, Commander."

"That's not what I mean. Only high houses have the resources to uphold the practice. High houses are still held to mandatory conscription laws...yet you have no service record."

Rohaan nodded his understanding. "You want to know why I didn't serve?"

"Yes."

Rohaan was quiet for long enough that Hinata doubted he would answer, but then a look passed over Rohaan's face, as if he had made a decision.

"When I was a child, I became very ill...it was an illness that not even the scientists at Medina could find a cure for. Many years were spent researching the sickness with no breakthroughs. I only got worse...It was only a matter of time before I would be called to Jannah."

Rohaan paused, his gaze turning to the viewport scattered with stars. "Then the new wave of archeology hit. The station was flooded with alien tech, and my parents bought up every piece of promising med tech. Finally, there was a breakthrough, and I was saved. I was twelve, and having spent a quarter of my life in medical and missing the early years of cadet school, I was excused from service. My parents had sent four children to the Navy. We had already proven our loyalty, and the UTA didn't need a sickly child, who they feared could relapse at any moment, to look after."

Embarrassment heated Hinata's cheeks at his brash question as he realized how intimate the story had been; the trust Rohaan had in him by sharing it. He shouldn't have asked. But now the scientist's obsession with Old World Tech made sense, why he and Skyla were so close. The thought of Skyla soured his mood once more.

"Thank you, Dr. Dar."

"Rohaan, there is no need for all of the formality." Rohaan waved a hand dismissively, a soft smile on his face.

"Let me know if you need anything for your project…Rohaan." Hinata moved to stand, but Rohaan held up a hand to halt him.

"There is something that we need."

"Name it."

"We need more of those high-tech nanites. Operational ones. You destroyed most of the ones from the fight with the mega-bot."

"We have nanites," Hinata growled. He didn't like where this was going. The bots that had attacked his ship were dangerous, and he didn't relish the idea of chasing after them.

"Not like these, we don't." Rohaan moved his datapad into position to pull up a holo. "These nanites are far superior to our own. They have advanced shielding that we are going to need if we are going to send them into a star to harvest energy."

"Can't you upgrade the shielding on ours?"

Rohaan paused to consider. "With time and resources, yes. But we are short on both."

"Fine, leave the nanites to me. You focus on getting that power source ready."

"Where will you find them?"

"I'll figure it out." Hinata's poor mood darkened further at the thought of the one man on his ship who knew where those bots had come from.

Rohaan set his jaw. "Very well." He nodded and excused himself.

Hinata exhaled, letting the exhaustion slump his shoulders as he relaxed into his chair, his eyelids pressing closed. None of this was going to plan.

CHAPTER 28 | FREYJA

INTERROGATION

Freyja watched Skyla with sharp eyes as she filled her in on everything that had happened while she had been missing. Skyla steadied her hands around a cup of coffee, but she wore her concern plainly on her face as she worried her bottom lip. They had settled into a quiet corner of the mess hall, but even at off hours, there was a low din and a continuous stream of soldiers streaming in and out.

Skyla was fragile; Freyja could see it in her eyes. Spending all of those months alone on Thule had changed her, but she wouldn't temper her words. Skyla needed to know what was happening. Freyja would not protect her from the consequences of her actions.

"He is never going to forgive me," Skyla whispered.

Freyja shrugged. "The man stole a stardestroyer and jumped it across the galaxy for you. I don't know if he can forgive you, but that's not nothing."

Skyla pressed her lips together, her eyes dropping to her cup.

"Besides, that's not anywhere near the top of our list of worries. Let's get you settled. We'll need to start working on a rescue strategy for Pele tomorrow."

The corridors were empty, only adding to the silence that permeated the air since Freyja had dropped Skyla off at her assigned quarters. Too many thoughts raced through her mind for rest, her feet moving her to wander. How had she ended up in this shit storm? She needed a strong crew to track down the signal, to face the Goliath she suspected was behind it all, but instead, two of her strongest assets were broken, and she wasn't sure if the damage could be repaired.

Heat raced over her skin as her anger flared. They would have to get their shit together. The universe did not revolve around them, and they had more important things to do than sulk over losses. If they were successful, there would be plenty of time once there was peace to stitch themselves back together.

Freyja rounded a corner and nearly slammed straight into Commander Azai, who appeared to be equally absorbed in his own ruminations. He grunted and moved to sidestep her, not sparing a word.

Freyja dodged to block him, narrowing her eyes as she took in his strange appearance. "What are you up to?"

"Nothing that concerns you," he snapped.

"If I'm not mistaken, I recruited you for this rescue mission, which means everything concerns me."

"Get out of my way, Freyja."

She crossed her arms over her chest and planted her feet. Hinata's eyes drilled into hers as the seconds ticked by until, finally, he relented.

"I have a prisoner to interrogate. Now if you will let me pass."

Freyja took in the commander's dark eyes and slightly disheveled appearance. He still met with the standard of the UTA, but not the higher standard she had always seen him hold himself and his soldiers to. He wasn't himself, and she wasn't certain she should trust him alone with a prisoner.

Worry pressed in at the corners of her mind. "What prisoner do you need to interrogate in the middle of the night cycle?"

"Drop it, Freyja."

"This is a joint venture, and you will treat me with the respect that I am entitled to. What. Prisoner?"

"Gabriel." Hinata growled the name, and Freyja was glad that she had held her ground. If he interrogated that sociopath in this state, she wasn't sure that Hinata wouldn't kill him.

She raised her brows in question.

Hinata shook his head, his annoyance mounting at the delay. His eyes darted around the corridor before he stepped closer, dropping his voice to a whisper. "Dr. Dar needs more of those advanced nanites to develop an alternate energy source for our ship. There is only one person here who might know where we can find more."

Freyja nodded. His explanation made sense, but she still wasn't going to let him speak with the gangster alone. "Alright then." She stepped to the side, gesturing for him to continue. "Lead the way."

"I don't need your assistance."

"I disagree." Freyja fell in step with him as they made their way to the brig. A low grumble escaped from Hinata, but he appeared to accept that he wouldn't be questioning Gabriel without her.

Hinata stormed past the guard on duty. The soldier sprang to attention, knocking a set of playing cards from the table he had been slouched over.

The guard brought a fist to his chest in salute, then quickly scrambled after Hinata.

"Commander?" the guard's voice wavered.

"Open the cell for Gabriel Tibaquirá."

"Yes, sir." The guard flattened himself against the wall to slide past Hinata's menacing form. Hinata held his ground, making no move to accommodate the man. The guard paused a few paces down the hallway and swiped his forearm in front of a panel, which triggered the door to slide back into the wall. The guard then stood at attention next to the opening, waiting for Hinata's orders.

Hinata strode into the cell. "That will be all, soldier. Seal the door and return to your post."

Freyja barely had time to slide in behind him before the door sealed shut once again.

The cell was small, with just enough room for the two of them to stand shoulder to shoulder. The majority of the dimly lit room was taken up with a cot where a man, far too tall for the cramped space, lay with his feet hanging off the end.

"Lights," Hinata commanded, and the lights brightened until they were almost blinding. Freyja squinted against the caustic brightness. The man on the bed still made no acknowledgement of the officers in his room.

"Get. Up," Hinata commanded.

Gabriel groaned and finally shifted his forearm off of his eyes, pushing to sit up.

"What is it, Commander? I wasn't expecting visitors." Gabriel's glib response earned a stern look from Hinata. The man was already on the edge, and Freyja didn't want to see what would happen if he snapped. She stepped past Hinata to take point on the interrogation.

"You are a prisoner of the UTA Navy and will answer what is asked of you," Freyja said.

"Or what? You'll stick me in a dark hole and forget about me." Gabriel laughed maniacally. "I'm already there, sweetheart." He flashed a crooked grin that betrayed the feral animal he was beneath the chiseled face and dark curls. The phoenix inked at his neck reared back and let out a silent screech before settling back into his skin.

"Admiral," Freyja corrected.

"What's that now?"

"Admiral Nygaard. You are a prisoner, and you will show respect to your betters, or I will give you a lesson in remembering."

"Whatever you say, love."

Freyja let the rage surge through her at his disrespect, backhanding him before he even registered the blow was coming. Gabriel let out another laugh as he wiped blood from his mouth.

"Whatever you say, *Admiral*." He twisted the words of her title with a smirk.

"Better, now shall we try again?"

Gabriel shrugged. "I'm not going anywhere anytime soon, *Admiral*."

"You were in possession of advanced robotics when you engaged with the *Takarabune*." She paused to see if he would respond, but he only nodded. "I need to know how you came by those bots."

"I was merely transporting them. A middleman if you will."

"And where might a middleman like yourself come across more inventory?"

"I don't give anything away for free, swe—Admiral."

"You are not in a position to make demands."

"I disagree, given that things couldn't get much worse than rotting in a UTA prison, and I apparently have something you want. I believe I'm in the perfect position to make demands."

Freyja ground her teeth so hard the muscle in her jaw popped.

Gabriel began to laugh again, and Freyja lost control, stepping close, her face dropping to meet his as she grabbed him by the throat. "And what is so funny, you syndicate piece of shit?"

"You are so much like her, you know." His words froze Freyja in place. "I can see the same calculating mind behind those piercing eyes. Same ruthless streak too." His gaze dropped to her hand at his throat. "But this—" His eyes flicked over her. "—the way you show your emotions. The way you lose control." He tsked. "I'm sure your mother would be quite disappointed."

The comment made the inferno inside her burn brighter, but she wouldn't give him the satisfaction. He was right. Her mother would tell her to stop letting her emotions show like a child, and she would be right. Loosening her grip, Freyja let her hand fall to her side as she took a step back. A cool mask of indifference slid over her features.

"Ah, there she is," Gabriel said.

Freyja felt as if she had been doused in ice. The way he looked at her chilled her to her core.

"Now you look the heir to a galactic empire, and so I will speak to you as someone whose interests align with my own. I am no good to you locked up in a UTA prison." He paused to spit a wad of blood on the floor. "Left to rot while war tears the UTA apart. I'm much more useful as an ally, and so I propose this: Let me go, and I will give you what you want."

"Not a chance in hell." Hinata stepped forward.

"Tsk tsk, Commander, the grown-ups are talking."

Hinata growled, taking another step to push past Freyja, but she held out her arm to stay his advance. She dropped her voice and spoke over her shoulder to him. "You remember how he was on Trogon. Let me deal with him."

"Ahh, yes, you and my Halcóncita did a number on my planet. You owe me for that. By the way, where is my little Gyr? Odd to see you two together without her."

"None of your concern," Hinata retorted.

"Aw, your eyes betray you, Commander. She *is* here, isn't she? Resilient little thing. I should have had the cojones to end her when I had the chance. I guess I'm just too sentimental for my own good. She is far more trouble than she is worth. I won't hesitate next time—"

In one swift motion, Hinata extended the blade of his katana, raising his arm, ready to strike. Freyja moved swiftly to block Hinata's blow.

"We still need answers," Freyja said.

"He doesn't need his limbs to talk."

Freyja wrapped her hand around Hinata's arm, firmly moving his sword to his side. "Not like this, Commander."

The muscle of his jaw feathered at the recognition of his own words repeated back to him. A fire she was all too familiar with burned through his eyes, but he relented, returning his katana to its place at his hip. He gave a curt nod, ceding control of the interrogation back to her.

"Impressive," Gabriel muttered.

"Stop goading the commander, or I will leave, and I don't think you will like what he has planned for you."

Gabriel's expression turned serious for the first time since they had entered his cell. He sat forward on the cot and nodded.

"I will give you what you want. All I ask for is my freedom."

Freyja shook her head slowly. She didn't want to let the gangster go. He would only cause trouble for her another day, but right now, he was the only lead they had on the nanites. Gabriel was a backwater thug. She could deal with him when the day came.

"Deal." She extended her hand to clasp forearms with him. She yanked him forward, bringing him close enough to hiss in his ear. "And if you cross me, you will find there are worse fates than having your limbs severed from your body. I promise you that."

Gabriel went stalk still at her words before letting out one of his manic laughs.

"You've got a deal, Heir to The Empire." Gabriel gave her a sardonic solute.

"I didn't agree to any of this." Hinata blocked Freyja's way as she turned to leave the cell.

"Do you have any better ideas?" she asked.

His silence was her answer.

"That's what I thought. For now, we need him, and he needs us."

"I don't make deals with criminals."

"You have to stop thinking in black and white and start thinking in shades of gray. My mother will not hesitate to break the rules to her will. You have already seen that, and if you insist on sticking to your rules, you will lose this war."

Hinata's eyes drilled into hers, hot burning embers in their depths. Eventually, he set his jaw and gave a tight nod before turning to lead them from the cell.

"Get us that location, and I will give you your freedom," Hinata said without turning back.

Hinata didn't wait for Freyja as he stormed out of the brig. Better to let him go burn off his anger. She knew how it was.

It was late into the night cycle as Freyja made her way back to her ship in the hangar. Kylian was waiting outside of her quarters. He kicked off the side of the wall where he had been leaning, blinking hard to dismiss his ocular display.

"Everything all right boss ma'am?" he asked in his heavily accented standard. The sound of his voice put her at ease. The way he talked when they were alone always melted the tension that clung to her.

"Fine." She tried to move past him to her quarters, but his muscular frame took up the bulk of the corridor. She sighed and looked up to meet his warm hazel eyes.

"Everything is fine, Kylian."

He searched her eyes for a moment before relenting, turning to let her pass. She raised her palm to open her quarters, and he snatched her wrist.

"You're covered in blood."

"Not mine." She tried half-heartedly to pull her hand back, but his grip tightened.

"Whose?"

"A prisoner's. We needed answers. I made sure we got them."

He looked for a moment as if he would pull her closer, but finally, he let go. She didn't spare him a second glance as she entered her quarters, but she heard him follow her as she moved to the sink to scrub away the blood.

"You don't have to do everything alone." His voice was soft, the tenor causing her heart to stutter.

"Yes, I do." Freyja focused on her hands and the red swirling down the drain.

Kylian reached in front of her to turn off the water. "Maybe that was true once. Not anymore. You are not alone in this."

Her hands began to tremble. She had been alone for so long. Since she was ten years old and lost her best friend. Maybe even before that, since the Empress had started to mold her heir with cruelty.

The pressure of Kylian's hands as they wrapped around hers stopped her racing thoughts, grounding her in reality. She looked up into his eyes and saw concern there and something else. There was a look in those eyes she had only seen at a glance. He had always been sure to hide whatever lay there from her, until now.

The intensity of his gaze made her skin tingle. The strange sensation made her uncomfortable. She wasn't willing to jeopardize anything about the life she had built for herself since they had set out on their own path, least of all her relationship with Kylian.

"Where is your idiot cousin?" She changed the subject.

Kylian dropped her hands. "Tristan is off fraternizing with the crew."

Freyja rolled her eyes. "Of course he is. Let's go find him before he gets into trouble."

Kylian shook his head, a soft smile pulling at the corners of his mouth. "He's a big boy. He'll be fine, Freyja."

He reached out like he might take her hand again, and she stepped back slightly. Kylian abandoned the motion, folding his arms. "Now promise me, we are in this together."

She shook her head. "I can't promise that. It's my duty to keep you safe."

"We're not kids playing in the Empresses' games anymore." He let out an exasperated breath. "Damn it, Freyja, you should have told us everything back at the Academy. You never had to do this on your own."

"I did. To keep you safe. To keep all of you safe."

Kylian stepped forward, so swiftly that she didn't have time to react as he looped a thick arm around her waist, tracing the lines of her face with the other. "And who keeps you safe, Freyja?"

She pulled back, and he reacted by pulling her tighter until her body was flush against his. His eyes were unrelenting. He would not let her go without an answer.

Tears brimmed at the edges of her vision as she relaxed into his arms. He nodded, accepting this small surrender, dropping his head until his lips brushed the shell of her ear.

"Let me in. Let me be there for you. I promise; Freyja, I will keep you safe."

The doors to her quarters snapped open. Kylian dropped his hold on her as she pushed away from his chest, spinning to snap at the intruder.

"Well, what do we have here?" Tristan staggered in, a slight sway to his step, his black tee-shirt haphazardly tucked and his belt left unbuckled.

"I think we should be asking *you* that question," Freyja snapped.

"You're not wrong." Tristan swayed and collapsed on Freyja's bed.

"Come on, cuz, I'll help you to your bunk." Kylian reached out to his cousin.

"But then you won't hear everything I learned from the crew. They are a chatty bunch after a few drinks, and I promise you want to hear this."

CHAPTER 29 | HINATA

BETRAYAL

A large holo of a star system shimmered in the space between Hinata and Tax on the circular war room table. Tax smelled of tequila, and his eyes had a glassy sheen he couldn't hide. Hinata decided to ignore the breach in protocol. Tax had turned a blind eye to plenty of his own questionable behaviors over the past few months. The least he could do was return the favor. Besides, it was late, and Tax had been off duty, but Hinata needed the distraction. With Skyla on his ship, his mind kept turning to the woman. Yet he wasn't ready to face what any of it meant for the two of them.

There was no *two of them,* he chided himself. He needed something else to focus on, and Gabriel had provided the routes that the Empress used to collect the advanced nanites.

A dark foreboding settled over him as he thought about the attack from deep space that had struck on their return trip from the megastructure salvage mission. They were undoubtedly the same nanites, but those had appeared from out of nowhere, as if of their own volition. Had the Empress sent the bots after the AI ships? If she had, why had the attacks stopped as they approached central rim space? Why had she let them go? He was missing a key piece of the picture, and it drove him mad.

"If we can get the solar sails operational, this location is within range." Tax's words brought Hinata back to the problem at hand.

"How long?"

"It will take us a week to get there."

Hinata rubbed the stubble that etched his lower jaw. A week was acceptable. The *Takarabune* was a large warship, fashioned after ancestral cruisers. It had a large hydroponics garden at its center and life support systems that could last a generation without major maintenance.

"Then that is where we will go once we exhume Pele. Send a probe to monitor activity in the sector and keep it dark. I want to know what we are walking into, but the last thing we need is for the Empress to know we are coming."

"Yes, sir—"

The sound of the war room doors sliding open cut off Tax's words. Freyja strode in, followed closely by Kylian and Tristan. Hinata took in Tristan's appearance. His shirt was only half-tucked, and there was a sway to his step that betrayed how much the man had drunk.

Tristan's eyes drifted to Tax, and a crooked smile flashed across his face before he noticed the commander watching. Tristan quickly washed away the expression and stood a little taller. Hinata glanced at Tax to find his cheeks flushed pink. Hinata sighed. It wasn't his business.

He shifted his attention to Freyja. "Thank you for your assistance with the prisoner. But it's late, and Lieutenant Commander Sato and I were just wrapping up for the evening."

Freyja widened her stance, crossing her arms as she shook her head. "You're going to want to hear this, Commander."

Her tone had his attention. "What is it?"

Freyja flicked her head toward Tristan. "Tell him."

Tristan stepped forward. "You have a problem."

"I have many problems, currently." Hinata narrowed his eyes. "Be more specific."

Tristan rolled his eyes and slid into one of the empty conference chairs. "Did you wonder how the Fenix forces targeted the *Takarabune* on our way to Jubokko?"

"Space is a dangerous place. It's likely they were staking out that route, waiting for a cargo ship worth raiding," Tax said.

Tristan shook his head. "Someone on board sent a transmission."

"What are you saying? That someone from my crew alerted the cartel?" Hinata leaned forward, his elbows pressing onto the table.

Tristan shook his head. He had a strange look in his eyes when they darted to Tax, like he already regretted what he would say next. "I can't confirm who the transmission was for, but it disclosed our location and that you intended to take this ship."

Heat burned under Hinata's skin. He was fully dedicated to his soldiers, and he expected their loyalty in return. "Who?"

Tristan hesitated a moment, his eyes darting briefly to Tax once more. "Callan Kobayashi."

"That's not possible," Tax snapped.

Tristan's gaze dropped to the table. "I'm sorry."

Tax shook his head. "No, Callan has been part of our squad since the academy. He would never betray us."

Tristan flicked his fingers, sending logs to the shimmering holo display between them. "After everything I heard, I had Kylian do a little digging. It's not just rumors. You can see it in the logs. He sent the transmission."

"Logs can be faked," Tax countered.

With another flick of his fingers, security footage pulled up next to the logs. It was a video of Callan sending a transmission. The timestamps matched the logs.

"We have already seen that video records can be altered. This isn't proof." Tax refused to give any ground.

"If you don't believe me, then ask him yourself." Anger laced Tristan's words.

Hinata had let this play out long enough. "You make a fair point. We will question Lieutenant Commander Kobayashi." As much as he didn't want to accept it, Tristan's words had the ring of truth, and he could not ignore such a significant threat to his ship.

Hinata opened a comm line. "Locate Kobayashi."

"Lieutenant Commander Kobayashi is currently in the mess hall," the computer system responded.

"Security, send a detail to meet me at the mess." Hinata rose from the table, leading the way from the war room. Hushed voices that were not meant for him reached his ears.

"I trusted you," Tax whispered.

"I do what needs to be done. I have no moral compass to restrain me," Tristan hissed back.

"All I said was that he was acting off, not that he was a traitor."

"And the logs proved it!" Tristan's voice rose in exasperation.

"The only thing that has been proven tonight is what a mistake it was to get involved with you."

"Tax..." Tristan's voice fell once again to the same hushed tones, but if Tax gave the man a response, Hinata didn't hear it.

No more words were exchanged on their way to the mess hall. A security detail awaited their arrival just outside the doors.

"On my orders—you are here for support only," Hinata said.

"Yes, sir," the guards replied in unison.

"Let's get this over with," Hinata muttered as he stormed into the mess.

Callan sat at a table in the far corner, an entire unit gathered around him—evidence of a night of drinking sprawled out on the table between them. Callan snapped to his feet as he recognized Hinata.

"Commander." Callan brought his fist to his chest in salute.

"Is it true?" Hinata asked.

Confusion clouded Callan's face, and for a moment, Hinata hoped that Tristan was wrong. "Sir?"

"Did you divulge our location and my intentions for this ship?"

The confusion melted away to clarity as Callan registered what Hinata was asking. Callan set his jaw, his stare turning hard, and any doubts that Hinata had harbored washed away.

"Why? You went behind my back, sold out this crew, and for what? Why did you betray your people?"

"I am not the one who betrayed our tribe. That honor belongs to you, *Commander*." Callan pulled out the title with mock respect, the liquor in his veins loosening his tongue.

Hinata shook his head. "I have always put our tribe first."

Callan laughed. "You were planning to steal this very ship!"

"To find answers that will end a war!"

"To go chasing after a woman who doesn't want you!"

The insult cut at his festering wound, and Hinata lost what little control he had. Drawing his sword, he held his blade out in challenge. Callan drew his own katana, and Hinata pressed forward in a flurry of slashes. The pace was frenzied and chaotic. Callan barely kept time with Hinata's endless fury and lost ground with each strike as Hinata forced him toward the corner.

"Your betrayal cost hundreds of lives."

"My betrayal!? You were the one planning on stealing a ship and leaving our tribe in the middle of a war."

"A war that we are losing! A war that we will lose if we don't adapt."

"You don't get to change the rules, Hinata. You don't get to abandon your tribe."

"I would never abandon my tribe," Hinata growled, swinging his katana in a powerful, downward strike. Callan blocked, struggling to hold the blade away from his flesh.

"Taking the *Takarabune* to this sun-forsaken system instead of following orders isn't abandoning your tribe?"

"There is more to this than you are willing to admit. If we abide by the rules of engagement, we will lose! We are already losing. Our enemy has changed, and we must change too, or we will perish."

Callan shoved Hinata's blade away. "You do not get to make those decisions. That is why I reported you to the council. If you are so confident in your course, you could have pleaded your case!"

Hinata froze. "You reported me to the council?"

"Yes! They were ready to detain you when we arrived at Jubokko. You would have had the chance to make your case. You are the son of Josei Tennō Azai. The worst you would have faced was a dishonorable discharge. But I doubt your mother would let it go that far. I was trying to save you from yourself."

"It was that transmission that led the cartel straight to us." Hinata's voice fell.

The shocked expression that twisted Callan's face was genuine. He hadn't intended to sell them out to the cartel.

"I didn't know." Callan gripped his katana in one hand, but raised the opposite in surrender. "I swear to you. I would never betray you like that."

Hinata let his sword fall by his side. "No, you would only betray me to my mother. The very person that I pleaded my case to. Who denied this expedition because she refuses to accept that the rules of engagement have changed. You would damn us all." Hinata returned his blade to its sheath, turning his back on the man he once called friend. "Detain him and his unit."

"Don't take it out on my unit," Callan called after Hinata.

Hinata paused but didn't turn. "Did they know?"

Callan's silence spoke for him.

"Then they will share your fate."

CHAPTER 30 | SKYLA

ON THE MAT

Skyla's skin itched with nervous energy. She shook her hands out at her sides as she made her way to the training room. It had been a week since her rescue. A week on the *Takarabune,* and yet she hadn't seen Hinata since that first day when she woke up in the regen pod. Why hadn't he come to see her? Agonizing over the possibilities had been a new kind of torture. The uncertainty was eating her alive. She needed a way to burn off all of this nervous energy, and since Hinata was avoiding her, she was left with training to quiet the noise buzzing inside her head.

A gentle nudge at her calf brought her mind back to the present, and she paused to scratch Fenrir's head. He looked up at her with those intelligent eyes, like he could read her thoughts, as if he knew she needed his presence to ground her. She sighed and gave him one last scratch under his chin before resuming her walk.

Ice washed through Skyla as she stepped into the training room—that same cold panic that she had felt when the sea beast tore her under the frozen ocean. *Hinata.*

Given the off hour, Hinata and his sparring partner were the only two in the facility. Sweat glistened off Hinata's tattooed back, the only indication of his effort. Both men moved with incredible speed.

At first glance, Hinata looked just like he did that first day she sparred with him, but as she watched, the differences became apparent. He was still lean, all hard lines, but he had put on more muscle than the last time they had fought. The way he moved betrayed hours of training, effortlessly blocking blow after blow from his second, Tax. The man was fast, but Hinata was faster.

Sweat plastered Tax's dark hair to his brow, the effort of trying to land a blow written clearly on his face. As if a switch had flipped, Hinata went on the offensive. Within three moves, he had captured Tax's arm, taken out his feet, and now held the edge of his foot to the man's neck, holding him in submission until Tax finally reached out and tapped the mat.

"Maybe you should spend a little less time drinking," Hinata said with a grin as he pulled Tax to his feet. Tax's eyes met Skyla's, and a sympathetic smile parted his lips.

"Or perhaps you need a drink yourself." Tax clasped Hinata by the shoulder then nodded to where Skyla stood, leaning against the wall, watching them.

As Hinata turned, the carefree look fell from his face, replaced by a dark storm. Skyla's heart beat frantically against her ribs. She hated the way he looked at her now. It physically hurt, like her heart might rip from its place in her chest.

Tax slipped his shirt back on and gave Skyla a nod as he exited. Pushing from the wall where she had watched the men fight, Skyla made her way warily toward Hinata.

"Have you been avoiding me, Commander?" she asked playfully, trying to get a glimpse of the man she knew hidden under the mask.

"It's not a large ship. How could I possibly?" His words cut. They were her own words, from when she had indeed been avoiding him, and the fact that the *Takarabune* was not a small ship in the least made them sting all the more.

Fenrir let out a loud yawn as he settled in to take a nap by the doors.

"What is that thing doing, stalking my ship?" Hinata focused his anger on Fenrir.

"What am I supposed to do? Keep him locked up in my quarters?" Skyla's grip on her own emotions started to slip.

"Fine," Hinata growled, turning from her to grab his shirt.

No, she had given him space. She had waited a whole week to seek him out. After dreaming of him every night for months, after clinging to the memory of him like a silk ribbon slipping through her fingers while all else felt lost. She was done being patient. He wasn't getting off that easy. "Spar with me," she demanded.

He turned slowly, those burning amber eyes drilling into her. "No."

He didn't want to talk with her? *Fine*. But he could spar with her. This was where they had been most comfortable before she left. On the mat, she had always known where she stood with him.

Skyla lunged forward, grabbing him by his neck and tricep. She twisted, putting all of her weight behind the move, and threw him to the center of the mat. Surprise had worked in her favor: she met no resistance from Hinata as she tossed him back into the ring.

"I said no." Even as he denied her, he took up a solid fighting stance.

"If you won't talk with me, then you will fight with me. The choice is yours!" Skyla took a step onto the mat to square up with him.

"Fine."

"Fine, you'll talk?"

"Fine, let's fight." Hinata rushed forward with a series of blows that drove Skyla back. She barely had time to block one strike before he was on her with the next. A moment of hesitation, and she saw it. He was holding back. Why was he holding back?

"Why are you holding back?" she screamed at him.

"You think you can handle me? Fine."

Skyla's vision went dark for a split second, and then she was on the mat. Her lungs ached from the force that had stolen her breath, and her head felt fuzzy. Once her eyes focused, they locked onto Hinata's. He held her against the mat, his breath so close it played across her lips, his eyes blazing with anger, yes, but there was something more there too. She had seen that look before, and her skin sparked with the tension between them. It was still there. He could deny it all he wanted, but she could see it plainly in the way his gaze bore into her, like he could see her very soul.

"Was that so hard?" she joked, her voice hoarse as she caught her breath.

The muscle in his jaw twitched, and her heart sank a little with his silence.

"Why won't you talk to me?" she asked, her voice raw with vulnerability.

He stared hard at her, letting the silence thicken until she thought it might choke her. He leaned closer, and her breath caught. For a moment, she thought he was going to break the tension with his lips. Instead, the moment was shattered by the loud thwack of his palm hitting the mat beside her head.

"I'm not doing this with you." He jumped to his feet, stalking to the corner where he had left his things. Shocked by the outburst, she raced to follow.

"What do you mean, you aren't doing this?" She planted herself firmly in his way, demanding his attention.

"This." He gestured between the two of them. "I am not doing *this*. Whatever this is."

Skyla's shoulders slumped as his words settled in. "Why?" she whispered.

Hinata rubbed his palm across his face. "You left."

"We both had responsibilities. I thought you understood."

Hinata nodded slowly. "And now? Have you fulfilled your *responsibilities*?"

"What is that supposed to mean?"

"Chasing ghosts and seeking answers beyond the edges of the Known Galaxies are not responsibilities, Skyla. You were running away. What is to keep you from running again? Obviously there is nothing here you value enough to stay, so once we rescue Pele, what is to keep you from disappearing again?"

"That's not fair."

Hinata shrugged. "Then tell me, what will you do once you are reunited with your ship?"

The question struck Skyla. What would she do? All those long nights she had spent alone, only two thoughts kept her sane, rescuing Pele...and him. How could she tell him that? How could she bare her soul—that it was the thought of him that had kept her going through all of those months alone—when he so obviously hated her for leaving?

"That. That right there. Your silence speaks volumes, Skyla, and that is why I can't do this." Hinata didn't give her time to respond as he pushed past her and exited through the training doors.

The tears came freely as Skyla collapsed to her knees, curling in on herself, hard sobs wracking her body. A soft head butted into her chin as Fenrir cuddled up next to her. Wrapping her arms around the creature, she buried her face in his golden fur. How had she messed everything up so badly?

DISTRACTION

The sound of soldiers entering the training room snapped Skyla back to her senses. She had sat there, curled into Fenrir, crying for far too long. Fenrir let out a warning growl at the newcomers, and Skyla leapt to her feet, running an arm across her face to wipe away the tears.

"Sorry about him," she mumbled as she maneuvered past the two soldiers. "He gets grumpy when he's hungry." A sly smile spread across Skyla's lips at the worried glances the two men exchanged as she and Fenrir slipped past them into the corridor.

Skyla blinked hard to activate her ocular display. A schematic of the *Takarabune* overlayed her vision, and she quickly identified the lab. It was just a quick lift tube ride away. Relief washed over her as she stepped into the lab to find Rohaan working alone. Her friend glanced up from the holo he was working on, and his expression softened as he took in her appearance.

"What happened?" he asked.

The signs that she had spent the better part of the past hour crying were still clearly displayed on her face. She slid onto a stool next to him and leaned her head against his shoulder.

"I've messed everything up."

Rohaan slid an arm around her shoulders and gave her a reassuring squeeze.

"There is nothing broken that can't be fixed," he said, leaning his head to the side to rest atop hers.

"I'm not so sure."

Rohaan knew better than to argue with her when she got like this, so instead, he sat with her quietly until she was ready to speak again.

"What are you working on?" she finally asked.

Rohaan dropped his arm from around her to position himself squarely in front of the holo once more. He manipulated the schematic with his hands, pulling out from the tiny details he had been inspecting, to reveal a dive suit.

"I'm almost finished programming the design for the dive suits. Based on the specs I pulled from the dive module, we could encounter depths up to 4,000 meters. These suits will be rated for a depth of 5,000. Plenty for us to be able to exit the dive module and get to work on Pele's repairs."

"When will they be ready?" Unease plagued her, growing with each day that passed without a firm date for the rescue mission. After Skyla had described the anomaly to Rohaan, they had worked together to find a way to identify the storms, and now that they could track them, they had found they were only getting worse. In days, the entire planet would be shrouded in the ice storms that—if their findings were accurate—would last centuries, making a rescue mission impossible.

"I'll need another day to print and test the prototypes, but I have the equipment to retrofit her engines ready, and my sim training with the pod controls has gone excellently. I don't see why we should wait any longer than that to go rescue our girl."

Skyla forced out a breath. "That's good."

"Yes, we don't need any more delays. I still find it strange that we didn't find any suits in the dive module when there is a hatch for deep water exit. It was built to take the researchers down and allow them to investigate. How were they supposed to do that with no suits?"

Skyla worried her bottom lip. She hadn't told any of them what had happened to the researchers. She hadn't been ready to talk about it. Even now, she wasn't sure she was ready to reveal what had happened on Thule. Yet the words came rushing out of her before she could think better of it.

"That's because the researchers died in those suits." Fresh tears built in her eyes, ready to spill over her still red cheeks.

Rohaan's fingers froze in mid-air as he turned to meet her eyes. His eyes asked the question he wouldn't voice.

Skyla nodded. "I found my father." The words came out as a choked whisper.

Rohaan reached out and pulled her into a crushing hug. "*Inna lillahi wa inna ilayhi raji'un.*" Once her sobs settled, he pulled back, holding her by the shoulders. "I am so sorry, Skyla. I'm sure he is in Jannah now."

She shot him a look.

"Or Valhalla," he amended.

Skyla nodded. "I hope so." She settled back into her seat as Rohaan moved over to a corner of the lab where he had set up a kettle, mugs, and a stainless steel canister filled with tea. He prepared them both a cup before returning to her side.

"Thank you." She sipped the piping hot tea. It burned her tongue, but the heat and the spices were a welcome distraction.

"Have you told him?" Rohaan asked.

"Told who?" Skyla ran a finger along the edge of her cup, focusing her attention on the heat that was near burning before finally letting her gaze drift up.

Rohaan gave her a look. "Don't play stupid. It doesn't suit you."

Skyla bumped her shoulder into his. "Hey, that's my line."

"Avoiding the question." The words may have been playful, but his gaze remained hard.

The brief smile fell from her lips. "I haven't told anyone."

"Skyla—"

"He won't talk to me." Skyla threw her hands up and stood from her stool to pace.

Rohaan placed a gentle hand on her forearm to halt her nervous movements. "He doesn't know what you've been through."

Skyla deflated, sinking back into her seat. "It doesn't matter."

"It does matter." Rohaan's deep brown eyes filled with worry.

Skyla dropped her head into her hands. "Some things are too broken to be repaired," she mumbled into her fingers.

Rohaan rubbed her back gently, waiting until she shifted her fingers and peered out at him before he spoke again. "And you think this is one of those things?"

"He thinks so," she sighed. "Just keep this between us for now, okay? I don't need pity. I need to get to Pele."

Rohaan stared at her for a long stretch before relenting. "As you wish."

Skyla relaxed a little, then mumbled, "I never should have left."

"On that point, we are agreed." Rohaan grinned at her, then scooped up his mug to hide his smug look behind his tea.

"Hey!" She feigned offense but couldn't help but smile, too.

"I'm not entirely sure that you can be trusted on your own. You seem to be finding your way into mortal danger lately," Rohaan said.

Skyla's shoulders slumped under the implication. He was right.

"Plus, we really could have used you on our expeditions. I've been to five ruin sites now. You better watch out. At this rate, I may see more of the Old World cities than you!"

She laughed, appreciating the change of topic. "We will see about that, Ears." She flicked his ear. "I thought you preferred listening—far more interesting things in deep space. I believe that's what you always said."

Rohaan waved her off. "There is still plenty of time for listening as we travel from planet to planet."

"True." Skyla's finger traced the rim of her teacup absentmindedly. "Find anything interesting?" she asked, hoping to keep the conversation light.

"Oh, yes. Lots." Rohaan paused to consider. "There is one thing in particular I think you will be interested in, though!" He excitedly dismissed the holo specs of the dive suit, trading them out for a strand of DNA.

"What am I looking at?"

"You can't tell?"

"Obviously."

"Don't tease the captain!" Zarah called from the doorway, her hands full with a try of cookies that she slid onto the counter before taking the holo into her hands and spreading her arms out wide to zoom the image out.

Rohaan chuckled, his attention fully on the beautiful scientist beside him. "Fine, I couldn't differentiate it from just a strand of DNA either."

Skyla rolled her eyes. The image transformed from a strand of DNA into a cell, then a cluster of cells, tissues, organs, and finally, it zoomed all the way out to a creature...her creature.

"Fenrir," she whispered. "You went to Alpha 4375?"

Rohaan shook his head. "No, this was on Eta 5309. We found these ruins with a largely intact biological pod system and extensive records—"

"It looks like his species was engineered as a biological asset for settlers," Zarah interrupted excitedly. "The planet had highly dangerous fauna. Creatures like Fenrir were made to be companions for the researchers, to keep them safe."

"Humans designed him?" Skyla absentmindedly plucked a cookie from the tray, her eyes flicking from the image to Fenrir curled up at her feet. His gaze met hers. Finding mischief reflected in his deep eyes, she promptly shoved the cookie in her mouth before he got other ideas.

Rohaan nodded. "Ancient humans, yes. There is something else." He zoomed back into the DNA strand once again; this time, when he flicked his hand, different sections were highlighted, mostly in blues, purples, and oranges, but there was a rainbow of colors splashed across the sequence. "Based on my records, these strands came from ancient Earth animals."

"Impossible," Skyla mumbled around another cookie.

"And yet the data suggests no other option." Rohaan pinned Skyla with a stare, but Zarah simply chuckled and scooted the plate closer to Skyla.

Skyla swallowed before continuing. "Ancient humans didn't have the resources to bring Earth animals with them when they went voyaging."

Rohaan shrugged. "I know the histories as well as you, and yet that DNA is distinctly Canis, and Caracal, along with bits from a dozen other species—"

"Ambystoma?" Skyla asked.

Rohaan paused and cocked his head to the side. "Yes, that one is strange." With the wave of his palm, the holo shifted to a little amphibian and ran through a range of its properties.

"That!" Skyla pointed at the display. "What was that?"

"Oh, yes, these little creatures have the amazing ability to regenerate limbs...you don't think?" Rohaan mussed.

A smile spread across Skyla's lips. "I don't think, I know! Ears! This explains it; how Fenrir regrew his leg."

Rohaan nearly choked on his tea at the statement. "He did what now?"

"Fascinating," Zarah whispered, crouching down to scratch Fenrir under his chin. He lifted his head, eyes pressing closed with contentment.

Bobbing her head with excitement, Skyla explained everything that had happened with Fenrir on Thule.

"Fascinating," Rohaan echoed Zara's statement as he took down notes. "Now that would be quite a valuable attribute."

It certainly was, but one thought plagued her. "Ears, you said that the DNA comes from Earth That Was...are you certain?"

Rohaan once again shifted the display back to the illuminated strand of DNA. "I'm certain."

They sat in silence for a long time as they contemplated how the impossible was clearly displayed on the holo before them. Two rounds of tea later and they still had no solid theories, but Skyla couldn't complain. The mystery of Fenrir's origins was a welcome distraction. Her mind had a puzzle to work on instead of facing the reality of her broken heart.

CHAPTER 32 | FREYJA

BATTLE OF WILLS

"Come on." Freyja kicked Kylian's bunk, then Tristan's. The hour was early, but she couldn't keep her mind from racing. The details that Gabriel had shared with them about the bot shipment ran through her mind, scenarios forming and playing out before her eyes. Those were her mother's ships. If they were going to successfully secure the tech they needed, she would have to come up with a plan. No one else knew the Empress like she did. Their fleet was small and damaged, and they couldn't go head-to-head with the Empress in this state. Not if they wanted to walk away. No, she would have to come up with something.

"Boss ma'am?" Kylian asked, his voice groggy with sleep.

"Fuck off and turn out the lights on your way, won't you?" Tristan mumbled from under the arm he had draped across his eyes.

"I will not. Now get your lazy ass out of bed, we have plans to make."

Kylian complied first, sliding out from under his blankets. Freyja's eyes fell to the lines of his exposed chest, where black looping lines of a cross were etched into his dark skin. Her gaze traced the cut of his abdomen, the lines of his hips. Her cheeks heated as her eyes flew to his. A slight smile parted his lips at having caught her admiring gaze.

"Get dressed and meet me outside," she snapped as she turned and stomped off.

The groggy men trailed behind Freyja into the lift tube that would take them to the bridge. Tristan snorted a stim, and Freyja rolled her eyes. That man was going to wear his body out before he ever had a chance to grow old. The thought stuck in her mind. Perhaps he had the right of it. Their life was not an easy one, and the likelihood that they would be around to worry about the consequences of their rough life in later years looked less likely every day.

The bridge doors snapped open. It was quiet with a minimal crew on duty at this hour, but she found Tax where she had expected him to be. His eyes were unfocused as he scanned through something in his ocular display. As she approached, he blinked hard to dismiss the display and turned to meet them.

His face turned hard as his eyes landed on Tristan. Freyja chanced a glance at her Berserker, and she was surprised to find hurt reflected on his face, even if only for the briefest moment before he plastered on a sly grin and leaned against the command console in front of Tax.

"Hey, handsome," Tristan said.

"Lieutenant Commander." Tax's words were tight. He wouldn't look at Tristan, instead turning his attention to the display.

"Lieutenant Commander, is it now? I seem to remember you calling me by something else the other night—"

"Admiral." Tax turned, looking past Tristan to focus on Freyja. "Is there something I can do for you?"

"Tax." All of Tristan's playful charisma leaked away as he pleaded.

Finally, Tax looked at Tristan. "No, I trusted you. I told you that in confidence. All I said was that Callan had been acting odd, and you go and accuse him of conspiracy!"

"To be fair, I didn't accuse him of anything. I found evidence that implicated him."

"You were only looking because of what I said."

"He was ready to sell you all out! Who knows what trouble he could have caused for us! I thought you were loyal to Hinata."

"I am. Right or wrong, I will stand by his side until the day I fall. But Callan was one of us, too. We've been together since the academy."

"And he betrayed that trust. I did you a favor." Tristan's anger and desperation had turned his words harsh.

Tax turned away from Tristan once again to focus on Freyja. "Admiral, if there is nothing I can do for you, then I have duties to attend to. There is still much work to do on the *Takarabune*."

Freyja laid a hand on Tristan's shoulder to silence the arguments she knew he still had. Tristan wasn't known to hold his tongue or to let things go.

"Of course," Freyja said. "Our next move is actually what I had come to talk with you about. I need access to the probe reports."

Tax hesitated. Those reports were classified, and even she hadn't been granted access. After what had happened with Lieutenant Commander Kobayashi, Freyja couldn't blame Hinata for tightening security, but she needed access to those reports.

"Of course, Admiral, I just need to clear it with Commander Azai."

Freyja clenched her jaw, willing the anger that bubbled up to settle. She had expected the response. "Does a commander outrank an admiral?"

Tax took his time to formulate a response. "Under normal circumstances, no, but I think that you and I both know that these are not normal circumstances."

Freyja locked eyes with Tax. A battle of wills played out between the two of them. Finally, Freyja sighed and turned away. "Send those files as soon as he approves access," she said over her shoulder as she moved to exit. When she reached the door, only Kylian was at her side. "Tristan, enough, leave the man alone." She motioned for her Berserker to fall in, and though anger radiated off Tristan, he complied.

CHAPTER 33 | HINATA

INTO THE DEEP

Hinata's eyes traced the lines of the bulkhead in the dark of his quarters. Sleep eluded him. His mind raced with thoughts of Callan and his betrayal, of the exchange he'd had with Skyla in the training room. There were ship repairs to oversee, the matter of their depleted energy cells and the alternate energy source Dr. Dar was working on, and the rescue mission to plan. All of these things sat in the shadow of the war that raged on the other side of the galaxy, and the mystery of the signal that Freyja was convinced was somehow behind it all. It all congealed into a mass that would not let him rest.

Hinata sighed. There was nothing to do but endure. With a thought, he signaled the end of his sleep cycle to his neural chip. Immediately, he was hit with a barrage of messages. Repair requests to approve made up the bulk of the communications, but in the sea of correspondence, he found a priority message from Tax.

Sato: Admiral Nygaard is requesting access to the drone files for the Omega quadrant.

Of course she was. The betrayal from Callan, one of his closest officers—one of his closest friends—had shaken him to his core. He didn't know who he could trust, and the admiral had never been high on his list. How could he trust someone who would do anything to get what she wanted? Yet, as far as he could tell, the admiral had been nothing but forthright with him since the destruction of Medina.

"While our interests align." Those had been her words. It was Freyja who had alerted him to Skyla's disappearance. She'd recruited *him* for this rescue mission and trusted him to help track down the signal. At the moment, their interests aligned, and he was desperately in need of allies.

Azai: Granted.

Hinata had enough to worry about. If Freyja wanted to dig into that probe data, let her. He sent the message to Tax before quickly working through the rest of the requests. The ship had been so badly damaged that his repair crew had to improvise half of the repairs. Nothing would be up to code, but she would hold together for a jump. At least he hoped she would.

After finishing the requests with brutal efficiency, his mind was left to puzzle through the rescue mission. He regretted working so quickly through the mundane tasks; he could have used a few more minutes of peace. Today they would return planetside to rescue Pele, and Hinata dreaded the close contact with the captain, almost as much as he dreaded what she would do once they had rescued her ship.

He had done his best to avoid her, and yet she remained a virus that plagued his thoughts. Waking or dreaming, it didn't matter; she was everywhere. Those ice-blue eyes that saw right through him. The soft bergamot and sea salt scent of her. The gentle touch of her lips.

Pushing up from his bed, he banished the thoughts before they took root. He was doing the right thing, keeping his distance, but his treacherous body still yearned to be close to her. It was worse when she was near. At least while he was avoiding her, he wasn't tempted to give in and take her in his arms, to kiss her so deeply she might forget about leaving him for her adventures, claiming her so thoroughly that she would never leave his bed.

Damn it. He was spiraling again. Time to get moving. It was much easier to keep his mind quiet when he was moving.

Cramming his feet into running shoes, Hinata was in the corridor before his thoughts spiraled out of control and prompted him to do something he knew he couldn't. A good run around the stardestroyer before the mission would sort his mind.

One hard blink and soft sunlit trees replaced the sterile corridors. The trail that cut through the woods around his home overlayed on his ocular display. The air still tasted of the recycler, and he had to imagine the smell of pine and water, but he instantly felt more grounded.

One, two, three—the kilometers ticked by. His heart beat strong in his chest, its rhythm a mantra that calmed him. Four, five, six—sweat cut rivers down his back. Seven, eight, nine—finally, his mind stopped drifting. Ten, eleven, twelve—he was grounded in his body. Thirteen, fourteen, fifteen—his comms broke his stride.

"Sir, we are twenty minutes out from launch. Is there anything further you need prepared for the mission?" Tax asked.

Shit—he had given into the hypnotic flow of the run and lost track of the time. "Yes, be sure the dive suits, bio-balls, and repair equipment are stored properly, and send a message to the team. I don't want any delays." The sooner this was done the better. The sooner she was gone for good, the sooner he would learn to live with this pain that would never heal.

"Yes, sir." The comms cut out, and Hinata started his run back to his quarters. He had just enough time to shower, change, and down an algae pouch before meeting the rest of the team on the docks.

When he arrived, his face was shaved, his hair braided tight against his scalp, his shirt tucked, and his boots shined. He looked the part of the UTA commander as he always did, no hint of the man in turmoil beneath the surface. To his surprise, Freyja and her men were already there. Tristan lounged on a cargo box, and Kylian was keenly focused on Freyja, whose focus was on the ship, where he spotted Skyla and Rohaan. His heart leaped into his throat at the sight of her, and he swallowed hard to dislodge the lump that had formed there.

"Nice of you to join us, Commander," Freyja said.

"I am on time." Hinata held his face blank, his voice emotionless. He was in control.

"Sure, sure...your dock crew already loaded and cleared the ship for launch. Shall we?" Freyja said.

"Why am I not on the expedition party!" Gunner yelled, stomping across the dock, Fenrir following close behind.

"Because we didn't have enough material to make you a suit." Skyla had to tip her head back to look her cousin in the eye.

Gunner's face turned red, his nostrils flaring as he crossed his thick arms. "I don't like it."

Skyla placed a gentle palm on his arm. "We will be fine...besides, I'm not even certain you would fit in the pod."

A smile twitched at Gunner's lips. "Fine, but next time there is a raiding party, I am on it."

"Deal." Skyla grinned at her cousin, then added. "Hey, watch out for Fenrir while I'm away, won't you?"

Fenrir plopped down on his haunches and cocked his head up at the two of them.

Gunner eyed the hybrid for a moment, then nodded, grasped her forearm, and pulled her close, his voice turning serious. "Stay safe, cousin."

Hinata turned away from the private moment and walked up the shuttle ramp with Freyja, her men a step behind.

"Let's get this rescue mission underway," Hinata affirmed as he slid into his seat...a moment later Skyla slid into the seat next to him. His pulse raced against his will as he buckled the crash harness. His traitorous eyes traveled to Skyla's. She gave him a weak smile. He found hope reflected in her eyes, along with another emotion he wasn't sure if he was reading right...sadness? He returned a tight smile and turned his focus to the viewport.

"Take us down," Hinata commanded.

The flight planetside was silent. Everyone's thoughts were focused on the mission ahead. The icy orb rose up before them. White clouds whipped across the viewport as they sunk into the atmosphere. The vast frozen ocean stretched out in all directions, only disappearing behind the horizon. Plates of ice reached up toward them like pale, jagged blades. There was no softness in this world.

Kylian piloted the shuttle to land near the dive site. Everyone worked with quiet efficiency to load the dive module. Dr. Dar settled into the controls, running through diagnostics to ensure the pod was prepared and ready to dive. Even Tristan, whom Hinata had never heard remain quiet for more than a short stretch, held his tongue.

Looking for something to keep his mind from wandering to the beautiful woman who had constantly worried her soft pink lips on the flight down, Hinata focused instead on Tristan's odd behavior. He hadn't missed the interaction between Tristan and Tax the other night. Narrowing his eyes, Hinata studied the man. Tristan's jaw was set, and his eyes were hard as he lugged a heavy cargo box toward the dive module. The man knocked shoulders with his cousin and kept going, not a spare second to apologize. Hinata hoped he was wrong. Tax deserved so much more.

Kylian paused by the commander, still rubbing his shoulder. "Everything is loaded and ready, sir."

Hinata nodded.

Kylian took in Hinata as he studied Tristan. "He's not all bad, you know."

Hinata's attention snapped to the man beside him.

"My cousin." Kylian rubbed the back of his neck. "I know he doesn't come off well. But he is a good guy, ya? He's had my back since we were kids...he had to step up too young. You know?" Kylian's voice dropped to just above a whisper. "Do things that no kid should have to do..." He cleared his throat before continuing with a smile. "The jokes, the swagger, it's his way of dealing. But he always comes through when it counts."

Hinata grunted. "I'll keep that in mind."

"Maybe you could put in a good word with your friend?" Kylian cocked a hopeful brow.

Hinata pinned Kylian with a hard stare.

Raising his hands in surrender, Kylian backed away, but that grin was still on his face. "Just think about it, boss man." With that, Kylian turned and returned to the dive module.

Hinata took one last deep breath, the chill of the frozen wind piercing his nose and clearing his mind before he sealed himself inside a six-by-four-meter pod with the one person in the universe that made him feel like he might catch fire, though from anger or desire, he wasn't sure.

Hinata sat next to Rohaan, where he focused all of his attention on the large view screen that took up the entire nose of the pod.

The floor vibrated through his boots as the suspensors under the pod rumbled to life, bringing the pod to hover a meter above the snow-swept landscape. Slowly, Rohaan maneuvered backward, bringing the pod out over the frozen ocean. Once through the narrow entryway onto the ice, Rohaan carefully spun the pod around and directed it to the search site. The pod raced across the frozen plates; a twang like metal cables snapping came through the speakers.

"What is that?" Kylian asked.

"The ice." Rohaan gave no further explanation, his focus locked on the fast-approaching dive site.

The pod slowed to a stop over a patch of ice that looked identical to the vast stretch of ocean they had left behind. There were no signs that the ice had been disturbed, but it had been months since the crash; all signs of the incident would have been frozen over and swept away with the wind.

"Deploying laser torches," Rohaan announced.

The exterior cameras showed a beam of light tracing the outline of the pod. Steam bubbled up from the edges of the ice where the laser passed through. As soon as the lasers stopped, the pod shot straight into the air where it hovered, suspended for a brief moment, before plummeting into free fall. The instruments on the bottom of the pod tucked away into its shell as they plunged toward the ice.

Hinata's stomach leapt into his throat, and he thought of how much he hated high-G maneuvers aboard Tentei. The image of Skyla's lips, quirked into a smile of pure joy as she piloted Pele, came into his mind. His stomach lurched again, and then the pod crashed through the ice, bringing him back to the present.

Their descent was slow as the ocean took its time swallowing the invader. Dark waves capped in shards of ice pressed in overhead, and soon the entire pod was shrouded in darkness.

Though they were insulated inside the pod, a shiver ran through Hinata as if the icy fingers of the ocean gripped him by the throat. He focused on his breathing, willing away the panic that clawed at the edges of his mind, working to will away the fear the endless dark instilled in him.

He had spent more than half of his life in space, yet this, *this* was different. His people belonged to the stars, and while he preferred his home world to space, the stars were like a second home—but this dark ocean was no refuge. Here, Hinata was an invader. He was some place he shouldn't be, and if he wasn't careful, he had the ominous feeling that he would never return to the surface.

Inhale, exhale, he turned his attention to his breath. This was a mission, no different from the hundreds of missions he had been on before. They would bring Pele home. He just needed to focus.

The ocean beneath him appeared to glow with tiny cracks, like broken porcelain, and Hinata was certain he was hallucinating, his mind playing tricks on him as he blinked hard to dismiss the image...but the lines only grew brighter.

"Dr. Dar," Hinata began, unsure of how to ask the question. Was what he was seeing real?

"I see it too, Commander. Deploying drones to investigate now."

The pod slowed as a fleet of drones deployed from its belly, dispersing quickly toward the glowing fissures below. A mosaic of drone footage rippled across the viewport.

"Amazing," Rohaan mumbled as the footage of the glowing trenches came into view. What had appeared as hazy, glowing lines in the distance transformed into a vibrant tapestry of colors, textures, and movement. The trenches were filled with alien organisms, ranging from tiny, pink fish to tall grasses with pulsing edges, and massive purple growths ran through with electric lines.

"The trenches are thermal vents," Rohaan said, his eyes switching back and forth between readouts from the drones and the enchanting images that filled the screen.

"How deep are the trenches?" Hinata asked, fearing the answer. The module was only certified up to a depth of 5,000 meters. If Pele had fallen down one of those trenches, they wouldn't be able to reach her.

"Scanning now." Rohaan flicked his fingers through the air, working through the incoming streams of data from the drones. He froze. "I cannot confirm depth...The drones have a signal range of 10,000 meters...and have not been able to confirm the depth of the trenches."

The scans confirmed his suspicion. If they couldn't find Pele on the ocean floor, then she was lost down one of the countless trenches that stretched into the darkness in every direction. Trenches that their equipment wasn't equipped to survey, let alone traverse. Would they be able to find her? Their time on this planet was already limited with the storms rolling in. If they didn't find her before the dangerous anomaly enveloped the planet, how long could he delay his call to duty while a war raged in the galaxy around them? Would they even be able to find another way to save her? It was an impossible choice: Skyla's ship—Tentei's love—or the countless lives that stopping this war would save. He couldn't delay forever. But he still had time. He prayed he wouldn't have to make that call.

A gentle brush across his hand startled Hinata back into the moment. Skyla had moved up next to him, so close her pinkie brushed his, and he had to clench his fist to keep his fingers from reaching out to interlace with hers. Worry lined her face as she studied the display.

"Dr. Dar, is the pod ready to take a scan of the ocean floor?" Hinata asked.

Rohaan snapped to attention as if just remembering his plan. "Moving into position now."

The pod sank another one hundred meters and then hung suspended above the ocean floor. The hull vibrated under them with a rhythmic beat. A wireframe model took form on the viewscreen before them, becoming more detailed with each pulse of the beat.

The pod lurched violently to the side, throwing Skyla from her feet into Hinata's lap. On instinct, he wrapped his arms around her, holding her tight to him. He inhaled and was hit with the aroma of bergamot and sea spray; the scent was her, and a memory of a moment she had spent with Pele. Hinata inhaled deeply, relishing the scent of her. *Fuck.*

The pod swayed sharply in the opposite direction, demanding Hinata's attention. He focused on the screen ahead, though he held his grip around Skyla's waist.

"Report," Hinata demanded.

"Move." Kylian shoved Rohaan out of his seat to take the controls. "There." Kylian zoomed the cameras in on a dark shadow as it whipped past the pod.

"What is that?" Tristan yelled.

The pod rocked hard enough to nearly shake them from their seats as the shadow swept past once again, this time accompanied by the screeching sound of sharp points wracked over metal.

"Whatever it is, we don't want to find out if it can puncture the hull."

"It is titanium, reinforced with a robotic repair lattice. There is no way an organic creature should be able to damage it," Rohaan tried to reason.

"Sure, in theory, yet that last swipe did significant damage. Even the slightest puncture will be catastrophic. We need to ditch this thing." Kylian threw the pod into motion.

The sudden acceleration flung Skyla against Hinata's chest, and he swore she must have been able to feel his heart pounding against her back. He hoped she would believe that it was the monster in the deep that made his pulse race when he knew the truth; that it was her. *Focus.*

"End the scan!" Hinata ordered. The wireframe model froze on the screen, still laid out over the gloom below, but the rhythmic pulses that worked to fill the gaps ended. The pod turned to the side as the shadow swooped past again. At least this time there was no sound of metal on metal.

"It's still focused on us," Kylian ground out between gritted teeth as he worked to stabilize the pod. "Out here in open water, we are easy prey. We need somewhere to lose it."

Rohaan lurched forward, throwing a file up onto the main screen with the motion. "Head for these coordinates. There appears to be a structure at a safe depth for the pod."

Kylian took them into a sharp turn as they shot past the shadow, the sudden maneuver giving them a precious head start. The view screen had gone oddly dark. The glowing fissures that took up most of the ocean floor were ominously absent.

"I don't see anything. Are you sure Dr. Dar?" Hinata asked.

"Something is there." As if on cue, strange shapes took form in the dark before them. Long lines topped with domes, too symmetrical to be organic. Rows upon rows of buildings stretched out ahead of them. Kylian navigated the pod through an archway, heading into the center of the underwater city.

Everything was dark, and they didn't dare turn on their lights. Instead, Kylian slowed as he maneuvered through the tight avenues, twisting and turning until the exit was long obscured from view. Finally, he brought the pod to a stop at the end of a corridor that appeared to open up into a large atrium.

The pod was oppressively quiet. Each member of the crew scarcely drew breath as they watched the readouts. Seconds ticked into minutes until, finally, Rohaan let out a long exhale. He clasped Kylian by the shoulder and nodded before sinking into a chair.

"I don't think it followed us. I have nothing on near-range scans," Rohaan said.

The uncomfortable feeling of eyes studying him brought Hinata's attention to the woman who sat in his lap, his arms still wrapped around her. His eyes caught on hers. He expected her to be angry, but she just looked confused. Clearing his throat, he reluctantly relaxed his grip. Skyla slid out of his arms to take the seat behind him.

"What is this place?" Tristan asked as he leaned close to the display.

"Heracleion," Skyla whispered.

While Skyla studied the wireframe model of the broken city, Hinata studied her. The line of her jaw, the fullness of her lips, and the way her eyes shone as she took in the ruins. How long could he keep pushing her away? How long until his resolve crumbled, and he submitted to this maddening draw he had to her?

CHAPTER 34 | SKYLA

WHAT WAS LOST

"What?" Hinata's soothing baritone reached Skyla's ears, but she was struggling to process, her full attention homed in on the display of the broken city before her. Her stomach turned into a gaping hole that threatened to swallow her as her breath caught.

She stepped close enough to brush her fingertips over the image. This was it. This was where all of her father's research had led her. This was the place he had spent his life looking for. This was the place he had left her for.

She shook her head. That wasn't entirely fair. Her mother had driven him away because of this embarrassing obsession, and yet it still stung, like he had chosen this place, his wild dreams, over her.

The familiarity of the thought caught her by surprise, and her eyes darted to Hinata, who sat studying her. Cold guilt washed over her as she thought, isn't that exactly what she had done to him? She had chosen obsession and adventure over...not love. She couldn't use that word. That word scared her senseless, but the sentiment still rang true.

"This is it, isn't it?" Rohaan stood beside Skyla.

She nodded. "It has to be."

"Anyone want to fill the rest of us in?" Freyja asked, annoyance obvious in her tone.

"This is what the researchers were looking for. My father believed that there was an ancient city under the ocean."

"Why?" Freyja asked.

"He found records. Everyone thought they were legends, but he believed they were real. According to his journals, he believed that ancient humans came through a wild wormhole millennia before the voyagers that populated the Old Worlds."

"Is that even possible?" Freyja leaned closer to the viewscreen, scrutinizing the display.

Skyla spread her arms wide. "It looks pretty damn possible." That pit in her stomach grew, and she desperately wanted to think about anything else. *Pele.* "We are here to find Pele. We can worry about this later. Ears, have your drones found anything?"

Rohaan snapped to attention. His hands flew through the air. "No sign of Pele. The drones have finished searching near the trenches where we came down. I'll recall them to our location now. If I distribute their approach, we should have a pretty good map of the city."

Skyla bit her bottom lip. She didn't want a better view of the city; she wanted to find Pele. She scanned the search grids as they formed on the screen. The drones had finished mapping most of the nearby ocean floor; the city and the surrounding area were all that was left.

Her heart sank. What if Pele had fallen down one of those trenches? She couldn't leave Pele in those crushing depths, but how would she get to her?

The minutes stretched on in silence as the grid filled in around the city's perimeter. Kylian had tried several times to engage the group in idle chatter, yet all he got in return for his efforts were a couple of single-word answers from Freyja and begrudging grunts from Tristan, who sat with his arms crossed and a sour expression on his face.

Skyla could feel Hinata's eyes on her, his gaze scorching her skin, and she almost wished the rest of the crew would break the silence—anything to break the intensity of his gaze. Every meter the drones covered, she prayed that there would be an anomaly, any indication of her ship. Just a sliver of hope was all she asked for.

"There!" Skyla's sudden cry caused the rest of the crew to startle.

"What is it?" Rohaan asked, enlarging the drone footage that she had indicated.

"That! Right there." Skyla pulled and pinched at the image until it zoomed in on the anomaly. "That damage isn't like the rest of the city! That's from a crash."

Rohaan shook his head. "You don't know that. This entire city is in ruin."

"I do know. I have seen this damage before. Look." Skyla pulled up several images from the drone footage. "See these buildings, they look shattered. As if they were made of glass and dropped from a height. I have seen this damage before, on other worlds. This is what the damage throughout the rest of the city looks like too, but this—" She once again enlarged the anomaly. "—this dome was punctured. The rest of the building is intact."

Rohaan nodded along. He could see it too, but when his eyes met hers, they were clouded with worry. "It doesn't mean that Pele's crash caused the damage."

Skyla's heart beat in her throat. She knew her friend was only being logical, and yet she pleaded with him to understand. She needed this. She needed that wreck sight to be Pele. She had to find her bonded; she needed to feel whole again, to have that gaping wound in her chest filled. She couldn't imagine life without Pele.

"It's worth investigating further," Rohaan finally concluded.

Skyla let out a sigh, then gripped her friend by the shoulder. "Thank you."

Rohaan raised his hand to cover hers and gave it a comforting squeeze. "We will find her."

Recalling the nearest drone to their location, Rohaan used it to plot a course through the city that the pod could safely navigate. The shadow creature may have lost interest, but they weren't certain if it had remained nearby. Best to keep the pod concealed inside the city until they were ready to ascend.

Kylian moved back into the navigation chair to steer the pod to the crash site.

"Are you kidding me?" Kylian mumbled as they approached a narrow opening into the next section.

"She will fit," Rohaan said matter-of-factly.

"Are we looking at the same passageway?" Kylian countered.

"I was very precise in my calculations." There was no ego in Rohaan's tone.

"Too precise," Kylian muttered as he slowed their approach. The margin for error had dropped to near zero. "There's just barely enough room for us to squeeze through." Kylian's hands trembled on the controls.

"I can make it fit, honey," Tristan said, cocking his head back over his chair with a grin, returning to his normal, obnoxious self.

Skyla rolled her eyes, but she noticed the tremors in Kylian's hands still, a slight smirk on his lips. She saw it now. Tristan was Kylian's rock, even if the man was severely unhinged.

They emerged from the dark chamber into a vast atrium. It was the largest space they had traveled through, stretching at least a city block. Glass domes encased the cavernous space, their dim lights glittering softly off the white stone supports. Three matching stone sculptures were spaced out through the center of the atrium, clearly humanoid carvings surrounded by what had likely been a pool of water, though everything now sat below the waves.

The pale, carved walls housed large doors at regular intervals. The place had once been the hub of a grand society. It was gorgeous and devastating. Mesmerizing and dark. There was no question that this place belonged to their ancestors, and to see the destruction that befell them was heart shattering. An ominous feeling settled over Skyla as she wondered if they, too, would be so easily forgotten. Here one day, then washed away by history the next. If a society this grand could fall, why not the UTA?

"We are almost there." Rohaan broke the spell. "Just one more passageway, and we will be at the anomaly."

Skyla swallowed the lump that formed in her throat, her spark of hope tempered with cold, hard fear. If Pele wasn't at the crash site, there was a very real chance she would never see her again.

The passageway opened up into a vast room. Unlike the atrium, this room had no windows. Only a faint shadow outlined the break in the ceiling overhead, the dark water barely lighter than the pitch black of the space around them. Their dim lights did little to wash away the gloom.

"Power up the lights." Skyla fought to keep her tone even, but it still came out as a plea.

Kylian looked to the scientist for confirmation. When Rohaan nodded, Kylian thumbed the controls, and the entire room illuminated in a ghostly pale light. It took Skyla's eyes a moment to adjust and fill in the details of the white-washed wreck, but then her vision blurred with tears as she took in the most beautiful sight she had ever seen. *Pele*. She had found Pele.

Happiness mixed with worry as she inventoried the damage. Pele's left flank was torn open from the rail gunfire. There was hardly any hull intact on that side. Her bow had long gashes from where she had broken through the roof with cuts so deep they ran all the way through her coral nanite structure.

Tremors racked Skyla's body. A warm hand slid into hers, steadying her; she startled at the touch, at who she thought it was.

Rohaan smiled at her and nodded, still holding tight to her hand. "We'll fix her. As long as her consciousness is still present, we can fix her."

Skyla's gaze dropped to find Hinata's fingers pressing divots into the armrest of his chair, his jaw set, and his gaze locked on her. She took a deep breath to steady her voice before she said, "Right, then let's get to work."

CHAPTER 35 | HINATA

TRUTH

Hinata watched Skyla carefully as they prepared to exit the dive module, only taking his eyes off her to prep his own dive suit. Spots flecked the corners of his vision as she asked Freyja to check her suit. Then he cursed himself for feeling jealous that she would ask Freyja and not him.

How far he had fallen in her eyes. He had asked for this; he chided himself. He had pushed her away. How could he resent her for respecting his wishes? A frustrated growl rumbled in his throat, catching Kylian's attention, who looked from the commander to the two women as they finished sealing their suits.

"You know it's not like that, boss." Kylian clapped him on the shoulder.

Hinata dropped his gaze to the floor. "Not like what?"

"She doesn't look at Freyja the way she looks at you." Kylian paused for a moment to consider. "I've known Karsten a long time. I don't think I have ever seen her look at someone the way she looks at you."

Hinata grunted. "Let's just get this mission over with."

"You know, it would be a lot easier on the rest of us if you two would just work through whatever this is." Kylian gestured to the space between Hinata and Skyla.

"Noted. Seals?" Hinata changed the subject.

Kylian smirked but said nothing further as he checked Hinata's seals.

Once suited up, they all crowded into the back of the pod, laden with repair materials. Kylian and Tristan carried a large cargo box between the two of them. Freyja held dual power cells in each hand, fully charged from the *Takarabune's* meager reserves. Rohaan carried a pack filled with algae cultures while Hinata carried a large box of pumps and Skyla a box filled with handheld tools. They had come prepared with everything they might need to repair Pele. After seeing the extensive damage, Hinata hoped it would be enough.

Rohaan opened a small chamber that barely fit the six of them. Once inside, the door behind them sealed, cutting them off from the main pod. A purple, shimmering force field appeared before the back of the pod spiraled open like an iris, the shiny metal replaced by the dark waters of the deep. The water pressed up against the force field, but the barrier held.

"The suits are coded to pass through the force field. Once you exit the pod, you might feel some pressure, but the suits will take the brunt of it," Rohaan explained.

"Yes, we all got the debrief, Doc," Tristan said.

"Enough talking. Let's go get my ship." Skyla didn't wait for acknowledgment before stepping through the force field out into the dark.

"Stay sharp out there. We still don't know what attacked the ship. See something, say something," Hinata said over the comms before activating the artificial gravity component of his boots and stepping out into the deep.

The second he exited the pod the entire weight of the ocean bared down on him, pressing in all around him; there was no escaping her might. Dr. Dar may have undersold the whole experience. He fought against the tightness in his chest that accompanied his rising panic at being trapped under an entire ocean with only a thin dive suit between him and certain death.

The feeling of the void was nothing compared to this. In space, he felt free. A spacewalk was vast and empty, but this, this was a terror he had never known. Here he was an invader in a world where he didn't belong, and he risked the ocean's wrath at the intrusion; how her will demanded his destruction—how she would crush him into oblivion if given the opportunity. Taking in a deeply unsatisfying breath of recycled air, he focused his attention on the task at hand.

Skyla was already several meters ahead of him, bounding forward with each step she took. Her gravity stabilizers turned low as she vaulted through the water, then disappeared into a hole in Pele's side.

"Are you all right, Commander?" Freyja asked as she stepped up to his side.

"Yeah, you need a hand with that little box? Are the new muscles just for show?" Tristan quipped as he and Kylian passed on Hinata's other side. The large cargo box hung between them.

"I'm fine. Let's see what the damage is."

Once inside Pele's cargo bay, the crew set down their supplies and began their inspection of the sunken starship. Pele was pristinely preserved, one of the few benefits of the frigid waters. Beyond the damage done by the crash itself, she looked to be in good condition.

"If I can get her powered up and her engines running, the rest of the work can be done back on the *Takarabune*," Rohaan said over comms.

"We'll check the engine room." Tristan hit Kylian.

"I can tap into her main systems from here," Rohaan added.

"I'll finish mapping the hull damage," Freyja said before pushing off and swimming out of the cargo hold.

Hinata realized Skyla was nowhere to be found.

"Skyla?" Hinata said over comms. "Captain, report." Nothing.

"I'm good here," Rohaan mumbled by way of dismissal.

Pulling up their trackers in his ocular display, Hinata searched for Skyla. According to her ping, she was on the ship, though the water distorted the signal, so he wasn't entirely sure where. He would have to find her the old-fashioned way.

The water resistance slowed his motions, but he still preferred to walk the dark corridors in search of the missing captain. It gave him some sense of normalcy in a world where nothing felt right. A deep sadness burrowed into him as he ran a gloved hand over the lifeless walls. The memory of the night Pele had guided him to Skyla's room with pulsing, blue bioluminescence pushed into his mind. That was the night he had lost control and fully given in to his desires. The night he had taken her in his arms and consumed her with a kiss, ready to claim every last centimeter of her—that was the night she had stopped him because they were too different and would never be together.

Pausing in the empty hallway, he pressed his palm onto the hull. "You didn't believe that, did you, Pele? I'm sorry this happened to you. I promise you, we will get you home, back out to the stars with her." Emotion clouded his next words, "Even if she decides to take you and leave—" *Me.* The last word sat unsaid.

Hinata searched Skyla's quarters, then the kitchen. She wasn't in either place. It wasn't until he came to the bridge that he finally found her, sitting in her captain's chair, her gloved fingers tracing the panel where the neural link cables would connect her to Pele. But there was no life in the ship, and the golden cables remained hidden in their compartment.

"Rohaan is checking on her systems now." Hinata opened a private commline with Skyla.

"I heard." Skyla's voice came out monotone, as lifeless as her ship.

"She's still there."

"You don't know that...I let her down...again." Skyla's emotions broke through.

Hinata chanced, taking a step closer. "Rohaan was able to bring her back from a tech-killing virus; this is nothing."

Skyla stiffened. "If she is still there to revive." She slowly turned to face him. "What if she gave up? Sent her signal back to Earth That Was?"

"Pele would never willingly leave you." The last of his resolve broke as Hinata came to stand beside her.

"What if I've let her down one too many times? I wouldn't blame her. She was stuck down here, in the dark, all alone, for months, her power slowly draining away. Too cold to repair, no sunlight." Skyla shuddered, and it took all of his will not to wrap his arms around her.

"She's still here, Skyla. I can feel it."

Skyla squinted at him. "Since when are you such an optimist?"

"I'm not, never have been. She's still here. Give Rohaan a chance to find her." Hinata tentatively reached out his fingers to brush her arm, but then clutched them into a fist at his side, remembering to keep his distance.

Skyla nodded slowly. "Sit with me?"

Hinata swallowed hard but slid into the seat next to her. Time slowed, and even the tiny particles that danced in the beams of their torchlights appeared to still. He wasn't sure how long they sat in the dark bridge before Rohaan's comm came through.

"I've got her! She evacuated all systems save for her backup hub. It's going to take some work before we can reintegrate her consciousness with the rest of the ship, but we've got her!"

The tension in Skyla's shoulders eased, and she leaned forward in her chair, splaying her arms wide across the control panels. "Thank you, thank you, thank you. Thank you for waiting for me. I won't let you down again. I promise."

Hinata gave Skyla a moment of privacy. Pele couldn't hear her, but he knew she needed this.

Finally, Skyla came to her feet.

"Well, Captain, it sounds like we have some work to do."

For a moment, the smile that lit her eyes made him forget that he was preparing for her to leave.

***

The next few hours passed in a blur of activity. Rohaan connected an external power source to Pele's hub, and insisted that it was safest for Pele if they waited to reintegrate her with the rest of the ship until she was safely onboard the *Takarabune*. Rohaan was working on getting her subroutines running so they would be able to manually fly her up into orbit.

Freyja had finished mapping the damage and applied bio-balls to the worst of the structural damage. Pele just needed to be stable enough to make it into orbit. The worst of it was her engines. The rail gun had shredded her port engines. Tristan and Kylian had their work cut out for them, retrofitting her engines with enough power to break atmo. The damage was extensive, and time was tight, but Rohaan assured them that they would be able to get her off Thule and back to the *Takarabune* before the strange ice storms took hold of the entire hemisphere.

The countdown read three hours and nineteen minutes in Skyla's ocular display.

"That is all I can do here." Rohaan looked up from the control panel. "Status check on the engines?"

"Fuuuuuuuuuck—" Tristan's voice came through the comms.

"Um, best give us a little more time, Doc. I'll let you know when she's ready, ya?" Kylian said in hushed tones before he cut comms.

"I'll go check and see if they need anything. It's probably best if you all just give them some space," Freyja said, heading for the engine room.

Rohaan's eyes unfocused for a moment as he checked his ocular display. "I think Kylian may have been a little generous in his use of the term 'a little time.' By my estimate, they are going to need a minimum of two hours before we can take her up."

Skyla shifted uncomfortably at the news.

"Don't worry, we still have plenty of time. Maybe we should do something to take your mind off the repairs while we wait." Rohaan turned to Skyla, and Hinata didn't miss the sparkle in the scientist's eyes. He had seen that look before on the megastructure. "How often does one get the chance to explore a lost, underwater city?"

Skyla shook her head, then slid down the wall to sit on the floor. "I'm needed here."

"Skyla, she is running on subroutines right now while she undergoes repairs. Her power was completely drained, and the damage was extensive. She is not conscious yet; she doesn't know you are here," Rohaan insisted.

"No, I said I am staying. Go ahead, Ears. I'll be fine." Skyla folded her arms and leaned her head back against the bulkhead, the lights from her helm casting deep shadows across her features.

"I can stay here with her," Hinata said softly.

Rohaan shook his head, taking a step closer to where Skyla sat on the floor. "If you don't come and see the city, you will regret it for the rest of your life. This is the culmination of your father's life's work. The last thing you will get to share with him. I don't want you to miss it. He wouldn't have wanted you to miss it."

Hinata stiffened at Rohaan's words. "What?"

Rohaan squared his shoulders, his glance passing from Skyla to Hinata as if they were children in a spat. "Her father died here. *This,*" Rohaan gestured toward the sunken city. "His research. This is what she has left of him."

Hinata's hand twitched at his side as he resisted the urge to reach out and touch her. He ached to hold her, to take away her pain, to make everything right in her universe—and then it hit him. The realization of everything she hadn't told him.

She had lost her father. She had been trapped on this abandoned planet with his corpse. Alone. For all of those months…And she hadn't told him. She hadn't been able to tell him because he couldn't get over himself and let her in.

The muscle in his jaw feathered. He took a step closer and dropped down to kneel beside her. "If you want to stay, I will stay here with you. Whatever you need. The choice is yours." His voice caught in his throat as her tear-rimmed eyes finally looked up. "But I don't want you to have regrets."

Hinata thought of what he would do to feel close to his brother one last time. Two decades dead, there was so little left of Akio in this universe.

"These moments don't come often. If this is your last chance to feel close to your father, I don't want you to miss it," he whispered.

Skyla remained quiet for a long while, but her eyes never left his, and the heat of that stare lit a flame in him. Finally, she gave a tight nod.

Hinata rose to his feet before extending a hand to her. She hesitated only for a moment before she slipped her hand into his, allowing him to pull her to her feet. Even through the material of the dive suit, sparks radiated across his skin where they touched. He didn't want to let her go. But he gave her hand a tight squeeze, followed by a reassuring nod before he let go and turned to Rohaan.

"Well, Doctor, lead the way."

CHAPTER 36 | SKYLA

THE CRUSH

The dark edges of the city rose up in the water around them, silhouettes cast by the eerie glow of the trenches. They stepped out of the passageway into the large atrium.

"Look here." Rohaan slowly floated along the wall as he ran his fingers along a pattern etched in the white stone. "I think I know what this is. I saw something similar at the Eta site. I think they used bioluminescence for lighting...in fact..." Rohaan's artificial gravity brought him back to the ground, and he walked toward a large building on the other end of the atrium, his eyes glued to the wall, studying every centimeter.

"Ears, where are you going?" Skyla killed her own gravity to swim after him.

"If I am right, this next building should be a biotech hub. If it is still intact, we might even be able to power up the city."

Hinata jogged to catch up with them. "Is that such a good idea? We don't know what attracted that creature that attacked the pod."

"It wasn't light." Rohaan waved a lazy hand. "If they were attracted to light, they would be gorging on the creatures in the trenches. Here." Rohaan stopped in front of a once grand set of double doors.

"All right, Ears." Skyla landed next to Rohaan with her boots firmly planted. "You have my attention. What are you waiting for?"

"Well, normally I'm not allowed to go in first." There was a tinge of embarrassment in his tone.

"Let's go in together?" Skyla reached up to take one door handle in her hand. She paused, waiting for Rohaan to take the other. Hinata tensed behind them, ready to take the lead if something waited behind those doors.

Rohaan took the other handle. "Three, two, one."

They both threw their weight back, pulling hard against the doors and the resistance of the ocean. The doors grated against the stone floor as they opened into a pitch-black room.

Skyla stepped into the dark first, Rohaan following close behind, and finally Hinata strode through.

"Lights," Skyla commanded, and the full array of lights across her helm shot out into the dark.

"Are you sure?" Hinata asked.

"It's perfectly safe, Commander," Rohaan said before powering on his suit.

Reluctantly, Hinata's lights powered on behind her, the beams arching through the darkness in controlled patterns.

"Yes!" Rohaan paced quickly, windmilling his arms to speed his progress along a wall that was filled floor to ceiling with giant tubes. "It's almost identical! Over here." Rohaan rushed to the far wall, where he found what looked like an ancient control panel. "This." Rohaan wrapped his hand around a lever. "If the system is still intact, it will illuminate the city."

"Wait—" Hinata threw a hand out to stop the scientist, but Rohaan had already lowered the lever. Nothing happened.

"Hmm...too bad. Their algae cultures must not have been able to survive the cold down here," Rohaan mused.

"Dr. Dar." Hinata's words were steady as always, but they held the weight of his anger. "I will respectfully ask you not to initiate any Old World Tech that we don't understand while we are on this rescue mission."

Rohaan's gaze dropped to the floor as he shuffled his boots along the stone surface. "Of course, Commander. My apologies. I let my excitement get the better of me."

Skyla smiled at the interaction, but then Hinata nodded and turned to catch her observing him. Her cheeks heated at the way he looked at her. He blinked slowly, and she knew she should break their heated stare, but she couldn't look away.

Were her eyes playing tricks on her? She could have sworn his skin glowed softly. Between his ethereal appearance and the way he looked at her now, she was certain he had never been more beautiful.

"Oh! The cultures didn't die after all! They are just slowly metabolizing the nutrients we released because it is so cold down here! Fascinating!" Rohaan rushed to the wall beside Skyla where the intricate designs softly came to life, with the pale blue glow of bioluminescent algae. All around them, the walls took on a soft glow, not unlike the trenches cut into the ocean floor beyond these walls.

In the dim light, Skyla could now make out the rough shape of the room; it was crowded with large tubes, just like the ones near them.

"What was this place?" she whispered.

"It's their biotech hub!" Rohaan responded a little too loudly as he extended cables from his wrist unit to insert into the control panel beside him. "This is where they housed and grew all of the biological tech they used to settle this planet."

"Why would anyone choose to settle here?" Skyla's legs weakened as she flashed back to those moments that were almost her last when she lay nearly frozen to death in this wasteland.

"I have a hypothesis, but I'd like to get to their central hub first, see if we can get some more data." Rohaan snapped his cables back in place, then motioned for them to follow. "This way. According to the system schematics, the hub is just on the other side of the atrium."

Skyla froze as she stepped back into the atrium. What had once been looming, black towers in the gloom, were now softly illuminated walls, intricately carved and glowing with an otherworldly light that made this place feel sacred.

Skyla's throat grew thick as she took in the outlines of buildings and the tops of turquoise, domed roofs stretching out in all directions. What would her father have thought of this? Pain radiated through her sternum, as if a fist had closed around her heart, knowing that he would never see it. It was beautiful, even in its current state. Would it have lived up to his expectations...would she?

Hinata's hand brushed the edge of her own as he stepped to her side, breaking her trance.

"It's truly magnificent," Skyla said in awe.

"It is." Hinata echoed her statement, but when she turned to look at him, his gaze was focused only on her. She let her eyes linger on him a moment before she nodded and hurried to catch up with Rohaan, who was already halfway across the vast atrium.

Once they reached the opposite side, they came across another set of ornate doors. This time, there was no hesitation as they pulled them open. The command hub was already softly lit with the algae Rohaan had released into the city.

"Perfect!" Rohaan rushed over to a large circular console in the center of the room. He wasted no time connecting to the main system. While Skyla knew he would download most of the data to analyze later, Rohaan pulled up holos in the center of the circular display for them to watch as the time passed.

The first image was a rendering of the city in all its glory. The paradise was so different from the frozen wasteland it was now. It was an enormous city that stretched along the edge of an azure sea, all glittering limestone and turquoise-topped domes, nestled between pale sand beaches and verdant green foliage.

Little ships of an unfamiliar design, similar to their land skimmers, flew to and from the city. Time passed in quick succession as the daily activities of the city unfolded in a matter of seconds. Then the display zoomed in on a launch.

A wide rocket took off from Thule, and the holo zoomed out to follow its trajectory into space. It traveled to the edge of their solar system, then deployed a device. The space in front of the rocket warped and rippled, the very fabric of space-time unraveling and reforming into a wormhole. The ship passed through the wormhole to reappear in an unfamiliar solar system. It passed a swirling, blue orb, rimmed by a faint vertical ring, then a deeper blue orb, followed by a yellow one with thick horizontal rings that stretched out into space. Next was the largest of all; the orb was a kaleidoscopic of yellows, blues, and oranges, with an angry red storm that raged around its equator.

Where in the universe was this place? Why was it important enough for the space it took in the archives? They passed a small, red, rocky body, and then Skyla's heart stopped as they approached a blue and green orb, shrouded in wisps of white. The unsettling feeling of déjà vu washed over her as she recognized the planet she had only ever seen once before.

This was the planet that she had traveled home to in her near-death hallucination when she had been left to die in the void of space all of those years ago.

"That's not possible," Skyla whispered.

"What is it?" Hinata asked.

"Ears, what is this?"

Rohaan waved her off, his eyes focused on the archives in his ocular display.

Skyla stepped close enough to the image for the tips of her gloves to pass through the pixels.

Simulation Ended.

The words replaced the holo. It took Skyla a moment to understand that it hadn't been a recording; it was a simulation, but why? What was so important about that planet? Skyla's thoughts were interrupted by the next image on the holo.

A large bird materialized on the screen, unlike any bird she had seen on her adventures, yet its form was familiar. It was all hard lines and planes, nothing about it felt organic. As the creature shifted its wings, its colors shifted from the soft yellows and reds of sandstone to those that rippled like an oil slick, with prominent pinks and purples settling around the edges of its crystal-like feathers.

The creature looked as if it was an amalgamation of electricity, light, and crystal. It was beautiful and alien, and a deep sense of foreboding settled over her as she watched the creature move in the holo.

"Is that..." Hinata whispered, more to himself than to her.

"It looks just like the bots that attacked us in deep space," Skyla finished for him.

"Yes, but also entirely different." Hinata stepped up to her side to better inspect the image.

"What are—"

A deep rumbling cut off Hinata's words.

"What was that?" Rohaan asked.

"I think it's time to go," Hinata answered as he moved to the door.

"I could use a little more time with the mainframe," Rohaan countered.

"Time's up, Doc. We have company." Hinata's eyes tracked the space above the atrium. Icy tendrils of fear snaked down Skyla's spine at the recognition of the shadows darting over the city. The surge of energy had called to the creatures of the dark.

"We need to get back to Pele now." The command in Skyla's voice was enough for Rohaan to break his link with the tech and fall in line, though he looked back longingly at the console. Skyla wanted answers, too, but it wasn't worth their lives. Whatever he had gotten would have to be enough.

Regret held Skyla in place a moment longer as she looked one last time at the holo, which now displayed a vast array of star charts. This was her father's dream. A dream that she would have to leave to its frozen grave, forgotten beneath the ice, just as her father had been forgotten on this frozen world.

"Stick to my shadow and stay out of sight." Hinata's words brought Skyla's focus back to the moment. She swallowed the lump that formed in her throat and focused instead on the shadows above. There was a pattern to their movements. They were searching. She reached out, taking Rohaan's gloved hand and giving it a squeeze.

"Stay close," she said, then followed Hinata out the doors. The commander crouched low, moving slowly to stay tucked against the wall.

Skyla turned around just in time to catch Rohaan by the shoulder as he prepared to launch himself into the atrium. She shook her head, then pointed to Hinata before crouching down and mimicking the movement. They moved painfully slow. The creatures appeared to be attracted to vibrations. Best to keep any disturbance to a minimum.

They were halfway to the corridor that would lead back to Pele when a soft current washed across Skyla's suit as Rohaan stumbled forward.

"Sorry," he mumbled, the tenor of his voice trembling.

The shadows above froze. Skyla's heart thundered in her ears.

Time slowed to an agonizing crawl as she willed the creatures to move, to go back to their search patterns. Finally, one shadow darted at another, crashing into the massive form. The aggressive move sent the rest into a frenzy as they collided with one another.

"Move," Hinata hissed through the comms. This time, he lessened the gravity in his boots and dove forward, using his arms to slice through the water.

A terrible crack sounded as a tangling pair of shadows slammed through the roof of the atrium. The force knocked Skyla into the wall. Her shoulder ached, and her head buzzed. Her body floated up aimlessly until a tight grip around her chest anchored her in place. She thrashed against the creature as panic set in. A vision of the sky turning to water as a tentacle ripped her under the ice flashed in her mind, and a scream crept up her throat—

"Captain," Hinata whispered through the comms, and his voice brought the world back into focus. He held her tight as he crouched near the wall, his boots fully engaged to anchor them in place. His focus was on the dark behemoths that tussled in the center of the atrium. Rohaan crouched low at her side, his eyes blown wide and visible tremors running through his gloves.

No one dared move as the creatures tore into each other. They were each the size of a large shuttle, with long tails that tapered before jutting out into a propeller shape that looked sharp enough to cut. Their bodies had matching, blade-like appendages, three on each side, and their heads narrowed into gaping maws, filled with rows upon rows of sharp, elongated teeth. Their thick hides were so dark they appeared to swallow the soft light of the atrium, still appearing as shadows, clashing in the center of the room.

The larger of the beasts whipped its tail around, the force of the movement traveling through the water as the blades at its tip sliced a trail along its opponent. Thick, dark blood oozed from the wound, clouding the water and turning it murky. The smaller beast retaliated, slamming its head into its opponent and driving the pair closer to where Skyla, Hinata, and Rohaan had hunkered down.

"Move," Hinata shouted over the comms. He released Skyla, shoving her forward. Skyla stumbled into an awkward combination of swimming and pushing against the stone floor. She hadn't made it far when she glanced over her shoulder to find Rohaan still frozen in place. Hinata grabbed Rohaan by the arm, trying to break the hold that fear had taken on the scientist, but Rohaan's eyes were locked on the creatures.

"Ears!" Skyla screamed over the comms. He gave no sign of recognition. She turned to swim back to the men.

"For once in your goddamn life, can you follow my orders?" Hinata growled through the comms. "I've got him. Get to the ship."

In one swift movement, Hinata grabbed Rohaan in a cross hold and threw his weight back. Hinata pushed off the floor and kicked toward her, towing Rohaan with him. A sharp fin slammed into the wall where they had been moments before.

Seeing that Hinata had Rohaan firmly in his grip, Skyla turned, heading once again for the corridor. She pulled herself through the water, kicking off the ground with as much force as she could muster with every bound. She was nearly there when she chanced a glance behind her. Rohaan now swam on his own and was close on her heels, but where was Hinata? The water was a blur of beast and blood and murky water so thick she couldn't make out his form in the churn.

"Where is Hinata?"

"I...I...I..." Rohaan stuttered, shaking his head from side to side.

Skyla twisted to grip Rohaan by the shoulder. "Get to the pod, now!" Skyla yelled at him before dashing back into the mayhem.

"Skyla!" Rohaan called through the comms, but she didn't answer. She had a singular focus; Hinata may not be hers, but the beasts couldn't have him either.

She dove for the ground as a fin came careening through the murk. The power of the movement rippled against her as it passed just above, the force washing her back several meters before she was able to regain her orientation. Again, she charged forward. She had to find him.

"Hinata?" she yelled into the comms, but there was no answer. She kicked so hard her quads burned, and each breath was a starved gasp, begging for more oxygen. She swam low to the ground as she worked her way back toward the wall. The water was so thick with black blood that Skyla couldn't see further than the distance to her gloves. Fear sharpened her senses. She wouldn't see an attack coming through this. Would she be able to find Hinata in the darkness?

Feeling along the ground, she inched forward, fearing her efforts were futile but unwilling to give up. Her hand snagged on a jumble of rocks, chunks of the wall that seeped blue, glowing algae into the water as the bioluminescent carvings faded from its surface. There among the rubble was a dive suit.

"No, no, no," Skyla muttered to herself as her panicked fingers removed rocks from on top of the suit. She brushed away debris from his waist. His suit was in one piece. A large boulder pinned down his right shoulder, obscuring half of his chest. Skyla pulled at the boulder, but it didn't budge.

"No," Skyla said firmly to herself. "I am not leaving you here." She repositioned, wedging her back under the boulder. A desperate scream raked across her throat as she pushed with all of her strength, her legs threatening to give out, then a surge of adrenaline flooded her veins. Finally, the boulder shifted and fell to the side.

Skyla searched the suit in a frenzy, only stilling when she was certain that it was intact. She worked her way up to his faceplate. Her fingers trembled as she lifted a large rock from his helmet, her insides twisting at what she would see underneath.

Cracks spider-webbed across the surface, distorting his face with speckled red lines, but it was intact, barely. A rush of water threw her back from Hinata's prone form and brought the world into sharp focus as she remembered they were not out of danger yet. She had to get him back to the ship, *now.* That suit couldn't take any more damage, and at this depth, even a small puncture would mean death.

Skyla looped her arms through Hinata's armpits to clasp her hands at his chest, then hauled him toward the corridor, scanning the water overhead as she went. It was too dark to make out their forms, but the water around her shifted as the shadows danced in the murk above.

The repercussions of their fight overhead threw her to the ground, once, twice, three times. Each time, she tightened her grip on Hinata and moved them a step closer to safety. Finally, she threw herself backward, and they tumbled into the dark corridor as a thick tail slammed into the doorway behind them. The frame cracked, then collapsed.

Skyla's breaths came in quick waves as she fought to regain control. If she had been a second slower, they would have been trapped in the atrium with those things, with no way back to Pele. Skyla tightened her grip on Hinata, the responsibility of getting him back to the ship her only focus. They might be safe from those monsters for now, but this was far from over.

Her movements were awkward as she used a combination of kicking and bouncing off the floor to drag Hinata back to the pod.

"I am the blaze in the flame.

I am the calm in the storm.

I am the force behind the machine.

The choice is mine.

Fear has no power over me."

The mantra matched the pounding of her heart. Her voice wavering, the litany poured from her lips. If only she could will it to be true. She was so focused on her task that she didn't notice she had rounded the corner into the storeroom.

"Skyla, let go. We've got him." Freyja's voice came through her comms. It was only then that she registered Freyja at her side, her hands clasped tightly around Hinata's shoulders while Rohaan had taken his feet.

Skyla fought the instinct to clutch Hinata closer, slowly loosening her fingers. As soon as she did, Freyja and Rohaan were moving. They were through the shimmering force field of the dive module and out of sight before she could move.

"Come on, Karsten." Tristan looped an arm under her shoulders to help her to the pod. Normally she would rather crawl than let Tristan help her, but as she limped forward, the adrenaline fading from her bloodstream, leaching away her panicked strength and replacing it with the pain of her battered body, she was grateful for the support, as much as she hated to admit it.

"It's going to be okay. We finished Pele's engines. We're all getting out of here." Tristan's voice was surprisingly sincere, and Skyla wondered for the first time about the man behind the pompous remarks. Maybe there was a good man in there after all, though she got the distinct feeling that it was a side of himself that he did a very good job of hiding.

Overwhelm froze Skyla in place as they passed through the force field into the pod. Rohaan worked at the controls, where he had dual trajectories pulled up on the screen, one for the pod and another for Pele. Kylian rubbed at his ribs with a grimace before shifting next to Freyja, who worked furiously over Hinata.

With his suit stripped down to the waist, the material beneath cut away, the pulverized flesh that had once been his shoulder was on full display. Dark, angry bruises blossomed across his pale skin. The rise and fall of his breath was so shallow, she nearly missed it; her ocular display pulled up the medical readout. Skyla wanted to look away as all of his systems flashed red.

Collapsed lung.

Punctured lung.

Broken: ribs, humerus, scapula, clavicle.

Rhabdomyolysis.

Organ failure: imminent.

"Crush injury, it had to be a crush injury," Freyja muttered as she opened up nanite bandage after nanite bandage, slapping them over the mess that had once been Hinata's shoulder. Kylian pulled an injector from the med kit and added medical nanites to Hinata's bloodstream, but all systems remained red.

"We need to get him to a regen pod. The nanites will buy us time, but…"

Tristan muttered obscenities under his breath as he helped Skyla over to sit beside Hinata.

"What are you waiting for?" Skyla demanded.

"It's not that simple," Kylian said.

"What do you mean? He's going to die if we can't get to a regen pod. It's crystal! Get us out of here!" Skyla yelled.

Rohaan cleared his throat. "Pele isn't ready."

Skyla's heart sank. "Give it to me quick." Skyla's voice dropped to a whisper, "I am not losing him."

"She still needs twenty minutes before she has enough power to ascend to the surface."

"What are you not saying, Ears?"

"She can't navigate to the surface on her own, and we don't have a strong enough signal to guide her from the surface—" Ear's voice dropped to a whisper. "—and the pod was damaged by the blast; we won't be able to attempt another dive unless we can repair it." Though he didn't say it out loud, Skyla heard his meaning—*if* they could repair it...and then there were the storms. They were out of time and out of options.

Skyla came to her feet and secured her dive helmet once again. "That is not a problem. I am not choosing between the two of them. I'll stay with Pele and guide her up. You get Hinata to the *Takarabune*."

Kylian shook his head. "There's more. She will only have one good engine...and she can't fit back out of the hole she crashed through. We set up charges to open up the roof, but when we overpowered her engine, we must have accidentally set one off. The explosion attracted those things. The hole still isn't large enough for Pele, and if you blast your way out, you are going to have to fight your way to the surface."

"Are her weapons operational?"

"I don't know." Tristan glared at his cousin. "We didn't get that far before this idiot tried to blow himself up."

"If you had uploaded that software patch like I had asked you to, then the energy flow between the power cell and the engine would have been properly regulated, and there would have been no explosion," Kylian said.

"I was a little busy fixing the ship!" Tristan yelled.

"Enough! I'll figure it out. Save him." Skyla raked her eyes over Hinata's broken body one last time before she moved to the back of the pod.

"Skyla," Rohaan's eyes pleaded with her not to go. "If this doesn't work, if you can't get Pele to the surface…"

Skyla set her jaw and nodded. "Then I go down with my ship."

Rohaan moved to the back of the pod to grasp Skyla's forearm.

"You don't have to do this," he whispered.

"Yes, I do."

Rohaan hesitated only a moment before nodding. "Be careful out there."

Skyla brought Rohaan close. "Don't let him die." Then she let go and limped through the force field.

Skyla shuffled inside Pele's cargo bay and turned to watch the dive pod disappear through the hole in the ceiling. Relief tempered her anxiety. They would get Hinata to the *Takarabune*. He would live. The uncertainty threatened to drown her, but she had to believe that he would make it. There was no other possibility, even to entertain the thought of it would break her. No, she needed all of her focus here, on getting Pele to the surface.

Skyla ran a gloved palm along the bulkhead as she walked down Pele's corridor. "We've been through worse. We will get through this, I promise."

Worse than being trapped at the bottom of a frozen ocean, surrounded by creatures strong enough to pierce aerogeluim plating? Skyla imagined

Pele's quippy reply, the thought of actually being able to talk to Pele again bringing fresh tears to her eyes.

"Keep it together, Karsten," Skyla muttered to herself as she made her way to the engine room.

Kylian hadn't lied. The engine room was a mess. Pockmarks marred the far wall, damage from the recent explosion. Skyla checked the stats. It would only be enough to help with navigation. Next, she moved on to the twin-engine on the other side of the room, which was slowly absorbing energy from the portable cell. Nineteen minutes left on the transfer.

"Alright, nineteen minutes to make sure we have something that can shoot at those monsters." Skyla split her time between the cannons on either side of the ship. Finally, a bit of good luck on her side: she found the mechanisms intact. She just needed a way to control them. It took a solid five minutes of hacking to sync the weapons with her neural chip, but she would have control, as long as she could relay a signal. A repeater set up at the midway point between the weapons and the bridge should do the trick.

With her work finished, Skyla settled into her captain's chair on the bridge. Her fingers idly traced the panel where the neural link cables were housed. She ached to connect with Pele. The bridge was deathly quiet, and Skyla had never felt so alone.

Pulling up the status of the energy transfer in her ocular display, Skyla was relieved to find they were nearly ready. She cycled over to her weapons controls, now that she had connected them to the rest of the semi-functional system. Skyla frowned at the display. There was barely enough power to get Pele to the *Takarabune*. No reserves, which meant she only had three shots with the plasma cannons, max, before she risked losing power before breaking atmo.

"Damn it." They had come prepared for a rescue mission on the ocean floor, not a hostile attack from oversized alien creatures while navigating a sunken city. Skyla blew out a heavy breath as she ran her gloved palms over the console.

"We are going to make it out of here, you hear me?" Skyla paused. "I don't care what Ears says, I know you can hear me." Then her voice dropped to a whisper. "Any help you can send me is appreciated. We are going to need more than a little bit of luck."

Skyla checked her controls one last time. The energy transfer was complete, and the weapons were operational, or as operational as they were going to get. Finally, she pulled up the trajectory for their ascent.

"I guess the only thing left to do is go." Skyla triggered the charges that lined the opening in the roof. The walls crumbled away, leaving just enough room for Pele to rise through the opening. Nerves on edge, Skyla scanned the murky water for the dark shadows she feared the explosion would summon.

They had just risen above the city when the first shadow darted past, so massive that its wake caused Pele to wobble and waver from her trajectory. Skyla fought to correct their course with the barely functioning engine. She didn't want to feed it too much power and burn it out entirely.

Another shadow darted out of the gloom, washing Pele to the other side. Two more joined the growing frenzy, darting around the ship in semi-circles. None were bold enough to attack her, yet.

"Come on, come on, come on." Sweat clung to Skyla's brow beneath her helmet as she fought to keep control of Pele's course. The effort of moving a ship filled with water through the ocean on minimal power caused her to grind her teeth together. Their movements were slow and clumsy. The missing neural link and second consciousness weighed heavily on Skyla.

A shadow broke from its circling, growing bold enough to take a swipe at Pele's wing with its nasty teeth. Skyla rocked in her seat, swearing loudly at the beast, though it couldn't hear her.

The creature came in for a second pass. Skyla wasn't sure how much damage Pele could sustain in this state and still be spaceworthy. She had to take the shot.

The plasma cannon took mere moments to power up, and she fired. The superheated plasma tore through the shadow, leaving nothing but dark, murky water saturated with oily, black blood.

Skyla hoped that would be enough to deter another attack. The shadows went into a frenzy around the carnage, snapping and tearing at one another as they fought for a taste of scorched flesh.

"Please, please, please, just a little further," Skyla muttered as the water above her shifted in color, the weak sun peeking through the ice sheet above. Skyla took aim with the plasma cannon and blasted a hole through the ice. Pele breached the surface. Immediately, the cabin was filled with the loud whir of mechanics as the pumps Kylian installed to empty Pele of water before lift-off picked up. The water on the bridge now only came up to her waist. A few more minutes and they could launch. Hope swelled in her as she took in the wide, open sky. They were going to make it.

Something massive slammed into the bottom of the ship, sending Skyla careening into the console in front of her. She reoriented the cameras to find that the shadows from the deep had followed her to the surface. Skyla checked her power reserves. She had enough energy to fire off another round, but it wouldn't leave her any reserve for the launch.

A large tail raked across the bottom of Pele's hull. She didn't have a choice. Skyla took aim and fired. The plasma round ripped through the creature, and Skyla didn't waste another moment. The pumps worked hard to overcome the water coming in through the freshly torn hole in the hull, and she could see more shadows approaching, attracted by the scent of blood. They had to go, now!

Skyla pushed Pele's engines to their max capacity. The sudden surge of power threw her back into her captain's chair, where she fumbled with the crash harness before taking the controls. Pele rocketed into the sky, the ice plating of the ocean already blurring into one continuous sheet of white beneath them. The surrounding struts whined from the pressure, and the engines strained against the extra weight of the water that she hadn't had time to evacuate before launch.

The power cells drained at an alarming rate.

"We aren't going to make it...think, think, think." She needed to offload weight, fast, if they had any chance of breaking atmosphere.

Skyla tipped the ship until she was nearly vertical then opened the cargo bay. The change was almost instantaneous as hundreds of cubic meters of water streamed out the back of the ship behind her. She tried not to think about what else she had lost from the cargo bay with that maneuver. Instead, she focused on the trajectory lines that now glowed green as they guided her out of the atmosphere and in line with the *Takarabune*.

Manic laughter filled her helmet as tears of joy streamed down her cheeks.

"I won," she shouted back at the planet. "You tried to take Fenrir, you tried to take me, and you tried to take Pele, but you can't have us. I beat you," she screamed at the ice planet. "I beat you."

The joy leached from her voice as she thought of the life that still hung in the balance, the man that Thule still might claim. "You can't have him," she whispered, though she knew the choice wasn't hers to make.

CHAPTER 37 | FREYJA

GRAVITY

"**I** need an emergency med crew on deck when we land," Freyja called through the comms, her eyes dropping to Hinata, who had gone deathly still. All of the color had leached from his face behind the oxygen mask, and dark blood pooled in his chest, bruising his skin an angry shade of purple.

He began to convulse as he made a sick, sucking, sputtering sound with each breath. His body struggled to take in oxygen as his functioning lung filled with blood. He was drowning from within. She had applied every medical nanite they had to the crush site. The nanites were already working overtime to keep his organs from shutting down. There was too much damage and too few bots.

"Have a regen tank ready." She sent the next transmission.

"This is Lieutenant Commander Sato."

Tristan went stock still beside Freyja.

"I need to hear from Commander Azai."

"Open the bay doors and get me that regen tank if you ever want to speak to Commander Azai again," Freyja snarled.

The comm line went silent for several moments. Freyja's temper flared as the *Takarabune* grew in the viewport, but the bay doors remained closed.

"Cleared for berth, alpha-5," the lieutenant commander finally said, and though he tried to hide it, Freyja caught the emotion in his voice.

"Hurry it up!" Freyja yelled at Kylian, having already burned through what little patience she had.

"Unless you want me to crash this shuttle into the berth, this is as fast as we can land, Admiral," Kylian voiced in his perfect standard.

Damn it. Though he had always sounded like that while he was under her command, she had grown fond of his Merc accent, which he tended to slip into more often than not lately. His transition back to the good soldier hurt; the fact that it was her fault hurt more.

She knew she shouldn't lose her temper with him, just as she knew she didn't have the patience to do better right now. Saving Commander Azai's life was her focus; anything else she could fix later, but Hinata was running out of time. She snorted at the irony. Who would have thought she would hold Commander Azai's life in her hands, and with that power, she would fight to save him?

A gentle rumble signaled their landing, and she immediately activated the suspensors on the gurney beneath Hinata, rushing down the shuttle ramp before it had a chance to hit the deck.

"Where is my regen tank?" she roared.

"We can take it from here, Admiral." Dr. Pinot stood at the head of a swarm of medics as they descended on the gurney. Deft hands moved across the commander's body, attaching wires and removing the patches she had haphazardly slapped all over his skin.

They administered medications, then transferred Hinata's limp form from the gurney into the egg-shaped regen pod. Hinata's crushed shoulder hung awkwardly as they moved him, and Freyja fought the wave of nausea that the sight incurred. It was less than a minute since they had landed, and the pod slid closed around the commander. Soft hex lights illuminated around the pod as Dr. Pinot programmed the machine.

Freyja took a step closer. "What's the verdict, Doc?"

Dr. Pinot shook her head. "You gave him the best shot he's going to get. The nanites can repair him, but the damage is extensive. He's going to have to want to stick around long enough for them to do their job."

Freyja ran a hand over the pod. "You are the most stubborn bastard I've ever met." She hissed, "If someone is going to give death a run for his money, I'd put my bet on you." She then leaned in closer to whisper, "Don't you dare give up."

Balling her hand into a fist, she bumped it against the side of the pod. The medics navigated the regen pod off to medical, and Freyja was left alone on the dock with her crew.

Moments after the commotion of the medics' exit, a cadre of officers entered. Lieutenant Commander Sato stormed over to Freyja and the rescue crew, flanked by two officers Freyja didn't recognize.

"What did you do?" His voice was controlled, but danger hung on the edges—so much like Hinata, but Tax didn't have the same edge as his commander.

"You better check yourself, Sato, before I put you in your place." Freyja crossed her arms as she widened her stance. She felt Kylian and Tristan move up behind her.

"My commander is dying in a regen tank right now. What happened?" Tax gritted out from behind clenched teeth.

Tristan took a step forward but froze in place at the icy stare Tax gave him.

Freyja let the malice drop from her voice. "It was just supposed to be a rescue mission. We weren't ready for what was down there." She let her arms fall to her sides. "Let's just say the indigenous species are far from friendly. Commander Azai got the worst of it, but the regen tank—"

"The doctor says he won't make it through the night."

Freyja shook her head. "He'll make it. Now, if you will clear my ship, we left a member of our crew on planet."

Tax's gaze swept across the crew for the first time since entering. He shook his head. "You are confined to quarters until I can verify your story."

"Don't make me pull rank on you."

"We succeeded. There is no pulling rank, *Admiral*. I am not in your Navy, and you hold no rank here."

"Have you figured out who is missing yet?" Freyja let a sneer twist her lips. "If he wakes up and finds out that you left her on that planet, what do you think he's going to do?"

Tax looked over the crew once more. Fear and indecision held his tongue.

"Listen, he's going to pull through, and when he does, Skyla is going to be on this ship." Freyja stepped forward and clasped the man by the shoulder. The gesture appeared comforting, but the pressure she pushed through her fingertips was a warning. "Now, clear my ship."

"Fine." Tax shouldered out of her grip and stormed off the deck.

"Get Selkie ready, and let's go get our girl." Freyja didn't wait for a response as she led the way to her ship.

Rohaan ran to catch up. "Freyja, we won't have time to make another dive. If she didn't make it up on her own..."

"That girl's a survivor, Rohaan. She made it up."

"We have a ship exiting the atmosphere." Tax's message came through the comms.

Freyja threw an arm around Rohaan. "See! I told you!"

"It appears that the ship has lost power and is in an unstable, low orbit around Thule." Tax's next comm came through.

"How much time before gravity brings her down?" Freyja asked.

"Minutes."

"Let's move," Freyja shouted.

Selkie was ready for them, and they exited the *Takarabune* mere moments later.

"Selkie, take us into a synchronous orbit with Pele."

"Her trajectory is unstable."

"Just get us close."

"And then what?"

Selkie was a warship; she was loaded with armaments but nothing that would allow them to tow Pele to the *Takarabune*....there had to be something; she just had to think.

Freyja's gut twisted as she realized what she was about to ask Skyla to do. "Just get us close enough to catch her when she ejects and get Skyla on comms."

Thule quickly grew to fill the viewport as Selkie approached the planet. Pele appeared as a blemish against the bright white planet, her hull dark and damaged, her trajectory wobbling as gravity threatened to pull her back down.

"Gravity always wins," Freyja muttered, her skin boiled. She couldn't accept that there was nothing she could do. She hated this helpless feeling; she hated giving in.

"Skyla," Freyja sent through the comms.

"I never thought I would be so happy to hear your voice!" Skyla's response came through immediately.

The relief Freyja felt turned quickly to guilt at what she was about to ask Skyla to do. "Skyla, I need you to trust me."

There was a long pause. "What is it?"

"Pele's orbit is too low."

Silence.

"Skyla, do you understand what I am saying? She is going to crash...and there's nothing we can do to stop it."

"No."

"Skyla—"

"No, I don't accept that! She is leaving Thule."

"I wish there was something we could do, but there isn't. I need you to get your ass out the cargo bay so we can pick you up."

"I am not leaving her."

"Skyla."

"I meant what I said. If Pele goes down, then I am going down with her. I am not leaving her." Skyla cut the comms.

Freyja slammed a fist into the console. "Damn it!"

CHAPTER 38 | SKYLA

GOODBYE

Adrenaline buzzed through Skyla's veins. The rush soured her stomach and set her hands to shaking.

Think. Think. Think.

She meant what she had said. She wouldn't leave Pele. Not again. The survival rate for pilots that lost their ships was better than that of ships that lost their pilots, but Skyla was done running. They would both come through this, or neither of them would.

"We are doing this together," Skyla forced through gritted teeth as she initiated a manual upload of Pele's consciousness. "We are not going out without a goodbye."

A high-pitched screech tore through the haul. Skyla's palms clasped her ears as the sound threatened to shatter her eardrums along with her heart. Slowly, the sound eased until the bridge went silent.

"*Skyla?*" Pele's voice was tentative, scared.

Emotion threatened to choke her, but still Skyla managed to whisper, "I'm here, Pele." Tears streamed down Skyla's face, blurring the controls in front of her. "I'm here." A soft smile stretched across Skyla's lips as she sucked in a deep breath. Reigning in her emotions, she focused on opening the control box and initiating the link with Pele.

Two processors, one mind.

If they had any hope of coming through this, they would do it together.

"Skyla," Pele's voice was steady now. "I don't feel right...I don't feel anything."

Skyla choked back a sob. "I know. I'm so sorry. I'm so sorry. We'll get you all fixed up, I promise. But right now, I need your help if we are going to get out of this alive." Skyla grunted as she finally levered open the panel that concealed the neural link cables.

The cables, which normally shone gold and danced like live wires up her skin, sat pale and limp in the console.

First, Skyla removed her helmet and gloves, then the top half of her suit. Goosebumps raced across her flesh; whether from the thin freezing air or the fear that the fragile repairs that kept her from the vacuum of space wouldn't hold, she wasn't sure.

Skyla removed the cables from their housing, then carefully unwrapped the delicate tendrils, prompting them to fuse with her flesh. At first, they wrapped around her fingertips with tendrils fragile as pea shoots, but once the first connection sunk into her skin, the cables grew brighter, more lively, until they shone with a brilliance beyond anything Skyla could remember as they twined around her shoulders and inserted into her neck.

The shock of the link knocked the air from Skyla's lungs. Panicked gasps left her feeling empty, because half of her body was gone.

"*Skyla.*" Pele's voice was a soothing balm in her mind. The only part of the link that felt right.

"*Pele.*" Skyla settled into the link. Remembering that Pele had lost function, Skyla grounded them both in her body.

Both minds settled now that they had a physical space to occupy.

"*I'm sorry,*" Skyla said.

"*It's disorienting,*" Pele responded.

Skyla shook her head. "*I'm sorry it took me so long to get to you.*"

Ice pressed in around Skyla's body, and her vision tunneled until she could barely see the controls in front of her. Her mouth filled with salt, and it took her only a moment to recognize that this was the last memory Pele had before she shut down.

As suddenly as the feeling came, it ended, replaced with a warmth that made Skyla's body tingle.

"*I always knew you would come,*" Pele said.

"*I will never leave you. Never again,*" Skyla sighed.

"*What is it? What are you not saying? I can feel it, you know.*"

"*We made it off the planet. But we used too much fuel, and if we can't find a solution, we are going to crash...again,*" Skyla said.

"*You had enough control to get us up here, right? Take us back down and give me time to take control of my systems—*"

Skyla shook her head. "*The planet is passing into some anomaly that is kicking up violent storms all over the planet. If we go back down...We aren't coming back up.*"

"Skyla, stop ignoring my comms!" Freyja's voice filled the bridge.

"Did you come up with a solution?" Skyla asked.

The comms quieted until finally, Freyja responded. "No, there is no solution where you both walk away, but she wouldn't want you to—"

"If you aren't going to help, then leave us alone and let me think." Skyla killed the comms.

"Skyla..."

Skyla could already feel the reprimand coming. There was no hiding their emotions when they were connected like this.

"Skyla, what are you not telling me?" Pele asked.

"Selkie is here...and a stardestroyer, and I don't accept that we can't figure our way out of this." The words tumbled out as fast as Skyla could think.

"And what does Freyja want you to do?" Pele sent a warm surge through the bond. She already knew. The comfort, the gentle words—she was preparing to tell Skyla to leave.

Skyla nodded toward her discarded helmet. *"The dive suit is more than enough to last in a vacuum. She wants me to abandon ship. But I won't. I won't do it again. I won't leave you. It is you and me until the end."* Skyla's thoughts rushed through the bond.

Warmth wrapped around Skyla. She was floating in an azure sea as the waves lapped against Pele's hull. *"I know what you are doing."* Tears threatened to drown her.

"I loved this world," Pele said.

"I did too." The thought was reverent in Skyla's mind.

"When this is done, go back there for both of us."

"No!" Skyla shouted. "I am not leaving you."

"Skyla, you once made me leave you. Do you remember?"

Nausea bubbled up in side her with the memory. Three days she had floated in space before she was rescued. Thought dead by her crew. Left for dead by her lover. It was the worst memory of her life.

"Of course I remember," Skyla whispered.

"You would not let me stay and fight."

"I had to save you. I had to save all of you," Skyla whispered.

"I know. That's why I listened. I knew you would never forgive me if the whole crew died to save you. But if it had been just you and me, I never would have left."

"I still would have sent you away."

"No, you wouldn't. The survival rate for unbonded ships is less than ten percent, and what kind of life is that anyway? To only be half of a whole? No, I would go down at your side any day."

Skyla smiled through her tears. *"Then we are agreed."*

"No."

"But you just said—"

"I said that ships are not meant to live without their hosts. It does not go both ways. The survival rate for pilots is inverse at over ninety percent. You know this, Skyla."

"I don't care."

"Skyla, I have lived more than any AI I have ever met. I have adventured across the galaxy, seen countless worlds, and shared my life with the most amazing human. I have loved, and I have lived, and if it is my time, then I will return to The Great Consciousness with nothing but pure joy to share with the collective. But you, Skyla. You are not done, and I will not let you give up."

Skyla wrapped her arms around herself and gave into the sorrow that threatened to drown her. Wracking sobs ripped through her body. "I can't—"

"You can."

Skyla peered up through tear-lined lashes at the sound of Pele's voice coming through the speakers.

"Skyla." Pele gently flicked her lights. They were dim, but there.

Skyla's eyes went wide. "How much control do you have?"

The dim lights went dark. "Not enough. Now get your suit on. It's time to say goodbye."

Skyla shook her head. "You always were bossy, you know that?"

Freyja's voice came through the comms. "If you're ready to stop acting like a martyr, then I might have a solution…It's risky though."

"How risky?" Pele asked.

"Pele!" A heavy exhale followed Freyja's words. "I wasn't expecting—it's good to hear your voice again."

"How risky, Nygaard?" Pele asked again.

Another forced breath came through the line. "It's fifty-fifty."

"Fifty-fifty what?" Skyla asked.

"Fifty percent chance it works, and we all go home heroes," Freyja said.

"And the other fifty percent?" Skyla asked.

"You know, the other fifty percent ends with all of us dying a fiery death," Freyja said nonchalantly.

"No, I am not putting anyone else in danger. If it's something Pele and I can do on our own, then we will risk it, but—"

"Just shut up and listen, Karsten. No one is leaving your ass. We all go home or none of us. Now, can you bring Pele's nose up and stabilize her trajectory?"

"I can try. What did you have in mind?" Skyla asked.

"We are going to link the ships. But we only have one shot, and time is almost up. Are you ready?" Freyja asked.

"As I will ever be." Skyla straightened in the captain's chair, taking the manual controls into her hands. Pele was slowly taking control of the systems that were still intact, but she didn't have enough control to pilot the ship yet.

Skyla strained against the yoke. Slowly, she brought Pele's nose up. The shift in position sent turbulence through the cabin. Her teeth clacked together, and she tightened her jaw as she worked to stabilize their orbit. The bridge continued to rock under Skyla; her adjustments weren't enough.

"Can you even her out anymore?" Freyja asked. Skyla heard the worry in her friend's voice.

"I'm trying." Skyla grunted against the strain as the controls fought her every movement.

"Alright, looks like this is as good as it gets. Initiating the connection." Freyja gave the command.

The bridge pitched left, throwing Skyla from her seat. The neural link tore through her flesh.

Skyla snarled, struggling back into her seat. The golden tendrils traced over her torn flesh, smearing blood along her skin as it snaked back up over her arms.

Skyla clutched the yoke once again with white knuckles, fighting to keep them stable.

"Connection is at thirty percent." Freyja's update came over the comms.

Another violent rock threw Skyla once again to the ground. Pain seared through her nerves, and she couldn't stop the cry from escaping her throat as the cables ripped free once again.

"Skyla, you don't need the neural link to fly the ship," Pele said as Skyla once again slid into her seat and connected to her ship. With the link reestablished, worry flooded the bond.

"We are in this together. If we go down, we go down together. Now let me concentrate." Skyla took the controls and focused on the viewscreen.

"Connection is at twenty-five percent." Freyja gave the update.

"Weren't we just at thirty?" Skyla yelled.

"The turbulence, it's breaking the connections as fast as the tech can make them."

Skyla heard what Freyja wouldn't say: this wasn't going to work.

"Cut the connection," Skyla gave the command.

"You're not in charge here!" Freyja bit back.

"Freyja, my oldest friend—"

Pele's lights flicked in annoyance.

"You know what I mean," Skyla whispered to Pele before continuing. "I am grateful for all that you have done for me. You came for me when I left. You saved Pele when it put you and yours at risk...you saved me even when I had nothing but hate for you. I will miss you. But you can't come where I am going now. I'll save a seat for you at Odin's table. Now disconnect the link."

"What is that?" Freyja's comment didn't sound like it was meant for Skyla. "A ship. There's a ship approaching from the *Takarabune*."

Skyla squinted at her view port, but she couldn't see anything from her vantage point.

"I have spent an eternity with you, and it is not enough." A voice came through the comms. While she didn't recognize the voice, Skyla was overcome with emotions, longing and love and joy. Pele's lights flickered, and then Skyla heard a name, *Tentei*.

"I will not let you fall," Tentei's voice came through the comms. "Disengage your connection. Move to the coordinates I have sent, reengage, then we will push her out together."

"Who put you in charge?" This time Selkie responded.

"Do as he says, Selkie," Freyja prompted.

Without further argument, Selkie released her hold on Pele.

The bridge vibrated violently in response.

Tentei's voice came once again through the comms. "Three, two, one."

Skyla clutched onto the arms of her captain's seat, crashing her eyes closed as she braced for the pain of another violent blow that never came. Instead, the vibrations dampened. She cocked one eye open, then the other.

"Well, I'll be damned," Freyja mumbled. "Connection at fifty percent and climbing. Fifty-five percent, sixty percent...sixty percent..."

Rohaan finally spoke up, "That's all we are going to get. She is too low in her orbit. We won't be able to further strengthen the connection unless we get her up and stabilized."

"And will it hold?" Freyja asked.

"With two connection points at sixty percent, I'd put our odds of success at roughly seventy-three—"

"Good enough, Doc," Freyja interrupted. "Let's do this."

As if Selkie and Tentei shared their own connection, the two ships lifted in unison.

The support structures ground under Pele, and Skyla held her breath.

This was it. This would work. Or they would fall.

Slowly, the bridge settled under Skyla. The steady rumblings faded to a constant vibration that faded to a strange lack of motion that left Skyla numb.

Skyla bit her lip. The sound of her breath and the loud thump of her heart was all she heard.

"That's how it's done!" Freyja yelled.

Skyla closed her eyes and let out a soft chuckle. "That's how it's done."

"You could have crashed," Pele's voice came angry through the comms.

"And you would have," Tentei countered.

"That was not your decision to make. I am ready to transmit—"

"As am I. But I am not ready to live in a universe without you."

Pele went silent at Tentei's rebuke.

Tears Skyla could no longer hold back fell as the words hit home. If Tentei was alive, then *he* had made it. *He* was still here.

"I don't want to lose you," she whispered.

CHAPTER 39 | FREYJA

JUST A MEAL

It took the better part of an hour for the *Takarabune* to deploy shuttles to tow Pele into her own berth. By the time Freyja disembarked, she was sweaty and hungry and exhausted, but there was work to do.

"Kylian, get me Lieutenant Commander Sato's location," Freyja commanded as she stomped into the lift tube.

"I forgot something back on Selkie." Tristan turned and darted back to the docks.

The doors to the lift tube slid closed behind him, leaving Freyja alone with Kylian in the confined space. Freyja stood with her back to him, impatiently waiting for the lift doors to open. His gaze burned across her skin. She had known him for years, practically her whole life, so why did her skin now tingle under his gaze?

"Location. I need to know where to send the lift," she snapped.

"Freyja." Kylian's voice was soft as he took her shoulders, gently turning her to face him. "Hold lift," he gave the command to the computer system. "You need rest."

"There is no rest for people like us."

Kylian closed his eyes and inhaled deeply. "Nothing has to happen right now. We are in a safe orbit with plenty of supplies. The solar sails are collecting energy. We don't have to make a move tonight."

Freyja shook her head. "We don't have the luxury of time. Every moment we waste, the factions are tearing each other apart. People are dying. Now that we have Skyla and Pele, it's time to get to the bottom of the signal and end this."

Freyja fought back panic at what answers would mean. It was one thing to suspect her mother had made a play to tear the UTA apart. It was another to prove it. How would she take on the most powerful woman in the Known Galaxies? How would she face down the monster who created her?

Kylian lowered his forehead to rest against hers. Freyja's spiraling thoughts snapped at the treacherous flutter in her belly. That same resolve to keep him at a distance settled over her. She would keep him safe, even from her. But Freyja held her tongue. He was tired, they all were; she wouldn't break him by correcting his behavior, not now.

His voice came out soft as he ran his fingers along her jaw. "You have taken on the weight of the universe, but it is not your burden to bear alone." His touch making her shiver. "Let me lighten your load. Let me take care of you," he whispered.

Freyja tensed at his words. She couldn't let him in; she couldn't let anyone in. Caring for others was a weakness—a weakness her mother wouldn't hesitate to exploit. "I can't." She moved to pull away from him, but he slid his arms around her, holding her tight.

"So stubborn," he muttered. "I just want to feed you and put you to bed. Can you handle that?"

She relaxed slightly at the simple request. Her empty stomach rumbled, and her eyelids grew heavy as her weary body rebelled against her will.

"Fine," she growled, but she carefully wrapped her arms around his waist, relaxing against him. "I could use a good meal."

Kylian directed the lift tube back to the docks, where he sent Freyja off to shower and change before meeting him in the small ship galley.

The hot water scalded Freyja's skin. After the hours spent beneath the ice of the frozen wasteland, Freyja relished in its warmth. She tried to clear her mind, to center in the moment, but she couldn't keep her thoughts from wandering. What would happen if Hinata died? Tax had already shown that he wasn't inclined to submit to her command.

The bloody battle on the *Ormen Korte* flashed across her closed eyelids. She had lost so many of her soldiers to that ambitious piece of shit, Borg. She wasn't itching to battle for another ship, but this mission couldn't end with Commander Azai's death. If he died, she would have no choice but to assume command. Whether that be by negotiation or by the blade remained to be seen.

Freyja tried to push the thoughts from her mind as she dressed. Kylian was right. There was no move to make tonight. While Hinata fought for his life, she would rest, recoup, and plan. If he lost his battle, she would be ready.

All thoughts of commandeering the *Takarabune* flew from Freyja's mind as her eyes caught on Kylian working over the stove. He wore only a pair of black shorts, water droplets still drying on his muscular back. Freyja leaned against the door, enjoying the view too much to interrupt, a rare genuine smile pulling at the corners of her lips. The smell of peppers mingled with onions, garlic, and a combination of spices she couldn't identify.

Finally, her curiosity got the better of her. "What are you making?"

Kylian jumped and spun around. "Damn, Admiral, you gave me a scare."

"No more Admiral, remember?" She bumped her shoulder against his playfully as she stepped closer to watch Kylian stir fresh herbs into the thick sauce.

Kylian paused, his eyes gliding up to meet hers. He smiled. "Right, Freyja." He admired her for a moment more before turning his attention back to the stove.

"So, what are you making? The galley has never smelled this good!"

Kylian chuckled, "Étouffée."

Freyja scrunched up her nose. "What?"

"Étouffée, it's one of my favorite dishes. My mama always makes it for me when I'm home." He looked up at her with a conspiratorial grin. "Mine's better though, but don't tell her I said so."

"I didn't know you could cook. How come I didn't know you could cook?"

"I guess it never came up."

Kylian turned his attention to serving the meal. There was something he had left unsaid as he changed the subject. "Sit." He pointed a large serving spoon at the stainless steel table.

The delicious smells, combined with Freyja's exhaustion, kept her from arguing. It wasn't like Kylian to order her around, but when he slid a steaming bowl in front of her, accompanied by a glass of tequila, she decided maybe it was okay, just this once.

"To family." He raised his glass.

Freyja slowly raised her glass. The next line was usually Tristan's. Where was he? She cleared her throat. "To those bound by blood."

"And those forged in it." They said the line together.

The mood sobered as Freyja realized how many of her Berserkers were now gone. They had claimed the motto as their own at the academy. The alcohol burned on the way down. Freyja wasn't sure if the burning in her belly was from the tequila or the embers of her rage fanning at the reminder of who they fought for.

"Eat," Kylian prompted, snapping Freyja's mind back to the moment.

She took a bite; a moan escaped before she could stop herself.

"Good, huh?" Kylian smirked.

"My gods, good is an understatement," Freyja said between mouthfuls. "This has to be one of the best things I've ever tasted."

"I'm glad you like it." Kylian's eyes stayed on Freyja, studying her as she ate her meal.

"Now that I know you can cook, you're going to have to cook for me more often."

"I could be persuaded. If you think you could make room in your life for me."

Freyja choked on her tequila. "I've spent almost my entire life with you Kylian, how much more were you thinking?"

His face fell a little, his fingers drifting to the knot of metal that hung from the silver chain around his neck. Grasping the key in his palm, he quickly hid his disappointment behind a smile. "Of course, Admiral."

Guilt pressed in on her once again. Every time he reverted back to her title, it hurt a little more. No...she shut the thought down. *This is good; this boundary keeps him safe.*

They finished their meal in silence, and it wasn't until Kylian moved to clear the empty plates that she spoke again.

"I think we are going to have to take the *Takarabune* from Sato. At least I think we should be prepared—"

Kylian pulled Freyja to her feet and gently pushed her toward the doorway. "Dinner, then bed."

"Kylian, this is important. I think—"

"I think the deal was dinner, then bed." He gently nudged her down the corridor toward her quarters, only pausing once her doors sprung open before them. Freyja whirled around to face him.

Damn, he was handsome. The soft night cycle lights accentuated the cut of his muscled chest, casting shadows over the deep black lines tattooed over his heart that matched the knotted silver cross hanging from the chain around his neck. Her gaze drifted over the deep lines of his abdomen—not Kylian. Not her rock, not her sunshine. She wouldn't risk breaking what they had. Their bond was deeper than romantic feelings, but she had no doubt that a failed romance would shatter it.

She forced her eyes to meet his. "Hinata likely won't make it through the night—"

Kylian held a finger to her lips. "Shhh."

This version of Kylian, the version that stood up to her, that talked back to her, that took care of her was infuriating. Heat pooled in her belly at the audacity. At least, she tried to convince herself that was what was making her skin burn under his heated gaze. Freyja's resolve wavered. She turned her body to the side, fighting the need she had to invite him into her quarters.

It hit her hard as she took in the quiet moment alone with him: how many times she could have lost him. Beneath the ice, in the explosion, on Trogon, on the ring. Her eyes caught on the thick white scar across his neck. Was pushing him away really keeping him safe? Or was she wasting what precious little time they might have together?

"Do you..." She trailed off, gathering the courage to ask what she really wanted.

Kylian leaned against the doorway, his face dropping close to hers. He ran his fingers over her shoulder, across the shimmering rune tattoos that inked her skin, down the length of her arm to take her hand in his own. Gently, he brought the backs of her fingers to brush his lips. "Dinner and bed. That's all I asked for tonight, Freyja." With that, he turned and disappeared into his quarters.

CHAPTER 40 | FREYJA

CODE STACK

When Freyja awoke the next morning, she was especially irritable. She tried to convince herself that it was the task at hand that brought her blood to a boil.

Barging into Kylian and Tristan's shared bunk, she turned up the lights and shouted, "Time to go!" Only to find Tristan alone, tangled in his sheets. The scent of alcohol wafted out of the room, and she was certain he was still half drunk as he stumbled to his feet, naked. Freyja turned and stomped down the corridor. "Get yourself cleaned up. We have a ship to commandeer!"

She found Kylian in the galley, fully dressed this time. Her cheeks heated at the thought. She snatched a cup of coffee from him and leaned against the counter.

"Status update on Hinata?" she asked.

Kylian's gaze went soft as he pulled up records in his ocular display. As the minutes dragged on, Freyja grew impatient.

"I'm not sure. The records have been restricted."

"Damn it." Freyja fought to suppress the roiling of her stomach. If it were her, she would have sealed the records too. Keep the commander's death quiet. Keep control of the ship. It's what she would have done.

"Come on, let's go find out for ourselves what we're dealing with."

Freyja stormed ahead of her men all the way to the med bay. Both men knew better than to try to reason with her when she was like this. Freyja paused outside of the med unit, her brow furrowed in confusion as she failed to open the door.

"Kylian, get these doors open," she snapped.

Again, the seconds ticked into minutes, and Freyja neared losing control.

"I'm locked out."

Tristan's face crumpled with guilt.

Kylian didn't miss the expression. He glared at his cousin. "What did you do?"

Tristan held up his hands. "I-I-I don't know. I went to see Tax last night, and I got so drunk. I don't remember. He's so mad at me I...I'd do anything to get him to listen to me, even for a minute—"

"What did you do?" Kylian's normally carefree tone had turned to stone.

"I might have given him your code stack."

"You did what?!"

"I don't know. I mean, I might have...I don't remember. I just remember he was interested in your hacking skills. He's a coder too. I don't know. I just wanted him to talk to me."

"And how did that work out for you?" Kylian bit out the words.

"Well, I woke up alone in our room, so how do you think it turned out for me?"

"Shut up." Freyja pressed her forefinger and thumb to the bridge of her nose. "It's done. Kylian, where is Sato?"

Kylian referenced his ocular display, "Lucky for you, your boyfriend didn't lock me out of all of the systems."

"Not my boyfriend," Tristan murmured.

"He better be your boyfriend if you'd give up my code stack to get him back. Otherwise—"

"Bicker later," Freyja said from between gritted teeth.

"He just left the engine room. It looks like he is headed for the bridge. If we hurry, we can get there before he does."

"Move."

A short lift tube ride brought them to wait for the lieutenant commander outside of the bridge doors. As she had suspected, they were locked out of the bridge as well. Crossing her arms, Freyja leaned against the bulkhead to wait. It wasn't long before Tax came around the corner. If he was surprised to see them waiting for him, he hid it well. He approached the bridge doors as if they weren't there.

Freyja moved with a singular purpose as soon as Tax was within reach. She punched him hard in the face, then grabbed him by the collar and wound up to deliver another blow. Tristan caught her arm mid-swing.

"Think about what you are doing," she growled.

Tristan didn't let go of her arm. He didn't say a word, but his eyes pleaded with her to stop. Freyja let go of Tax, shoving him a few paces back down the corridor.

"What gives you the right?" she shouted at Tax.

Tax took his time in answering, dragging the back of his hand beneath his bleeding nose, likely broken, his eyes never once leaving hers. "I am the commanding officer of this ship. You and your men pose a security threat, and I acted within my rights to mitigate that risk."

"By locking me out of the ship?"

"This is not your command. You are free to take your ship and leave."

"Like hell. We have to get to the bottom of that signal. What are you going to do now that you are in charge? Are you going to finish what Hinata started?"

Tax stiffened at the mention of Hinata. His reaction confirmed Freyja's fears. Tax was in charge now, and he didn't know how to operate outside of the UTA. He didn't know how to break the rules. He didn't have what it took to see this through.

"As ranking officer, I am taking command of this vessel. I will finish what he started."

"You have no rank here." Tax had finally found his spine, squaring his shoulders and raising his chin. "Hoshiko is an independent tribe."

Freyja laughed, "You still think you are Hoshiko after your commander stole this vessel." She shook her head, drawing her sword. "You are alone."

Tax drew his katana to match her stance. Each held their blade at the ready, eyes boring into one another, daring the other to make the first move.

"Enough."

Freyja froze at the familiar voice. Lowering her blade slowly, she turned to meet the specter.

Standing behind her was Hinata, and her assessment that he must be a ghost wasn't far off. His skin was so pale it was nearly translucent. Skyla stood at his side. She looked poised to catch him if he collapsed, which Freyja believed to be a very real possibility. His right shoulder was one dark, angry bruise, a disfigured, swollen mass held in place by a sling.

"Hinata." The tension melting from Freyja's muscles surprised her. "You're alive." She resheathed her sword and turned to face him. "Although, perhaps not for long." She appraised him.

"Don't joke." Skyla glared at Freyja, who only smiled and clasped Skyla by the arm.

"All joking aside, I'm glad you made it through." Freyja took a step closer, lowering her voice. "We need to make a move. I've analyzed the Empresses' shipments. We can ambush the next one, but only if we move now."

Hinata nodded in agreement, taking a step toward the bridge. He wobbled, and Skyla grabbed his good elbow, her other hand moving to his waist to steady him.

"Where do you think you are going?" Skyla asked.

"To my bridge," Hinata said.

"Like hell, they only pulled you out of regen for surgery."

Freyja held up a hand to silence them. "We both know you are in no condition to lead right now."

Hinata grunted.

"Hand over command to me until you are cleared for duty."

Hinata shook his head. "Lieutenant Commander Sato is more than capable of running things until I can resume command."

"That might have been true before, but we both know that man doesn't know what to do outside of the confines of the UTA Navy."

All eyes landed on Tax. He stood straight and proud, ready to take orders.

Hinata sighed, "And what will you do if I give you command of my ship?"

"I will finish what we started. We will get those nanites that Dr. Dar requested, and then we will get to the bottom of the signal." Freyja straightened and smiled. "Maybe I'll even stop a war."

Hinata snorted at that.

Freyja shrugged. "That's the plan, anyway." She put her hand out, waiting to see if he would accept her offer. Hinata extended his good arm to grasp her forearm.

"While our interests align?" Hinata asked.

"I think we are past that, Commander. To family."

Skyla's eyes darted up to meet hers. Skyla had never been one of them, but she recognized the oath. Freyja nodded her head for Skyla to join arms with them.

"To those bound by blood." Kylian reached out to grasp their interlocked arms.

"And those forged in it." Tristan grasped them next.

Hinata nodded slowly, then relaxed his grip. Their arms fell to their sides.

"Lieutenant Commander Sato," Hinata said, and the group parted for Hinata to meet his second.

"Yes, sir." Tax stood at attention.

Hinata moved close, grasping the man by the neck with his good hand. "You did well, my friend. You will report to Admiral Nygaard until I resume duty." He held Tax's gaze, something silently passing between them before Hinata released his second-in-command.

Tax chanced a glance at Freyja before answering, "Yes, sir."

"Now, can you help me get him back to medical?" Skyla asked.

"I can get myself back to medical." Hinata took a shaky step, an arm wrapped around Skyla's shoulders for support.

"Clearly."

"You can accompany me if you are so inclined, Captain. I need Tax to stay and help Freyja."

Skyla sighed. "Lucky for you, I was heading that way, anyway."

"Yes, lucky."

Freyja fought against the smile that tugged at her lips, watching the two of them go. They deserved to be happy. She hoped this near-death experience would snap some sense into them, inspiring them to get out of their own way. Her eyes caught on Kylian as she walked into the bridge, her gaze traveling from his eyes to catch on the thick, white scar across his neck. Prying her gaze away, she refocused on the display before her. Some people deserved to be happy; others deserved vengeance. She held no illusion as to which was her destiny.

CHAPTER 41 | HINATA

DUMPLINGS

Pain ripped through his mind, turning the med bay hazy as Dr. Pinot gently rotated his shoulder.

"And this?" she asked, her deep brown eyes studying him.

"Fine." Hinata managed to keep his voice steady as he forced the word out. The sweat that beaded on his brow betrayed the pain he tried to hide. He wasn't fooling anyone.

"Mhmm," Dr. Pinot hummed as she gently returned his arm to its sling, her eyes tracking back and forth, no doubt reviewing his chart and adding notes.

With the load taken off the damaged joint, Hinata hid the pain well. "See, perfectly functional. Now if you can go ahead and clear my return to duty—"

"Do you think I'm stupid?" Dr. Pinot trained her full attention on the commander.

The question caught Hinata by surprise. "No, of course not—"

"Good, because with an MD and PhD you would be a fool to think so, and given that you are no skilled actor, I'm certain that we both know I can't clear you for active duty."

Hinata swallowed his shock. Dr. Pinot was usually so reserved; he had hardly heard the woman speak. "Of course, Doctor, but I think we both know these are not normal times. I am needed at my post."

Her eyes softened. "Yes, I'm well aware of our situation, Commander, and it's my duty to ensure you are capable of returning to this fight."

Hinata's brow rose in anticipation.

"Which you are not."

His face fell. "Well, given that I have commandeered this ship, I don't strictly need you to sign off on my return." Hinata shifted toward the front of the med bed, ready to make his escape. Dr. Pinot placed a dainty hand on his damaged shoulder. There was no force behind the movement, but she held him in place all the same.

"Commander, we have all chosen to follow you. I believe in this cause...I believe in you. But now I need you to listen to me. Your body needs time to heal. That new joint I placed needs time to fully integrate with your organics."

She gently poked her thumb into the center of the joint. Even the slight pressure sent fire racing through his nerves, and he ground his teeth to keep from wincing.

Dr. Pinot nodded. "Just as I will follow your command to end this war, I need you to follow my orders now. You are not another piece of war machinery. I cannot simply 3D print your parts and send you back into battle. Take this time, Commander. You cannot end this war if you are broken before it truly starts."

Hinata considered for a long moment, letting Dr. Pinot's words sink in. He was not a machine made for war...he didn't know if he believed it.

The med bay doors snapped open, and the beautiful woman behind the doors stole all thought from his mind. Skyla's worried eyes met his, a soft smile spreading across her lips as she assessed him. Dr. Pinot patted his shoulder, prompting him back into the bed, and just like that, the fight left him. He settled back into the med bed as Skyla pulled a chair up beside him.

"I'll leave you two." Dr. Pinot turned but then called over her shoulder, "He is not to leave medical." She added for good measure before letting the door to her office slide closed behind her.

Hinata smiled and shook his head.

"Well, the good doctor is rather feisty today, isn't she?" Skyla joked as she set a container on the bed beside him.

"Yes, it appears that everyone has grown rather opinionated on this journey." Hinata turned and smiled at Skyla, then his gaze dropped to the container. "What did you bring today?"

This had turned into an easy routine between the two of them over the past week. She had been there when Dr. Pinot had pulled him from the regen pod for surgery, and he swore he had never seen a woman more beautiful, even with her face puffy and eyes red-rimmed from her vigil at his bedside. The last thing he remembered before everything went dark beneath that frozen ocean was regret that he would never see her beautiful face again. He had never been so happy to be wrong.

Skyla had come every day since, bringing something that she had whipped up. Hinata had chuckled the first day when she reminded him of her hatred for 3D printed meals and swore that he needed real food to help him regain his strength. He hadn't complained; it was an easy excuse to spend time with the woman, and she was a surprisingly good cook.

"Mushroom dumplings," Skyla announced as she popped the lid off the container. The savory aroma instantly filled the air between them.

"My favorite." Hinata's mouth turned up in a half grin. "How did you know?"

Skyla's cheeks flushed pink. "I had Pele ask Tentei."

Hinata's pulse quickened at the gesture. He took his chopsticks, clumsy in his non-dominant hand, and popped a dumpling into his mouth to hide how much it affected him.

A low moan escaped his lips. "These are really good," he said around a mouthful, causing Skyla to giggle. His cheeks heated at his lack of decorum. He swallowed before speaking again. "They would be even better with chili oil, though."

Skyla smirked at him and then slipped a small bottle from her pocket.

Hinata took the little vial in his fingers, his eyes widening. "Where did you get this?"

"I have my sources. But hey—" She snatched the bottle back from him as he poured a generous portion on his next dumpling. "It's extremely hard to get, so go easy, okay?"

She eyed the blob of chilis and oil dripping down the side of his dumpling. He popped it in his mouth before she could protest and delighted in the way it burned. He couldn't remember the last time he'd had chili oil. It was something he could have gotten on his home world, but he had never thought to. He was always so focused on his duties, on honing the war machine that was his life; he had thought it frivolous to do things for the joy of it.

Unscrewing the cap, Skyla topped each dumpling with a dollop of chili oil.

"What do I have to do to get more, Captain? Fight another sea beast? A flock of murder bots?"

She rolled her eyes but couldn't hide her smile, and so he continued.

"Cash in a favor from a notorious outlaw?"

Now she snorted to cover her laugh. "You wouldn't consort with such people."

"This one is particularly charming." Warmth spread across his chest at the way she bit her lip before responding.

"You would cash in your favor for more hot sauce?" Skyla kept her tone light.

This peace between the two of them was fragile, and neither of them wanted to break it. He considered for a minute, then nodded. "Yes, right now, I think I would." He took another dumpling in his chopsticks, but Skyla laid her hand on top of his, halting the motion.

"Free of charge, Commander." She poured more chili oil on until it matched his first dumpling, then she released his hand.

He pressed his lips together to hide the smile she elicited, but he knew she could read everything he tried to hide as her eyes caught on his. A piece of his long, dark hair slipped from behind his ear, obscuring his vision. He tilted his head to the side, trying to will the rebellious lock back into place. He was aware he looked rather ridiculous, but with his right arm in the sling and his left occupied with the chopsticks, he didn't have a lot of options.

"Here." Skyla's cool fingertips brushed across his brow and traveled along the edge of his face as she secured his hair behind his ear once again. Goosebumps ran over his skin at her touch.

"Thanks," Hinata whispered, the dumpling hanging forgotten in the space between them.

"I've never seen you wear it down," Skyla said, eyeing his loose hair that hung past his shoulders.

"Yeah, it's hard to braid with my shoulder like this." He slightly raised his arm in the sling, careful not to move it enough to trigger the wave of pain and nausea he knew would come if he overextended himself.

"Right." Skyla studied his arm for a moment. "You don't have your range of motion back?"

He shook his head, the lie catching in his throat. He hadn't told her how bad the injury was. That it was likely his shoulder would never function properly again. He stuffed the thought down before it took root and crushed him.

"Here." Skyla shoved the box of dumplings into his lap. "Turn."

Hinata raised a brow.

"Turn, I'll braid it for you."

"You don't have to—"

"Just turn, Hinata." She gently nudged him, and this time, he complied.

Another wave of goosebumps followed her delicate fingers tracing over his scalp, partitioning his hair into sections and gently tugging to weave them together. How had he ended up in this position? It was too intimate, having her hands on him, making his pulse race while he sat vulnerable before her.

"So tell me something about home," she prompted, as if she knew he needed the distraction.

Hinata thought for a moment. He needed a safe topic, something that would distract him from the captain's hands on him. Without thinking it through, he blurted, "There is this trail through the woods behind my home."

Why had he chosen that topic? It was the place he felt most grounded, but it was also a place that was just for him. He had never brought anyone on those long runs through the woods, not even Tax. But he had started, and now he couldn't stop, so he told her about the trail and the trees. About the scent on the breeze and the way the light played through the canopy. About the bend in the river where the water swelled and grew lazy. Where he would stop to swim on hot days ever since he was a boy.

He shared every detail of his sacred place with her, and in that moment, he knew she had undone him. He couldn't resist her any longer. If she left, it would shatter him, but if she chose him, he would not deny her. He was already hers.

CHAPTER 42 | SKYLA

NO MORE RUNNING

The walls press in around her. The icy breath of death steals the air from her lungs—a cold so deep it freezes her in place. Lifeless faces flash before her, horrifying with their pale blue skin and serene expressions. Her body has turned to stone, stuck forever in an icy tomb. The cold is so oppressive it burns. Permeates her bones. Freezes her screams in her throat. The silence is deafening. Tears carve frozen tracks over her cheeks, and everything turns to a black so deep it swallows her whole.

Skyla shot straight up in her bed, choking on her screams. Her fingers tangled in the sheets, sweat slicked her brow; she tried to settle her racing heart. It was just a dream. She wasn't trapped on Thule. She wasn't sealed inside the dive module. He had come for her.

As much as she tried to hold it back, a sob ripped through her. He had come for her. Even after she had left, after months of silence. He had come. He had commandeered a starship for her. Gone against his duty to find her. He had nearly died for her. She didn't want to be alone anymore.

Before the fuzzy edges of her mind could sharpen, she sprung from her bed, slipped on her boots, and stumbled into the hallway. A singular focus drove her down the empty corridors. She had spent every day with him in medical. They had kept it light, casual conversation over cups of green tea and warm meals she brought from her kitchen on Pele.

He was finally talking to her, and she hadn't wanted to ruin it. He had told her about his favorite running trail on his home world, and she had told him about her favorite adventures with Pele. They hadn't talked about the fact that she had left, or that she had almost died on that planet; that he had almost died on that planet.

Medical had released Hinata a couple of days prior. She ached to check on him in his quarters, already missing their daily ritual, but she wasn't sure where they stood. Would he welcome her in? Or was that too intimate? Then there were the nightmares, which had only gotten worse since Pele's rescue. Before she knew what she was doing, she had triggered the alert at his door. Shifting uncomfortably from one foot to the other, she held her breath and listened for movement on the other side. It was late.

Anxiety started to creep up her back. He was asleep. Of course, he was asleep. He was still recovering. He wasn't going to answer. She shouldn't have come here. Just as she was about to turn and slink back to her quarters, the door slid open.

Hinata leaned against the doorway, his dark hair, once again unbound, fell across his bare chest. He wore only a pair of black sweatpants, and Skyla's cheeks heated as she hungrily took him in. He rubbed the sleep from his eyes, which widened as soon as he registered the woman standing before him.

"Skyla." He turned, inviting her in. "Is everything okay?"

Folding her arms, she rubbed her palms over her bare skin as she slipped past him into his quarters. She hadn't thought this through, but she was here now.

"I," she hesitated. "I had a dream. I was still on Thule..." Her self-conscious brain cut off the words. Was she really running to him over a nightmare? She wasn't a child. "I'm sorry; I should go."

He caught her arm as she turned to leave, pulling her closer.

"Stay." The understanding in his eyes melted her resolve, and she let her body relax into his touch. He folded her in his arms, her cheek pressed against him. The strong rhythm of his heart prompted her own to slow as he rested his chin atop her head and stroked a gentle hand down her spine.

"Do you want to talk about it?"

"The dream?" The image of cold dead faces flashed behind her eyelids. She pressed closer to Hinata's warm solid presences. "No."

"Your father?" he prompted, running his hand soothingly over her back.

Skyla sucked in a long breath. "He left. He left when I was nine years old and I never saw him again until..." She unearthed his corpse.

"I'm sorry," he breathed.

She pulled back, just enough to look into his amber eyes. It was more than just words of condolence. Confusion pulled at her brow. None of this was his fault. It was hers. She had left him, put Pele in danger, gotten herself stranded on that damn planet. She should be the one apologizing. "For what?"

"That I didn't come sooner. That I didn't listen. That I wasn't there for you...That I pushed you away."

She shook her head. "You couldn't have known—"

"I should have. I should have realized. I should have at least talked with you. I was so angry. I thought you left...me. That you weren't coming back. That none of it meant anything to you. That I was a fool..." His voice trailed off, barely more than a whisper. "Losing you, broke me. I couldn't go through it again...I can't go through it again."

She reached up to trace the curve of his jaw, shaking her head. "I promised you I would come searching for you. I just got a little lost along the way."

His eyes closed as he leaned into her touch, nodding gently.

"It wasn't nothing. Not to me," Skyla whispered. "I'm sorry." She ran her hands up his chest to grasp his face. "I am here...I'm not going anywhere."

Hinata tightened his grip around her waist, bringing her flush against the hard planes of his body as he crashed his lips into hers. The breath stolen from her lungs, she collapsed into him, surrendering—she was done running. She brought her arms up to circle around his neck as he lifted her from her feet. Her legs wrapped around his waist as they tumbled into black, silk sheets.

She let the fire of their passion consume her. Her skin caught ablaze as his fingers traced the line of her jaw, then grasped gently around her throat, before moving on to trace the line of her sternum, brushing the swell of her breasts as his hands traveled lower, questing for the space between her legs.

With his touch, the blaze burning under her skin turned into an inferno. She pushed her hips into him, arching her back and dragging her nails down his smooth skin. She moaned against his lips, which pulled back into a smile.

"What was that?" he mumbled against her mouth as he prompted another indecent noise from her throat.

"Shut up," she said breathlessly.

He peppered kisses across her lips, her cheeks, her brow, then whispered in her ear, "You are wearing entirely too much clothing."

"Maybe we should rectify that." She hooked one of her legs behind his knee, and in one fluid motion, she flipped him onto his back as she straddled his hips.

Surprise flashed through his eyes, the look quickly replaced by a burning fire she had seen only once before. A fire that he held only for her.

She slipped her tank top over her head, and he froze, drinking her in with his eyes before reaching up to trace his thumb across her lips. His hand moved down her throat, then between her breasts. He took one in his hand, circling his thumb over her nipple. The other hand he pressed into the small of her back, bringing her close. He took the other in his mouth.

He flicked his tongue, eliciting another moan. She ground her hips into him. She needed more—more friction, more of his hands on her, more of him.

He let out a moan to match hers, pulling back to look at her, a smile gracing his lips.

"What?" she asked.

He shook his head. "You are fucking perfect."

Heat flushed through her cheeks as she shook her head, looking away from him.

He sat up, cupping her face in his hands, pressing his forehead to hers. "You are." He punctuated the sentence with a kiss. "Everything I want." Another kiss. "And I want all of you." Kiss. "Just the way you are."

He devoured her with the final kiss, and all of her walls came tumbling down. She hooked her fingers under her waistband, removing the last of her clothing. Hinata's eyes widened, studying her body, studying her intention, the thin material of his pants the only barrier left between them.

He wrapped a hand around her waist, his fingertips pressing divots into her hip at his restraint.

"Is this what you want?"

She could hear what he had not said. The pain he would endure if she said no. The respect he held for her; he would stop if she told him to. But his eyes were begging her not to.

"I want all of you."

That was all he had to hear. He tore the last of his clothing away, his hands tight around her hips, cupping her ass. His eyes locked on hers—it was still her decision, even now. She held his heated gaze as she closed the last of the distance between them, lowering herself onto him until she completely enveloped him.

Hinata's head rolled back into the pillows as she ground against him. A feral growl ripped from his chest. He moved one hand between her thighs, building the sensation at her core until she shattered against him.

Wrapping a strong arm around her, he flipped her onto her belly as he reentered her from behind. Tangling one hand in her hair, he pulled her head back toward him, pressing kisses to her skin with every thrust. Her jaw, her neck, her shoulder.

"You are mine." He nipped her ear. "Say it."

"I am yours," she gasped into the silk.

"Again." He tightened his grip in her hair.

"I am yours. I am yours. I am yours." The words poured from her like a litany, and she meant it with every fiber of her being.

His other hand slipped beneath her, finding that spot once again, and she moaned. Every nerve ending in her body lit on fire.

"Hinata." This man would break her. He built her up again, and this time when she fractured, he came with her.

Collapsing to the bed beside her, he pulled her close, not letting even a centimeter of space come between them. She traced gentle circles over the arm that held her. If she could live forever in this moment, she would.

Time froze, and eventually, his muscles relaxed, and his breath deepened. Certain that he had fallen asleep, she whispered to the darkness. "I don't want to be alone anymore."

His arm tightened around her, startling her as he brought his lips to brush against her ear. "Never again. You are mine, and I am yours, and I will never let you go."

Tears welled in her eyes as she pressed back into the warmth of his body and nodded. Never again. She wouldn't leave and nothing in the Known Galaxies could come between them.

***

Skyla's eyelashes fluttered open, and for a moment, she forgot where she was. The normal panic that hit her most mornings when she realized she was on Thule failed to come because she was no longer trapped there.

A smile quirked her lips as she reached out her fingers to trace along the green lily pads inked across Hinata's back. A particularly bold living ink koi followed her fingertips across the muscled contours of his back, and Skyla giggled when it appeared to nibble at her fingertips.

"Mmm, that feels good," Hinata mumbled into the pillows.

"I didn't mean to wake you." Skyla kept her voice soft, hoping he could drift off again.

"It's okay, I'll wake up to your touch any day." He turned to face her, cracking open one eye. "So it wasn't just a dream," he teased.

Skyla turned her attention back to his tattoo. "Why the koi?" she asked.

Hinata turned to his side, taking her hand and lacing her fingers between his, stroking his fingertips over the back of her hand and down her arm. "Back home, there is a garden. It's one of my favorite places, and in the pond, there are four koi. My father brought home a new koi for the birth of each of his children."

"So the koi represent you and your sisters?"

Hinata's hand halted its path along her arm. He took a deep breath and nodded. "Yes, the orange and white one is for Yui, my little sister, and the big black and silver one is for Sakura, my older sister. The smaller orange and black one is mine, and the larger one..."

There was one more orange and black koi swimming lazy circles across Hinata's back, slightly bigger than the other. Skyla waited for him to continue.

"Is Akio's, my brother."

Skyla furrowed her brow in confusion. "I thought you only had sisters. You never talk about him."

"He died."

The pain was evident in his voice and she cringed when she had nothing better to say than a whispered, "I'm sorry."

"It was a long time ago before I left for the academy..." His eyes pleaded with her for understanding before he continued, "It was my fault."

Skyla moved closer to him, bringing their clasped hands to press against her sternum. "Before you left for the academy? You were a child. It couldn't possibly be your fault."

"It was. I had this crazy idea when I was a kid that I was going to be a starship racer."

Skyla snorted at that. "You? You're a terrible pilot!"

Hinata rolled his eyes. "I'm not that bad."

She pinned him with a stare, and he finally relented.

"Fine, I wasn't always. I stopped flying after the accident."

Skyla's breath caught. "What happened?"

"I had to be the best...Akio was six years older than me, and he was better at everything, except flying...because I would fully link with Tentei."

Skyla's eyes rounded in surprise as the pieces fit together. So much about him made sense now. Why he was so harsh with the AIs. Why he always followed the rules.

"Akio held the record for the Tenzan Ishi run, a dangerous course through a limestone quarry near our home. While he was away at the academy, I smashed his record...It was so important to me that I beat him. He was fuming when he found out. When he came home on leave, he had only one thing on his mind. He had to take the record back from his little brother, but he didn't have the reaction times I did, not without a full link. He crashed into a quarry wall going three hundred kilometers an hour. He never had a chance."

Her grip tightened around his hand. "That's awful."

Hinata pressed his eyes closed against the memory, against the shame.

Skyla took her fingers from between his to push his hair away from his face. "But it's not your fault." A tear ran down his cheek, and she swiped it away with her thumb. "It's not your fault." She repeated the words, cupping his face in her hands as she kissed him again and again.

"I've never talked about it. My family...we don't talk about that night."

Her heart ached as she realized that he had carried this burden alone all of these years. Tortured himself over the foolish mistakes of his youth, taking the burden for both his and his brother's mistakes.

Skyla rolled over to straddle him, and she kissed him fiercely, wishing she could take away his pain. He wrapped his arms around her waist, wincing slightly at the movement. She pulled back; her eyes moved to the scar at his shoulder. Thick white lines radiated out from the center like a starburst. She traced a finger over them.

"Does it still hurt?"

"It's not bad. Dr. Pinot loaded it up with nanites before she discharged me."

She watched the effort it took for him to lift his arm and trace his fingers across her lips.

"It's fine," he said. "Come here."

"It's your sword arm."

"And it's fine." He slipped his hand between her thighs, his fingers finding that spot that made it hard for her to concentrate.

"Did Dr. Pinot say it was fine?"

"I didn't hear you complaining last night," he teased as he stroked a little faster.

She grabbed his hand to stop the movement, almost instantly regretting it, but she needed a real answer from him. "Will you be able to wield your sword again?" His skill as a swordsman was a core piece of who he was. She remembered their first sparring match on Medina, and she felt the full, crushing weight of his omission when he wouldn't meet her eye.

His silence spoke for him.

"Hinata," she whispered.

"I have everything I need right here." He wrapped his arms around her, squeezing her close before rolling to pin her to the bed. He kissed her deeply as he interlocked his fingers with hers, pinning her hands above her head. He kissed along her jaw, then nipped at her earlobe. "My father once told me that I was more than just a tool for the UTA." His teeth grazed along her neck as he moved to trail kisses along her collarbone. "I didn't believe him then...but I do now." He pulled back slightly to look at her, his eyes trailing up from her navel slowly, until they locked with her gaze. "There is more to life than the Navy. I want that life with you."

"I love you." The words were out of her mouth before she could think, but she didn't regret them. They were true. She did. She loved him. As much as she had tried to fight it, as much as it scared her, she had fallen for Commander Azai, the last person in the Known Galaxies she ever would have dreamed of for her, but he was perfect, everything she wanted.

"I love you." He returned her words as he pushed inside of her, filling her. Releasing one of her hands, he traced his fingers along her arm, along her ribs, and over the line of her hip where he gripped her tightly. "I love you." He accented the words with the rhythm of his hips. "I love you with the intensity of a thousand suns." He thrust deeper into her, eliciting a moan as her tension built. She arched her back to press into him, needing more. "I feared that I would burn in your chaos. I'm not afraid anymore." She ached for more, so close to her release. "If I burn, then I burn with you." He brought her over the edge, and as she shuddered around him, he came with her.

CHAPTER 43 | FREYJA

TENSION

"It appears that Commander Azai doesn't understand the meaning of bed rest. I will not clear him until he meets the minimum physical requirements for active duty." Dr. Pinot raised her chin defiantly and glared at the commander. For such a slight woman, she could be quite intimidating when she wanted to be.

"I assure you that I have taken your medical advice very seriously, Dr. Pinot. I haven't left my bed in a week." Hinata smirked, and Freyja decided she didn't like this version of him. Skyla's eyes dropped to her hands, which fiddled with her coffee cup; her cheeks flushed pink with an embarrassed smile of her own.

Freyja glared at the two of them, certain that Hinata had taken the medical advice too literally. "I need Commander Azai cleared. The *Takarabune* is too large to hide on route. I will deploy with Selkie, and I need Commander Azai to take his post as commander of this ship."

"Sorry, Admiral, that is not going to happen. I'm this close to sticking him back in a regen tank."

"We don't have the resources for that, and you know it," Hinata countered.

Dr. Pinot fumed, and Freyja was certain that she had never seen the petite woman so angry. "Then I recommend you take my medical advice seriously before I have to take matters into my own hands."

Hinata ignored the doctor's outburst and focused on Freyja. "Lieutenant Commander Sato can handle the *Takarabune* while you're gone."

Tax straightened in his seat beside Hinata and gave a slight nod.

Freyja narrowed her eyes as they locked onto Tax's. "I don't like you."

"The feeling is mutual," Tax replied.

***

"Why aren't we moving!" Freyja yelled the moment Tax came into view. The man stiffened at the sound of her voice. They had worked efficiently to prepare the *Takarabune* for the mission ahead, but the tension had only grown since their first altercation outside of the bridge.

It hadn't helped that Kylian had reprogrammed the 3D printers in the mess hall to only serve burgers and beer after the upstanding Lieutenant Commander Sato had commented on Tristan's poor nutritional choices matching his lacking moral code. Or that he had managed to slip a dye tablet into Tax's shower, staining his skin maroon.

Tristan's eyes had gone wide as saucers when he saw Tax in the mess hall, stained from head to toe. Freyja had thought he might apologize for his cousin, beg forgiveness like had done an embarrassing number of times since he had outed Callan as a traitor, but he raised his beer and said, "It looks good on you. I'd still tap that."

Kylian spat his beer across the table, and Freyja did nothing to hide her smirk. She hadn't seen Tax in the mess hall since and she had to assume he was living on algae pouches, the less-than-appetizing diet probably adding to his contentious attitude.

Tax shifted to pull up a holographic display, the skin around his knuckles still stained. Freyja fought the smile that pulled at her lips. Sometimes working with Tax and Kylian felt like working with bickering teenagers, but it did have its perks. Watching Kylian torture Tax over the stolen code had been rather amusing.

"There was damage to the retraction mechanism of the solar sails that we weren't aware of. My mechanics are working to rectify the situation as we speak."

"It's been three hours! If we delay much longer, we will miss our window!" Freyja smashed her hand through the display, which crumbled to pixels underneath her wrath.

"I understand, Admiral. We will be underway as soon as the sails are retracted." The words sounded compliant, but Freyja heard the sour taint of his bad mood. She had no patience for it.

She leveled Tax with a seething stare, one he returned unflinchingly. "You have twenty minutes."

"Admiral, my mechanics are working as quickly as possible, but—"

"Twenty minutes." Freyja ground the words out through gritted teeth.

"Yes, Admiral." His dark eyes still burned, but he said nothing more.

Freyja left the engine room with the flames of her own rage stoked into an inferno. She had thought Hinata a pain in the ass, but he was downright flexible compared to Tax. Tax was Hinata's right hand, trained to rigid conformity, but that applied to Hinata's command, not her own, and she had found the man lacked creativity, or a willingness to break the rules. *Damn, Hinata.* She had been expecting him to resume command by now.

CHAPTER 44 | SKYLA

HOME

"Gunner." Skyla clasped her cousin's hand. The massive man pulled her in for a bear hug, smashing her face against him as he patted her shoulder roughly. She returned the gesture, and he released her.

"I hope Pele isn't giving you too much trouble." Skyla ran her fingers along the nanite coral walls of her ship. Their soft pink color had returned, and her ship was well on her way to mending.

"What type of trouble could I possibly cause Gunner?" Pele strobed her lights in response.

Skyla chuckled softly. "No offense intended." Truth be told, she was relieved to hear Pele was getting back to her usual self. Those first few days of early integration had been hard on both of them.

"Pele and I have always gotten on just fine, isn't that right, girl?" Gunner grinned at the ship.

"Yes, you are fine company, Gunner. Speaking of which, I have another batch of cultures ready. I'll send you the coordinates where they need to be applied."

Gunner rolled his eyes but patted the bulkhead affectionately. "On it boss." He flashed a smile at Skyla. "It's nice to be home," he said before leaving to tend to Pele's request.

Home. The word stuck in Skyla's throat. Every single long night on Thule, she had ached to be back aboard Pele. But since her rescue, Skyla hadn't spent a single night aboard her ship. At first, it was because the damage was too extensive, and it was best for both of them if she stayed in her lodging aboard the *Takarabune*. And then everything had changed. That night she went to Commander Azai's quarters. Now that she had finally found her way back to him, she couldn't imagine a night without him.

"What is that look?" Pele asked.

"Hmm?" Skyla responded.

"That look, you look guilty. What did you do now?"

"Why do you assume I did something?"

"Skyla?" Pele dimmed her lights.

"Fine." Skyla hesitated. "Are you sure you're okay with me staying aboard the *Takarabune*?"

"You mean, am I okay with you shacking up with the commander?" Pele strobed her lights pink.

Skyla's cheeks heated. "Pele!"

"Are you not spending every waking moment with the commander?"

"And not waking," Skyla mumbled unintelligibly.

"What was that? I didn't catch that," Pele teased; she heard everything that happened within her hull.

"You're insufferable."

"You love it."

Skyla's mood turned serious. "I do love it. And I love you. And if you're not okay with—"

"I didn't spend countless hours paving the way for you and the commander to get together just so you can feel guilty about a sleepover. I have my own life, Skyla, and I am very much happy to have some privacy of my own."

Skyla rolled her eyes; of course she had noticed that Hinata's AI ship had moved into the berth next to Pele's. "You and Tentei?"

Pele's lights flickered softly.

Skyla sighed. "So you're really okay with all of this?"

"Of course I am. You didn't really think it would be just you, me, and the stars until our dying day, did you?"

Skyla's gaze dropped to the floor, toeing a misplaced wire stripper with her boot. "Kind of."

"Skyla, it will always be you and me. We are bonded, for life. But that doesn't mean there isn't room for more."

Skyla nodded slowly. She had dreamed of being reunited with Pele and Hinata. The dream had kept her going. "I guess I hadn't thought of how getting both of you back would change everything."

"Nothing has changed, Skyla. It is still you and me to the end, but perhaps it is better if we bring along our family for the ride."

Family. After being alone for so long, the thought that this rag-tag crew had grown into her family caused her throat to thicken and her eyes to sting. "Family," she whispered, and as the word left her mouth, she knew she would do anything to protect them. She was done running, she was done being alone, she would see this through to the end. Wherever it might lead.

"Well, look who decided to grace us with her presence!"

"Wout!" Skyla turned to clasp the grizzled mechanic's extended arm.

"Good to finally see you down at the docks!" The smug expression on Wout's face didn't suit him.

"I don't know what you are talking about. I've been here every day." Skyla lifted her chin to meet Wout's eye, crossing her arms.

"You've been a bit busy with the commander, from what I've heard."

Gunner reappeared at that moment, chuckling hardily at Skyla's expense.

"You better watch all of that gossiping, Wout." Skyla squinted at the head mechanic, only half joking.

"And what is a little thing like you going to do about it?" Wout leaned forward until they were nearly eye level, that annoying smirk plastered to his face.

Skyla leaned forward. "I'll take all your standars for starters." She winked, and this time Wout threw his head back and laughed.

"I'd like to see you try. I've been stuck playing with all these greenie recruits, and while they might know war, they sure don't know cards. I could use the mental stimulation."

"Hey, I played with you just last night, old man," Gunner said.

Wout smiled and looked the younger man over. Gunner was the only member of the crew that Wout didn't tower over. "I said what I said, boy."

Gunner laughed and clapped Wout on the back. "I guess I'll just have to prove it to you by wiping out your wallet."

"You, kit, sure like to yip. Come back when you have some bite." Wout snapped his teeth shut. "Anyway, you have work to do. I approved your rec order this morning. You can collect your materials in the port printing bay."

Gunner thanked the mechanic and excused himself to collect the freshly printed replacement parts.

"Since when does the head mechanic have to authorize simple print requests?" Skyla asked.

Wout's eyes darkened. "Since he almost lost his ship to a mega bot and ended up stranded at the edge of known space with barely enough supplies to patch her back together."

Guilt pressed in that the *Takarabune* was funding Pele's repairs when they didn't have enough materials to properly fix their own ship. "I'm sorry, Wout. Pele can manage a lot of her own repairs—"

"Don't be ridiculous." Wout batted a hand in the air. "You know I care about our girl here. I'm happy to contribute where I can. You hear that, Pele?"

"Of course I do, Wout..." Pele's indignant tone turned soft. "And thank you."

Wout held up his thermos of homemade stout in mock cheers before taking a drink.

"By the way." Skyla eyed the stainless steel container. "You wouldn't happen to know where I could get a bottle of whiskey, would you?"

Wout snorted. "Didn't I just tell ya that everything is in short supply?"

"What if I told you I knew where to get enough liquor for your whole crew to get drunk off their asses for a week?"

"I'd say why do you need my bottle of whiskey, then?"

"I have a promise to keep."

CHAPTER 45 | HINATA

Promises

Blinking hard, Hinata dismissed his ocular display and laid back to stare at the bulkhead. Tax had blocked his access—on Dr. Pinot's orders no doubt. The doctor had become a thorn in his side.

The doors to his quarters sprung open, and Skyla strolled in, a sly grin on her face and her arms held behind her back. Warmth spread through him at the sight of her. Even if everything in his life had fallen to pieces, she was the glue that held the broken bits together, and she shone as bright as gold between the cracks of his fractured soul.

Skyla sauntered closer, her arms still obviously held behind her.

"What do you have there?" He smiled at the heat in her eyes as she shook her head.

"Wouldn't you like to know?" She gazed up at him through her lashes.

In one swift movement, he looped his arm around her waist and twisted to lay her out on the bed beside him. He ran his fingers down her arm until they wrapped around the object clutched in her hands. When he pulled it into view, he was surprised to find a full bottle of whiskey. A bottle of whiskey that he had been holding onto for months, hoping that the mysterious woman he had fished out of the stars at Medina would find her way back to him. That is until he had heard Wout asking around for a bottle for the outlaw. He couldn't help himself; he had handed the bottle over to Wout, wanting to see how it would all play out. It had all started as a game for him back on Medina, watching her, dissecting the way she fought and the way she thought, looking for clues as to who this mysterious woman was and now...he saw every part of her, loved every imperfect piece. He had thought he was addicted to her all those months ago. He had had no idea.

He arched a brow, enjoying the game too much to ruin it. "You know you don't have to get me drunk to take advantage of me."

Skyla pushed against him playfully, then retrieved the bottle.

"I am keeping a promise," she called over her shoulder as she retrieved two cut glass tumblers, pouring two fingers of whiskey in each before returning to his side. She pressed the glass into his hand before tapping hers against it and downing the shot.

Hinata watched her carefully, taking in the soft expression on her face and the way her lips pressed together before kicking back his own glass. "And what promise is that?"

She turned to straddle him, running her fingers through the loose strands of his hair. His skin sparked under her touch, eliciting goosebumps across his bare skin.

"I swore that the next drink I had would be a celebration."

"And what are we celebrating?"

"That I found my way back to you."

Gripping her hips, he pressed his lips to hers, not coming up for air until she fully surrendered to him. The taste of whiskey on her lips and the feel of her fingers along the stubble that peppered his jaw made his head swim.

"Mmm, I could get used to this," he whispered against her lips.

"What, lying around naked in bed all day?"

Wrapping an arm around her waist, he growled and turned to pin her against the bed. "Yes." He kissed her again.

Skyla rolled her eyes, running her fingers across his collarbone. "Do you even get dressed anymore?"

"What's the point?" He shrugged. "Dr. Pinot locked me out of the training room, and Tax won't even hand admin duties over to me without her sign-off."

Her eyes bore into his. "Don't you have physical therapy?"

He groaned and turned over to lay beside her. "I need to get back to training, not some silly stretches in the clinic."

Skyla pinned him with a serious stare. "Those silly stretches are how you get back to training."

Locking his gaze on the ceiling, he clenched his jaw. He didn't want to talk about the injury or his rehab.

Finally, Skyla changed the topic. "Have you reviewed Freyja's plan?"

"Yes, I don't like it." The conversation had turned from bad to worse.

"It's the best shot we are going to get."

He could feel Skyla staring at him, but he refused to look at her. "It's too risky."

"Pele gave the mission a seventy percent chance of success. Those are some pretty good odds, Commander." She nudged him playfully, but his mood had soured.

Finally, he returned his gaze to her. "I don't want you on that mission."

The smile fell from Skyla's face. "Freyja needs me."

"It's too dangerous."

"I can handle myself."

"If you are going, then I am going with you."

Skyla shook her head, slowly tracing the starburst scar on his shoulder. He saw her fingers glide over the lines cut into his skin, but the tissue was still numb.

"We both know that you can't go."

He stared deep into those ice-blue eyes of hers, begging her not to go.

"It's just a mission, Hinata. I'll come back to you."

He worked hard to swallow the lump that formed in his throat, lacing his fingers in her hair and bringing her close. "I can't lose you."

"You won't." Her whispered breath played across his lips.

He kissed her deeply before finally relenting. She had never been his to command; he wasn't sure what he expected now. "Okay." He traced the planes of her face, memorizing every line.

"And while I am gone, you will go to physical therapy."

Groaning, he flopped back on the pillows.

"I'm serious. You want to go on missions again, then you have to get that arm functioning."

"It works just fine," he grumbled.

Her gaze bored into him until he relented.

"Fine."

CHAPTER 46 | FREYJA

REVENGE

Space debris whizzed by the face shield of Freyja's armored space suit. Chunks of ice, rock, and precious minerals streamed past her in a glittering mess of destruction. The Eos belt had been a planet eons ago. Now this was all that was left of it, the sum of its mass scattered across millions of kilometers of space—a hazardous zone of detritus that separated the Theta quadrant from the uncharted space beyond.

It would have been beautiful if Freyja had been safely onboard her ship instead of hurtling through space at sub-light speeds in nothing more than an armored spacesuit. But this had been her plan, and despite the risks, she still believed it was their best shot at claiming the nanites that Dr.

Dar needed to complete the quantum entanglement reactor without more bloodshed.

Freyja pressed her eyes closed against the debris that shot past her, refocusing her mind on the mission ahead. It had taken a week of sub-light travel to make it to the intercept site. With the delays, they had barely made it in time to raid the next run.

The press of a close encounter shocked her eyes open once again as a chunk of ice flew past, close enough to feel its proximity through her suit. That had been too close, but she had no choice but to trust the algorithm Kylian had programmed into her suit. Navigating the Eos belt at these speeds required particularly sophisticated calculations with faster adjustments than any human could account for.

Looking for a distraction, she searched the void for her crew. It took a moment, but she found her cluster of shadows streaking through space around her. The hours of silence traveling through the nothingness had left her mind prone to wander, and she couldn't help but think of how she had tried her best to get Kylian to stay behind.

"I want you to stay on Selkie," Freyja said. It was just the two of them on the bridge. Everyone else had retired to their quarters to rest before the drop-off. It would only be a matter of hours before Selkie sent them hurtling through space toward the Eos belt.

"Is that right boss ma'am?" Kylian folded his arms and gave her one of his crooked grins that made her skin heat.

"You don't need to go on this mission." Freyja bit her lower lip, willing her racing heart to slow. "You can stay on Selkie, make sure the pickup goes smoothly."

Kylian shook his head. "And what good am I to you waiting on a ship that can handle herself?"

"We won't be able to transmit while we're en route to the Empire vessel. It's not like you could make any adjustments to the code on the fly."

"Aye, and when you enter the vessel? Who will hack the security system? Find the nanites in the logs? Cover your tracks?"

Freyja growled, "You can write a protocol to do all that." She waved her hands in the air. "There is no need for you to be on site."

Kylian took a step closer, clasping Freyja's hands in his own and drawing them to rest against his chest. A soft smile spread across his lips. "I appreciate your faith in me, but it's not that simple. I need to be on sight to know what systems they have. To counterattack if their security officer notices my worm."

Freyja sighed, "I can't have you there."

"Why?"

"You are a distraction."

Kylian snorted, "Since when? We have been a damn efficient unit for going on two decades. You wouldn't know how to operate without me."

"I just—I can't see you get hurt. Not again. There have been too many close calls."

Kylian shook his head. "That's the job—"

"Kylian—"

"For all of us. I won't stay behind. It compromises the mission."

Heat burned through Freyja, and she wasn't sure if it was from losing the argument or the feeling of his hands clutched around hers.

A soft beep from Freyja's ocular display pulled her mind back to the present. Three hours in flight, they were still on trajectory, and the Empire vessel should be visible on scans soon. Freyja exhaled hard. All this time in silence, with nothing else to focus on, was getting to her.

Before her thoughts began to wander once again, a ship entered range. Finally, Freyja had somewhere to focus her scattered mind. With subtle bursts of air, Kylian's algorithm used the micro jets on her suit to realign her trajectory to match that of the approaching ship. This was it, the moment they would find out if they had got their calculations right.

It had been quite the mathematical feat ensuring that they didn't smash against the debris of the Eos belt while hurtling through space at speeds fast enough to latch onto the Empire vessel, since they wouldn't be able to bring their thrusters online without risking detection. Timing their intersect point just outside of the Eos belt was key. If their calculations were even slightly off, they would miss the ship.

They couldn't fail. According to Gabriel, The Empire made the supply run only once a month. The very idea of sitting idle in space, wasting away the days until the next window, made her blood boil. No, the mission would succeed. They would take the tech from right under her mother's nose, and no one would be the wiser.

The ship grew closer. Another few minutes and it would be upon her. It was finally close enough to make out its class; it was a stardestroyer. Realization struck like a live wire. It wasn't just any stardestroyer; it was the *Ormen Korte*.

Black spots lined the edges of her vision as her rage boiled over. It wasn't just any smuggler; it was *her* ship. A wild cackle ripped from her throat, resounding through her helm, and she was grateful that the comms were silent. The *Ormen Korte* had been declared destroyed at the battle of Medina. She knew Medina hadn't had the firepower to destroy the vessel. It all made sense now. The Empress had taken the opportunity to move the crown jewel of the Stjarna fleet off the playing field and into her private militia.

The blood of her Berserkers splashed across the bridge of the *Ormen Korte* flashed before her eyes. The battle haunted her every nightmare, and now the ghost of her ship brought it all back to vivid reality. Freyja set her jaw in grim resolve. The plan had been to sneak on, commandeer the nanites, and sneak off with no one the wiser, but that was before, when they had expected a common smuggler frigate. Finding out it was a stardestroyer—and not just any stardestroyer, but her ship—that changed everything. She had lost the *Ormen Korte* once. Now she had come back to haunt Freyja, and the admiral would not let this opportunity slip through her grasp. She would take back her ship.

The shadow of Frejya's former warship passed overhead, blocking out the pinpricks of light cast by distant stars. This was it, the moment where it would all come together or all fall apart. Freyja rotated so that she aligned with the bottom of the ship, her arms and legs splayed out wide. The blur of metal took up her entire field of vision.

Before she had a chance to overthink it, the magnetic field that ran the surface of her modified suit initiated, slamming her against the hull. The force of the impact knocked all of the air from her lungs. Her ribs ached, and her ears rang, but she had done it.

A quick scan confirmed that their entire crew had made contact. A cluster of aerogelium-clad barnacles stuck to the bottom of the ship. Now that she had the *Ormen Korte* in her grasp, Freyja had no intention of letting her go. Switching from a full magnetic field to the grips in her palms and feet, Freyja began her scuttle across the belly of the ship.

The loss of security twisted Freyja's belly into knots, she became keenly aware of every sway and shudder of the ship beneath her. They needed to get inside before one false move tossed them back into the void.

Freyja checked her coordinates. She was a mere twenty-five meters from the nearest maintenance hatch. With slow, calculated movements, she inched her way along the hull, alternating between the magnets in her gloves and feet.

Freyja's hand slipped as the impact of a thousand fragments across her suit threatened to tear her from the hull. Without hesitation, she re-initiated the full magnetic field. Once again pinned to the bottom of the ship, she took stock of their situation.

Debris rushed by, the inertia of the larger pieces activating the ship's shield array, but the small pieces passed through, and while they were harmless to the ship, they were large enough to pry her crew from their precarious perch along the belly of the vessel if one were to hit at the right moment. If only she could open a comm line with her squad, warn them to watch their scans—but she couldn't, not until they were inside and Kylian could block their signal from the ship's systems. She would have to trust them to be vigilant. The scans showed an endless ocean of scattered detritus. They couldn't wait; they needed to get inside now.

With an eye on her scans to watch for large projectiles, Freyja once again began the climb to the maintenance hatch, small pebbles pinging against her suit in a light staccato as the effort of the climb brought beads of moisture to the surface of her skin.

Sweat trickled down Freyja's brow, stinging her eyes as she finally pulled herself through the maintenance hatch. Within minutes, half of her ten-person raiding party was laid out around the maintenance door, taking in labored breaths. Kylian went to work on the ship's systems, his eyes going hazy and his fingers flashing through the air while Skyla and Gunner knelt around the hatch to help the rest of their crew inside.

Tristan took up position at the door with his sword drawn. A muffled scream echoed through the maintenance room, snapping Freyja's attention to the hatch. Adelice had been halfway through the hatch, and then she was gone, ripped from sight.

"No!" Freyja screamed, lunging toward the open hatch. Kylian grabbed her around the waist, pulling her back from the opening before the torrent of rocks and ice that scraped along the hull could tear her out into space next.

"Selkie will pick her up." Kylian's voice came through the comms.

Freyja wasn't so sure. The look of terror on Adelice's face burned into Freyja's mind. That debris had been enough to damage a suit, and if the suit was compromised, Adelice would be dead before Selkie came through to extract them.

Forcing deep breaths in through her nose and out through her mouth, Freyja fought to regain her composure. There was nothing she could do now. She had to focus on the mission. If Adelice gave her life, then Freyja would add her name to the rest of her Berserkers tattooed across her ribs, and though the thought brought bile to the back of Freyja's throat, she could not mourn, not now. No, this sacrifice would be more fuel for the fire that drove Freyja to end this.

Freyja shoved Kylian away from her. "Report."

Hurt reflected briefly in his eyes before the mask of the dutiful soldier settled into place. This is who she needed to be to end this war, and the sooner he learned that, the better.

With a swipe of his hand through the air, Kylian sealed the outer hatch. "I am in the ship's systems. No one knows we are here."

"Good," Freyja said. "Now I need a path to the bridge."

Kylian froze. "That's not the plan."

"Plans change."

"You're right; plans change," Skyla cut in, "and right now we need to take control of the engine room so they won't be able to pursue us when we extract. Otherwise, there's no way we are escaping this stardestroyer."

"Or we take the bridge and don't have to worry about detection at all," Freyja countered.

"You were always reckless, but this is downright suicidal!" Skyla argued.

"I'm reckless? Best not throw stones, Skyla, glass domes and all that." Freyja waved an annoyed hand through the air, turning to the exit.

"We don't have the firepower to take the ship." Tristan moved to cut her off.

Undeterred, Freyja took a step forward, bringing their helmets so close they nearly touched, and though she stood half a head shorter than Tristan, there was no mistaking the dominating gesture. "The *Ormen Korte* has been delivered back to me. I am not letting her go." Her words were so sharp they cut like glass, but when Freyja locked eyes with the man, she found her own anger and reckless abandon reflected there. He wouldn't fight her on this.

"I have a route to the cargo bay where the nanites are being held." Kylian pulled up a holo display.

Freyja threw an angry backhand through the image, the pixels distorting around her blow. "I said, get me a path to the bridge."

"Freyja—" Skyla tried again, but Kylian cut her off.

He shook his head, taking a step closer to Freyja so that the others couldn't read his lips, then switched over to a private line. "Freyja, I know. I know how much retaking this ship means to you—"

"If you did, then you wouldn't try to stop me," Freyja growled.

Kylian reached out to take her hand, but she yanked it out of his reach. "I was there too, Freyja. You think I don't want to go and kill those bastards right now? I would end them in a heartbeat if I thought we could win, but there are only nine of us. We couldn't beat them when we had twice the numbers. If we try to take the ship back now, we will fail." He paused, judging how his words had landed. When she didn't respond, he continued. "Listen to me. We get the nanites. We accomplish the mission. We get to the bottom of this signal, and then I promise you, I will follow you into the fires of hell if that's what it takes to get this ship back. I will serve you Borg's mutinous head on a platter. He will pay for the blood he has spilled. I promise you."

Freyja trembled with rage at the mere mention of the mutiny, but seeing her own anger reflected in Kylian's eyes centered her. To feel seen, to feel understood, to see that her ray of sunshine held some of that fire that raged through her freely, it anchored her. He was right. As much as she wanted the ship, as much as she ached to seek her revenge, their mission was bigger than one man; it was the chance to stop this war, to make sure that her Berserkers had not died for nothing. With Kylian's hazel eyes still burning into her soul, she gave a stiff nod.

"Make me a path to the cargo bay."

Kylian turned from her, his fingers flying through the air once more as he hacked into the systems of the *Ormen Korte*. "I've secured a route." Kylian turned to Skyla, flicking data over to her. "And your team has a clear path to the engine room. You can handle the security system from here?"

Skyla's fingers raced through the air. "I've managed this long on my own."

Kylian nodded, then turned to exit as the single door of the maintenance room snapped open. "Nanite crew on me. Fall in." Kylian led the way, his eyes roving from the unseen path outlined in his ocular display to the empty corridors before him.

Freyja and Tristan pressed in on either side of Kylian. Just a step behind, Loic took up the rear. While Kylian kept his hands free to navigate the code, the rest walked with hands on their hilts, ready to eliminate any threat before they could raise the alarm. A deep sense of unease swept over Freyja. The halls were quiet. She should have felt relieved that they were already halfway to their destination without incident, but something was off.

"Kylian, why is it so quiet?"

"From what I can tell, they are running on a barebones crew. But I jammed the doors along our route just in case."

"Won't that give us away as much as running into a bunch of Berserkers in the hall?" Tristan hissed.

"Not if it looks like a maintenance issue, which it will," Kylian hissed back, his anger toward his cousin evident.

"Save it for later, boys." Freyja had never seen the two at odds like this, and right now wasn't the time. She needed them focused on the mission.

Kylian stopped short, and Freyja nearly ran straight into his back. Tristan did.

"Damn it—"

Kylian cut him off, "Shhhh."

"What is it?" Freyja whispered.

"Someone is trying to come through that door." Kylian nodded just ahead of them.

"Well, it's a good thing that they will think it's just a *mechanical* problem then, right?" Tristan's words dripped with sarcasm.

"Yeah, until they try to fix it. We need to move. Keep quiet." Kylian crept forward.

Freyja tightened her grip around her sword as she eyed the closed door beside her, placing each step carefully as they moved on. It wasn't until they rounded the next bend that Freyja let out a long breath, the tension easing from her shoulders. They had made it to the cargo hold.

Kylian paused in front of a wide door frame. It was only a moment before the panel slid back, exposing the vast cargo bay beyond, draped in deep shadows. They slipped inside, Freyja and Kylian taking up a defensive position to the right of the entrance while Tristan and Loic took up the same stance on the left.

"Secured," Kylian said as he lowered his hands, and his gaze sharpened on the room in front of them.

Freyja strode forward. Stacked crates stretched out in either direction for over one hundred meters. A fully stocked stardestroyer could carry enough supplies to last years if rationed properly, and the *Ormen Korte* had been filled to the brim.

"How are we going to find the nanites?" She turned to her squad, who had gathered behind her.

"Accessing the ship's manifest now." Kylian's eyes went glassy.

With this much cargo, she wasn't sure how long it would take Kylian to find the records *if* there were records to find. "Spread out. See what you can find," she ordered the rest of them.

Tristan happily obliged, sauntering down the nearest walkway and then out of sight. Loic walked in the opposite direction. It was just the two of them now. Kylian was entirely focused on his ocular display. A thread of fear wove through Freyja at the thought of leaving Kylian in this state. He was completely vulnerable. She knew the fear was unfounded. The doors were sealed, and they were alone in the cargo hold. She was wasting time.

Freyja inched forward into the stacks, only pausing once she could go no further without losing sight of Kylian. She hesitated, and then anger flared in her. This is why she didn't let people in; she couldn't be worried about him when her focus should be on the mission. As hard as she fought to keep things the way they had always been, somehow he had chipped away at the mortar of her walls, and she knew now it was only a matter of time before they would crumble—

"I'm fine, Admiral. This could take a while; go take a look around," Kylian called down the aisle to her. He was still wholly absorbed in his display. *How could he read her like that?* The thought infuriated her, but his prompting was enough to push her around the corner and on to the next section of cargo.

Freyja's ocular display highlighted a manifest with the contents of each crate as she walked. The first section was filled with rations, enough to keep an army well-fed for a year, next were uniforms and other linens, followed by medical supplies. The medical supplies stretched on for three rows, far more than was standard on a UTA vessel—no one went through that many meds, not in peacetime.

What she read on the next crate halted her steps. Weapons—but it wasn't the standard issue nanite handhelds or munitions for the ships projectiles. No, the weapons in these boxes were illegal under UTA law. She had only ever seen these weapons once before, when she had faced off with the cartel. Guns.

What were guns doing on the *Ormen Korte?* Freyja traced her fingers along the boxes as she continued. Rows and rows of guns. The anger that coursed through her sent tremors through her hands. This was the future her mother had prepared her for. The future that saw humanity devolve into chaos. The future where only the strong would survive. The future that she would one day inherit.

Freyja's stomach churned. She didn't want anything to do with it. If she had once harbored any doubts, they were now gone. She would end this war before her mother could rip them apart. This couldn't be the only way.

"It's not here." Kylian's voice came through her comms.

"What do you mean, it's not here?" Tristan was quick to respond.

"I. Mean. It's. Not. Here." Kylian annunciated each word.

Freyja rolled her eyes. "Where are the nanites, Kylian?"

"It looks like they haven't been logged into the cargo manifest, which means they likely haven't been moved up from the ship's docks yet."

"You couldn't have saved us all some time and checked that first?" Tristan whined.

"Sorry, I was a little busy hacking into the system and making sure that no one found us. If you wanted to help out instead of giving away trade secrets, I would happily let you figure out where the nanites are."

"Save it for later!" Freyja fumed. "Kylian, I need a location, now."

The longer they stayed on the *Ormen Korte,* the greater the risk that they would be discovered, and while she desperately wanted to kill something, the mission came first. The best thing for all of them was to get those nanites and get the hell out, quickly.

By the time they had reconvened on Kylian's location, he was fairly certain he knew where the nanites were.

"This way." He marched off toward the far end of the cargo hold. "The *Ormen Korte* docked just a few days ago. I am willing to bet it was the pickup for the nanites. If I am right, then the cargo should still be on the shuttle."

"And if you're wrong?" Tristan squinted at his cousin, a nasty grin on his lips.

"Then you can figure out where they are!"

Freyja knocked her shoulder into Tristan's, throwing him off step, then leaned in close while the others continued on. "I don't know what your problem is, but pull it together now."

Tristan took in a deep breath. "Yes. Admiral." He remained silent as they rejoined the group, slipping back into the corridors and finally making their way to the loading dock.

Here, they would have to be on high alert. Kylian couldn't lock down the docks without arousing suspicion. They would need to blend in. A couple of mechanics worked on a starfighter a few berths over from their target, but no one gave them a second glance.

"That's the one." Kylian indicated the squat shuttle ahead.

It was the normal height of a shuttle but was twice the width and length, the additional size designed for hauling cargo. The ramp at the back was down, though it was dark inside. Freyja took point, drawing her sword as she walked carefully up the ramp, Kylian to one side, Tristan to the other, and Loic took up the rear. The hold was filled floor to ceiling with containers. She glanced at her ocular display, but there was no manifest for its contents.

The sound of a thick, bioplastic cargo lid striking the floor froze her in place. She darted a glance to either side, but the disturbance hadn't come from her team. Squinting into the gloom ahead, she made out the sheet of plastic in the walkway, the box to its side now open. Freyja gestured to her soldiers. Before advancing, Kylian and Tristan peeled off to make their way behind the open crate. Loic covered Freyja's position.

Freyja inched forward until she could see around the corner of the crate. Anger flared in her as her eyes landed on the man hunched over the open crate. *Borg.* Freyja ground her teeth so hard they nearly cracked. She fought the instinct to charge out and take his head from him right then and there—her eyes drawn to movement in the box.

Borg dipped his hand through a shimmering purple force field into the crate. A seething tide of black waves washed up his arm. The nanites coated his skin as he pulled them through the force field, the loose bots falling back into the container. He held up his hand, watching as the nanites solidified into plated armor contoured to his forearm. They wound their way up his biceps—Freyja had had enough. She moved with swift efficiency, severing his arm at the shoulder before the nanites could travel to the rest of his body. Borg screamed, his good hand clutching at the wound, trying to stanch the spray of blood. Freyja held the tip of her sword to Borg's throat.

"You," she seethed, triggering her helm to retract. She wanted Borg to know who had come to claim his life.

Borg's eyes bulged with recognition. "Freyja—"

Borg moved to draw a pistol from a holster at his ribs, but Kylian was faster. He slammed the pommel of his sword into the back of Borg's head, and he collapsed forward, his torso hanging limply over the box of nanites that now rolled like an angry sea during a storm as they appeared to consume the severed arm in a haze of fine red mist.

Freyja raised her sword. One stroke was all it would take to end him.

"Freyja!" Kylian shouted, halting her blow. Her eyes darted to his, the anger so thick in her bloodstream that red pressed in on her vision. He shook his head. "Not like this. If he bleeds out, so be it. But I know you. If you take his head now, it will haunt you."

Turning away from them, Freyja doubled over and yelled, her voice tearing across her vocal cords until they burned, until there wasn't a milliliter of oxygen left in her lungs.

"We need to go," Loic said from a few paces away, his eyes darting to the back of the shuttle.

"Get that piece of shit out of my sight, comm Skyla's team, and let's go get Adelice." Freyja stormed off toward the front of the shuttle before any of them could say another word. They would do as they were told.

Freyja locked the bridge doors before sinking into the captain's chair and running through pre-flight. Her anger still hung like a thick fog across her mind, making it hard to concentrate. Kylian was right; she knew he was right, and yet she couldn't help but hate him in that moment for taking her kill from her.

CHAPTER 47 | SKYLA

IMPROVISING

Skyla's nerves tingled as she pulled up the schematics of the *Ormen Korte.* It all came back to her so easy, leading a team, and yet the feeling was unsettling. She had promised never to be in this position, never to hold lives in her hands again after she had nearly gotten her whole crew killed by the Fenix Cartel, but things had changed. This war had torn the tribes apart, and sitting on the sidelines was no longer an option. Not when she had the skills to help put a stop to the madness. Failing to act now made her just as comparable as killing those soldiers herself.

A tremor traveled through her hand as she sealed their route to the engine room. No matter what, there would be blood on her hands. She only got to choose how. Clenching her hands and then releasing them, the tremors settled. She had already made her choice. No more running away.

"On me." Skyla extended the ends of her staff, the round metal sliding into place as she led her squad to the engine room.

Hacking may not have been Skyla's primary discipline at the academy, and in a head-to-head cyber-confrontation, she held no illusion that she could best Kylian or Tax, but she had been on her own a long time and could hack a system with the best of them.

She locked down the doors along their route. Her eyes flicked between the reality in front of her and the camera on the other side of those doors. Throwing up a fist, she called her group to halt as her ocular display showed a crew of mechanics approaching their position from an adjoining corridor.

Her fingers flew through the commands, and the lights flickered on the other side of the door. Next, she killed the lights and redirected all of the power to the control panel, which erupted in sparks mere moments later. The crew swore as they stumbled back from the door.

"It's busted," one of the mechanics said. "I have enough work on my docket for today."

"Don't we all?" another responded.

"Take the long route and pretend we didn't see anything?"

The second nodded, and the small crew retreated down the corridor.

"Clear." Skyla waved her squad forward, and it wasn't long before they were huddled outside of the engine room.

"I have five engineers on the other side of those doors," Skyla reported. "We need to overtake them before they can alert security that we're here. Gunner, you and your squad take the two on the left. Kaito, you have the right. I'll cover the middle."

Gunner clasped her by the shoulder. "It's leaving too much to chance. Even if we move fast, they could set off the alarm before we restrain them."

"You're right." Skyla couldn't keep the frustration from her voice. It wasn't Freyja's fault that it had been a stardestroyer carrying the nanites instead of a frigate, but she hadn't prepared them for this possibility, and now they were improvising.

"I can overload one of the cores." The idea came to Skyla.

"I know your reckless cousin, but I'm not ready to join Odin's Hall yet."

Skyla rolled her eyes. "You always were dramatic. I'm not going to let it blow, just reroute enough power to set off the safety sensors. The crew will be distracted. We can take them before they know what's happening."

"Are you sure you can shut it down before it blows?" Gunner questioned.

Skyla hesitated a moment too long. "Ninety percent sure."

Gunner glared at her.

"Eighty, I don't know. Let's not make problems where there aren't any yet. If you have any bright ideas, share them now. We are running out of time." Skyla let the silence stretch for a full minute. "It's settled then."

The soldiers behind her shifted into position, their weapons held at the ready.

"Rerouting power now." Her ocular display shifted to show the heat in the auxiliary core beginning to climb. "Approaching critical levels."

A klaxon wailed in the engine room. The doors snapped open before them. All the engineers had gathered around the defective core, rushing to disable it before it blew. Skyla cut the lights and rushed forward.

An engineer sprinted through the dark toward his control panel, but with one swift sweep of her staff, Skyla halted his mad dash. The crack of bone accompanied the strike to his ankles. Guilt pushed into the sides of her mind. *No time.*

She spun and hit another engineer, who had tried to escape into the corridor, flat against the back. The woman collapsed to the floor, wheezing. Skyla reset into a fighting stance to survey the room, but it was already over. The rest of the engineering crew stood with their hands in the air, sword tips held at their necks.

"Lights," Skyla commanded, and the doors to the corridor sealed shut behind her. In the light, she found her squad intact. The only injuries appeared to be those she had dealt. Once again, she had to push away the guilt. They would live. That was more than could be said for many.

"Restrain the crew." Skyla gave the command as she worked to lock the bridge out of the engineering controls. Gunner pulled a handful of pale goop out of the utility belt at his waist. Kaito followed suit. They spread the putty over the hands of the engineers, instructing them to hold their wrists together. Fear flashed in the engineers' eyes as they tried to guess their intentions. Gunner wrapped his wide palm around both fists of one of the engineers, then brought his fist down for a bone-breaking blow.

The man slammed his eyes shut against the impending injury, but instead, the putty expanded, absorbing the kinetic energy. Gunner repeated the process until the engineer's wrists and most of his fists were locked in place.

With the engineers immobilized, Skyla turned her attention back to the ship's schematics. The other team was already at the docks. Perfect. Time to get off this ship and put some distance between them and the *Ormen Korte* before Selkie came to pick them up. An alarm ripped through the quiet.

"What the Hel is that?" Gunner yelled, his hands clasped over his ears.

Skyla shook her head. "I don't know." She moved to the last power cell; its readouts pulled up instantly in her ocular display. "What? That can't be right. I reversed the energy flow..."

"What is it?" Gunner stepped up to her side.

Skyla's fingers flew through the air as she tried to reprogram the power cell. Energy continued to flow in the wrong direction. At this rate, the cell would blow in minutes. Despite all of her efforts, the heat output on the core continued to rise. "The conductor appears to be damaged. I can't shut off the energy flow."

"We need to get out of here now." Gunner grabbed Skyla's arm, pulling her toward the exit.

Skyla slipped out of his grasp. "There's no time. Besides, if one blows, it will set off the rest. The entire ship will go, and we don't have time to clear of the blast radius."

Gunner swore, slamming a fist into the bulkhead.

Skyla was once again working through her controls. "I can jettison the core."

"Will we be able to clear the blast?"

She shook her head as she finished hacking through the security proto-cols. One last tap of her fingers and the defective core disappeared into the floor.

Skyla cursed as she worked to kill the exterior sensors. She might have cut the engineering room off from the rest of the ship, but the exterior sensors were sure to pick up the jettisoned core, and then The Empire would know they were here.

It was no use. The floor shifted under her boots as the energy blast from the core hit the *Ormen Korte,* tossing the ship off course.

"Time to go." Skyla rushed into the corridor, her squad close on her heels with weapons drawn.

"Kylian, is our escape route secure?" Skyla called through the comms.

"We have a ship on the docks, but..."

"But what?"

"They locked down weapons control. If we launch, they won't hesitate to blast us to particles."

Skyla wanted to scream, but what good would it do? Instead, she leaned into years of training—she had been a soldier most of her life. Their plan had gone to hell. Time to improvise. "What are our options?"

Freyja's voice replaced Kylian's on the comms. "We take back my ship."

"We discussed this. We don't have the numbers."

"That was before. Now the only way off this ship alive is if we take the bridge."

CHAPTER 48 | FREYJA

PAID IN BLOOD

A maniacal smile twisted Freyja's lips. An unfamiliar feeling threaded through the rage and hate that fueled her; was it joy? She should be angry that their plan had gone to hell—that she would be risking the few Berserkers who still stood at her side—but she found the thought of taking back what was hers invigorating. She would take back her ship, or she would join her soldiers in Valhalla.

"Fall in. We are taking the ship."

Kylian grabbed Freyja's arm, pulling her close. His voice dropped to a whisper. "We already discussed this. We don't have the numbers to take the ship."

Heat flared under Freyja's skin as she pulled her arm away from him. She was still angry with him for stopping her from killing Borg. "Can you take control of their weapons system without us taking the bridge?"

Kylian's shoulders slumped. His eyes fell to the floor as he slowly shook his head.

"Then we don't have another choice." Freyja opened up the comms once again. "Meet us at the bridge." She sent the command to Skyla's team.

Kylian took control of the local systems as they passed through the corridors. The ship's security may have rerouted all essential systems to the bridge, but it couldn't hold control over local systems against Kylian's malware. Still, he only had control over a fifty-meter radius from their location, which meant it was only a matter of time until enemy forces found a way to head them off.

As if her thoughts had summoned them, eight soldiers with swords drawn blocked their way as they turned the next corner. Eight wasn't so bad, especially since they hadn't been expecting a boarding party and wore simple uniforms instead of armored space suits.

Freyja yelled a battle cry as she rushed forward, the corridors only just wide enough for her to fully extend her sword. She moved without hesitation, driving the edge of her blade through the clavicle of the soldier nearest her. The woman screamed, dropping her sword as blood poured down her chest. Freyja kicked the woman off of her blade with a heavy boot, the crack of bone sounding through the air.

Freyja drove forward in a frenzy, making room for Kylian and Tristan to take up the fight at her side. She narrowly blocked a blow as a heavy broadsword crashed into her own. Her muscles strained under the force as the brute put his weight behind the blade.

Freyja took a quick step forward, rotating to the side and dropping low to send the man careening forward. She slashed his hamstrings before he could regain his balance, and the hulking mass of a soldier fell to the floor. One quick stab through his spinal cord and she was certain his fight was over. With a quick exchange of blows, Freyja finished the final soldier standing in her way. The young man was fast but inexperienced, and in the end, he paid with his life for dropping his guard.

The melee was over within seconds. The Empire forces were no match for her Berserkers, even outnumbered. Crimson blood streaked across the once sterile, white walls of the stardestroyer, bodies now cluttering the walkway. Despite all of the gore, her soldiers stood unharmed in the aftermath. She nodded. Good—it wasn't going to get easier from here.

Freyja's muscles grew taught, the foreboding of a warrior's death settling over her. The bridge was still three floors and another three kilometers away; they were too far; they would be overwhelmed before they made it even half the distance to the bridge.

Leading the way, Kylian rounded the next bend, which would lead them to the center of the ship. Freyja stopped mid-step.

Making a snap decision, she halted their advance. "Suit up!" Freyja yelled. Her own helmet unfolded from her collar, reforming around her head and sealing her suit. "Stick to the perimeter. Kylian, keep an eye on the camera's aft and forward of our position. If you so much as see a shadow, vent the corridors." If they stuck to the perimeter of the ship until they were parallel with the bridge, maybe, just maybe, they could pull off this crazy mission.

They proceeded along the perimeter, Z-grav boots enabled to keep them from being sucked into the vacuum of space when it came time for Kylian to vent their position. They had made it half the distance to the bridge when the sound of boots marching cut them off. Fifty meters ahead, the corridor was blocked by a platoon of soldiers at least ten deep and three wide. Freyja and her crew were severely outmatched.

Freyja's face set with a grim determination. They wore the same uniforms as the last set of soldiers they had encountered. They hadn't taken time to suit up, and given that there was no breach, she couldn't blame them. Their folly would be their undoing.

"Now." She sent the command. The nearest maintenance hatch sprung open, and Freyja had only a split second to watch the look of surprise and terror wash over the face of the nearest soldier before she was ripped from sight. Within seconds, the corridor was clear once again.

Kylian had control of this section, which meant command hadn't seen what they had done. But soon sensors would pick up the bodies floating in space, and it wouldn't take much to put it all together. They had bought some time, but the next wave they encountered would be ready. They needed to take the bridge now.

"Move out!" Freyja yelled over the comms and set the pace at a steady jog. As the bridge doors came into view, Freyja could feel her victory in her bones. This was it. One last fight and the *Ormen Korte* would be hers. She scanned the halls and began to worry as she noticed that Skyla and her crew were missing.

"Skyla, report your position," Freyja called over comms.

An aerogelium plate fell from the ceiling. Freyja jumped, the discarded plate narrowly missing her. She held her sword, ready to strike, when a familiar voice came through her comms.

"Nice of you to join us," Skyla said as she hopped down from the hole above. The rest of her crew followed suit, and they now stood nine strong outside the bridge doors.

"Did you have a plan, or did you just think they would open the doors if we made it here?" Skyla asked. Her tone was light, as if this were a training simulation back in the academy, back before Freyja had tried to kill her, back when Skyla thought everything was a game.

"Yes, I figured if I knocked real nice, they might open up," Freyja said sarcastically.

"Okay, but seriously, this isn't a raiding party. We don't have plasma torches to cut through the aerogelium core."

"I'm thinking," Freyja snapped.

Gunner cleared his throat. "Excuse me, kin, but perhaps I could be of some assistance." Gunner pulled out a lump of the field dressing goop, his childish grin at odds with his hulking mass.

"Gunner, I know you love that stuff, but now is not the time," Skyla responded.

"Thanks for the vote of confidence, cousin." Gunner held one end of the goop, letting it stretch toward the ground, then he reached his arm high and slammed the end into the floor.

The gel solidified into a long rod. Gunner repeated the process. Now with a rod in each hand, he pivoted to wedge them between the seal of the blast doors. "If you want to help out instead of just watching, that would be appreciated," he said as he pressed one rod into Tristan's hand and threw his considerable weight back against the other.

The squad split between the two rods and pulled back hard, trying to pry the doors open.

"This isn't going to work." Skyla's words were strained by effort.

"Sure it will. We only have to be stronger than the gears holding it shut, not the aerogelium plating itself."

"Sure, unless the rods snap first," Skyla responded.

"That's where you're wrong. Dr. Pinot showed me the specs on this stuff. It's nearly unbreakable without the solvent to dissolve it."

Freyja nearly lost her footing as she staggered back, the door easing open a notch.

"That's it; let's drive it home!" Gunner yelled, and they all heaved back with every ounce of strength they had left. The gears snapped under the pressure, and the doors slid fully open. Freyja quickly regained her balance and drew her blade. This was it, one last battle.

Freyja stepped onto the bridge to find most of the officers still seated at their consoles, hands raised in surrender. As she scanned their faces, she recognized many of them. They had been junior officers under her tenure, not part of Borg's rebellion. Her heart sank as she realized the toll the war had taken. The only reason for them to be promoted was to fill the positions of their fallen leaders. They were barely out of the academy. Her quarrel wasn't with them.

A woman stood from the captain's chair to face her. As she turned, Freyja recognized her battle-scared face, Bodil. Bodil lifted her chin in defiance as she stared at the armored force that threatened to take her bridge. With their helmets in place, they were faceless terrors, warriors of myth and legend.

Freyja retracted her helm, squaring her shoulders with her opponent as she raised her blade. "Do you yield?"

Recognition flashed in Bodil's eyes, then a twisted sneer contorted the woman's face. "Freyja," Bodil spat, "I thought you were dead."

"I'm harder to kill than you might think. You, on the other hand, will be easy to kill, yield."

Bodil drew her sword. "You might be a *princess* in The Empire, but out here...you are nothing." Bodil drove forward, intending to impale Freyja, but her execution was clumsy. With one swift motion, Freyja side-stepped the attack, bringing her sword around to sever Bodil's head from her shoulders. Warmth splattered against Freyja's cheeks as Bodil's body collapsed to the floor in a pool of crimson.

"Anyone else?" Freyja demanded.

An officer sprang to his feet, his fist snapping to his chest. "We are at your service, Admiral." His voice wavered with fear, but he held eye contact. Freyja's gaze swept over the remainder of the crew. Slowly, each of them came to their feet as well, hands fisted over hearts, their eyes locked on hers.

Freyja smiled at the show of fidelity, then nodded. "I accept your service; resume your stations."

***

Freyja stepped into her quarters on the *Ormen Korte*. A strange satisfaction overcame her as she took in the space. She had claimed her prize, and she had no intention of letting it go. The adrenaline faded from her veins, replaced by a deep exhaustion.

The door snapped open behind her. Turning, she pulled her hand back into a fist to strike the intruder, but halted the punch at the last moment as Kylian raised his hands in surrender.

"Just me, boss ma'am."

Freyja let out an exasperated sigh, letting her hand fall limp at her side. She turned away from him, stalking across the vast quarters. She hadn't forgiven him for halting her hand on the shuttle.

"Freyja." He chased after her, grabbing her wrist to stop her escape. She whirled around, striking him hard on the shoulder, but his grip only tightened.

"Let go," she growled.

Instead, he pulled her closer, his free hand cupping the side of her face as his thumb smeared spattered blood across her cheek. "Are you okay?" His eyes scanned her face, then her body, before finally locking onto her own.

"I'm fine." She tried again to pull away from him, but he only held her tighter. "You shouldn't be here. Go reclaim your quarters and celebrate with the rest of the crew."

"I don't want to celebrate with the rest of the crew."

"Well, I don't give a damn what you want. I want you anywhere but here. That's an order!"

Hurt flashed in his eyes before they set with determination, his hand tightening around her jaw as he brought her face close to his—so close that she could feel his breath against her lips as he spoke.

"You order me around out there." His eyes flicked to the side before locking onto hers. They burned with an intensity that scared her. "But not in here; in here, you talk to me."

"You don't want me to talk to you right now, Kylian."

"Why?"

"Because right now I hate you!"

Understanding flashed in his eyes, and then he smirked. "You don't hate me for saving your humanity."

"I do." The words came out forceful, but already she was losing her resolve, and he could see it. She inhaled the scent of him: fresh rain, fern leaf, and pear blossoms. He smelled like her dream of a garden on a quiet planet, like life, and peace, and home. It was infuriating and intoxicating, the way it made her muscles relax against her will, sending heat to coil in her core.

Kylian shook his head, his nose brushing against hers. "You know, you were always easy to read."

"You think you can read me?" Freyja knew he could. She hated how well he could read her, but she wanted so badly to defy him, even as his fingers against her skin set her ablaze. "Then what do I want, Kylian?"

He hesitated for a moment, his eyes searching hers, and then his mouth was crashing into hers as he drove her back, pinning her against the wall.

All reason escaped her as she parted her lips and kissed him back, their tongues tangling as each fought for dominance. Kylian ground his hips into hers, one hand still tightly gripping her jaw as the other hand slid under her shirt to cup her breast.

She shoved him away just enough to grab the edges of his shirt and rip it over his head; he was back on her before she could take a moment to drink in the sight of him. He grabbed her by the hips and lifted her as she wrapped her legs around his waist, her fingernails scraping trails across his back as his lips traveled down her neck.

He growled, pressing his hips into her touch as she slipped a hand beneath his waistband. Freyja smirked at the moan she elicited from him as she stroked him. He turned suddenly, carrying her toward the oversized bed in the corner.

He stopped at its edge, setting Freyja on her feet, and kissing her gently before he pulled her tank top up over her head, followed by her bra. Then he stepped back just enough to drink her in. She ached at the way he looked at her, like a man who was dying of thirst and had finally come across an oasis. No one had ever looked at her that way before, and she hated the way she trembled under his gaze.

Kylian's eyes locked with hers as he lowered to his knees. He traced his fingers along the waistline of her pants before unbuckling her belt, popping open the snap, and then slowly lowering the zipper. His hands moved with reverence as he hooked a thumb in the edges of her garments, removing the last of her clothing with one fluid movement.

She stepped from the discarded pile, and his hands wrapped around her waist. Running her fingers through the short strands of his hair, Freyja ignored the voice in her mind that whispered this was a mistake. She knew this was wrong, and still, she couldn't stop. The way he gazed up at her, the look in his eyes, was unmistakable. The man worshipped her, and it scared the shit out of her. Never before had she felt so vulnerable as she did now under his adoring gaze.

Her desire warred with her conscience, and then it all came crashing down as the sound of Freyja's quarter doors sliding open shattered the moment. Rage replaced her moment of vulnerability.

"Get out!" she yelled as she turned to see who had interrupted them.

Tristan gave them a sly smirk as he swaggered into the room. "Well, this is not what I was expecting."

Freyja slid her muscular legs back into her pants and replaced her tank top as she yelled again, "I said get out."

Tristan slouched into one of the overstuffed armchairs, unphased.

"Sorry, boss, as much as I would love to leave you two to your fun—" He lifted his eyebrows suggestively.

Kylian slapped his cousin on the back of the head. "Asshole, how'd you get in here, anyway?"

Tristan grinned up at the dark cloud of a man towering over him, then held up his datapad that glowed with a strand of code. "Look familiar, cousin?"

Kylian pressed his thumb and index fingers to the bridge of his nose. "Betting my code stack on a game of cards against you has to be the worst decision I've ever made in my life."

"Yes, it really wasn't prudent, was it?" Tristan laughed, then waved his hands to dismiss the topic. "Anyway, not why I'm here. Freyja, we have a problem that needs to be dealt with now."

"What is it?" Freyja took a seat across from Tristan, pouring herself a glass of tequila from the decanter on the table between them.

"It turns out Borg had a loyal crew of officers; they were planning to break him out of medical and make an escape, or maybe even make a last stand. Not sure which; they haven't been very forthcoming since I caught them."

Freyja washed the news down with the bitter taste of liquor. "Have you rooted them all out?"

"Hard to say. I think the best course of action is to make a show of force now, with the ones we've caught. We deal with the treacherous bastards and scare any of their ranks that are still hidden into submission."

Freyja kicked back her drink. "Very well, I trust you can take care of the arrangements?"

"It would be my pleasure."

A nasty grin twisted across Tristan's face, and Freyja was reminded of the brutal boy she had met all of those years ago. The man behind the jokes and swagger, the man who delighted in brutality, the man who sought the strictest justice for tyrants like those who he had been too small to fight when he was young. This was a task that he knew all too well, and she trusted his judgment completely.

***

The entirety of the crew stood at attention on the docks. Orderly rows for each unit took up the majority of the open space they had cleared between the ships. In front of them, the dock doors stood open, the sheer purple shimmer of a force field the only thing standing between the crew and the void. Lined up in front of the force field stood Borg and twenty officers, all closer in age to Freyja's mother than to her Berserkers, all she recognized as loyal soldiers of The Empire.

Freyja strode up the aisle between units, dressed in a crisp, black dress uniform, the gold emblem of admiral embroidered at the mock neck of her collar. Her boots were shined and her hair shorn into a mohawk. She was the picture of a UTA admiral as she halted before her prisoners.

"You have been found guilty of mutiny against your commanding United Tribal Axis officer. How do you plead?"

Borg looked weary, but then he laughed. "There is no UTA anymore." He spat at her boots. "There is only The Empire, and I am a loyal soldier of the Empress."

Freyja shook her head. "Then you will be sent to stand trial before the Senate."

"Didn't you hear me, *girl*? There is no Senate; there is no UTA; there is only the Empress, and only she can judge me!"

Freyja took a step closer. "If you will not recognize the authority of the UTA, then you will recognize my authority as heir to The Empire."

Borg's eyes widened as the realization of the meaning behind her words hit him.

"I challenge you." She stepped back, drawing her sword.

Tristan stepped forward, pressing the hilt of a sword into Borg's single, remaining hand. "This death is more than you deserve," he snarled, then stepped back.

Borg's eyes flicked from the weapon to Freyja. Without his dominant arm, he didn't stand a chance against the admiral in a duel, and they both knew it. Acceptance settled on his features as Borg raised his weapon. He had barely lifted the blade when Freyja kicked the weapon from his hand. The sword went crashing to the ground. Already he was left defenseless.

Freyja lifted the tip of her blade to his jugular. "Yield, and I will show you mercy. I will allow you to stand before the Senate as is your right."

Borg was silent a moment before his eyes locked onto hers. "I. Will. Not. Yield."

"The choice is yours." Freyja's blade swept through his neck in one swift motion. Before his lifeless body shifted, Freyja kicked him, sending the body hurtling back through the force field and out into space. The sound of his head hitting the floor echoed his exit into the void.

She turned to his officers, their faces frozen in horror.

"I give you the same choice I gave your commander. Yield and stand trial, or meet your fate now," she growled.

The mutinous officers stood in shock for a long moment before the first fell to his knees. He held his palms out and his head bowed. "I yield." One by one, each of the officers took a knee, surrendering to the admiral.

Freyja turned to watch as the mutineers were secured and hurried out of the cargo bay to the brig. That rage that always burned inside her, a feeling as familiar to her as her beloved plants, a beast she could barely keep caged, always hungry, was sated for now. She could do this; she could bring peace to the compact, and she would do it with honor.

CHAPTER 49 | HINATA

DEBTS AND HONOR

Hinata paced the short length of the lab Dr. Dar had commandeered aboard the stardestroyer. Fenrir shadowing his movements. The strange creature hadn't left his side since Skyla boarded Selkie, and while he wanted to complain, he had found comfort in having Skyla's beast close. The away team was due to hit the rendezvous at any moment, and while he looked forward to having Skyla back aboard the *Takarabune* where he knew she was safe, the waiting was driving him mad.

Unused to being sidelined, he had worried from the moment she boarded Selkie. The fact that he was still not cleared for duty or physical activity had made matters worse. How was he supposed to deal with these emotions when he couldn't throw himself into work or burn off the thoughts rattling through his mind with training?

"Anything?" he asked Rohaan. The way that Rohaan looked up from his display and shook his head made Hinata think that perhaps he had asked one too many times.

Once again, Hinata turned to pacing. After a few more minutes of Hinata's nervous energy permeating every meter of the lab, Rohaan eventually sighed and dismissed the holo. The enlarged image of a nanite dissolved as Rohaan moved to the corner of the lab and prepared two cups of tea.

"Come, Commander, join me." Rohaan extended a cup to Hinata, who obliged, sliding onto a stool next to the scientist, Fenrir curling up beside his feet.

Wrapping his long fingers around the cup, Hinata let the warmth settle in as he stared into the dark depths of the tea, but he didn't drink.

"She's okay, you know," Rohaan said.

"How do you know?" Hinata lifted his gaze, hoping to find some confirmation behind the scientist's words.

Rohaan shrugged. "Skyla always comes back. She might be wild and impulsive and reckless, but she always comes back." Rohaan clasped Hinata by the shoulder, squeezing once before letting go. "They will be here soon." Rohaan pulled up the image of the nanite again, "And I have the specs all ready to modify the nanites for our quantum reactor." Hinata knew that Rohaan was merely trying to distract him, and he appreciated the effort.

"Assuming they come back with the nanites, what's our next move?" Hinata asked.

"I will need to wipe their programming and replace it with the protocols Dr. Aman and I have developed for the quantum reactor." The holo shifted to show a cluster of nanites. Electric pulses ran through their shells, and Hinata assumed that was the re-programming protocol Rohaan had described.

"Ah that." Rohaan locked onto Hinata, studying the holo. "Interesting isn't it?"

Hinata wasn't sure what he was looking at. Tech had never been his specialty, so he cocked a brow at the scientist, prompting the man to continue.

Pointing to the holo, Rohaan slowed the progression of the image, highlighting every little detail as a pulse ran in slow motion across the nanites' shell. "When I reprogram them, they send off a pulse. I didn't notice it at first. There is no reason for them to send a transmission upon re-programming, so I wasn't looking."

"A transmission?" Hinata furrowed his brow, watching the image on repeat. It was eerily familiar. "Like the AIs do?"

Rohaan paused to consider. "Yes, very much like that, but the direction of the transmission is not in the direction of Earth That Was."

"How can you be so sure?"

Rohaan smiled and gripped the air around the holo, rotating it until it zoomed out from the pulsing nanite to display a vast star chart. Little blue waves traveled through the dark, emitting like a beacon dispersed into the void.

"See the direction they are headed?" Rohaan gestured to the image.

When Hinata nodded, Rohaan pulled an ornate, gold compass from beneath his tunic and placed it next to the image. With a wave of Rohaan's palm, the compass unfolded, and swirling liquid, silver lines washed over a star chart like a current, running in the opposite direction of the holo.

"And do you see where the compass is pointing?"

Hinata nodded. "What is it?"

Rohaan smiled and collapsed the compass once again, tucking it away beneath his tunic before answering. "That is the direction of qibla and the great mosque on Earth That Was. That is how I am certain they are not transmitting back to Earth That Was, like our AIs do."

"What does it mean?" Hinata asked.

"I am not sure yet." Rohaan's face fell a little with the confession.

A heavy unease settled over Hinata, but he was looking for a distraction, so he merely nodded for the scientist to continue. Satisfied with his explanation of the nanite transmissions, Rohaan returned the holo to the specs for the reactor.

"We will need to deploy the modified nanites into a suitable host star. I believe our best option is this one here." Rohaan pulled up a star map. There was a highlighted star just at the edge of their current fuel capacity.

"That's a ring star," Hinata observed, and he considered for a moment if they should just take the *Takarabune* through the ring for repairs and resupply.

He halted that train of thought as soon as it began. He had taken this ship; there was no guarantee he would be allowed to continue on his mission if they took it back to Hoshiko space. Few, if any, other tribes would be willing to repair the warship. No, they would continue on as planned.

"Yes." Rohaan went on to describe what made the star a suitable choice, followed by a detailed description of the tech specs and what he and his team would need to deploy the prototype.

Hinata tried to pay attention, but his mind kept wandering to Skyla. *She should be back by now.* He tried to stuff down his rising anxiety at the thought of her disappearing off the map with no way for him to find her.

"We have ships on long-range sensors." Tax's voice came through the comms.

"Ships?" Hinata asked.

"Yes, Selkie and a stardestroyer class."

Something had gone wrong. "I'm on my way." Hinata stood abruptly. "We are needed on the bridge," he said to Rohaan.

"You are not cleared for duty!" Dr. Pinot called out from the corner of the lab. She had been wholly absorbed in her work, so much so that Hinata had forgotten she was there.

"I'm done sitting around, Dr. Pinot. If you want to stick me back in a regen tank, then good luck."

By the time Hinata and Rohaan arrived on the bridge, the ships were close enough for a visual. Sure enough, Selkie flew in the shadow of a stardestroyer.

Hinata squinted at the image. "Is that..."

"The *Ormen Korte*," Tax finished for him, "yes."

"We are receiving a hail from the *Ormen Korte*," the comms officer said.

Hinata slid into his captain's seat, the contours a familiar comfort after so long away. Though Skyla's creature at his side was new. "Put it on the main display."

"Hinata!" Skyla's beaming face greeted him from the bridge of the *Ormen Korte*, along with Freyja and several of the team that had been sent to retrieve the nanites. "I see you were finally cleared for duty."

"Not exactly." Hinata exchanged a guilty look with Rohaan. "I see that your mission didn't exactly go to plan."

Freyja cut in. "Not exactly, but the outcome couldn't have been better. The *Ormen Korte* is now under my command, and we have supplies enough to support both the *Ormen Korte* and the *Takarabune* crew."

"And an auxiliary energy core?" Hinata asked hopefully; this could be even better. If they could use the *Ormen Korte's* auxiliary core, the fate of this mission no longer rested on an experimental reactor.

Freyja grimaced, and it was Skyla's turn to look guilty as she shook her head. "We had to eject the auxiliary core. It was damaged and nearly took out the ship."

Hinata hid his disappointment behind his usual façade. They had commandeered the ship, which meant... "You secured the nanites then?"

"Yes, we have everything we need for Doctors Dar and Aman to proceed with the quantum reactor."

Hinata nodded. "We proceed as planned then."

***

Hinata had moved his nervous energy to the docks, where he now paced in anticipation of Skyla's shuttle landing. She was safe; she had come back to him as she promised she would, and yet he feared the universe would tear them apart. He needed her in his arms, needed her close. As much as he knew she was a capable woman, he hated not having her by his side.

A shuttle passed through the purple-tinged force field at berth alpha-3, and Hinata was at the shuttle ramp before it fully extended. Skyla emerged from the back of the ship, a warm smile spreading across her lips the moment she saw him. She ran down the ramp to pause in front of him, those ice-blue eyes gazing up at him with a fire that reflected his own.

"Commander." She canted her head to the side, a soft smile on her lips.

Hinata moved so suddenly her eyes went wide in surprise as he scooped her into his arms and kissed her. Wrapping her arms around his neck, she relaxed into him as she kissed him back.

When she finally pulled away for air, she said, "I believe that is against protocol."

"You are not mine to command, and I am not cleared for duty, so protocol be damned."

She laughed, and he kissed her again.

"Maybe you two can save this for later." Freyja waved a hand at the couple as she exited the shuttle. "We have preparations to make."

Hinata unwound his arms from around Skyla, slipping her hand into his and interlocking their fingers. "I trust that you can handle those preparations, Admiral." He tugged on Skyla's hand, prompting her to follow him back to his quarters.

"You can't avoid your responsibilities forever!" Freyja called after him. She didn't even try to hide her annoyance.

The words hit home. Hinata paused for a moment. He looked into Skyla's eyes and saw everything he wanted reflected in their depths. She was his responsibility; she was his home, his entire universe. The sting of Freyja's words rolled off like rain.

"Take it up with Dr. Pinot," he called back without turning to face Freyja. He was done playing the pawn in someone else's game. He was no longer a tool made only for war. He had chosen Skyla. The moment he stole this ship, he had chosen her; there was no going back.

***

A week had passed at sub-light travel, during which time, Hinata had barely left his quarters. His strength was returning, and his shoulder ached less, although it was no more coordinated than it had been in the weeks following the rescue on Thule. It was now only a matter of time before he was finally cleared for duty, and he wanted to spend every precious moment he had left with Skyla.

Before, his focus had been on the fleet, and their focus on finally uncovering the truth behind the signal. It was the quiet before a storm and the tension filled the air. They were close, and Hinata found the prospect more unsettling with each day that passed. What would they find out in the vast ocean of dead worlds?

As they approached the ring star, Dr. Pinot finally conceded that Hinata was well enough for active duty, although she had been very clear that he was not cleared for combat. Hinata flexed his right hand at his side before rotating his shoulder back. The sting of damaged nerves ran through his neck. He couldn't blame Dr. Pinot. The arm was barely functional, and he doubted if he could hold a sword, let alone wield one.

Dismissing the thought, he let his mind wander while he waited for the task at hand. He stood at the central evacuation port of the *Takarabune*. The time had come to send any of the crew they couldn't trust through the ring. This mission was dangerous enough. He didn't need a mutiny on his hands. All crew had been given the option to return to their home quadrant rather than continue on, and Hinata had been relieved to find most of his crew were more loyal to him than the Hoshiko Tribe. There were a handful of crew members who felt the pull of their duties at home too strongly to continue on this mission. They would be sent home through the ring along with all of the prisoners he would send to the capital to stand trial, and then there was the one prisoner that would be sent to the Beta quadrant.

Hinata's anger flared at the mere thought of the man, but Gabriel's intel had panned out. They had the nanites they needed to end this conflict, and true to his word, Hinata would send Gabriel home.

Gabriel approached from the far end of the corridor, shuffling along between two armed guards, his hands restrained and anchored around a belt at his waist. The gangster paused in front of Hinata, a cocky grin on his face.

"Time to make good on that promise, Commander?"

Hinata gestured to the pod. "Yes, I'll send you back to the Beta quadrant with a trajectory set for Trogon."

Gabriel frowned. "In that? It will take months!"

"I promised you I would let you go. I made no promise about the arrangements."

"You're a son of a bitch. I will destroy you. I'll make you watch while I bleed *her* dry—"

Hinata drew his sword for the first time since the injury. He focused hard to keep the blade from quivering in his grip as he held the tip of his katana to Gabriel's throat.

"You only live now because unlike you, I have honor. But make no mistake, the next time our paths cross, only one of us will walk away."

Gabriel set his jaw, raising his chin in defiance; he glared at the commander, but he held his tongue.

Hinata nodded to the guards, who helped Gabriel into the evacuation pod, which was little more than a spaceworthy cryo pod.

Worry flashed in the gangster's eyes. "Commander, does your honor extend as far as sending a signal to Trogon to retrieve my pod...and disabling my signature?"

"Worried someone else might pick you up before your people find you?" Hinata's face remained impassive. "I guess you will just have to hope your luck holds out."

The pod lid snapped shut before Gabriel could respond. With a nod from Hinata, the pod slid into place for launch.

"Disable his signature," Hinata commanded the guard at the evacuation controls. He would honor Gabriel's request. The idea of letting a rival destroy the pod before his side of the arrangement was fulfilled didn't sit right with his honor, but he didn't mind that Gabriel's last thoughts before cryo would be his doubts of ever waking up again.

The pod disappeared, ejected into space, en route to the ring. That was the only pod he would send to the Beta quadrant. The rest of Gabriel's crew would stand trial at the capital with the traitors and mutineers.

A new pod clicked into place, and it was time to face the moment he had been dreading. The next prisoner stood before Hinata, shackled and guarded like the crime lord before him, but looking into this man's eyes and sending him off into space hit Hinata like a punch to the gut. It hurt almost as much as it had when Hinata had learned of his betrayal.

"You will stand trial at the capital for your treachery. I do you the service of telling you to your face rather than going behind your back because I once called you a friend."

"Commander—" Callan began.

"There is nothing you can say to change my mind."

"Hinata, I am your friend! It is you who has strayed from the path. Nothing would have happened to you! You would have been sent home—"

"Tried, convicted, and stripped of rank," Hinata snarled.

"You don't know that. Your mother would never let that level of dishonor come to your house."

"You don't know my mother. I have disappointed her one too many times. I would have lost everything. Been grounded and unable to end this war—"

"You are still using that as an excuse for your actions! You threw away your future to chase after that woman! A woman that made a fool of you—"

"Watch your tongue, Callan. I have little patience left for you."

Callan shook his head. "This was never about ending the war; admit it."

"That's where you're wrong. This has always been about ending the war, and part of that involves having Skyla at my side."

"Send me to the Gamma quadrant. I will speak to the council on your behalf."

Hinata snorted, "And what will you say of me that will gain the council's favor?"

"I will tell the truth...as you see it. That you have taken the ship to track down this signal, to end this war."

Hinata hesitated, his heart at war with his head. He still cared for Callan. Decades of service together had forged a bond that he had once thought unbreakable before the man had betrayed him, cost dozens of lives, and nearly ended his chance of saving Skyla. His anger warred with his love, but he could see it in Callan's eyes. The man had thought he was doing the right thing, still thought he was doing the right thing. If Hinata sent him to the capital, who knew what would happen to his old friend? The Hoshiko Tribe had succeeded. Callan would likely be held as a prisoner of war until the conflict was over. The thought of it didn't sit right with his honor, but could he trust him? Could he trust what he would say to the council on his behalf? His conflicting desires must have shown on his face, because Callan spoke again.

"Nii, brother."

Hinata flinched at the unexpected sting of the words.

"Please, my intention was never to betray you. Let me prove myself. Let me regain my honor in your eyes. I will speak true to the council."

Unease settled in Hinata, but he nodded. He would grant Callan's request. Only time would tell if it was a mistake.

Callan nodded. "Thank you, my friend." The guards helped Callan into the pod, and within moments, he was gone.

Hinata continued the process of ejecting those who had stood by Callan's side in the conflict, deciding they, too, would be granted the same grace as Callan. They were still his people. Next, he moved through the prisoners from the *Ormen Korte* and the Fenix Cartel crew. No such mercy would be granted to any of them. They were sent straight to the capital for trial, where Hinata hoped justice would be swift.

With all of the prisoners sent on their way, there was only one thing left to do: deploy the prototype, and pray it worked. If the nanites would power the quantum reactor, they could end this now.

"Ready the probe," Hinata commanded over the comms. Not wanting to attract unwanted attention, the *Takarabune* held its position—a week's journey at sub-light speeds from the ring. The probe that Dr. Aman and Dr. Dar had developed was small and lightweight, keeping pace with the escape pods. Hinata hoped that the flurry of activity around the escape pods would mean the crew stationed at the ring would miss the probe on their scans as it dipped into the star's corona to deploy the nanites.

***

The week passed in a flurry of activity as the crew worked to transfer supplies from the *Ormen Korte* to the *Takarabune*. Repair efforts were once again underway as the new supplies provided fresh poly-matter for the 3D printers. Both the *Ormen Korte* and the *Takarabune* deployed their solar sails, collecting energy to fuel their trip home in the event that the quantum reactor didn't work. There was plenty to prepare while they waited, and if this worked, the *Takarabune* would be ready.

Hinata stood on the bridge, all of his senior staff in attendance as they awaited the first test of the probe.

"Our equipment indicates that the nanites have been deployed," Rohaan announced as he took control of the main display. The entire viewport filled with an endless sea of fire, the violent corona of the ring star licking along the cameras of their probe. "We are ready to commence testing."

"Proceed," Hinata said.

Rohaan's fingers flashed through the air, and the viewport went blank for just a second before the fire was replaced by an expanse of stars. The probe rotated slowly, and the image of a star with a giant ring beside it came into view.

"The probe has successfully sustained a wormhole for a five-kilometer journey. Test one is complete. Initiating test two."

Again Rohaan sent commands to the probe whose camera winked into darkness before coming to life again. The probe rotated to show the image of the *Ormen Korte* and the *Takarabune*. Cheers resounded through the bridge, though Hinata remained quiet. It was one thing to make small jumps. These were the types of jumps their current reactors could sustain. It was another entirely to cover the distance of light years.

"The final test, Dr. Dar." Hinata held his voice even.

Rohaan's beaming smile was replaced by the serious countenance of a scholar as he recomposed himself. "Of course, Commander. Commencing test three."

Again the image blinked out and when it reappeared, the viewport framed a world with swirling white clouds, small streaks of blue, and large swaths of gold and red.

"We have confirmation of the signal origin," Rohaan said reverently.

"Scans," Hinata commanded.

"Yes, Commander, we will have a full report in ninety minutes," Reina reported.

"Well, that gives us plenty of time to celebrate while we wait." Tristan took a swig straight from a clear bottle before Kylian snatched it away from him to pour a glass for Freyja, then himself. Kylian offered the bottle to Rohaan, who held up his hand in refusal, instead turning to converse excitedly with Zarah. Kylian shrugged and moved on to Skyla, who smiled at Hinata before pouring two glasses. She passed a glass to Hinata, who also refused.

"Will you deny me, Commander?" She smirked at him over the edge of her glass before taking a sip.

He moved so that his lips brushed against the curve of her ear. "You know I cannot deny you, but this is not over yet. When I celebrate, it will be with you alone." He kissed her temple, satisfied by the goosebumps that spread across her skin at his words. He meant what he had said. He would celebrate when this was over, not yet.

By the time the probe reported back with scans of the planet, Tristan was sloppy drunk and had long since stopped being subtle with his gaze, which locked longingly on Tax. The rest of the crew had shown a modicum of decorum as they sipped tequila and exchanged stories, waiting to discover what it was they were dealing with.

"Scans are in," Rohaan announced as he pulled up the results on the screen. "Air, temperature, and gravity are all within suitable ranges for humans."

As Hinata had suspected. If someone had set up a base of operations there, the question was who? Rohaan fell silent for so long that Hinata finally prompted him to continue.

"And what else, Dr. Dar?"

Rohaan turned from the screen to look at the commander. "There is no sign of higher intelligence life forms...just ruins."

"That signal must be coming from somewhere," Hinata said.

"It is. It appears to originate at the center of the largest ruin." Rohaan shifted the display to show a vast expanse of red desert rocks.

"I don't see anything." Skyla took a step closer to the display.

"We did a quick pass. This is the site where the ruins are. We can send the probe back around for a closer look," Rohaan said.

"Do it. I want to know what we're dealing with before we go down," Hinata commanded.

Freyja frowned. "You think we can still find answers, even without an active base on the planet?"

"That signal is at the center of their communications web. Maybe no one is there now, but I'm willing to bet they have left plenty behind for us to pick up their trail." Hinata turned. "Prepare to make the jump, Dr. Dar."

"What's the point?" Tristan slurred. "Maybe there is something to be said for knowing when you've been bested."

"There is honor in knowing when to abandon a futile quest, but I'm not ready to concede yet." Hinata rose from his seat. "Make the jump, Dr. Dar. We'll prepare a landing party."

Skyla followed Hinata into the corridor. Once they had made it around the first bend, she grabbed him by the arm, turning him to face her.

"I think you mean I will prepare the landing party," Skyla said.

Hinata shook his head. "I said what I meant. You are not leading that party without me."

Skyla rolled her eyes. "It's an abandoned planet, my specialty. How much trouble could I get into?"

"If your record holds, quite a bit."

She punched him playfully in response. "Those were very specific cases. I've led plenty of uneventful salvage missions solo."

Hinata shook his head. "This is my command, and I will be in that landing party."

The smile faded from Skyla's face as she traced her fingers along his shoulder, where the starburst scar lay beneath his uniform. "You're not ready," she whispered.

Hinata took her hand in his, bringing her knuckles to brush against his lips. "I thought you said it wasn't dangerous?"

"You can't even hold your sword."

"My armor can support the weight of the sword."

"And can your armor wield the sword for you?"

Hinata shrugged, turning away from her to continue down the hall. "It doesn't matter since it's not going to be dangerous, right?"

CHAPTER 50 | SKYLA

ANSWERS

Despite Skyla's protests, Hinata held firm that he would be joining her on the surface, and eventually, she acquiesced. And while she grumbled about it the whole trip down to the surface, she was glad to have him at her side.

The warm buzz of a new adventure raced through Skyla as red dirt crunched under her boots, crushing loose pebbles underfoot as she stepped out of Pele's shadow to take in the vast stretch of alien landscape. It was all red sand and towering limestone cliffs; precariously placed hoodoos; and sparse, silvery plant growth.

"It's beautiful," Rohaan whispered at Skyla's side. In the end, Skyla had agreed to take Hinata, Rohaan, Gunner, Freyja, Kylian, and Tristan, although she would have rather left him back on the *Takarabune*. The reality was that Freyja and her crew had spent the better part of the last nine months scouting Old Worlds and had proven themselves apt archaeologists.

"Yes, it is." Skyla stepped up next to her friend, taking in the beauty of the strange planet for just a moment longer. "All right, team, the signal is coming from a ruin site just two kilometers beyond those cliffs. Let's go find out who is causing all of this trouble."

The group walked in silence, taking in the sweeping landscape that was almost too grand to be organic. It was because of this reverence that they noticed the first bird, a dark speck that landed on a hoodoo in the distance ahead of them. It was forty meters above them and barely distinguishable, but something about the way it moved felt eerily familiar.

The next bird landed on a ridge to their left, this one a little bit closer. A sinking feeling settled over Skyla as she peered up at the creature. Its movements were too sharp as it observed them. They continued on toward the ruins, all eyes scanning their surroundings.

The next bird landed on a spiky plant twenty meters ahead of them. The sight of its hard planes and matte black exterior froze Skyla in place. Her suspicions were confirmed as several more birds gathered a safe distance from the landing party, their angled exteriors so dark they absorbed the light as their sharp eyes observed the crew. They were not birds at all; they were bots.

"Those are the bots that attacked Pele," Skyla whispered.

"What are they doing all the way out here?" Kylian asked.

Rohaan took a few careful steps forward. The birds watched him as he walked, but didn't move. "I'm not sure why they're here, but they appear to be observing us."

Freyja drew her sword and the rest of the crew followed suit. "If they are observing us, who are they reporting to?"

"Only one way to find out." Skyla nodded in the direction of the ruins. "What do you want to bet we get to the source of the signal; we get to the bottom of all of this?"

"A bottle of tequila," Tristan said. "I bet you a bottle of tequila that we don't find shit."

Skyla rolled her eyes, turning back to the trail. "Make it a bottle of whiskey, and you're on."

The bots continued to observe their progress, only taking flight to readjust their position. They rounded the cliffs, and Skyla sucked in a breath as the ruins came into view.

They were unlike anything she had found before: a vast city of megaliths that appeared to be constructed entirely out of crystal. The grand structures rose high into the sky, and while there were geometric holes cut into the surface at even intervals, Skyla couldn't make out any doorways. Similar geometrical holes dotted the cliffs that surrounded the crystal city, with whirling, angular designs taking up the space in between.

The reverence of the place was crushing, the feeling of both a shrine and a tomb.

"I don't think we're meant to be here," Rohaan whispered while his eyes searched the space hungrily, recording every little detail.

Skyla agreed, but there was no turning back now. This was the last promise they had of finding any answers. "The signal is strongest just ahead."

They passed through a series of angular arches, the crystals casting prisms across their path. The archways lead them into a domed, crystal cathedral that gave the appearance that it was entirely encompassed in light. A thousand tiny rainbows danced through the structure, and at the very center was one large crystal that appeared to pulse with electricity, pink and purple and orange lightning bolts streaking across its surface in a rhythm that matched Skyla's pulse, thundering in her ears.

She walked until she was almost near enough to reach out and touch the structure. Her ocular display confirmed that the crystal that towered above her was the source of the signal.

"What is it?" Freyja whispered.

Skyla shook her head. "I've never seen tech like this—"

The fluttering of metal wings silenced any further speculation as the bots that had followed them from a distance swarmed into the structure. They rushed in circles around the room, kicking up tiny, red dust devils as they whirled around and around. Their movements were sudden and powerful, yet they maintained their distance. Not a single bird ventured near the crew.

The birds dissolved into a dark whirlwind that started at the edges of the room, then slowly compressed until a dark tornado of nanites swirled just in front of the crystal.

The shimmer of a holo projected at the center of the whirling mass.

It displayed Freyja on the bridge of the *Ormen Korte*—glitched—then separated into two sets of the admiral. Only one image gave the order: "Take Medina; use lethal force. No one leaves the station."

"The deepfake signal," Freyja whispered, entranced by the eerie image of herself. The replica was so precise it was indistinguishable from the real thing, and yet they all knew she had never sent that transmission.

The holo shifted to show the Empress, her image glitched in and out. One second it was there, the next it was empty space, but her voice came through clear. "I have a job in the capital. It requires a specific set of skills I believe you can fulfill."

The face of the Empress morphed and became Gabriel. "Is that right? And what's in it for me?"

The image split into two sets of figures; a conversation between the Empress and the cartel war lord played out, though the voices only matched the glitchy transmission, one half of each pair.

"Change is coming," the Empress answered. "You will be paid for your part, and when I rule over all of humanity, I will leave you your backwater solar empire."

The holo shifted again. This time it showed the Hoshiko ring. It was once again whole, with Hinata's forces stationed before it. Hinata tensed beside her as the battle between him and the Empress played out. The image shifted and broke into two; the one on the left played out as Hinata had described, while the one on the right displayed a twisted version of reality where there was no surprise attack. The Empress didn't jump her forces into the ring, Hinata simply lost.

The holo zoomed out to show Senator Azai, disappointment displayed clearly in the lines of her face as she watched the replay of the battle in her chambers alone.

"That's not what happened," Hinata whispered.

The images fractured into a thousand transmissions, a thousand different faces across the tribes, their voices tangling into an indistinguishable web, and then just as suddenly as it had appeared, the cloud dispersed. The nanites sat heavy in the air like water droplets forming before a thunderhead. The dark storm roiled and reformed, condensing into a humanoid figure before them.

Skyla threw an arm out protectively in front of Hinata as she took a step back, extending the ends of her bō staff and creating space between her crew and the humanoid figure that materialized from the cloud.

The bot was all hard angles, like it had been carved from onyx. It raised its hands placatingly. "Peace, Earth child." It took a step closer, its blank face swiveling from side to side, appearing to take in the crew, even without eyes.

"There is no need for fear. We are but the archivists. We are simply a guide. Violent species always forge their own path to destruction."

THANK YOU

Thank you for reading! If you enjoyed this story, I would be so grateful if you would leave a review on Amazon and Goodreads, or wherever you like to review books! This is such a huge support for authors and helps get our stories out into the world. It doesn't have to be anything fancy, a couple of words will do.

ACKNOWLEDGEMENTS

Wow! I can't believe we are here. The journey to publishing this second installment has been a wild ride and I couldn't have done it without the amazing people who supported me along the way. Thank you to my partner, Hoz, for supporting me in this crazy dream. To my children who are my biggest cheerleaders. To my critique partner Qilanna Quinn who is supportive and always willing to chat about my many crazy ideas! To my beta readers, without whom, this story wouldn't be nearly as good! Amanda Simas, Amber Bolognesi, Merra R., Heather Doig, and Christine Jones. To my editors Kate Black and Ed Crocker, thank you so much for making this manuscript shine.

And thank you to you, reader! Thank you for taking time to dive into this world with these characters that I hold dear to my heart. I hope you enjoyed the journey and that you are ready for the next adventure! If you enjoyed this story please consider leaving a review on Goodreads, Amazon, or wherever you like to share your love of books. Reviews go a long way to helping this story find new readers.

Snag a copy of Hinata's lost transmissions to Skyla when you subscribe to my newsletter at ambertoro.com

GLOSSARY

CHARACTERS

Azai Akari - member of the Hoshiko tribe. Senator of the United Tribal Axis. Mother of Azai Hinata.

Azai Hinata - member of the Hoshiko tribe. Commander in the United Tribal Axis. Commanding officer of Medina Outpost. Bonded to the AI ship Tentei.

Elodie Pinot - member of the Etoile tribe. Doctor, bio-medical engineer, foremost expert in bio-mechanical integrations. Stationed at Medina Outpost.

The Empress - member of the Stjarna tribe. Self made monarch of mining. Mother of Freyja Nygaard.

Berserkers - Adelice, Basilie, Loic, Makena, Ona'je

Fallen Berserkers - Dakara, Kofi, Ekon, Amari. Members of the Stjarna tribe. Members of Freyja Nygaard's elite squad of soldiers. Fell at the battle of Medina during the mutiny of the *Orman Korte*.

Freyja Nygaard - member of the Stjarna tribe. Admiral in the United Tribal Axis Navy. Daughter of the Empress. Leader of the Berserkers. Bonded to the AI ship Selkie.

Gabriel Tibaquirá - Leader of the Fenix cartel. Ruler of the outer rim world, Trogon.

Gwen Karsten - member of the Stjarna tribe. Senator of the United Tribal Axis. Mother of Skyla Karsten.

Huang Bo - member of the XingXing tribe. Captain in the United Tribal Axis Navy. Ally to Senator Karsten.

Ivar Borg - member of the Stjarna tribe, Lieutenant in the United Tribal Axis Navy. Loyal to the Empress. Leader of the *Orman Korte* mutiny.

Kaku Caishen - member of the XingXing tribe. Senator of the United Tribal Axis. Astrophysicist.

Kobayashi Callan - member of the Hoshiko tribe Lieutenant commander in the United Tribal Axis Navy. Third in the chain of command under Commander Hinata Azai.

Kylian Aimé - member of the Stjarna tribe. Lieutenant commander in the United Tribal Axis Navy. Second in the chain of command under Admiral Freyja Nygaard. Cousin to Tristan Cylien. Expert hacker.

Nazhi Aman - member of the Taaralog tribe. Research Scientist working on the quantum entanglement energy transfer project. Father of Zahra Aman.

Rohaan Dar - member of the Taaralog tribe. Research scientist at Medina Outpost. Dual PhD's in astrophysics and computer science. Specializes in alien technologies and signal decryption. Best friend of Skyla Karsten. Bonded to the AI ship Cista.

Sato Tax - member of the Hoshiko tribe. Lieutenant commander in the United Tribal Axis Navy. Second in the chain of command under Commander Hinata Azai.

Skyla Karsten - member of the Stjarna tribe. Former captain in the United Tribal Axis Navy. Current outlaw archaeologist specializing in salvage of Old World tech. Ace pilot. Bonded to the AI ship Pele.

Sten Magnuson - member of the Stjarna tribe. First counselor to the Empress.

Tristan Cylien - member of the Stjarna tribe. Lieutenant commander in the United Tribal Axis Navy. Third in the chain of command under Admiral Freyja Nygaard. Cousin to Kylian Aimé. Weapons expert.

Wout Verhaert - member of the Verloren tribe,. Chief Petty Officer in the United Tribal Axis Navy. Head Mechanic at Medina Outpost under Commander Hinata Azai. Original pioneer of the UTA settlement effort.

Zahra Aman - member of the Taaralog tribe. Research Scientist working on the quantum entanglement energy transfer project. Daughter of Nazhi Aman. Assistant to Rohaan Dar.

Events

The Exodus - When all of mankind left Earth That Was.

Secchi Conference - annual astrophysics, materials science, and deep space analytics conference held at Medina Outpost.

The Wandering - the ten thousand year period between when humanity left Earth That Was and the founding of the United Tribal Axis.

GEAR

Armored spacesuits - spacesuits with additional armor for space warfare.

Arogelium Armor - armor made of aerogelium. Worn by space station peacekeepers.

Bio Ball - a nutrient rich algae gel used in the repair of bio-ships.

Mechs - armored mechanical battle suites. Small enough for standard UTA vessels to carry, but larger and more heavy armored than armored spacesuits.

Suspensors - a tool that creates the effect of hovering by locally disrupting gravity.

Z-grav Boots - produced a localized gravity field for the wearer.

PLACES

Aleppo - Black market hub favored by archaeologists.

Amalthea Galaxy - home to the United Tribal Axis central rim.

Central Rim - the solar systems under direct control of the United Tribal Axis.

Damascus - United Tribal Axis planet.

Fazenda - Perdida tribe moon farming community. Sabotaged by Freyja Nygaard in retaliation for attacks on farming stations owned by the Empress.

Gefion - Capital planet of the United Tribal Axis.

Amaterasu - Hoshiko home world.

Jubokko - Hoshiko prison planet.

Kensho - Hoshiko military academy.

Known Galaxies - the galaxies mapped by the United Tribal axis.

Medina Outpost - Taaralog research station.

Mirmir Academy - Stjarna military academy.

Old World Planets - abandoned planets thought to be colonized by ancient humans who left Earth before the exodus.

Tamatori - Hoshiko mining world.

Tenzan Ishi Run - a dangerous starship racing route on Amaterasu.

The Silk Road - a network of United Tribal Aixs controlled worm hole rings used to unite the Known Galaxies.

Thule - ice planet on the edge of known space.

Trogon - Fenix cartel controlled planet on the outer rim.

Upsala Station - Stjaran space station.

Starship Classes

AI bio-ship - fully sentient starship that is a bio-mechanical hybrid. Typically constructed with a coral titanium hybrid hull and other biological integrations, including vast DNA storage and an organic quantum computer. AI bio ships remodel and grow with their human hosts. They share an intense bond with their human hosts.

Corvette - small warship.

Cruiser - large warship.

Frigate - large civilian class ship.

Starfighter Carrier - Largest warship. Made for transporting starfighters.

Star Destroyer - Large warship with the heavyset armaments of any UTA class ship.

Starfighter - single occupant warship.

SENTIENT STARSHIPS

Cista - AI ship bonded to Rohaan Dar.

Pele - AI ship bonded to Skyla Karsten.

Selkie - AI ship bonded to Freyja Nygaard.

Tentei - AI ship bonded to Hinata Azai.

TRIBES

United Tribal Axis - the governing body that united the twelve tribes of humanity.

Tribes ranked by power:

Stjarna

XinXing

Hoshiko

Etoile

Zvezda

Sterkind

Verloren

Taaralog

Perdida

Zirka

Setareh

Pirntirri

WEAPONS

Atomics - explosive utilizing nuclear fission, nuclear fusion or a combination. Outlawed under the UTA.

Plasma Cannons - projectile weapon utilizing plasma discharge.

Railgun - high velocity electromagnetic force weapon used against stardestroyers.

Sonic Riffles - weapon used by peacekeeping units. Can

safely be used on space stations and ships without damaging the structures.

Nanite Hand Held Weapons - weapons made of nanite technology that links to a user's neural chip and can transform shape. Includes swords and bō staffs among other hand held weapons.

ASTRONOMICAL TERMS

Parallax - obseRvEd change in posiTion of an object due to a change in vantage point by the obseRver.

Umbra - Latin fOr "shadow." The part of an eclipse where all liGht is excluded. The daRkest pArt of a shaDow, whEre all light is blocked.

ABOUT THE AUTHOR

Amber Toro is a data scientist at machine learning startup working to make the world a better place with AI. She is a big believer in using tech for good.

Always dreaming, Amber writes epic sci-fi and fantasy.

Amber grew up in Seattle with a great love of the outdoors. She now calls Utah her home and when she is not writing or coding, you can find her biking, hiking, and camping in the mountains with her amazing partner and two tiny humans, or curled up with a good sci-fi/fantasy book.

Discover more at ambertoro.com or on social media @amberraetoro

ALSO BY AMBER TORO

SENTIENT STARS

Umbra

Parallax

Retrograde—coming soon

AETHER AND BONE

Aether and Bone—coming soon

BALLADS OF BEMOND

Fragments of Perfection

Ashes Fall Like Snow—coming soon